BEAR

MC SHIFTER ROMANCE
VERA FOXX

FOXX FANTASY PUBLISHING

First paperback edition: January 2024

Book design by: Etheric Designs

Model: Tony Brettman

Publisher: **Foxx Fantasy Publishing LLC**

Editing by: Chloe Leggatt

DEAR READER

Please read the following trigger warnings and other important information regarding this book.

This book contains:

Dominate male.

Submissive female: This does not mean she is weak and fragile.

Size Difference. Large male, small female.

Baculum (Bone in male shifter penis in human form)

Mentions Sex Trafficking.

PTSD, Depression

Blood, gore, torture.

Detailed consensual sex scenes.

Biting, marking

Breeding Kink.

Primal Kinks.

Obsessive MMC.

Strong Language.

Traumatic experiences regarding dreams, memories, family loss

CONTENTS

CHAPTER ONE

Nadia

Drip, drip, drip.

Eight hundred and ninety-two, eight hundred and ninety-three, eight hundred and ninety-four.

The incessant drips echoed throughout the small, dimly lit room as I swayed back and forth, matching the beat of the tiny sink in the corner. The sound of the drops hitting the metal basin was the only thing that broke the eerie silence. The air was thick with musty, damp smells, and I couldn't help but shiver as a chill ran down my spine. I had lost track of time, but the dim light that enveloped the room made it seem like an eternity had passed. The only things I could feel were the cold mattress on my feet and the dampness seeping through my clothes.

I just knew when my body was tired, when it was ready to be awake, when I needed to eat, and when it was full—which was exceedingly rare.

I didn't remember the last time my stomach felt full or distended. Now it was concave. I could easily count my ribs, and my hip bones were nearly piercing through the skin. The one thing I was grateful for was that there was no mirror. I couldn't imagine what my hair and face looked like.

I rubbed my nose, feeling the cold drip of liquid trying to fall to the upper part of my lip.

All those times my parents sat me at the table when I was young in our small apartment—telling me to eat my beans, the sweet potatoes with butter and brown sugar—that some poor starving person would love to gobble this meal up in a heartbeat seems really silly right now.

I'd scold that little girl who sat there all those years ago. *"Yeah, you will be the one starving down the road,"* I'd tell her. *"You will be the one wishing for this moment. Get some meat on them bones, girl. Savor every bite."*

I sniffed; my nose was still runny despite wiping it. As I breathed out, my glasses became foggy, and I had to take them off to wipe them clean.

Eight hundred ninety-nine. Nine hundred.

I continued to rock, no longer counting, just going along with the drips from the sink. I was tired of counting, tired of rocking, tired of sitting in this concrete cell every day. Most of all, I was tired of living.

They kept me alive just enough—just enough so that jerk wouldn't break a promise to Mrs. Delilah. She wasn't here now. She never wanted Master Shane Cunningham. Mrs. Delilah didn't want him. I still heard her crying when I slept.

Her cries still haunt me.

My body topples over, my face buried into the soiled mattress filled with tears, sweat, and mold. I just wanted to help her, and I did. Then why do I still suffer? How did I get caught when I was so quiet?

The scraping of my nails on the mattress echoed through the silent room. I winced when they made a noise.

Shh, cannot make any noise.

My eyes darted to the door in panic. No movement on the other side came, no door unlocking.

I was safe, for now.

No one was supposed to notice this tiny mouse. It was my *thing*. My mother gave me this cute nickname for her tiny daughter who would sneak into the kitchen in the middle of the night and make an old Russian dessert. It was a family recipe of blini and smear it with chocolate and powdered sugar.

But this time I wasn't so lucky. I pressed my luck and got caught in the biggest trap of them all. I didn't outwit the hunter.

My teeth bit into my lower lip, piercing the chapped skin. Drafts had a hard time penetrating this room. The walls were cold, with no ventilation to bring in fresh air. The seals around the door were so tight it surprised me I could still breathe since the door had been shut for so long.

I didn't need the whole door opened; I just longed for the slot at the base of the door. It was wide enough for a food tray, but even that slot had a lock on the other side.

Leaning over the side, I gazed longingly at it, my fingers twitching with anticipation. I flicked my finger, beckoning it to flip over and a tray to slide underneath it. *Come on,* I chanted in my head. *Let today be the day.*

If I had a concept of time, it was maybe five days since they fed me last. Master Cunningham must have given up now. His rescue mission had to have failed, or Mrs. Delilah refused to come home.

Not that I blamed her. I wouldn't come back here. This place was hell. Drugs, weapons, parties. Thankfully there was nothing but consensual sex around here thanks to Mrs. Delilah, but still, this place was full of danger.

I was one of the lucky ones. No one dared mess with me, anyway. I had stayed in the shadows, stuck near the walls of the mansion, cleaned the rooms, dusted the chair railing, books, and unused rooms. I wasn't one to be looked at, anyway. Not tall, too child-like, too small, to be anything beautiful for these men.

Master Cunningham sauntered down to the depths of the mansion and to my prison cell days ago. The light blinded me when he came inside, and I slid to the furthest corner away from him, hiding away from his imposing body.

He said he was going to find his wife and wouldn't have me fed until he returned. He wasn't providing me much, anyway. Just the scraps off the plates of his guests.

"Nadia, you behave." He chuckled, gazing over the room.

His voice was like a sledgehammer, pounding into my eardrums with each word.

I curled my arms around my knees, averting my gaze from him. The pungent smell of cigarettes mixed with his cologne filled my nostrils, making me crinkle my nose. I didn't dare look up at him. For what reason would I? I felt like the grime caked onto the bottom of his polished shoes. His appearance was striking, with his slicked-back blond hair and tailored suit. The tapping of his shoes against the pavement echoed in my ears. On the other hand, I was dressed in nothing but my shabby maid uniform, reduced to tatters after scrubbing it with the water in the dingy sink. "I'm proud of you for keeping quiet. Quiet as a mouse, huh? You've truly kept up to your nickname." He leaned over me, grasping under my chin and squeezing my cheeks, and pulled me up so I gazed into his frightening eyes.

There was something off about him since the first day I came to the mansion. They were piercing, more like a hunter ready to sink his teeth into his prey. His face was pale, and he had an ungodly amount of strength in just his hand.

I wanted to cry at the pain in my cheeks. Instead, I let the tears gather in my eyes, trying my best not to make a sound. Ever since I'd remained quiet about how I got Mrs. Delilah out, he didn't want to hear any word escape my lips, and now I was afraid to talk, and after what he had done to me, I swore I would never speak again. "I expect you to remain quiet during the duration of my departure. None of that banging on the door, like you did in the beginning, hmm?" He cocked his head, and my eyes widened in fear.

Mrs. Delilah requested little from Master Cunningham, but she requested no female be sexually abused or hit, which he hadn't done to me. Instead, he came up with other ways to punish me instead.

With his hand clamped around my face, I nodded my head the best I could. "Good little mouse, I shall return."

I'd always been a quiet person, but after coming here I was more of a recluse, and even more so since helping Mrs. Delilah escape. I didn't regret what I did. I only regretted not leaving with her.

If only I hadn't been so foolish in thinking I could help others escape. What kind of person would I have been if I had left? The guilt would have been too much. I would have crawled back, trying to help others that wanted my help.

No, this was the right decision. This was what I was supposed to do. Help others, like my mother and father were doing before me.

If I looked at it in a positive light—this place had become my home since they threw me in here. It was small and dimly lit, but if you looked at it with the right attitude, it could be homely. It was large for my size, six by nine feet. It could be smaller if I really thought about it. The walls were cold and grey, but at least they weren't stark white and blinding.

The small window that opened and shut by the door would occasionally let light in if they didn't close it all the way, and when the light came in, it was welcome. The bed was uncomfortable, but if I cried on it just right, it would soften the mattress. The blanket was soft when dried after a few days of washing it in the sink. And after a good washing, the air would pull the water out of the blanket, giving the air some humidity, some sort of warmth if I concentrated really hard.

The metal toilet flushed. Not much more I could say about that really, but at least it was not a bucket.

It was—quiet in here. I'd grown to like it. The soft sounds were soothing and helped me sleep.

With the sounds from the outside world, the banging of doors from the hallways, and the click of the lock, I could very well rupture an eardrum.

If I was let out of this cell now, I didn't know if I would survive out there. All the sounds rushing in, my hearing just might—explode.

Again, I beckoned the food slot to open with my finger, wishing and hoping it would move. Instead, a tear trailed down my cheek. A useless tear.

I left my arm hanging off the cot, listened to the continued dripping of the sink, and let my lifeless body lay there.

As much optimism as I tried to display, as much as I tried to look at the bright side of things, today was a lot more bleak with my stomach yelling that it was hungry. Right now, the darkness was closing in, and I was hoping I didn't wake up.

I was too chicken to do it myself, too prideful to hit my head on the sink. But what if I just closed my eyes and my stomach just began to eat itself?

Would it hurt?

Because no help is really coming.

No one knew I was here besides the hired help, and they would never help me, not after what they witnessed the day I was caught. Master Cunningham made sure to make an example out of me.

My lip curled, and I rolled onto my back, staring at the lone lightbulb hanging from the ceiling. Yeah—it was a great run. Too bad it had to end like this.

At least Mrs. Delilah got out. At least she didn't have to live with that evil, crazy man anymore. She had to live with him for years before I came along, and I've only known him for a few.

I let out a deep breath, my eyes fluttering closed.

Maybe I could dream of something nice for once.

Maybe the nightmares that liked to haunt my dreams while in this room wouldn't come this time.

Maybe, just once.

CHAPTER TWO

Bear

Grim bit his lip, his tongue playing with the bruised skin as he hunched over the genetically altered vamp tied to the cement support beam of the club's basement. Delilah's ex-husband and step-brother, the leader of one of the largest crime syndicates in the eastern part of the country, was bleeding out for what seemed like the twentieth time this week.

Vamps were like cockroaches-they kept coming back to life no matter how many damn times you tried to kill them.

That didn't stop Grim. He was patient. He enjoyed this part of his job. It was in his blood to torture, to destroy, to mutilate those who had done wrong. And somehow he was blessed with a second chance mate that supported it all—as long as those he killed deserved it.

Lucky fucking bastard.

While Grim tortured the shit head, Grim was sporting a hard-on. Some might think it was because of his love for inflicting pain, but really it was because his mate, Journey, was close by. He took her everywhere, never out of his sight.

Which is what a fit male should do. Never let your female be far from you. Protect what was yours, and if I had one, I would do the same. In fact, I would never let mine leave my side, but to each their own. Grim had a job, and so did his female. She was the goddess' priestess now, the direct line of the goddess of the moon.

Journey was sitting in the corner, oblivious to the mayhem occurring in the basement. She read, drew, or whatever the hell she did behind the partition, so she wasn't triggered because she'd been through her own pain as well. Grim protected her because he wasn't just the enforcer and protector of this club, but hers as well. He sheltered her, fucked her, treated her like a goddamn princess, and even provided her with pink headphones so she couldn't hear a fucking thing.

And we all cared for her. We cared for all the females we saved. They had been through as much as we had been.

Shane, the wretched prisoner, let out a piercing howl that echoed through the prison walls. His fangs, once menacing and sharp, now lay detached on the grimy floor, lost amidst the crimson pool and chunks of flesh. The stench of iron hung heavy in the air, and the sickening squelch of torn skin filled the room. It was a gruesome sight, a scene that would be etched into the memories of any witness. "Just end me!" he gargled.

"Not until you give us the codes to the security footage of your mansion." Locke flicked a cigarette into the pool of blood like it was a sight he saw every day of his life.

Locke's eyes were bloodshot, pupils dilated. He wasn't in a mood to be toyed with. He was licking his lips, balling up his fists repeatedly, and groaning at the sight of every drop of blood falling to the floor.

I tightened my brass knuckles that were molded to fit my large hand. They were created with claws to match the length of my grizzly's. I held them up, picking the extra skin away from the point.

I missed my claws. I used to be powerful and didn't have to rely on weapons or create them to give me the feeling of what I once was. Now I must sit back in the shadows and help when I could. I was still huge, still more muscular than most, but now that Grim was mated he was at full strength with his wolf. He was—more.

I was nothing and becoming weaker by the day. Soon my grizzly would wake and not for the reason I wanted—to find a mate. It would wake to take over my body and force me to go insane.

Shane spat and drooled the thick, congealed blood from his mouth. "Idris sealed it in my memory."

Locke hummed disapprovingly, not believing him. He lit another cigarette and nodded his head at me. I tightened my fist, used my hand with my brass claws, and punched him right into the gut, twisting the sharp points inside him.

With a grunt, Shane passed out, and Grim shook his head, retreating to his table of instruments and pulling out a large machete from the pile of tools.

The prospects and brothers cheered from the side of the room, clinking beer cans together. Not one area of the basement was empty watching the show, except the corner where Switch set up his equipment.

Switch was tapping away at his computer, trying to break into Shane's mansion's security. Switch was sweating; I didn't think I'd ever seen him so angry. He was the silent type, reclusive for a wolf, but smart, and being unable to break into a security system was doing him in.

Finally, someone else feeling frustration around here other than me.

A prospect took an ice bucket of cold water and threw it on Shane. We backed up, and Shane gasped for air, his body stark white from the lack of blood. "It's bound in magic!" he cried. "It's bound by Duke Idris' magic," he repeated with a dramatic sigh and hung his head.

And that was when everything fell apart. Locke barked orders to get

Tajah and Bram—a witch and a warlock—to break down whatever spell was cast over the security system.

All while I stood there, watching Grim growling maliciously, ready for the kill. His wolf fangs descended below his mouth, hair sprouted on his arms, claws lengthened on his fingertips.

My heart thundered in my chest in jealousy. I wanted that. I wanted to feel my bear. I wanted to feel the animal inside me that slumbered, that hibernated for years now. I was left with only the obscene amount of hair for a human and my tall, wide stature that put off not only humans but also other supernaturals.

But what I wanted more than anything besides my animal, the power, the closeness of nature, was a female.

I glanced at the partition that concealed his mate, then to Shane, the prisoner we were destroying in honor of Delilah, Hawke's mate and beloved friend to the club.

I. Wanted. That.

As I watched Grim, I lifted my lip in a snarl and waited for Locke's call to finish off Shane. Grim smiled maliciously, licking his lips.

"I'm in," Switch announced when he slammed his finger on the escape button of his computer.

Locke snapped his fingers, signaling for the final kill. Shane was of no use anymore.

Grim wouldn't have to kill Shane anymore and place his head back on his body for us to torture again each night. This would be the last time that Shane's head would be removed from his body, permanently.

Grim leaned back, his fingers digging into the fabric of Shane's shirt. He pushed his claws into Shane's chest, and with a sickening squelch, he pulled out his heart. The sound of beating reverberated through the silent basement. Grim lifted his foot and brought it down hard on the still-beating heart. The smell of blood filled the air, and the leather of Grim's boots was slick with it.

If my bear was awake, he would roar with excitement for the kill. Another enemy caught, another destroyed.

My thumb ran over the brass claws, my heart filled with loneliness that I couldn't celebrate this moment with him while the crowd cheered. No matter how full this room was, everyone in it would continue to feel lonely on the inside.

I swallowed, watching as Hawke walked down the stairs, just arriving in the basement. A smile on his face as he bypassed Grim, patting his shoulder and leaning over Switch.

Grim licked the blood off his claws, a smile on his face as well.

Hawke had his mate, and so did Grim.

I fucking wanted one too.

I growled, running my hand through my beard.

When was it my turn?

Grim's machete cut through the air, chopping off Shane's head. It toppled to the floor. Sounds of footsteps walked across the cement floor, the hose turning on to flood the blood down the drain, the wheelbarrow hinge squeaked to recover the body, and it rang in my sensitive ears.

I shook my head, scratching at it as if I had fleas. As the ringing died, murmurs of excitement and replays of the days of torture continued to fill the room.

All I could think of was—when could I get my chance?

I stepped forward, bending over and picking up Shane's head by the scalp. I held it away from my body, keeping the blood from drenching any more of my clothes. Shane's mouth and eyes were still open, bruises on his cheek and cuts on his forehead.

I straightened my shoulders and put on a face of pride to show Locke, my president, as I sauntered to the corner of the room where they finally broke the security code to the mansion across the country.

We were going to mount this whole ass head like a fucking deer mount, but I needed further orders on what to do with it. I needed to show that I was a capable brother and put my needs and wants behind me so I could show my president—acting alpha even if he could not hold that title without his wolf—that I cared about this club and the broken souls in it.

I still had my pride to maintain.

"Hey, Pres, where do you want me to put the head?" I gazed down at the head again and winced at the blood dripping out of the mouth. When I looked up again, Switch's head moved away from the computer, and I got the perfect view of the screen.

It was a grainy black-and-white picture of a female huddled on a cot in a small cell with no windows and only a door. She was rocking herself back and forth with a mass of curly hair and a tiny body.

My heart stopped in my chest when I saw her. An overprotective instinct surged inside me. It wasn't enough to wake the grizzly that slumbered, but my body instantly reacted, and my hand that gripped the decapitated head tightened.

"Who is she?" I whispered. I tried to remain calm.

I was anything but. This woman needed to be rescued, and that was the whole point of why the Iron Fang was founded. To save those in distress, to regain redemption for ourselves so we wouldn't be completely damned.

We were gaining redemption, some of us getting second chances, but this woman sitting in a cell, alone, was doing something to me.

No one answered, and my heart pounded again. This time when the blood regained its movement, it boiled in my veins.

"Well?!" my voice thundered, filling the basement with my urgency. Even Locke took a step back when my eyes narrowed at every one of them.

It wasn't my intention to lose control. I know I could be a damn dick, but not to the leaders of the club.

"She's our next target," Locke said, fumbling with a new cigarette. "Gonna send a squad in to extract her."

"I want in," I said with no hesitation and dropped the head to the floor.

The head rolled away from me. I didn't look back and stomped away from the group, feeling their heated stares on my back.

CHAPTER THREE

Bear

I stormed down the dimly lit hallway, the echo of my footsteps reverberating off the empty walls. My heart pounded in my chest as I approached the door to my room. With a forceful push, I flung the door open and stepped inside. The air was still and stale, with a faint scent of mustiness lingering in the space. I took in my sparsely furnished room, the only sound being the rustling of my duffle bag as I dragged it out from underneath the creaky bed.

I stayed at the club only because the gym I owned was in town. On the weekends I liked to go to my cabin to get away from everyone. Bears didn't like to spend much time around other people, which may be why I wanted to go on this mission.

Get away from all the mates around this damn place.

As I yanked open the drawers of the old pine chest, the sweet smell of polished wood filled my nostrils, making me feel like I was in a forest. I rummaged through the contents, my fingers brushing against the rough texture of black clothing, the cold metal of weapons, and the softness of ski masks. The creaking of the chest's joints echoed through the room, blending with my heavy breathing. Suddenly, a flicker of movement caught my attention, but I chose to ignore it, slamming the drawers shut with a loud thud that reverberated around the room.

"I'm here to check on your health, Bear," Bones said as he walked in. The club doc set his bag on top of my pile of shit, and I scowled when I saw his stuff over mine. He lifted it, shaking his head and placing it on the bedside table. "You know you shouldn't leave. It isn't wise."

I scoffed and pulled the claws from my knuckles, feeling the sharp edges graze my skin. I ran my fingers across the cool metal, then tossed it with the rest of my stuff. "Who says? You? You help more wolves than you do bears. Bears do better off alone. I do fine when I go off for a few days and come back here."

"You don't know how long you will be gone on this mission. You still need the strength of others." Bones opened his bag, pulling out a stethoscope, a blood pressure cuff, and a needle and syringe.

"I'll be with the stealth team. It will be fine," I argued, throwing my hands up. "They are broken like the rest of us. It doesn't matter who I'm with."

"They're different. They are trained for this and have their own bond with each other." Bones grabbed my arm and pulled me to sitting, wrapping the cuff around my arm. Once wrapped, I flexed and let the Velcro rip apart.

"Bear," he chastised.

"No!" I bellowed, ripping it off. "I'm going, no matter what you say." I stuck my finger into his chest. "I'm going to help rescue that woman whether you say I can or not. You or Locke can't tell me otherwise." I knocked his bag on the floor and grabbed my clothes, stuffing them inside the duffle.

Bones stood, holding his stethoscope in his hand, fiddling with it. I continued with my task, not bothering to fold anything, and retreated to the caddy I took with me to the communal bathroom and stuffed my toiletries inside as well.

"Bear?" Bones asked.

I grunted, zipping up the duffle. "Is she your mate?"

I sank my hands into the plush queen mattress, feeling the softness and warmth beneath my fingertips. With my head drooping heavily between my shoulders, I took in the sight of the disheveled blankets scattered haphazardly across the bed, remnants of a restless night's sleep. As I closed my eyes, the silence of the room enveloped me, broken only by the sound of my own breathing.

My grizzly didn't wake up, didn't claim that female, so what? But my protective instinct awakened. I wanted to help someone. I needed a reason to live. A passion, a drive to do something good. On the last mission, when we found Journey, I was losing that spark and will to do good. Seeing that battered girl, I found meaning again, a will to wake up. The candle that was burning out inside me had sparked again. I didn't want to let it go; it gave me motivation to live until I found my mate.

"No," I replied.

Bones' shoulders slumped, and he picked up his things. "I can't recommend you go. Bear or not, you will be away from the club, away from your support group. What if something happens? You can't heal quickly. What are you even lifting now? Has your strength dropped? Be honest."

I pushed away from the bed. "Ten pounds less from my previous best."

Bones pulled out his tablet and typed it into his notes. "Bear, what if you go rabid? You are going on a plane; what if you go rabid on the—"

"Listen," I said calmly. "I know. I've been an ass for the past couple of weeks."

Bones put the tablet away and pinched the bridge of his nose. "That's an understatement."

I rolled my eyes. "I've been slipping, I know that. I gave Journey hell in the beginning about this second chance thing. I've been snapping at Anaki when he asked me if I believe in all this second chance stuff since Hawke has Delilah now. The thing is, I do believe in it. I think I'll get a chance, but"—I pulled on my beard—"I don't know if I'll get my chance in time. I'm getting jealous, irrational and can't hold back my emotions like I used to. I want a mate. I want her now.

"Past missions haven't done it for me. I normally get a rush, a sense of accomplishment. It fills part of the void since my animal is not there. But then I saw her. That woman on the screen. For the first time in a long time, I had a protective urge, an instinct to go and rescue someone. I need to do this, Bones. Keep my mind off finding a mate and protect someone. And I don't need you or Locke's damn permission to do it. I'm going because if I don't, I'll lose myself more than I already have."

Bones stared at me for a long moment, his eyes never leaving mine. "I can only tell Locke what I know about your physical abilities. I can't tell him what you want to do. I can't put you on a plane with the team and put them in danger. It's for their safety and yours. I'm doing this as your friend. I hope you see that."

Bones was a doctor, sure. Trained through human and supernatural ways of medicine, and he took a damn oath to protect all of us. Most of all, he was our friend, keeping us safe as rogues to protect the brotherhood.

That didn't matter to me now. I was pissed as hell. I needed this. I needed to save that woman. My entire being was telling me I needed to be there for her. I stepped forward, my bloodied boots sticking to the floor with blood, and my hand reached out ready to grab Bones's neck.

I knew I wasn't thinking right; I was losing it. I could very well be going rabid right now, but nothing was going to stop me from saving this woman.

Bones stood there unafraid, his jaw tightening.

"What are you going to do, Bear? Strangle me? Hurt me? Prove to me and to this brotherhood even more that you can't handle being out there? That you are maybe too far gone than we all realize."

My face twisted into a snarl, my nostrils flaring as I felt a dull ache pulsing behind my temples. I could almost hear the sound of my bear's heart pounding against his chest, as if he was waking up from his winter slumber. A shiver ran down my spine as I felt the muscles in my arms and legs twitching, as if they were preparing for a fight.

A trampling of footsteps came down the hall, men shouting, going to the communal showers, shutting and opening doors.

Locke's scent of cigarette and ash stopped at the door and slammed his hand on the doorway. "Bear, shower, and get some sleep. You and the Moonlight Outcasts are leaving tomorrow."

Bones scoffed. "I don't think that's a good idea, Pres. I don't think Bear has a good hold on his emotions. He might be closer to going rabid than we think."

I growled. Bones backed up, heading to Locke. Locke chuckled, playing with an unlit cigarette in his mouth. "Nah, he'll be fine. Won't you, Bear? You won't screw this up for Delilah's sake, will you?"

"No, sir," I said and grabbed my duffle. "I won't."

Bones scoffed and Locke put his hand on Bones's shoulder, leaning in and he whispered something in his ear. Unfortunately, my grizzly's hearing was long gone, so I pulled out my toiletries to shower.

Bones's eyes widened and nodded. "Fine. Do what you will. But I'm requesting that I go along too."

Locke smirked, leaning on the doorway. "Why is that?"

"For the safety of your crew and for the woman. She's in bad shape from what I saw on the cameras." He gripped his bag tight. "I'm willing to risk my life to help someone in need, just as Bear is."

Locke rubbed his brow. "If you think that it is necessary, I trust your judgment. Stay on the plane. Bear and the crew will bring the female to you."

Bones nodded and stomped down the hallway.

I huffed, pulled off my clothes, and threw them in the laundry basket. "Thanks, Pres, I owe ya." I walked naked to the door, and Locke shook his head.

"Yeah, no problem. Just be careful where you aim that thing." He pointed to my dick, and I rolled my shoulders back.

I chuckled. "I'll clear out the shower room for ya." I walked down the hallway, and once I stepped into the shower room, the space filled with groans and whines. Everyone was jealous of this dick, and they washed up pretty quickly when I came into the room.

That, and they hated my hairy body. But fuck them. Nothing was going to ruin my mood now. I was going on a mission that was going to turn my life around. I could feel it in my gut.

As a bolt of lightning split the sky outside the airplane window, the ear-piercing sound of thunder shook the entire plane. My fingers instinctively curled around the armrests, my blunt nails digging into the luxurious leather of the private jet. The smell of ozone wafted through the cabin, adding to the already tense atmosphere. I let out an exasperated huff as the storm raged on, the boisterous laughter of the team completely unfazed by the tumultuous weather.

Once more, a brilliant flash of lightning illuminated the world outside my window. I gazed in awe as the electric bolts danced from cloud to cloud, lighting the night sky. The thunder that followed rumbled through the air, shaking the plane's floor. As I looked on, I saw the lightning strike the ground below. The earth trembled as the light spread like wicked witch's fingers, clawing at the ground below. My stomach churned as I watched the terrifying display of raw power.

I reached over the two seats that separated me from the window and slammed the movable blind shut, noticing that I left three scratch marks on the plastic. I pulled my hand away, looking at the three tiny claws protruding from my fingers.

The hell?

An unexpected hand landed on my shoulder. My own reached over and grabbed the wrist at the sudden touch. The opposing hand pulled back quicker than I could get a hold of the stranger, and they held it up in surrender. "Hey now, I'm just checking to see if you are alright," Cyran said as he rubbed his wrists. "We can smell your sweat from the back, and shit"—he looked at his wrist. Tiny drops of blood beaded on his skin—"you scratched me. Since when did your nails get so sharp?"

I gazed at my hand again. It was only on a few fingers, my index, middle, and ring finger. Not enough to do any harm to anyone, not as long as my grizzly's, but it was enough to get my heart pounding.

The nails were dark; all of them were on my left hand, meaning they weren't nails; they were my claws growing. I scratched the back of my head. The thunder rolled in the distance while I continued to stare at the phenomenon, at what this could mean.

Was Bones right? Was I going rabid?

I never thought I would see them again. The last time I saw my claws was at least five years ago when I came to the Iron Fang looking for a support system. Back then I thought I was close to going rabid, but being around others going through the same hardship I was going through slowed down the process.

Broken souls thrived together.

Joining the Iron Fang gave my grizzly something to hold on to before he fell into an infinite slumber. It also gave me some hope that shifters like me didn't have to be alone and suffer in silence. Staying together as a mismatched pack or community gave us enough strength to rely on each other. Even if bears stayed in solitude more often than not.

"Whose bleeding?" Quillian snapped. He grabbed Cyran's forearm and sniffed. "Gods, you haven't eaten in a while either. Go to the back fridge and eat before we land."

"It's chunky when it's cold," Cyran complained. "Do they at least have a blood bag heater in here?"

Cyran and Quillian were part of the Iron Fang's special ops forces Locke put in place a few years ago. They go under the guise of the Moonlight Outcasts, a rock band that "traveled" around the country. They weren't bad. They played decent music and kept humans entertained when the brothers and sisters of the club scouted for their mates on Friday and Saturday nights.

"Shut the hell up, just drink it. Not unless you want to bleed out, and I have to carry your sorry ass out of that hellhole. Better yet, I'll just leave you on the mansion floor," Quillian shouted, shoving Cyran out of his way.

Quillian sat next to me, his metal chains clanging against the armrest while his black mesh top rustled with every movement. He looked like the epitome of a rock band lead singer, but it only infuriated me. I despised how effortlessly they put on a façade, blending into their roles too seamlessly. Maybe it was because I loathed vampires, or maybe it was the sharp metallic scent of Quillian's chains mixed with the musty smell of his leather pants that made my skin crawl.

The Iron Fang didn't condone any racist judgment shit. Locke said that from the beginning. Anyone who was rejected was welcome to be there. Vampires had more time on their hands than the shifters before they went damn crazy after a rejection, though. They had better handle on the demons that inhabited them, more will to live, or maybe they acted more human. Hell if I knew.

They still gave me the creeps.

Quillian pulled a vape that hung around his neck and stuck it in his mouth. He puffed on it several times and let the vape gather around us. "Tell me why Locke let you come with us?" He looks me up and down. "You aren't really stealthy, can't squeeze into small spaces, and being quiet isn't your strong suit." He let out a puff of his vape.

I glared at him, my grizzly growling in his sleep. "A favor to Delilah, to save the woman that helped her escape her ex." I looked forward and concentrated ahead of me. I didn't owe him any other explanation. I didn't need to talk to him.

Out of the corner of my eye, I see Quillian smirk. He twirled the vape in his fingers and leaned forward. "Rumor has it that the little lady put you off on the camera feed," Quillian taunted. "That you went damn near feral when you saw the state she was in. It differed from all the women you've saved before. Your eyes glazed over and turned yellow—"

I balled my hands into fists, and my lip curled.

Quillian sat back in his seat. "Then again, that was all rumors and speculation." He waved his hand and was handed a blood bag. He let down his teeth, sucking in the blood until it was completely drained. "Fuuuuck, good shit. Hit me with another," he asked another bandmate.

I've saved plenty of women, men, and even children from uncertain death and trafficking over the years since coming to the Iron Fang. It was what we did, trying to seek one last attempt at redemption until our animals took over our bodies and killed everything in sight.

We wanted to try to get whatever redemption we could before going rabid. That was before. Now that Grim, Tajah, and Hawke got another chance, we were more hopeful. Things were looking up, great things were happening, people were believing again.

And I was impatient as hell.

I saw this mission as a distraction in my obsession with finding my second chance. That's all this was. It was just a chance to help Delilah rescue the nameless female who helped her escape her ex-husband's mansion and somehow didn't make it out like she promised Delilah she would.

Delilah was one of my good friends, and before I left, I promised her I'd bring her little savior home.

I'd be the bear to make sure this female was free and started a new life. A new apartment, a job, and safety, to be with the Iron Fang where she would be protected and looked after until she was well.

The image of her tiny body, her arms wrapped around herself, shaking, was enough to strengthen my dozing grizzly's heart from a few beats a minute to pumping more regularly. Maybe that was why my claws were appearing.

Another rumble in my chest appeared, and the lightning flashed outside the window.

The private jet, stolen from Delilah's now-dead ex-husband, hit an air pocket and fell hundreds of feet. I gripped the seat, my soul leaving my body as the vampires cheered, feeling the weightless bodies fly about the cabin until the pilot leveled out the plane.

"I don't know many bears that like to fly," Quillian joked and took another long draw out of the blood bag.

"We don't." I gritted my teeth.

The plane continued with its turbulence. My head leaned back into the seat as the vampires and one wolf shifter, who had been adopted into the Moonlight Outcasts years ago, laughed and joked with one another while they put their drinks away and got ready for the descent.

They put on their gear, all black, their slim, lithe bodies completely covered in knife-cut-resistant material.

My grizzly was unsettled as he slumbered, my nails turning blacker as I continued to concentrate on what mission I had before me. This was supposed to be a stealth mission, not my forte, I'd admit.

I gripped my Glocks under each arm holster and pulled them out, switching the safety on and off. Silver, holy water, and dogwood filled bullets were in various clips on my belt. Not just humans, but other supernaturals could be inside.

I let out a breath, tightening my belt as we lowered through the clouds, the rain pelting on the plane. This was it. Soon we would be landing on the private runway.

Get in, get out.

Shit, this is what I wanted. Feel the rush, get the girl, get her home.

Then why was I nervous as hell?

CHAPTER FOUR

Bear

My heart pounded as I raced across the darkened lawn of the estate with the other five Moonlight Outcast members. The small runway was far enough from the mansion so it wouldn't disturb anyone on the property, and the pilot could land with no lights on the runway.

The pilot had to be compelled over a dozen times over the trip across the states because none of the vampires' compulsions would last more than an hour. Much less than it usually would if they were at full strength before their own rejections. Rejection could rip your soul in half, and even their powers were crumbling like the rest of us.

"Forty minutes. We need to be back on the plane," Quillian said as he stared down at the side door of the conservatory. He's wearing night vision goggles to enhance their vision like the rest of us. It doubled as cameras, which gave access to a feed so Switch and the rest of the club could watch at home.

Switch didn't cut off all the alarms upon our arrival, so no one in the mansion would question any changes in the house. We were going to open and close doors one at a time, making sure to be as stealthy as we could. We weren't sure if Duke Idris would take up residency or even knew if Shane

Cunningham was dead. Running into the dark fae would mean certain death for all of us.

"You're clear," Switch said through our comms.

We all stepped inside and found ourselves in the conservatory. The vines wound up the glass, keeping a lot of the moonlight out but still giving us enough cover.

"Remember to stay together," Quillian reiterated.

I growled, rolling my eyes. I was ready to move, ready to blast in there with guns blazing, claws out, and fucking kill them all.

"See that is not what we want," Quillian snapped at my huffing. "This isn't a Locke mission. He isn't here. I'm the one in charge." His black leather gloves stretched around his hands and grabbed onto my night vision goggles, pulling them toward him. "Don't fuck up my system, Bear."

I snarled, showing my teeth, and he let go, his eyes widening for a fraction of a second. He shook his head and threw out some hand signals only his guys would know.

Locke had his own hand signals, and I went on missions with him, not with these guys. So I just followed behind them, my hand on my Glock with a stupid silencer, and listened through the comm.

Switch spouted off directions, his voice calm, cool, and collected as he gave out orders. It was like he was right there with us, reading the map. He knew what was around every corner, if a guard was nearby, telling us when to wait, when to grab someone by the neck and take them out.

All was done in silence, not a single disruption and not another guard alerted of our presence.

As we moved through the house, we entered the massive hallway. It did not surprise us as we entered a den area with sleeping human bodies scattered around the couches and TV blaring with infomercials per Switch's description. There were no women. Just beer bottles, lines of cocaine, drugs, glass pipes, and bongs lying everywhere.

We continued through the house, taking one man down at a time. The entire pack back home was watching on the big screens at the bar, watching our every move as we went through the house. It was deathly quiet through the comm as we grew closer to the kitchen.

I clenched my hands tightly, feeling my nails digging into my palms as my heart thumped wildly against my ribcage. The sound was deafening, like a muffled drumbeat echoing in my ears. But it wasn't just my own heartbeat that I could feel—there was a low growl emanating from the depths of my being, a primal sound that rumbled in my chest like thunder. I could smell the musky scent of my own fear mingling with the sharp tang of adrenaline, making my nostrils flare. And beneath it all, I could sense the stirring of my grizzly, restless energy that pulsed through me like a live wire. It was both exhilarating and terrifying, and I wasn't sure what it could mean.

As my claws grew longer, they shredded through the leather with a faint scratching sound. Quillian and the others were completely oblivious to the transformation happening to me. They were staring at Cyran, who was sniffing their air, pulling off his goggles and reaching for the kitchen door.

When I glanced down at my hands, the sight of my elongated claws was both mesmerizing and terrifying. The smell of freshly ripped leather hit me, and my eyes widened at the sight of my elongated claws. As I attempted to wrap my fingers around the trigger of my gun, the length of my claws made it difficult to maintain a steady grip, causing a sense of clumsiness and unease to wash over me.

Shit.

And everyone back home just saw it.

"Hey, big Bear," a familiar voice came on the comm and it was none other than Journey.

Grim's woman was the club's priestess. The Moon Goddess blessed her when she willingly listened to the Goddess months ago when no one else would. She damn saved us all and is trying to get our stubborn asses to find our mates—not that I would ever reject a second chance. But, now that she was talking to me, maybe it was too late.

"We are on a private line, Bear. It's just us," she soothed.

I swallowed hard as the team watched Cyran staring at the kitchen door.

"Can you ask her to give me more time? I'm trying here."

Hell, I was. The goddess couldn't take me now. I'm trying to live, trying to get my chance.

I could almost see Journey's smile. That's how bright she was. A giggle came from her line. "I think I can do that. Just don't stress, okay? Things are going to work out."

Cyran pushed the door open, and the blinding light threw our night vision goggles back to daytime mode. Cyran's throat made a growling, purring noise, and he projected his voice across the room. "Sleep," he commanded.

In a sudden frenzy, he bolted across the spacious kitchen, barely avoiding colliding with the female who accidentally hit her head on the sharp edge of the island. Crimson blood trickled down her temple, creating a stark contrast against her pale skin. Without hesitation, he swiftly lifted the unconscious female, whom he had previously commanded to sleep, and cradled her delicately against his broad chest. A low, comforting purr emanated from him as he held her close.

"Beloved." He smiled and rubbed her cheek with his thumb.

Fuck, everyone gets their female.

"This wasn't part of the plan, Cyran." Quillian took off the goggles and shoved them in his bag. As he approached, Cyran held the female tighter and hissed at him.

Quillian stood back and held his hands up. "Quite right. Yes, well, congrats to you, old chap, but we have a mission now, and you're out since you're compromised. But what's that around her neck?" He pointed to the black collar with a red blinking light.

Cyran growled, and his fingers wrapped around it, ready to pull.

"No!" Phineus, one of the other vamps, comes barreling around the corner of the kitchen island. "If you take it off, it might trigger an alarm. Just wait for us outside. We will take it off of her when we get the other female and get on the plane."

"You go with him. Best stay in twos," Quillian said. "The rest will be carried out. Congratulations again, Cyran."

Cyran didn't pay attention. Instead, he was sniffing her hair, licking her wound, and groaning. I scoffed, my anger rising that I again was without a mate. I thought this mission would give me a break from seeing so many mated couples at the club, but this was not the case.

Does the Goddess want to curse me more?

My grizzly stirred inside me, his head jolting back and forth as if trying to break free from his slumber. The slightest sounds echoed in my ears, amplified and distorted. Virgil stood by the door, his silhouette barely visible in the dim light. He fiddled with his night goggles, the sound of the toggle switch growing louder and more grating by the second. The acrid smell of burnt plastic filled my nostrils as the goggles emitted a high-pitched whine. I winced, my eardrums vibrating with each click of the switch. Desperately, I reached for my comm, pulling it out of my ear and rubbing it vigorously to relieve the discomfort.

Quillian ignored me, too caught up in Cyran and Phineus leaving and motioned for us to follow him.

"Stay put. We won't be gone for long," Quillian commanded Arlo, the sole wolf shifter of the group. Arlo nodded firmly, his jaw clenched beneath the second skin wrap he wore, and he gripped his gun with a sense of purpose.

And then we descended, leaving the kitchen behind. Switch guided us further into the abyss that was not a basement but a dungeon that seemed to be an afterthought of the glorious mansion that we traveled through.

This place reeked of death, the pungent stench of blood and ammonia making my nose wrinkle in disgust. My heart pounded painfully in my chest, the worry that we might be too late to save the poor female making my stomach churn. My grizzly companion's eyes snapped open at the same moment that the thought crossed my mind, his keen sense of smell detecting the acrid odor that permeated the air.

As we reached the bottom, I put my hand on the wall, my claws scraping against the bare cement walls. My grizzly shook his fur, dust and debris casting out of his thick and mangy fur.

Gods, he was rough and depressed looking, but fuck, he was awake.

Please don't go rabid now.

Quillian and Virgil continued their walk, unaware I was no longer behind them. Their flashlights in their hands looking into each room as they passed by.

"*Keep going,*" I whispered to myself.

I could worry about my bear waking up later. As long as he wasn't going rabid, trying to hurt anyone, if I was strong enough to hold him back until I could get the girl on the plane, then they could take off. Let my grizzly go wild in the house and attack all the assholes that remained.

I cleared my throat. Quillian and Virgil looked behind me. Their steps faltered as they saw me staggering toward them.

"This is it. Found the room." Quillian nodded to the door. "You wanna look while we work on the lock?"

I put the comm back in my ear and heard Switch blowing out some curses. I lowered the volume for him to mumble off that the prison security system wasn't connected with the house.

"*Break it down. Grab her, get out,*" Locke snapped through the comm. "*She doesn't look like she has much time.*"

I frowned and opened the small window that shut automatically if you don't hold it open, and what I saw threw my stomach into knots.

The woman was adorned in threadbare clothes that barely covered her skeletal frame. The sound of her labored breaths filled the room, accompanied by the faint creaking of the poor excuse of a cot that struggled to support her weight. There was a pungent smell of sweat mixed with the musty odor of unwashed fabric. Her arm dangled off the side of the cot, exposed to the chilly air, with a blanket of nothing but rags to provide warmth.

Gritting my teeth, I felt my grizzly rising to the surface with alarming speed. He took over my mind, and I let out a guttural growl as I pounded on the metal door with my fists. The sound echoed through the hallway, and I could feel the walls shaking beneath my furious blows. The metallic taste of blood filled my mouth as my knuckles scraped against the rough surface of the door. I could feel the heat of my rage rising within me.

"The hell is he doing!" Virgil reached out his hand from my peripheral, but Quillian pulled him away.

"He's going to break down the door, go down the hall, check for any guards," Quillian hissed.

Virgil updated everyone and ran in the opposite direction while he spoke with Switch on the comm for updates.

I, on the other hand, switched up tactics to get the door moving. My blood was pumping, my grizzly amping up the adrenaline coursing through my body, my strength coming in tenfold at seeing the body of the girl laying there lifeless. She hadn't even moved at the pounding of my body against the door.

I moved to ramming my shoulder, using my body as a battering ram until the hinges cracked, then I took my foot and rammed it two more times until the door pushed in and landed on the floor.

The dust flew from the concrete, and I stepped on the door, walking in. Quillian was right behind me. He rushed and tried to bolt in front of me to check on the girl, but I gripped him by the arm and held him close to my face. "Don't touch her," I breathed. I glanced at her body, her chest barely rising.

It was my job to take care of her. It was stuck in my head all along, and I would fulfill my duty and do just that. This vampire would not touch her.

Quillian, the asshole leader of the group, raised a brow to retaliate, but his eyes sunk back into his head, and his hands gripped my wrist holding onto his arm. "Your eyes, your bear—"

"I ain't just a damn bear. I'm a grizzly," I corrected. "And he's awake."

CHAPTER FIVE

Nadia

I knew their screams weren't real. The high-pitched, exaggerated cries they made for me echoed in the darkness. The sweet names they called me as a child—"little sweet," "mouse," "angel"—were now laced with longing. The enticing promises we would be together as a family once again were nothing but a distant memory, like the faded scent of my mother's perfume that lingered in the air. As I lay there, the coldness of the room seeping into my bones, I realized that the love and warmth I had once felt were long gone.

My skin prickled with goosebumps as I lay there in the dark, feeling as though something was watching me. The more I moved here in my dreams, the deeper the claws raked my skin.

Before I came to this prison in the basement of the mansion, I never felt pain in a dream. That was all different now, and I wasn't sure why. Here I felt everything, and it was magnified.

"Nadia, please, we are over here." I could hear my mother's thick Russian accent echo through the darkness, and Papa's grunts beating away whatever was pulling him and Mama away from me. He wasn't fighting anything because I knew he wasn't really there.

I knew because I tried for the longest time to find them in the darkness, and while I did, the long claws of whatever held me in place would dig deeper into my skin, making me scream, making their own cries that much louder.

I lay there, feeling the sharp claws sinking into my skin while their cries and my tears mingled together. Being awake or asleep, either way, was torture. There was no rest, and I thought—or at least hoped that when I closed my eyes this time, I would meet my maker.

Suddenly, my dream was interrupted by a loud bang and an unfamiliar growl that echoed in my ears. I winced, covering them with my fists, and the claws retracted as I did so. The cries of my parents stopped, and they left me alone in the darkness.

Warmth surrounded me, filling me with a sense of peace and contentment.

Oh god, so much warmth.

My body was lifted, and I felt weightless. The heat was all too welcoming, and I swore this was it. This was how I died, and thank god I was heading toward the sun.

My eyes slowly opened and adjusted to the brightness. It was so bright and maybe I just got to heaven for all the suffering. But then there was a slam and another man shouting in the distance. I balled up my fists and blocked out sounds.

So. Much. Noise.

"Basement is secure. All guards taken down. Let's get to the jet." A male voice came from my right, and I tried to open my eyes again.

A rumbling, deep and motor-like, came from deep within the wall holding me. I wasn't put off by the deep vibrations; it reminded me of the many times riding in the old car my parents used to drive around when I was a child to put me to sleep. The wall itself was vast and soft, and I uncovered my ear to inspect what I was leaning up against.

It wasn't just a wall, but a clothed chest. It was breathing heavily, and it was muscled. I pulled my hand back, squinted my eyes against the bright light, and looked up at who was clenching me in the thick blanket surrounding me.

It was a man, but not just any man who had me in his arms. Instead of finding a clean-shaven mafia man like I usually see, this one had a thick, dark beard and was tall with a wide chest. His eyes were golden yellow, not normal in the slightest, and despite the furrow in his brow and his clenched jaw to make him look intimidating, I didn't feel he would hurt me.

In fact, I felt the opposite.

The burly man held me tighter, and a whimper escaped me. I was too weak to think clearly, too tired to care.

"You're safe," he said in a hushed tone.

He took his hand and brushed my tangled hair away from my face. It took him a moment to get the hair to unwrap from around my glasses, but he did it with ease with just one hand while his other arm held me steady.

This guy must be strong and huge to hold me so steady.

"I'm going to get you out of here." His deep, heavy breathing, combined with a rattling in his chest, was soothing. My eyes grew heavy, but I dared not close them again.

"We've got a clear shot to get out of here. We are going to head out the back of the kitchen," a man said behind him.

I put my hand back on my ear to muffle the noise, and the man carrying me turned, and we shuffled out of the room. The turning, the racing up the stairs, and the heavy footsteps were all movements I wasn't ready for. Luckily, my stomach was empty, and the noise was minimal.

Once outside, I took in my first breath of fresh air. My eyes widened, and I dared to open them all the way and saw the brightest moon I'd ever witnessed. It wasn't completely full, but it was the most beautiful thing I'd seen.

As I leaned against the towering figure holding me, I gazed up at the vast expanse of the sky. The cool evening breeze swept over my skin, carrying the scent of blooming flowers. With a heart full of gratitude, I silently whispered a thank you to the heavens above. I let out a contented sigh, feeling the soft fabric of the man's shirt beneath my fingertips. It was as if his embrace was shielding me from the harshness of the world. The rhythmic sound of his steady breathing was a soothing lullaby, lulling me into a peaceful state. At that moment, I realized I felt safe for the first time in what felt like an eternity. Perhaps it was because his touch was the first human contact I had experienced in so long, or maybe it was because he had chased away the darkness from not just my dreams but my reality as well.

I could die happy now.

He tightened his hold on me. My head fell back into his chest, and I smiled, so happy to be out of the prison. Wherever these people were taking me, may it be another prison—I knew I wouldn't last long. I could pretend this man was my savior. That there was some part of good in the world, even if it was just for another day.

The area was dark as the men slinked their way across the courtyard. They were quiet, guns in their hands and looking all around them. They were trained and skillful in what they did, but the giant holding me stood out more than the others.

He was taller and broader; he didn't fit in with the rest of them. He didn't duck behind statues or trees; he walked like he owned the estate, and his jaw was set so tense I feared he might break his teeth.

"Bones, have the medical bed ready," he spoke. I jumped in his arms, and his thumb rubbed over my cheek. "Easy," his voice rumbled. "We have a doctor on board ready to look at you when we take off."

I swallowed hard and balled my fist into his shirt.

Why help me? I wanted to ask.

Once we arrived, there was another woman in the arms of another. I'd never seen her before, but she was wearing a uniform that was like mine but newer, and she had a collar around her neck. "Break it and get in." I heard behind me as I was carried inside.

The plane engine roared, and I covered my ears again, the sound overwhelming. My heart raced at the new surroundings and my body shook with the anxiety of not knowing what was going to happen to me. For years I'd spent time in the same space, and now I was out—which I was grateful for—but where was I going?

The male set me down in a chair, the blanket still wrapped around me. He knelt in front of me and buckled me in. It was all I could do to sit upright. My body shook and tilted, trying to lean on the wall next to the window. My teeth chattered, my body already losing the heat from his body.

The man frowned. I couldn't look him in the eye; I was too ashamed, too weak to do anything more.

He lifted my chin. "My name is Bear. What is yours?"

I opened my mouth, but no words came out.

I shook my head, my hair covering my face. "Shh, it's alright," Bear's soft words for a giant comforted me. He unbuckled my seat belt, picked me up again, and brought me into his lap.

I didn't protest. I soaked up the massive amount of heat that he radiated. I wanted it, craved it, and I buried my face into his chest. My bones didn't ache. My body warmed. I wanted more of it.

Only because he's warm. It's for survival. I told myself as I buried my face in his chest.

His arms wrapped around me, his breathing deepened, and a loud growling noise radiated from his chest. He petted my hair and ran his fingers through it, and I melted.

The plane went into motion, and soon enough, it was airborne, and the shaking in my body soon subsided.

It was better than food.

As soon as the plane stabilized and the distinct clicking of seatbelts being undone filled the air, I instinctively brought my hands up to my ears. I winced at the high-pitched noises, burying my face further into Bear's chest.

"What's wrong? Are you in pain?" Bear asked. He tried to pull my hands down, but I refused and kept them close to my ears.

Too much noise. Too much.

Bear growled deeply.

I'm becoming a problem.

Bear unbuckled our seat belt, picked me up, and traveled to the back of the plane. Bear tapped on a door, and it opened rapidly, revealing a gentleman with salt and peppered hair.

I say gentleman because he looks well put together and nothing like the other men I saw who were dressed in assassin black clothes. This man looked put together with his black button-down shirt and dark jeans.

"Bear, I was about to come get you." I winced, turning my head away and back into Bear's chest.

Bear put his overly large hand over my ear and kept me glued to his body.

"Lower your voice. She can't handle loud noises," Bear grumbled, pushed the gentleman to the side, and barged in.

The soft voice Bear used on me earlier was gone, and now I felt more guilty for causing problems. But maybe it was all because he was trying to get me on the plane and be compliant anyway.

I didn't know what they wanted with me yet.

Bear sat me on the medical bed; it was stark white and sterile. I frowned knowing I would just stain it with my dirty clothes as Bear sat me down with a blanket wrapped around me. I swayed, unable to sit up, so I lay on the bed, not looking at either one of them.

I could feel the heated stare from Bear and saw his fists at his sides. He was angry, that much was for sure.

I swallowed, trying not to look at him. Even if he felt warm and safe while he held me, I couldn't expect him to continue to do it.

"Hi there, I'm Bones. I'm a trained medical professional." He did his best to smile, but it looked like he didn't do it much. "I'm going to check you over. See if we need to get some antibiotics in you or anything else to get you healthy, okay? We are also going to start an IV with some fluids to get some food in you too."

I nodded a few times, wrapping the blanket tighter. "Can you tell me your name?" Bones sat down on a stool, so I was looking down at him. It made me feel taller, like I was on the same level as him, but I was still uncomfortable. I had two men in the room and then me, a girl, with no way to communicate.

I shook my head and fiddled with the blanket.

Bones's brow furrowed.

"She hasn't spoken since we rescued her," Bear interrupted, crossing his arms.

"Do you want to tell me your name?" Bones reworded the question.

I nodded.

Bones pulled out a clipboard, flipped over a piece of paper, and handed me a pen. I held the pen as best I could with my hand, but it shook so badly I could hardly keep it steady. I bit my lip, trying to concentrate, but my bony fingers were unable to grip. I dropped it several times until Bear came to my aid and sat me up before pulling me into his lap.

His big, burly body engulfed me. A rush of heat flooded through my body and gave me strength. Sitting up so fast, along with the heat and my starving body, I had no more energy to spend.

With the last bit of energy and with Bear's help, he used his hand to steady my grip on the pen and I was able to write out my name. *Nadia.*

CHAPTER SIX

Bear

*M*ine.

That was exactly what I thought when I took in her scent, lying there, helpless. When I saw Quillian try to step in front of me to get near her, it was a grave mistake. I had gripped his arm and threw him across the room. He laid in a crumpled heap. It was invigorating. I tried not to roar with triumph with my strength returning.

As soon as I realized she was mine, I felt a sudden surge of strength coursing through my body. I knew instantly that it was all because of her. I could smell the heady aroma of freshly picked wild blackberries dripping with sweet, sticky honey. The scent was so strong that it filled my nostrils and permeated every inch of my being. It was the most delicious smell I had ever experienced, and it brought back memories of my childhood. I could almost taste the sweet, juicy berries on my tongue and feel the sticky honey dripping down my chin. It was like being transported back in time to when I ate it as a cub, carefree of the world and the dangers that surrounded me. The sensation was overwhelming, and I knew I would never forget this moment for as long as I lived.

Unfortunately, my mate was being offered to me on a worthless, crumbling cot. She should be laying on an altar, ready for me to worship her for the goddess she is, but no, she was wasting away.

My bear reared his ugly head, shook whatever fur left of our emaciated body, and set off a deafening roar that alerted the guards. I knew Quillian and his men would deal with them quickly because Quillian ran out the door while I scooped my mate in my arms and paid them no mind.

I had her. I finally had her.

I cradled her, smelled her, buried my nose into her neck. She woke up once and showed me deep blue eyes, and I knew she had me wrapped around her finger. I'd do anything for her, and right now, I needed to get her to a safe place.

My bear let out his loud hum, one that was much louder than the wolf shifters. She didn't shy away; instead, she curled up into my arms more, and damn, did my grizzly feel that much more prideful.

As we went to the plane and her grip on my shirt tightened, I hoped she would remain awake so she could answer my questions. I could know her name, know who she was, and finally hear her voice.

As we gathered on the plane, I knew I had to calm myself as well as my grizzly. He had to know we could not push her and claim her like any other type of bear. She was a human, scared and very weak from her time spent in that damn hell hole.

My anger rose thinking about that fucking prison. I should get her seated, go back, and take care of the bastards.

My touches stayed gentle when I sat her in the seat, carefully wrapping the blanket around her body. Her body swayed, and she leaned up against the wall of the plane, her body shaking.

My heart nearly shattered when I saw her like this. My grizzly was damn near rabid to reach out and pull the blankets away from her, pull off my shirt, and let her skin take up my warmth. There was no way I could leave her to seek vengeance now. I had to take care of her, keep her safe.

Fucking hell. What kind of sick bastard could do this to a woman?

I frowned. The doors slammed, and I didn't even care anymore if I could go back and kill someone. All I wanted was to keep her safe now. I would. I swore to my bear we would. He undoubtedly agreed, and there would be no shame in keeping her away from everyone.

When she gripped her ears, and I heard her near-non-existent whimpers, I couldn't understand what was wrong.

I couldn't understand why she found them so loud? Why had she not said a word? More worrying thoughts. My grizzly was restless, and waiting for Bones was no longer an option.

Now, seeing her lying in front of me, with the excitement of finding my mate now fading and reality setting in, she was worse than I feared. My mate had no meat on her bones, her feet bare and dirty, her tiny body lay there so helpless, and my grizzly was just at the surface. He wanted to demand they turn the plane around and gut every last person in that mansion.

My heart raced as my fists clenched, my nails digging into my palms. My breathing became shallow and erratic as I struggled to contain my anger. My vision narrowed as I focused solely on the frail figure before me, my mate. It took all my willpower not to let my grizzly take over and wreak havoc on everything around me.

I tried to calm myself, knowing it would be best for both me and my mate, but that was proving difficult.

As I reached out to touch her, my hands trembled with a mix of emotions. I felt both a fierce protectiveness and a deep longing to connect with her. My grizzly roared inside me, demanding that I claim her and do it swiftly.

Being the levelheaded one, I knew better than to do that.

The only thing I could do was to vow silently to protect her and provide for her, ensuring that she never suffered again.

I didn't care if I got harmed in the process, but it would seek vengeance on every damn bastard that ignored her.

She wouldn't—couldn't speak.

I held enough rage to strip down thousands of forests as she sat there trying to write. I lunged forward, pushing Bones away, and pulled her into my arms. I wrapped my large hand around hers, my cheek leaning against her forehead.

Already her touch soothed the animal inside me.

The humming in my chest eased her quivering breaths as I helped steady her hand, and she wrote out her name.

"Nadia," I breathed out. "What a beautiful name."

Suddenly she fell limp, and I cradled her back in my arms. "Nadia?" I gently shook her. "Nadia?" I said it louder, but she did not wake. With her resistance to sound, my panic surfaced, and I lost hold of my bear.

We laid her gently over the table and hovered over her in a protective stance, glaring at Bones like he was the culprit. He held his arms back, showing he wielded no weapon, and backed away.

"Easy there," Bones soothed. "Everything is going to be fine." He pressed his comm to his ear, and I snarled.

He was calling for backup.

He was going to take her away from me.

Quillian and Phineus opened the door, their hands on their side where their guns were held. I growled in warning.

"Bear, what's going on?" Quillian said quietly, not making any sudden movements.

"The female, Nadia. She passed out from exhaustion. Bear just got a little excited," Bones answered. "I need to get an IV in her, get her stable. I just need Bear to calm down a bit."

I lifted my lip back, showing off my teeth, and Phineus showed me his fangs in return. Quillian grabbed his wrist and pulled his man back. "Bear's grizzly is back. We need to show some respect," Quillian said and didn't keep his eyes off me. He tried to pull Phineus behind him.

Bones darted his gaze between Quillian and me. "That true, Bear? He's woken up?"

"Yes." I gritted my teeth.

Bones smiled. "I guess Journey was right again. Nadia is truly your mate, isn't she?"

"Mine," I snarled, holding her closer.

"And I found mine too!" Cyran called from the other room

Bones jumped up from his chair, clapping his hand loudly. "Another found their mate! That's amazing!"

The quick movements pissed off my grizzly. He took control of my arm, reared back, and went to swipe Bone's chest. Phineus pushed Quillian away and jumped in front of Bones, catching the brunt of the claws. Fabric and skin ripped, causing blood to drip onto the floor, and my grizzly let out a menacing roar as I pounded the medical bed.

Nadia whimpered under me, my body hovered over hers as I nuzzled my nose into her neck. She calmed, her body warming under my touch.

"That was the most idiotic thing you could do, Bones. You call yourself a doctor?" Quillian hissed from the other side of the room. "Damn you." Quillian took slow and deliberate movements, showing he had no weapons in his hands.

I watched Quillian as he picked up Phineus, who stared at me with wide eyes. I would not say sorry. He should have let Bones take the hit, the dumb bastard.

Quillian cursed at his friend, ordering him to drink two blood bags, and led Phineus out, but continued to stay by the door. "Now, Bones, do you know about bear shifters or not? Specifically, a grizzly because they are nasty fuckers to deal with."

I growled again, and Quillian kept his gaze on Bones.

Bones rolled his eyes and raised his hands. "Right, I'm sorry, Bear, Quillian." Bones gave a curt nod. "Now, I need to check on your mate. She's malnourished. I don't know if she's hydrated, and I need to get some blood samples before I start a feeding tube."

I weighed my options. I didn't want to leave her or let anyone touch her, but I knew staying on top of her to protect her would do nothing for her body. I could feel the bones in her arms and wrists. I couldn't be selfish, and I had to trust.

Bones was trained. He brought the supplies needed to take care of a human in such a condition. I growled once more, gently getting off of my mate.

Quillian watched from the doorway. My eyes stayed on both of them, and I kept at least one hand on my mate.

Bones got to work, taking his time, treating me as if I was the patient, explaining in complete detail what he was doing and why. I was grateful because my grizzly was just bubbling above the surface and to shift on a plane, even in his weakened state, would not fare well.

My animal was still sick, but since finding his mate he would fight anyone, no matter what power they wielded, to keep her safe, especially after what she had been through. Nadia would never leave my sight, and when she woke, that would be a hard pill to swallow for her.

Quillian watched at the end of the medical table, his arms crossed and brow furrowed. "Is it necessary to put a feeding tube in her now?" he asked.

Bones continued to fiddle with the food bag, hanging it up along with the IV bag. "She is severely malnourished; you can see her body. Even though I cannot accurately weigh her, I listened with my stethoscope and found no food in her stomach. Even her lower intestines are empty, barely moving. Her internal organs are shutting down."

I wrapped my hand around my mate's torso, pulling her closer to me. "And what does that mean?" I asked.

Bones ran his hand through his hair. "It means if we had waited one more day, she wouldn't be alive."

My heart squeezed in my chest. My world is nearly crumbling around me. Nadia had an IV in her arm and a feeding tube down her nose that led to her stomach. Her skin was pale, nearly grey. There was barely life left in her body, but she was still beautiful to me.

"It's the bond," Quillian interrupted my thoughts. "You find her stunning even when she is on the brink of death."

"My mate will not die." I gritted my teeth. "She is my second chance."

Quillian chuckled. "I never got to caress the mate that rejected me so lovingly as you are doing, though. No, didn't give her the chance. I staked her instead." He gave a rueful smile.

Bones and I both sat in silence, not sure what to say.

"Yeah—but even in her final breath, until her blood ran dry—I thought she was the most beautiful creature." He paused and looked out the plane window. "But, Bear, your mate will make it. I am sure of it. Nadia is your second chance."

Quillian left the room, and I was left with Bones, with the quiet and the dripping of the saline bag.

Quillian, vampires in general were strange creatures. Dark, void of most emotion from their faces, the older ones anyway.

I was no doctor; I didn't understand the human body and how fragile it could be. I was a shifter, and even in my weakened state I was twice as strong as the strongest human male.

"What do I need to do to ensure her health?" A wave of determination settled over me. I would make sure my mate would be healthy. I rested my hand against her forehead and closed my eyes.

Bones pulled a bag from a drawer in his makeshift medical room and laid it beside my mate. "In here are cleansing wipes and clean clothes. Clean her up the best you can and dress her. I know you will not let me do such a thing."

Damn straight, he won't touch her. That's my job.

Bones rubbed the sweat away from his forehead. "I must rest. I will come back and change her fluid bag soon. By then, we will be close to home."

I opened the bag inside, seeing a pair of sweatpants and a sweatshirt along with clean underwear one of the females back home prepared for her.

Moon Goddess, give me strength.

"And Bear," Bones said from the doorway. "You being with her now is what is keeping her alive. Let the bond do its work."

With a heavy heart, I realized this journey would not be easy, but I was willing to do whatever it took to make my mate whole again.

CHAPTER SEVEN

Nadia

"It's been a week." The deep, fuzzy voice came from the darkness. My eyelids were heavy, but I still didn't open them. My body, though heavy as well, I didn't try to move either.

I knew I wasn't dreaming. I could feel crisp, clean sheets between my fingers, a cool liquid going up my arm, and that same wall of heat radiating into my face.

"Bear, give her time," another voice said.

Bear was holding me.

And strangely enough, I didn't hate it.

"It is going to take time. I told you this." The other voice was tired, exasperated, as I noticed my surroundings. There was a thump beside me, and he cleared his throat. "Please, Bear, go shower. That way, when she wakes up, you will be ready to tend to her. Trust me, her seeing you like this won't do you any favors. You haven't shaved; you look like death. At least look presentable."

Bear sighed deeply. He again sounded like a loud engine motor going off in his chest. I did my best not to sigh deeply into it. The sound was deep enough it didn't hurt my ears in the slightest. Instead, it was lulling me back to sleep.

"Fine, but you come get me if she stirs." Bear held me tight to his chest, his thumb rubbing up against my cheek.

The other male scoffed, which I assumed was Bones. I heard typing while I was gently laid back on a slightly raised bed with blankets strewn across me. Bear's large hand was placed on my forehead. It lingered there and a strange feeling warmed my chest.

Why in the world was this guy so taken with me? Had he laid some sort of claim on me? Was I some sort of product to him?

The mansion ran drugs and weapons—not humans. That was the one thing that was good about working there, at least when I was a housekeeper. I didn't know what it was like there now.

Bear holding me, and who knows for how long—why? Why would he do that?

I knew one thing: I felt better. My mind was not foggy, my mentality was better, my thinking was clearer, and best of all... my stomach wasn't eating itself. I wasn't starving, which was strange since I had been sleeping.

"I mean it, Bones," Bear growled from across the room. "I'm trusting you with her care if one hair—"

"I got it, oh possessive one," Bones scoffed. "Now go, you smell like a bear just out of hibernation that needs a good dip in the river, and take that bag on the table with you."

Bear made a grunting noise and shut the door.

A few moments passed while I tried to weigh my options of what I should do, but luckily, Bones answered my questions.

"Nadia, I know you are awake. Your heart rate spiked on the monitor the moment you woke up."

I fluttered my eyes open and saw him sitting on a stool next to a computer. He wasn't wearing a typical white doctor's coat; instead, he had on a black button-down dress shirt and jeans with a stethoscope around his neck.

"You are at my clinic right now, at the Iron Fang. It's a motorcycle club on the west coast of the country. You are far away from the Cunningham estate and will never have to worry about them again."

I fisted the surrounding blankets. They were thicker than the typical hospital blankets. They were flannel, smelled of pine, a winding river, and—Bear.

"You're safe, Nadia." Bones' words were soft, his eyes even more so. "You are here to get better, stronger. I thought you might feel overwhelmed with Bear being in the room. If you would like me to bring him back, I can."

I brought my legs up to my torso, keeping the blankets wrapped around me. The smell, the heat left over from Bear's warmth, soothed me enough to where I didn't feel so vulnerable.

And why was that?

Because he rescued me? Carried me out like some motorcycle gang Viking warrior person?

Bones nodded and pulled the stethoscope from around his neck. "If you are okay, I would like to listen to your lungs, make sure they are clear?"

I swallowed and nodded, unfurling my legs.

Bones spoke just like any physician as he checked my breathing on my back and my chest. I didn't mind him touching me, and he kept it professional. He also did the other tests, such as my reflexes, and checked my eyes, mouth, and throat. He explained the feeding tube that was threaded down my throat and gently removed it, saying since I was awake, I was in charge of filling my own stomach now.

He even pulled out my IV, carefully placing a hot pink band-aid on top of it, chucking to himself as he did so. "I do it to piss off the other bikers, but it looks good on you."

I smiled and swung my legs on the bed. As the minutes went on, I was more comfortable with Bones. I don't know if it was just a faux feeling and if I should put my guard back up, but after being locked away with no one to listen to but an evil boss for so many years, it was nice.

The large shirt hung over my tiny body. From what I could tell, there was a picture of a skull splattered with blood. The shorts I wore were oversized and rolled up but still came to my knees. They all smelled heavily like Bear, as did everything else on the bed.

Did he sleep in here with me?

"Do you know how tall you are, what you used to weigh before you were put in that terrible place?" Bones jotted down some notes on a clipboard, and I nodded.

"And you cannot talk? Did they—do something to your vocal cords, your throat?"

I shook my head, pursed my lips, and looked away from him in shame.

I can talk—

Bones patted my hand. "It's fine. We will work through it." He handed me the clipboard and had me fill out my height. Bones cursed. "Four, eleven, shit, you are tiny." He chuckled. "I'd like to get your weight now; do you think you can walk?"

I'd always been tiny. My parents were strikingly taller than me, closer to six feet, while I never grew. We were in the poorer lower middle class, lived in a modest two-bedroom apartment in New York, and they never had reason for concern about me being unhealthy, especially since I never went hungry. I was quieter than most kids, the weird introvert, but my parents didn't care.

I was loved.

My feet dangled as I stared at the floor, lost in thought. I sighed heavily, pushed myself close to the edge, and slipped off. Bones was right there, grabbing my upper arm and holding me to his side when I swayed. It was then we heard the door slam open and a heavy-breathing Bear staring at the both of us.

His hair was still wet from his shower. Water dripped on his bare chest; he didn't even bother putting on a shirt. Small pieces of white tissue paper dotted his chest with red dots staining the middle of them. He—shaved his chest?

As my gaze roamed down his chiseled physique, I noticed the glistening droplets of water trickling along his carved muscles, drawing my attention to his gray sweatpants. My quickening breath echoed in my ears as my heart thumped relentlessly against my chest, sending a rush of heat coursing through my body.

Woah.

I didn't remember a time in my life when I was *aroused*. I'd never found men attractive, good-looking, yes, but nothing that would get my body hot and needy. For a while I thought I might be into girls, but yeah, I didn't find them overly attractive either.

This sight, however, turned on an engine that had never been on before.

I bit my lip, trailing my gaze back up his body, and did not see a smiling face but a furious one. Bear's eyes were wild, brightly lit with gold sparkles until they dilated completely to black. His wet hair fell in front of his face, nostrils flared. His large white front teeth bared when he snarled, and my heart flipped in my chest.

He was savage-looking, very wild, and for a reason unbeknownst to me, I found it extremely arousing yet scary at the same time.

I stepped away from Bones, my hands fumbling with the bed to keep me standing. I kept my eyes on Bear while doing so. I rounded it until I put enough space between me and the angry-sexy-confusing-grey sweat-pants-wearing Bear.

"Easy there," Bones soothed. "We were just going to get a weight on her, get some vitals. No harm done."

Bear snarled again, his muscles rippling under his skin. I took in his body once more, and man, he was completely ripped. A claw mark tattoo dominated one side of his chest, and a full sleeve of tattoos on the other. Chills radiated up my spine at the sheer power this guy held. I couldn't help but find his strength alluring.

He held me with those big muscles.

Bear knocked over a lamp at the entrance of the room with his thundering stomp, his massive frame filling the doorway. He seized Bones by the neck, his fingers digging into the sinewy flesh. With a swift motion, he whirled the hapless victim around like a rag doll and hurled him towards the wall. The impact was deafening, the plaster cracking and crumbling under the force of the collision. A cloud of dust and debris fell. The room was plunged into a tense silence, punctuated only by Bear's heavy breathing as he stood, towering over his prey. "You said you would get me if she woke!"

Bones tightly clasped his hands around Bear's, his long, jagged nails digging into the skin as he attempted to loosen Bear's unbreakable grip. My body was curled up tightly behind the other side of the bed, trembling as I witnessed the incredible display of strength. The room filled with grunts and heavy breathing as Bones strained against Bear's unyielding hold.

"You do not touch her!" The roar of Bear was so loud that it drowned out all other sounds.

I winced with the echo of noise and tightly clasped my ears to block out the blaring racket.

Bones' face turned purple. My panic rose in my throat as I saw this man suffer. Bones was only trying to help, and I couldn't understand why Bear was trying to kill him.

I wanted to yell for Bear to stop, to let Bones go. Yet I still didn't have a full explanation of why they were helping me or where I was to go from here. But the act of kindness he had given me already was enough to do something.

Somehow, I rounded the bed, although shakily, and before I put my hand on Bear to get him to stop, more people flooded the room.

"Bear, let go!" A male with a mohawk threw himself on Bear, which made him roar loudly.

I let out a small whimper as the deafening noise filled the room. I stumbled and fell to the floor, instinctively covering my ears to block out the screams and snarls. The sound of people wrestling echoed through the room, making my heart race with fear. I crawled frantically towards the corner of the room, seeking refuge from the chaos. With my ears still covered, I rocked back and forth, trying to escape the overwhelming sensory overload. The memory of being in prison flooded my mind, and I longed for the silence and monotony of my cell. The only sound was the constant dripping of a leaky faucet, a sound that now seemed like a welcome relief compared to the chaos around me.

"You are upsetting her!" A female's voice screeched. My eyes remained closed, my nose remained in the corner, and I stayed there until the noise ceased and the shuffling of footsteps and bodies either left or stilled.

A gentle hand landed on my back. I flinched and curled my hands tighter around my ears.

"Hey there, Nadia? It's okay, it's me. Do you remember me?" Her voice was sweet, like a song. I remember that voice. She was always so nice, but I remember her cries.

Mrs. Delilah.

I squinted my eyes to get a good look at her. Her golden hair was shining, she had gained a little weight, and she looked so... happy.

I gave her a small wave, and she pulled me into her arms for a hug. So much hugging, so much touch. I sniffed and shyly hugged her back, realizing most of the noise was gone.

Once she let go, I shyly looked around the room and saw the audience there.

"Nadia, I am so sorry." Mrs. Delilah sniffed, brushing away my hair. "I thought you got out. You said you were going to leave right after me," she whispered. "Then Shane came after me, said he kept you locked up for years, and when we found out, my friends said they would get you out."

A tear rolled down my cheek.

Mrs. Delilah remembered me.

I wasn't forgotten.

"I'm so sorry," she cried.

I shook my head and pulled her closer to me. It wasn't her fault; it was mine. I got too cocky and thought I could help other women get out of the jobs they got sucked into, but that baffling man came back with Master Cunningham.

I could see Bear out the corner of my eye. He was breathing heavily, and Bones was rubbing his bruised neck. The other men in the room watched as Delilah and I held each other, and even though Delilah said these men were her friends, they looked questionable with their black clothes, leather vests, and animal skull patches.

Delilah sniffed and wiped her nose. "Let me introduce you to them. This is Hawke. He's my mate—well, boyfriend, husband. We are in it for life, I guess." She giggled, and Hawke came forward and kneeled on the floor. He was the one who tackled Bear. He was shorter than Bear and had tattoos covering his entire body.

"Pleasure to meet you, Nadia. I think I should thank you for helping get my sunshine out of there. Without you, I'd never have met her." He pressed a kiss on Delilah's cheek and rubbed her stomach. A tiny bump lay underneath, and I covered my mouth in excitement.

"Yeah, we are going to have a baby," Delilah gushed.

I smiled wildly and motioned to touch her belly.

Delilah smiled. It didn't reach her eyes, and she grabbed my hand for me to touch. It was still so small, but I swore I could feel it fluttering beneath my palm.

"Nadia? Did Shane hurt you? Did any of them physically"—she took in a deep breath—"sexually hurt you?"

I shook my head and pulled my hand away.

"But they starved you," Hawke grunted. "Anything else?"

I looked away and swallowed. That would be very hard to explain, even on paper. I sat back, leaned my head on the wall, and shrugged my shoulders, hoping that would be the end of that.

They didn't need to know everything. Delilah didn't need to know that burden. "Now might not be the best time," Bones interrupted. "She's had a busy afternoon. We should get her back to—"

Bear cleared his throat and stepped behind Hawke and Delilah. "Can I have her back now?"

I tilted my head farther back, staring at the man. He was certainly built like a bear, exceedingly tall, with broad shoulders, hairy arms, and a thick happy trail. As I studied him closer, I saw that the little white dots of tissue with red dots were knicks where he cut himself. They were gone now from the brawl; now he had a completely smooth chest.

I swallowed heavily when he lent me a hand and pulled me up to stand.

Now that I looked at him closely, bare chest and all, I felt extremely self-conscious. He was really handsome, sculpted from stone from the looks of it, and I looked like a little girl under his gaze. I could practically feel the heat radiating off his body, the loud hum of his chest, and I immediately wanted to curl back into his arms, but that would be insane and very—weird.

Not to mention he just beat up Bones. I probably should step away. So, I did, before I did or said anything stupid. He could like me one minute and then grab my neck, just like Bones.

Bear frowned down at me, his hand reaching out until another person spoke up at the door.

"I see that our special guest is awake." The man had an unlit cigarette in his mouth and a sweaty forehead. His eyes were empty, void of emotion like he was an empty shell. But he did his best to give a fake smile that reached his eyes to try and put me at ease. "Welcome. We are happy to have you here, Nadia. I'm Locke, leader of the baboons here." He tilted his head to me, and I nodded in thanks. "First off—Bones, you're an idiot." Locke pointed his cigarette at him.

Bones rolled his eyes. "It was faster to get her vitals while Bear wasn't in the room hovering over her. I stand by my decision."

"Still an idiot. Maybe I should let him choke you again." Locke lit his cigarette. "Don't do it again."

Bones nodded. "I understand, Pres."

Locke hummed and stepped toward me. Bear stood in front of me when Locke came closer and let out a growl.

A growl, like an animal.

"Bear, step aside."

Bear again let out a growl, his hands balling into fists.

"I am acting alpha," he whispered. "I give you my word I won't touch her or scent her."

I blinked, looking to Delilah for support. She grabbed my hand and squeezed, giving me the support I needed. Because right now, I really didn't know what was going on.

Bear stepped to the side just a little, and Locke smiled down at me. It wasn't a comforting smile, it was a smirk, and he pulled his cigarette away and blew the smoke away from me.

"Nadia, I heard you can't speak right now. Is that right?"

I bit my cheek and agreed.

"There are a lot of people we would like to get out of the mansion. We want to save them like we saved you."

My eyes lit up.

"We are going to need your help."

Bear shuffled closer. "She isn't ready to do that. She's still recovering."

Locke ignored him. "When I come to call you to ask some questions, would you be willing?"

My eyes darted to Bear, Delilah, and Bones. Not that I was seeking help or support, just to gauge the room. Could I trust these men? Could I trust everyone here?

They saved me because of Delilah. They helped me, but it had only been a week. I still had a long way to go to get better. I was still a broken mess on the inside, still a shell of myself, but who knew what other women were in that mansion suffering like I was?

Who else would help if not these men?

I was willing to take that chance. I needed to find my voice, not be afraid to speak.

Closing my eyes, I nodded to Locke.

I'd help him. I'd help everyone in the best way I could.

CHAPTER EIGHT

Bear

"What the hell happened to you?" Locke snickered, picking one of the red-stained pieces of tissue paper off my chest. "Get in a fight with a kitten?"

I groaned, swatting his hand away as he sauntered out the door.

Bones gave a not-so-subtle hint at the bag by the door when I left earlier. He thought I should shave or at least trim up my hairy body so I didn't scare my mate. I knew I was a hairy beast, but I was a damn bear. We were all covered in more hair than most humans and shifters, but I was beyond compare.

The humans who worked for the club thought I looked like a bear anyway because of my physical appearance. It didn't bother me as much because that is what I *really* was: a bear.

Now I was second-guessing because of my tiny little mate. So, I dug for the razors in the bag. Not one but multiple sat in there, and I knew the amount of hair on my chest was enough to dull the blades. I thought I should trim it at first, but then I realized that a lot of the shifters in the communal showers often shaved their chests bare, or at least shaved once a month to show off their bodies to prepare to meet their mates.

I thought I should do so too.

I just didn't know it would be so damn sharp.

My cuts were healing in places, but some still bled by the time I came back, and I wasn't expecting to see my mate up and moving.

And gods, she was a fucking beautiful sight. She was still thin, way too thin, but it would take me no time to fatten her up with good food and plenty of rest. I would make sure of that.

"She needs rest," I commanded the room, put my hand on her back, and pressed her to my side.

Nadia feared me after taking Bones by my paws, but I didn't regret it. She needed to see that I would take care of her and that my word was law when it came to her safety. Anyone who disobeyed me regarding her, I would punish. Same went for my reigning alpha—Locke. He held no true power over me now that I had a mate. I could crush him.

Nadia stared up at me, her eyes blinking several times with her glasses that were far too big for her tiny face. She didn't take a step away, but her movements were leery.

Delilah pulled Nadia into another hug, one that was too long for comfort for me. I pulled Nadia back to my side, and another questionable glance was thrown my way.

"I think it is best we talk to her about the club and its... details," Delilah said. "You know, about *everything*." She winked at me. "It would be for the best, considering the situation."

The situation being I would not let Nadia out of my sight.

Hawke grunted in agreement, wrapping his arms around Delilah. "Tomorrow morning then? We should have Journey attend as well. More females that have been through the same as Nadia is about to go through would be wise."

Nadia tugged away from me, but my fingers remained lightly clasped around her arm. I could feel the warmth of her skin and the slight tremble in her muscles. My other hand reached out to rest on her shoulder, feeling the tension in her body. I glanced over to the door where Delilah stood, her expression unreadable. Turning back to Nadia, I saw the fear etched on her face, and I released her arm. The air was thick with silence, except for the sound of our breathing.

"You're safe, Nadia. I promise you this," I told her. "I would risk my life all over again to make sure you are safe and cared for." I wanted nothing more than to hold her like I did the past week. Now that she was awake, now that she was able to think for herself and no longer on death's door, she wanted to live, which meant her fight-or-flight instincts had finally kicked in again.

"You are," Delilah said softly. "You are safer here than anywhere else. No one will force you to do anything. If you need to say something, talk, just motion for some pen and paper, okay? Bear saved you. He's your caretaker while you are here. If you want me to stay, I will."

Nadia glanced at Delilah's stomach, and Hawke's hand rubbed up and down her arm. She tilted her head until she finally shook it in reply. Nadia straightened her back and moved closer to me. My chest swelled with pride as she took Delilah's words to heart.

Everyone reluctantly walked out the door, giving backward glances to make sure she was alright. My jaw clenched that everyone would worry for her. My hands formed fists at my sides, a physical manifestation of my protectiveness over her. It was a familiar feeling, one that had been with me since the moment I first laid eyes on her. I would do everything in my power to make sure she was okay, always. She was mine to take care of, my mate, my responsibility.

The knock at the door made her jump when I tucked her into the bed. I growled lowly, staring at the door, but saw Anaki bring in a tray full of food. "Thought I would bring the little miss something to eat?" He held up the tray sheepishly.

I huffed, waving for my friend to come in, and I sat on the bed next to her. I took the tray from him and set it down in front of her. Her stomach growled, and instantly my guilt took over that I had not fed her sooner.

But I had to teach Bones a lesson.

"I thought grilled cheese and tomato soup would be best," Anaki said quickly. "Best for the stomach, very filling and easy. Also, there is chocolate fudge cake for dessert." He pointed to her food and my grizzly gripped his fingers.

My grizzly hated it when someone touched our food, let alone our mates.

"Fuckin' hell!" He pulled away, shaking his fingers.

Nadia grunted, near silent, grabbing my fingers and shaking her head. She pointed to Anaki.

Ah, at least she wasn't afraid to tell me no.

"Sorry," I grunted and grabbed the sandwich from the plate, easing it into her mouth. She stared at me while I held it there and tentatively took a bite.

"How is it?" Anaki leaned over, and I nearly punched him in the face.

"Leave!" I snarled. "You got to see her. Now leave!"

"But I want to make friends! She's so pretty." Anaki fluttered his long dragon lashes. "I can't wait to take both of your pictures and hang them on my wall."

He sounds creepy as fuck right now.

"Mine." I stood from the bed and hovered over him. I stalked toward him. He backed away closer to the door, and my hand reached out to strangle him just as I did Bones.

"N-nh!"

I darted my head behind me, listening to the pitiful sound. Nadia was waving her hand, her face full of terror. My shoulders slumped, and I glared at Anaki. "Leave. You are lucky she's here to save your hide."

Anaki scoffed and opened the door. "Thanks, little miss. I'll bring you extra sweets next time!" He shut the door before I had the chance to swat him on the head.

Nadia leaned back on the headboard and sighed, wiping her hand down her face.

Yes, she has me wrapped around her tiny little finger.

She ate the rest of her meal in silence. It wasn't awkward; it was peaceful as she ate. Nadia took every bite I gave her, and I think she ate more than her stomach allowed. Once we got to the cake, she looked longingly at it but shook her head when I tried to feed her.

"No because you don't want to eat sugar or because you are full?" I raised an eyebrow.

She raised her hand, showing off her second finger, and rubbed her stomach. I cleared the tray away, then removed the crumbs from the bed. I motioned for her to lie down and had her head rest peacefully on the blankets.

"You need rest. Do you need medicine for sleep?"

She shook her head, her eyes glassy. Was she going to cry? Fuck, I couldn't handle my mate crying. What did I do if she cried?

I swallowed, rubbed my hand down my face, and before I could ask her if she was going to cry, her eyes shut, and tiny snores came from her body.

Oh, thank fuck.

"The only good thing about her not talking is, you can't fuck up in the communication department," Locke says, leaning on the door.

It's two in the morning, and I can't sleep. Nadia slept right through dinner, and I didn't have the heart to wake her up to feed her. Bones said she would wake up on her own now that she was eating. The meal she ate earlier was heavier than what he fed her through a tube, so she should be fine.

I grunted, keeping my arms crossed as I sat in the chair. I was as close as I could get to her without being in bed, curled up and around her when she was completely unconscious for the week.

I hated it. I hated not being in bed with her, but it was strongly advised that I didn't. She had my blankets, my scent tucked up around her, but it wasn't enough. I wanted her to have my heat, bury my nose in her hair, take in her scent, and cradle her tiny body against me. I could regulate her body temperature much better that way.

"I guess," I grumbled.

Locke fiddled with his lighter. "Come out here. Need to talk to you."

It wasn't a request, and after my display earlier, it was best I yield. Especially since I know I would kick his ass if he tried to be a dick and come between my mate and me later. I got up from the chair, watching my mate as I strode out the door. I cracked the door, just in case, to monitor her and wait for Locke to talk to me.

"You really need to put a shirt on." Locke eyed me while he flicked his lighter on and off.

"Is that what you wanted to tell me?" I crossed my arms.

I had fucking razor burn, and it hurt like a bitch.

He laughed. "No, not the only thing." His face turned serious. "What I wanted to say was, I think it is best you work on getting Nadia talking, and fast."

My grizzly snapped, taking a step toward Locke. He put down his lighter, his eyes lit ablaze. "Remember who you are talking to, Bear."

"And you remember who you are talking to? I don't need to be here. I don't need to submit to you. Bears don't need a pack," I snarled.

"But your brothers need you. We are all family. I'm thinking about us as a whole, and she can write shit down, but I need emotion from her. That is where I'm going to get my answers. I can't tell if she is lying through writing," he snapped.

"Why would she lie?"

"We may have rescued her, but we stuck her in another room with no way to escape. And now you are hovering over her like you are going to eat her! Nadia probably thinks you have saved her, claimed her for yourself in some sick and twisted way!"

I backed away, punching the opposite wall.

"I claimed her. She is mine! She is my mate!"

"Yeah, but she doesn't know all that bond shit. And we don't know if she will believe it tomorrow either. You need to back off. Give her some space."

Give her space? Was he serious? Would he give his mate space? Hell no, he wouldn't. I wouldn't be surprised if he took his mate and marked her right there on the bar downstairs.

"She doesn't think badly of me," I muttered.

"How the hell do you know? Have you asked? Has she said, 'oh Bear, thanks for rescuing me. How can I ever repay you!'" He squealed in a girly voice. "No, the fuck she hasn't. She's playing it cool right now because she doesn't know what she's been dropped into. Nadia thinks this is the lion's den. She's biding her time, looking for an escape when the time is right. Think about it." He points to his head.

My claws lengthened, and my lip pulled up to a snarl. Locke has it all wrong. Nadia would never run because I wouldn't ever let her leave.

As we argued, a piercing scream echoed through the wooden door. My heart raced as I pushed it open, revealing the sight of Nadia writhing on the bed. The room was dimly lit, with only a faint aroma of wild berry scent lingering in the air. Nadia's face was contorted with pain, and her body glistened with sweat in the dim light. She appeared to be levitating a few inches above the bed until she suddenly dropped back down as I entered. She continued to thrash and grunt, her movements wild and uncontrolled. The sound of her screams filled the room, making my ears ring. It was a bone-chilling scene that left me feeling helpless and terrified.

I ran to her, screaming her name.

I pinned her to the bed so she didn't hurt herself, my hand cradling her face. She calmed, her body relaxed, and her breath calmed the more I touched her.

"Your female has a set of pipes on her," Locke said.

Bones runs into the room in just his boxers, panting. "What the hell happened?"

"Nightmare," I breathed, checking my mate's body for injury.

"You sure, you are on top of her while Locke is watching, are you doing something she doesn't want?" Bones yelled.

"Fuck no!" Locke grabbed Bones by the arm. "We do not do that to unwilling women. You are just an asshole today, aren't you?" Locke shoved

Bones into the desk. "Not even funny to joke about."

Bones ripped his shoulder from Locke's grip. "It was an odd scene to walk into, just making sure."

"She hasn't had a nightmare before this." I lay on the bed next to her. "She used her voice, and I swore she was—floating."

"Floating..." Bones sighed. "Maybe it isn't just psychological then."

I pulled my mate closer to me, wrapping her up into my body. She welcomed the touch, her face laying against my chest.

"What do you mean?" Locke paced the room.

"Nadia not speaking, I told you all it was something psychological. She was scared into not talking, but now I wonder if it is something more. If she's levitating"—he waved his hand to the bed—"then magic, dark magic specifically, could be involved."

CHAPTER NINE

Nadia

The bar was a desolate sight besides Delilah and a few friends—with chairs piled high on tables from the previous night's closure. The glasses were being stacked in the background by a few employees emitting a symphony of high-pitched clinks that made me wince slightly. Despite my sensitivity to noise, I couldn't help but notice the faint smell of stale beer lingering in the air. I had been in solitary confinement for so long that my senses were still adjusting to the outside world. However, I found solace in the deeper undertones, like Bear's constant grumbling, which provided a sense of comfort.

I liked him despite his violence against other men. He seemed to take his protection for me seriously.

I woke with my face plastered to his bare chest this morning. I wasn't sure if I should be frightened or delighted by that. He was warm, he smelled like the forest, and did I mention he was warm? I'd felt cold for so long I forgot what warmth felt like, and my dumb self relished in it this morning.

I should have scrambled away from the bed, shuddering in fear that this enormous giant was holding me through the night, but the fear and panic never came. His touch wasn't perverted, and had said nothing to warrant him a threat to me. Those around me, though, I worried about.

When I showered, I was concerned he would be a peeping Tom. He made sure to keep the door cracked, and he lingered by the door asking if I was alright several times throughout the shower. It was the first shower I had in ages, and I wanted to relax under the heat of the water, but that would not happen. He was a six-foot-five-plus man standing outside the door, pacing and cursing, asking if I had fallen when I dropped the soap in the enormous communal shower area. Everything echoed in the shower room, and my ears couldn't take it for long.

I couldn't understand why he cared so much about my well-being or if he was just an overly attentive guard with nothing better to do. But feeding me, sleeping in my bed? A little over the top if I say so.

This whole scenario was over the top. Delilah had already fallen in love and gotten pregnant so fast after being with Master Shane. I worried I had fallen into some sort of cult—not a motorcycle club.

Delilah stood from Hawke's lap. It was common to find a woman perched on a guy's lap around here, and I was no stranger to that. Even Bear had me on his.

Was I fighting it? Nope, I wasn't.

Why? I wasn't sure of that either.

"Nadia, there isn't an easy way to tell you this, so I'm just going to say it." Delilah threaded her fingers together nervously and stared at the floor. "These men here aren't really men. They are shifters, animals. They can turn their bodies into something that is not human. They can change into animals. Hawke and Grim..." She nodded to the terrifying man in the room. He looked like a Viking with a thick red braid down his back and beard. Perched on his lap was a woman with a blue crescent moon on her forehead, smiling at me.

Yup, I'm in a cult. And they drank the Kool-aid.

I wrinkled my nose and shook my head.

Delilah waved Hawke forward. He took off his vest, shirt, and pants. My eyes widened as he stripped off his clothes, and I turned my head away.

"You have to see," Bear whispered in my ear. As he spoke, his deep baritone voice reverberated through my body, sending shivers down my spine and causing a tingling sensation to spread throughout my body. The sound was smooth and rich, resonating with a power that went straight to my core. The air surrounding us was thick with the scent of his musk, which added to the overall effect. As I listened to him speak, I couldn't help but be mesmerized by the way his words seemed to dance in the air around me, each one carrying a weight and importance that was impossible to ignore. It was as though the very essence of his being was wrapped up in his voice, and I found myself completely entranced by the sound of it. "It will help you understand why I will never let you go."

I felt my throat close up at his confession. It wasn't just me feeling the undeniable attraction either then? I closed my eyes, my heart pounding in my chest. I've never had these feelings stirring in my body before, and it was just so... strange.

As I opened my mouth to respond, a sickening crack echoed through the air, and my attention was drawn to Hawke's arm. It had popped out of its socket, and he began to contort his body in an unnatural way. I couldn't believe what I was seeing as his form began to shift and change before my very eyes. The sound of bones snapping and crunching as he transformed into something out of a horror movie. Thick, coarse fur sprouted from his skin, and his face elongated into a snout. His body grew taller and more muscular, and he dropped onto all fours. The transformation continued, and a long, thick tail sprouted from his backside. The sight of this creature was both mesmerizing and terrifying.

My fingers grabbed onto Bear's shirt, my only form of comfort, as I watched the final formation of a large black wolf stand in front of me. And it was massive, terrifying, ears twitching and watching me.

"Ah—" my voice cracked to say something, anything, as I watched it come toward me.

I pulled myself closer to him, his arm wrapped around me, his head lowering to my ear. "He won't hurt you," he soothed, rubbing his hand up and down my back. "No one in this club will hurt you. Although I prefer them not to get near you because I am your protector." He growled back at the wolf, snapping at him with his teeth.

That's when I realized that Bear—he was one of them too.

I pushed him away, falling on my butt, and pointed at him. He sighed.

"Yes, I am one too. But I am a bear, a grizzly."

I swallowed heavily. He would be bigger than all of them.

My chest felt tight, and my heart was pounding so loudly I could hear it in my ears. My palms were sweaty, and I felt a wave of nausea wash over me. I tried to take deep breaths to calm myself down, but it only made me feel more lightheaded. I knew I was having a panic attack, and I needed to find a way to regain control before it got worse.

Delilah kneeled beside me, her arm wrapping around me, but I pushed her away. "Hey, it's okay. They aren't going to hurt you or me. They are good... they saved you. They saved me. They killed Shane. They are on our side. The Iron Fang, that's what they do. They save people that need help and bring them here and give them a new life."

They killed Master Cunningham?

Bear wiggled his fingers, his eyes filled with longing while he stared at me. He wanted to touch me. I could feel it. He stayed away, glaring at anyone else who tried to come over, but he nodded his head for Delilah to come closer.

Delilah sat with me on the floor while Bear hovered. They all waited patiently until my breathing evened out and let my mind process that this world I lived in for so long was not so normal.

They hadn't attacked me, hurt me, tried to kill me. I needed to, I don't know, not be too irrational about all this.

What else is out there?

I made a motion for pen and paper with my hands, and Bones already had it ready for me.

What else are there? Vampires? Fairies? I wrote.

"Yes, much more," Bear said as he scooped me up and held me in his arms. I could feel his body relax as he rubbed his cheek over my hair. His scent was so soothing it put me at ease. The calming fragrance filled my senses, and I felt myself relaxing even more in his arms.

This is so weird. Somehow, I've drunk the Kool-aid too.

Instead of shying away, I let him hold me. I gazed around the room, looking for odd glances, but they acted as if this was a normal occurrence.

I didn't have the strength to fight this man. I was still weak, still too broken, but I had been strong for so long. Maybe I wanted someone to lean on for once.

How long have these beings *been here on earth?* I scribble again.

"Always, as long as the earth has held humans," Bear replied. "We are not allowed to reveal ourselves. It is important you do not tell others about us."

I huffed a tiny laugh. *I don't think we have a problem.*

"Nadia, there is something I need to ask you. It's about last night, your nightmare—" Bones stepped closer to us.

Bear let out a warning noise, which I now knew was a growl. Bear stood up and stepped away, holding me tight to his body.

"Now that I don't have to hide what I am, you need to stay the fuck away from her," Bear snapped. "Get away and don't touch her. She's mine to protect."

"You asshole, she's my patient. I'm trying to take care of her!" Bones threw his hand in my direction.

"Nadia is my responsibility now!" Bear snapped.

I dropped the pad and paper and covered my ears.

Bear's shoulder deflated, and his large hand covered my ears. "I'm so sorry, Nadia. I didn't mean to hurt you," he whispered.

"See, you can't take care of her," Bones whispered. He pulled out earplugs from his pocket. "She can wear these until she gets used to hearing loud noises again."

The noise and footsteps from the second floor of the bar echoed down to where we stood. People—shifters—came stomping down the stairs, talking loudly, laughing, and pulling on their vests. The people and the noise were already becoming overwhelming the closer they came.

Along with being tired, weak, and overstimulated from just being told that fairy tale creatures were real, I felt a panic attack rising. I grabbed the ear earplugs from Bones' hands and shoved them in my ears, my fists curled up in Bear's shirt, and even with the earplugs, the faces, the large amount of people—shifters, vampires, and who knows what else—it was too much.

Bear

I felt her curling up into my arms—I could smell her fear.

She was here, seeking my strength. Nadia clung to me, using me to protect herself, and I would give whatever my mate wanted. Now was the time to prove to myself again that I would do anything to protect her, even if that meant taking her away from Bones and the club.

I held her tightly, pressing her head to my chest, keeping her ears covered.

"Quiet!" I bellowed, and all fell silent at the bar. My voice was loud but deep. My mate didn't shutter or whimper when I kept the tone of my voice lower.

As the bar lay still, I turned to Bones and Delilah. "I'm taking her to the cabin. I have my cell. You can reach us there."

"Her treatment…" Bones argued as he rushed to the door with me. "What about her nightmares, the levitation? We need to have her see Tajah and Bram. She may have a curse on her mind."

I grunted and pulled the heavy-laden door of the bar open. Winter was still in full swing. It was cold and blustery. Not much snow had fallen, but there was enough chill in the air that my mate would be cold.

I rounded the corner of the bar's building with Bones still on my tail. He was huffing and puffing, and I could hear him rubbing his hands up and down his arms to keep warm. Bones wasn't faring well, and working on a patient such as my mate right now was not good for him, anyway. He did the brunt of the work; I'd watched him over the week. It was my turn to take care of her.

"Anything I need to know about Nadia's care?" I stepped into the mud as we headed to the back of the bar property and closer to the mechanic area. Cars and bikes lined up ready to be used by any of the men, but I was looking for the ride I used to get up the mountain where I kept my cabin.

"Keep feeding her food, human food. She needs carbs and lots of them. Those protein shakes at every meal, two snacks a day, keep her warm. That's just the physical side. Her mentality?"

I reached in my pocket for my keys and clicked for the doors to open for my black pickup truck. Inside I already had blankets on the front seat for when I used to get cold.

I no longer needed them.

I set my mate in the passenger seat and wrapped blankets around her.

Confusion set on her face. "I'm taking you to my cabin. It's quiet there." Nadia looked back at the bar and then at me.

I reached over her, pulling a burner phone from the center console. "We will charge this. It's yours. We can put Delilah's phone number in it."

"And mine," Bones interrupted.

I rolled my eyes and huffed. "Yes, and if you want his, I guess I can put Bones' in there too."

And then Nadia did something I never thought I would hear... a laugh. She put her hand over her mouth to muffle the sound, but it was a goddamn laugh.

I smiled, and she bit her lips to keep herself silent.

"Do you even have enough supplies at your cabin right now?" Bones interrupted our moment.

I pushed Bones back and shut the truck door. "Of course. Anaki filled it with all I needed last night. Food for a week, clothes, blankets, plus all my hibernating shit is up there. We are fine. I'll call you if we need anything. Otherwise, don't bother us."

I rounded the truck, and Bones followed.

"Bear, what about her nightmares? We need to get that taken care of. You can't just take her away and expect everything to be fine."

"Everything *will* be fine," I argued back. "When I am with her they are gone. I'll be sure to stay with her always. Once I get her talking, opening up to me, you will get better answers, anyway." I started up the truck and put my hand on the door. Nadia was staring out the window, looking at the rows and rows of bikes in the garage.

"Call me," Bones ordered. "If anything changes, we will bring Tajah and Bram up there."

I saluted Bones and shut the door. I gripped the steering wheel and checked on Nadia again. She had rolled her window down, and Delilah poked her head in. "Bear will take good care of you," Delilah said softly. "It's really loud around here. The cabin is really nice and quiet while you recover. Bear has my number, and we can text. Any questions you have, I can answer them, okay?"

All I could see was Nadia nodding, and my shoulders slumped. I just damn hoped I was doing the right thing.

CHAPTER TEN

Bear

My mate tried to stay awake on the ride to my cabin, but her eyes were too heavy, and she fell asleep. Once we turned to the dirt road, I stopped and pulled her to my side so her head wouldn't hit the window and had her lean on me through the rough terrain up the small mountain up to my home.

For the past few years I've widened the path for a vehicle to pass through, knowing one day I would need to bring more supplies, but I never knew I would be so lucky to bring a mate up here so soon.

But I had everything ready for such an occasion. My subconscious must have known. Food, electricity, plumbing, everything she would need while she got better and away from unmated males and wandering eyes that tried to behold her beauty.

My grizzly was getting stronger by the day and my possessiveness of her was getting stronger. I could bear no one looking at her, even Bones, and he was the club's physician. The warlocks of the club wanting to conduct magical experiments and examining her concerning her levitation and nightmares seemed too much for my grizzly to handle right now. I could not keep him contained, and I worried for their safety, not just because I was being an ass.

The option of leaving her alone with them was not there either.

I just found her. I wasn't about to let her out of my sight.

Once we arrived at the cabin, Nadia stirred, but her body was plastered to mine. She was wrapped in my warmest blanket, her head nuzzled into my side. I was pleased that she did not fear me in sleep. It meant the bond was working in her subconscious, but while she was awake, I would definitely need to be patient. An attribute that was not my strongest.

I turned off the truck and pulled her into my arms, careful not to jostle her frail body. She was still stick thin, but I hoped to rectify that quickly.

All this time, my grizzly had been in protection mode, and our instincts were working in overdrive to see her to safety and regain her health. Once she woke and he saw she was feeling better, I knew my time was short before he would want to rut her senselessly.

I tried to keep those thoughts locked away. My dick hadn't been hard in years, and thank fuck, it hadn't started yet. My grizzly was severely weakened while it hibernated for so long, and he was concentrating on getting well and protecting and serving her.

Now that we were at the cabin and alone with our mate—her strength increasing by the day—I couldn't guarantee how much longer I would be able to hide my want for her.

I won't be able to wear sweatpants around her, that's for sure.

As soon as I entered the rustic cabin I had constructed with my own two hands, I made a beeline for the cozy bedroom where we would spend our nights. A sense of satisfaction washed over me as I carried her towards the space. The room held a grand king-sized bed I built myself. The hand-carved wooden furniture exuded a warm, earthy scent that filled the rest of the cabin. The thick, woolen rugs on the floor felt soft underfoot as I carried her towards the bed. Two softly glowing lamps illuminated the room, casting a warm, welcoming light that enveloped us as we entered. I couldn't help but feel proud of my creations as I looked around the space, admiring the details that I had painstakingly crafted myself—for my mate.

I was an ass to my brothers for a while. I told them not to get their hopes up, that Grim getting his second chance may have been a fluke. He could have been the only one lucky enough to have a second chance. But secretly I was hopeful and held on to that sliver of a chance.

I'm glad I was wrong.

Look at me now.

I have my mate here in my arms.

I placed her on my bed, complete with thick furs of animals I had hunted, killed, and skinned myself. The thickest blankets, the warmest you could find from around the entire town, were right here in my den, and now she lay in my nest of furs.

Nadia stirred and looked up at me when I placed the last of the furs on her tiny body. "Bear—" She slapped her hand over her mouth, her eyes widening.

I grinned, crawling onto the bed with her, and pulled her hand away. "You said my name," I whispered. "Please, let me hear it again."

She shook her head and scooted away.

I frowned, pulling her closer. "Do not run from me, Nadia. My animal does not like it when you run."

She froze, her heart racing in her chest.

"He is very possessive of you. He wants to keep you safe, as do I. When you run, it upsets both of us. We would never hurt you, but when you run, we will find you and bring you back here where it is safe, in our den, the cabin. Do you understand?"

Nadia nodded and glanced around the room.

"We just arrived, and you were sleeping, so I brought you to bed. You are more than welcome to explore if you wish?" I held out my hand for her to take, and she looked at it tentatively.

Nadia would come out of her shell far quicker here than she would at the club. I was hoping the bond would tie her quickly to me. It was selfish of me, but I knew I had to have her to myself for the safety of the club and for my sanity.

Grizzlies did not tolerate sharing. Nadia was mine, and these moments were precious to us right now as the bond strengthened between us. I would not mess this up like my last mate. Nadia would be mine.

Nadia's small hand clasped mine as we slowly crawled out of the cozy bed. The wooden floorboards creaked under the weight of her tiny feet as I led her through the dimly lit cabin. The main living space would soon be illuminated by the flickering flames of the large fireplace that would cast a warm glow over the room. The previously burnt-out embers could still be smelt in the fireplace. Mostly the cabin smelt of pine from the nearby forest. The bathroom's large tub and shower were visible through the open door as I pointed to the areas of the rugs' placement throughout the cabin to be careful of so she wouldn't trip over them while we headed to the kitchen. The cabin was simple, but it was enough to house my mate and me.

As for cubs—if she wanted any, I would be more than happy to give her—I could expand the cabin easily.

"Any questions?" I asked.

Nadia strolled leisurely around the spacious room, her footsteps echoing softly against the wooden floorboards. She made her way towards the vast windows of the living room, taking in the breathtaking view of the lush green forest outside. The natural sunlight streamed in through the windows casting a warm glow on the room, illuminating every corner.

Nadia's once dull and lifeless hair, when I found her in that prison, now shined. It held large curls that framed her tiny face. Her cheeks glowed with color; she was another woman, more lively, and with each passing moment she was coming further out of her shell.

The glasses that hid her enormous, innocent eyes gave her an extremely young look, along with her short stature. Her allure alone made me itch to always touch her, get to know her intimately.

Fuck, please don't be younger than twenty—

Nadia gazed out over the mountain. The cliff where my cabin sat had a perfect view of a cleared area below where several cabins and homes were being built. One was large, in the shape of a packhouse for unmated wolves—a place where Locke would stay once he had his mate and would control a band of rogues more efficiently.

Nadia tilted her head, pointed at the area below, and looked up at me questioningly.

I stood beside her, with my hand resting on the small of her back.

"That, down there"—I nodded—"is where the Iron Fang's new homes are being built. There is a lot more to the Iron Fang than just shifters, Nadia. A lot more." I sat in the leather chair next to her and motioned with my arm for her to come sit.

She stood there, looking at my lap. I waited to see if she would come on her own and, to my surprise, she came and sat with me. My grizzly purred instantly, and her lips curled into a smile, and leaned her head on my chest as she adjusted her glasses.

"A lot of the Iron Fang are single, as humans say. We shifters say *unmated.* Meaning they have no one to care for, be with, or to love. It is different with shifters because we do not have meaningless relationships. Shifters have been blessed with a soulmate. A piece of us is gifted to another soul. Supposedly a perfect match."

I could see the gears turning in Nadia's head, but she said nothing.

"There is a special name for us. We are not ordinary shifters, Nadia. It is best to tell you now. We are called rogues in our world. We are the rejected shifters, vampires, witches, and all. Rejected by our soulmates who didn't want us. They chose another, and they get to live while our soul withers."

Nadia's face paled when she gasped.

"I know, right?" I scoffed. "And when that happens... we slowly die. We lose control of our animals. We can hurt people, so we have to hide them, tuck them away, can't shift."

Tears welled up in my mate's eyes, and her lips quivered.

"Yeah." I tried to hide the emotion of my past betrayal. I looked away from her and gazed out into the forest. I didn't want Nadia to pity me for my past. I wanted her to be happy that she was here with me now.

My mate shook my arm for me to continue when I was silent for too long. It was just so hard to form the right words for what I was about to say.

Nadia mouths Hawke's name.

"He's got Delilah." I shrugged my shoulders.

"Oh right, Delilah and Hawke." I cleared my throat. "And we weren't supposed to have a second chance. We were just supposed to die, and many did. But Hawke and Delilah are mates. That is why they are together."

"How?" Nadia whispered excitedly. Her eyes shone with such curiosity.

I smiled, seeing how worked up my mate was getting and that she spoke. My claws broke free and lengthened. She gasped, seeing them over her thighs, and traced them with her finger.

"Journey, the one with the crescent moon on her head"—I tapped on my forehead—"came along. She was a human that prayed to the Moon Goddess. She's the goddess that matches souls to the supernaturals of our world and got her to help the rogues."

Nadia hummed and continued to stare down at the cabins and houses below.

"No one wants to stay in the Iron Fang bar forever. They want to have their own homes, their own places to live. It's no way to have a family." I shook my head. "We're part animal, demon, fae—we are best in nature. Once we have that part of ourselves back, we want to stay deeper into nature."

Nadia motioned for paper. I reached over to the coffee table and handed it to her.

Everyone will get a mate now then? She wrote.

"Yes, hopefully. If they aren't too far gone." I sighed. "Sometimes we have had to put members down because they have gone rabid. That means their animal takes over, and the human part of themselves is gone." I scratched my beard. "We stay together as a pack or club to help each other out. Being in a group seems to slow down the process of going rabid. Locke is our acting alpha or president. However, he isn't doing very well these days."

My mate frowned.

How is your grizzly? Will he go rabid soon? She gazed up at me with a worried look.

I shook my head and rubbed my hand through her hair. "No, mine is getting stronger now. I don't think I will have any troubles from now on."

Nadia blinked, tilting her head. *Why?*

Her stomach growled at that moment, and I took that as a sign that we should cease our questions for the day.

"Let's feed you first, and we can come back to questions, hmm?"

Nadia narrowed her eyes and pointed back at the paper. I smirked and playfully growled at her and set her on the floor.

"Later, come on, little bee, it's time to feed you."

Nadia raised a brow.

"Because you are small but mighty. You hit Shane where it hurt him the most, a powerful sting to the heart."

My mate's lip curled. "Just so you know, a bee's sting will not penetrate a bear's skin," I joked. She playfully punched me in my chest and jumped off my lap.

I watched her walk away and bit my lip as I stood.

I could not wait to taste her honey.

CHAPTER ELEVEN

Nadia

Just when he had my curiosity at an all-time high, he ripped the rug right out from under me.

My mind was still working through the details of the incredible world revealed to me. It was difficult to comprehend at first, but now it all started to add up.

For most of my life, I had been in the dark, unable to see the world around me. The chaos had settled, and everything was falling into place.

Papa had a particular set of skills he taught me when I was young. I was far too young to be taught these skills because I took them most seriously. It made me leery of people, unable to enjoy the blissful ignorance that most children enjoyed in their childhoods.

I didn't believe in Santa, the Easter Bunny, or the promises of being best friends forever with any of the other children. I didn't even believe it when a guy said he liked me for my mind or personality—no one liked me for me. They all thought I was weird and quiet.

None of them could trick me and try to make a fool of me either.

"Repeat it back to me, so I know you listened," Papa scolded, patting me on the nose with his index finger. I was rather bored with his Saturday morning

lessons. It was the same thing over and over for months, and I knew his words like the back of my favorite cereal box.

"Papa, I know it. I knew you lied to Mama when you said you liked her roast last Sunday."

Papa's eyes widened, and he placed his scarred hand over his mouth to cover his smile. For a personal driver, he had a lot of scars all over his arms and one cut over his eyebrow where the hair no longer grew. "You saw that, huh?"

I nodded and tried to hold back a smile.

"Then I guess you need no more of my lessons?" he said with a defeated sigh.

I shrugged and continued brushing one of the antique dolls my mama had given me from their home country of Russia. "Mama gives me lessons too when you are not around. Once I master it, she moves on to the next subject."

Papa's mouth hung open, and I leaned forward and pushed it closed. "Careful, Papa, you will catch flies."

He barked out a laugh and ran a hand through his salt and peppered hair. "You and your mama are sneaky little foxes. What has she taught you?"

I bit my cheeks, holding in my smile only to be attacked by Papa's tickling.

It was one of my fondest memories of my papa and I. There were many more to be had, but I always remembered his *search for truth* lessons, and now that I was more of a sound mind with food in my belly and proper rest, I could apply them better.

Bear explained that all these wonderful people—shifters, or magical beings, whatever species they may be—helped save me all for the chance at redemption. It tugged at my heartstrings. I believed every word he said without hesitation.

Bear believed in every word he said about a Moon Goddess, about Journey being a priestess. He believed it. Now if it was true or not, that was up for debate, but after seeing a wolf shift before my eyes, why not believe it?

I had more questions, and I needed more answers. Not speaking hindered that, but old habits, well, they were hard to break.

I'd slipped several times, and I hoped I was on the verge of breaking the cycle and not reliving Master Cunningham's special guest coming to reprimand me when I spoke out loud. I hated the flashbacks of being thrown into that dark corner of my mind and what happened that day when I defied his orders.

Bear helped me forget the tough times. My mind was put at ease when I was around him. I did not feel the impending doom when he was in the room. I was brought to the present. It made my body and heart feel things I've never felt before. He helped me trust, and for the first time in my life, I trusted a man… shifter… bear, whatever he was. He hadn't lied to me.

It scared me. The longer I was left alone with him, the closer I wanted to be with him. I wanted his touch. I wanted to know more about him.

Who was the woman that broke him, rejected him? He was a fierce protector. He didn't even know me but came to my rescue and brought me to safety. He'd even brought me to his cabin, and if I knew anything about animals, I knew they took pride in their homes.

Even now, as I sat at the table waiting as he prepared *me* food, he was speaking about how he cut down each tree, how he laid down every timber piece by piece. That alone must speak how much he considered his home a safe space and was proud he brought a stranger into it.

But why me?

And why hold me, keep me in his arms whenever he could?

Did he have any idea what sort of thoughts could be put in one's head when you invited them to sit on your lap, constantly touched them, and woke up with them holding you?

I took my hands and covered my heated cheeks. It didn't seem to matter when I was dying or alive. I reveled in his touch. I liked someone holding me because I felt less alone. How could he know that?

I was living, thriving now. He didn't have to do this; he didn't have to hover over me now. I was out of danger. Not unless he was purposefully trying to make me reliant on him.

And that wasn't good at all.

Bear's kind had mates.

I needed to shut down all the feels. Shifters didn't date casually. Not that I was looking for casualness; I wanted a love like my parents had. They were together until the day they died.

I just knew that someone as special as Bear wouldn't end up with someone like me.

I wasn't that lucky.

Bear talked to fill the void as he cooked. He spoke of his cabin and how he built it piece by piece. Chopped down trees, built the tables, the chairs, the bed frame. I stared at all of it with awe at how well he worked with his hands, and my mind wandered to other things he could do with those hands.

How would they feel on my bare skin?

His touch was fiery on my lower back when he guided me room to room in his home. When I sat on his lap, his thigh warmed me so much I swore I was sweating between my thighs but not because of his heat, but of my own.

His voice, his scent, his aura, his touch, my body reacted like it should have when I was a teen. Feelings from my body blossomed the more I thought about it. I wanted to see him shirtless again; I wanted to run my fingers over his chest, let my fingers explore parts of a man I'd never dared to think about.

Bear continued to talk. His baritone voice lulled me into a state of lust as he spoke of the forest he missed roaming as his bear. I would love to see his animal, see how big he truly was. Would he be that much bigger than he is now?

My heart raced as I imagined his body pressed against mine. My skin tingled with anticipation, and my breath quickened. I felt a flush of heat spread throughout my body, my cheeks turning red with desire. I couldn't help but feel a little embarrassed at how my body was reacting to his presence, but I couldn't deny the intense attraction I felt for him.

Every time he spoke, my knees weakened, and the thought of him touching me was like an electric shock that sent shivers down my spine. I knew I shouldn't be feeling this way, but I couldn't help it. My body was responding to him in ways I never thought possible.

I tried to push these thoughts aside, to focus on something else, but it was impossible. He was all I could think about, and the more I thought about him, the more my body responded. The flames of desire roared inside me, making it impossible to ignore.

I knew I had to do something about these feelings, but I didn't know where to start. All I knew was that I wanted him, and I wanted him badly. The thought of being with him was both exhilarating and terrifying. I couldn't resist the pull he had on me.

I felt my nipples harden against the loose T-shirt I wore. It was so large it went to my knees. The shorts underneath were borrowed as well, and I still had to roll them high on my hips. Now they were damp, thinking about how good his butt looked in those damn jeans.

Bear's back was to me as he stirred the sauce in the pot. I shifted my thighs, my nipples sliding against my shirt, and I felt my nipples tighten against the fabric.

They were... sensitive.

This was normal, totally normal.

And that was when I felt my clit pulse between my legs.

Oh god, it was happening. I was turned on.

I've read about it but thought the day would never come. I was getting turned on! It was at the wrong time, completely wrong, because it was actually happening while Bear was talking to me in his kitchen about the damn trees outside.

Bear stopped stirring and started sniffing the spaghetti sauce, then turned to me. His golden eyes set on me and then darkened to ebony.

I don't know why my face flushed, but it did. I felt so guilty. Like he could see right through me. Bear couldn't possibly know what I was thinking, could he? He was a bear. He wasn't a mind reader or a witch. He couldn't know that sort of thing... could he?

"Bathroom!" I squeaked and threw my hand over my mouth, pushing away from the table. The chair let out a colossal noise that echoed through the kitchen, and I raced across the carpeted cabin and pushed the door into the only bathroom.

I slammed the door shut and quickly turned the lock, relieved to be safely inside. Despite all that, my nipples were still hard, and my clit was still pulsing when my head leaned back on the door and thudded against it.

I was so turned on I could feel the dampness between my thighs. *This was so embarrassing. Why was this happening now? Of all times?*

Thudding footsteps came louder to the door. I stepped away, sat on the tub, and waited.

"Nadia? What's wrong?" His deep voice went impossibly deeper. I swore I could feel the heat of his breath seeping into the woodgrains of the door and coming inside. It was like he was right there, his breath fanning my neck.

What in god's name is happening to me?

"Nadia?" he snapped, and I shook my head, knowing good and well I would not answer.

He sighed, leaving the door briefly and coming back.

Bear shoved a piece of paper and a pen under the door. "Tell me what you are doing in there right now. What is wrong?"

I stepped forward and wrote the only reply I could think of: *I'm pooping.*

I shoved it under the door before I could take it back. That was so *not sexy,* and it would give him reason to leave me alone for a while so I could, I don't know, give me some time to cool down. "You wouldn't be telling me a lie, would you, Nadia?" Bear growled. The sensation caused my spine to shiver, and I instinctively fell back onto the carpet. "Open the door, little bee."

He shoved the paper back under the door, and I wrote on it quickly. *I'll be out in a minute.*

Bear grunted, and I heard big, heavy footsteps walk away from the door. I sighed, grateful for his departure, but instead of my body calming down, the throb between my legs was still there.

I was slightly disappointed he didn't knock down the door. I should be grateful that he didn't, but with Bear's protective instincts, I thought he just might do it, anyway. I stayed sitting on the floor, my legs slightly spread and my back leaning against the tub.

I'd never been turned on and didn't want to lose it. Didn't want to miss the opportunity to feel what an orgasm felt like, and the idea of Bear being somewhere in the cabin was... erotic.

Being asexual crossed my mind several times over the years, but now I was excited that I wasn't. I was excited to explore this part of myself, and I wasn't going to let it go. Not since I came across Bear.

I just needed inspiration. The big, bulky male who was way overbearing with a commanding voice that, with enough coaxing, could make me come on the spot.

My fingers sunk under the waistband, trailing between my untrimmed hair. I winced. I really hoped there was a razor somewhere in here for later. Lower I went, and I immediately found how damp I was, and soon enough, my fingers were coated in my arousal, and my clit was already begging to be stroked.

I gasped, rubbing the pad of my middle finger against my swollen clit that sat there. I dipped my finger lower, gathering more of my wetness, and continued to rub it in circles.

It felt so *good.* My toes curled, my back arched, and I got the great idea to have my other hand reach under my shirt to pinch my nipple. I bit my lip hard, breaking the skin to keep my whimpers at bay.

I must be quiet, not make a sound.

As I reminisced about Bear, the image of his massive frame with no shirt and only the sweatpants he had on last night flooded my mind. I could almost feel the warmth emanating from his body, and my eyes lingered on every curve and bulge. The sight of him was pure ecstasy, and my hands were itching to explore every inch of his skin, to feel the texture of his muscles and the heat of his flesh. I could smell his masculine scent, a mixture of sweat and cologne that made my pulse quicken and my heart race. Oh, how I longed to be near him once more, to bask in the glory of his presence and revel in the sensation of his touch.

What would I have done if he had come closer to me? His gigantic form straddling me over the bed, his hand cupping what little breast I had and kissing me down my neck?

I swirled my finger around my clit, every so often dipping into the hole shallowly. I flicked my clit quickly, and a rolling wave began to build inside my body. Further and further the wave built inside me, growing into a roaring tsunami. I pinched my nipple harder and harder, ready to pull it as soon as I reached the crest of the wave. Once I reached the top, so close to falling over and landing in the exotic waters below, the door burst open, and Bear stood in front of me, his eyes completely black, his breath heaving. He holds a doorknob in one hand and a screwdriver in the other.

I was too stunned to speak; too many emotions swirling around me.

I didn't know which emotion was more prominent. The frustration from not coming, the anger he opened the door, or the humiliation that I still had my hands on the most intimate parts of my body.

I pulled my hands away from my private areas and narrowed my eyes at him. "Bad!" I whispered and pointed.

CHAPTER TWELVE

Bear

I swore to myself I was going to be good while I nursed my mate back to health. It was proving difficult seeing her wear my clothing. When she sat at the kitchen table, I did my best to keep the air filled with the smells of our dinner and my one-sided conversation.

I was never good at talking, but obviously the Goddess was testing me.

My cock suddenly rose with newfound vigor, pulsating against the constraints of my denim jeans. The pressure was unbearable, so I turned away from her as I busied myself with cooking. I tried to talk about my home, how I built it with my hands to impress her with my strength and skill. I wanted to prove to her that I was worthy of providing the perfect den for her and our cubs.

I fought the urge to sneak glances at her donning my oversized shirt that draped down to her knees. My scent, my clothing, it was on her body.

My grizzly was purring in delight at the thought of taking the shirt back just to see her naked body. He hadn't seen her yet like I had, but it was purely to dress her and not in any sexual way.

As I put the rest of the ingredients into the pot and stirred, a smell that should not have infiltrated the kitchen filled my lungs. The scent of blackberry notes with hints of honey and sunshine wafted over the thick, heady scent of tomatoes easily. It was like a warm summer's day, the golden aroma coating the back of my throat the more I breathed it in. I wanted to taste it on my tongue and savor every drop, let it linger in my mouth until I had received my fill.

My grizzly took hold of my arm, turning off the burner of the stove, and turned around to see my mate with her arms wrapped around her legs. She's stunned to see me, her eyes dilated and wide. She was guilty, gazing at me like I could see right through her and what she had done.

And I didn't think she had done anything on purpose, but I believed her body was reacting to mine, and it gave me great joy that she found me attractive.

My cock leaked with seed. I could feel it pooling against the roughness of my jeans. Before I could get a word in, she took off into the bathroom. I barely registered what she said, barely able to listen or read the paper when she replied when I told her to open the door.

All I knew was she was in need, and I wanted to be the one to sate her.

Her scent seeped from under the door, whimpers of pleasure rang into my ears like the bells of human cathedrals. My fingers couldn't work fast enough to unscrew the doorknob, and when I finally opened the door, the sight before me nearly had me coming in my pants.

My little mate had been caught red-handed, her hand down her shorts, skin flushed, and her tiny nipples hard against the shirt.

"Bad," she whispered. She tried her best to look angry, but to me, she looked like a feral little tick mouse.

I chuckled and stepped further into the room. "My little bee has been busy," I rasped. Her face flushed a dark pink, her eyes lowering in embarrassment.

My mate had been bold today. She's spoken several times; it had been quiet, barely a whisper, but I'll take whatever voice she gave me. My hearing was impeccable now that my grizzly was awake, but I wanted to hear more of her voice, especially when the time comes to give her pleasure. My goal was to hear her scream.

"Are you making honey for the bear?" I knelt in front of her, taking her chin to look me in the eye.

Nadia pressed her lips together, her jaw tight. She would not give me an answer, but I damn well was going to get one from her.

I tsked. "My sweet little bee, are you going to be a good girl for me and tell me what you were doing in here?" Her lips parted, tension relaxing, and I picked up her hand that was delved between her thighs. It was still coated with her arousal, thick with her honey. I brought her finger up to my mouth and swallowed it whole.

As I took her finger into my mouth, my mate's heart raced, and her eyes widened. I released her finger with a soft pop and planted a gentle kiss on her wrist, savoring the salty-sweet taste of her skin. The sound of our breathing filled the air as I sucked on the tender flesh, the scent of her perfume mingling with the musky aroma of desire.

"You are my good girl? Aren't you Nadia?"

A nod was her only response, but it was enough.

"Then tell your bear why you ran to the bathroom?"

She looked around the bathroom and tried to motion for a piece of paper and pen. I shook my head, kissing her wrist again. "My little bee doesn't need paper. You've spoken several times today without it, haven't you?" I tucked her hair behind her ear. "Nothing bad happened, has it? No pain, no one came after you. And nothing will ever happen to you again, not with me here," I growled.

I felt the warmth of her skin as she leaned into my hand. As my mate trusted me, my grizzly purred loudly, a deep sound of contentment.

"Now tell me, why did you run? You made my grizzly chase after you. You are lucky I didn't break down the door."

Nadia's face flushed again, and I pulled her off the bathroom floor and took her back into the living room. I sat her on the couch and cupped her face again, making her look at me. "Tell me."

I was being a bastard. But I needed to know.

I should drop this right now, but I was too curious to see how far she would go. She trusted me. I knew that much. I could feel the intensity of her emotions as they radiated off her in waves. The bond between us was growing stronger with each passing moment, and I knew that I had to be careful not to let it consume us both. As I traced my fingers down her arm, I could feel the goosebumps rising on her skin. Her breathing became rapid.

I knew I should stop, but it was like a force beyond my control was pulling me closer to her. This was all too much too soon for her. Hell, it's only been a week since I'd rescued her, and I find her touching herself on my bathroom floor.

But this was a bond—our bond. We were meant for this.

She wet her lips. "My body was reacting to some thoughts about you. Thoughts that I have never had a desire to have until you. Then you looked at me. I felt like you could see right through me and knew what I was thinking."

I smirked, remembering how I smelled her arousal.

"Thoughts about me?" I smirked.

She nodded.

"And you have never had these thoughts before? These desires?"

What kind of woman doesn't have these thoughts? She is human. All living creatures can experience some sort of desire.

She shook her head. "No. I've never been a sexual person. I've never been attracted to anyone, had no urges." She blushed, and it went down her neck and disappeared beneath her shirt.

I would like to see how far it went, but I wouldn't push my luck, not today anyway.

My mate looked away from me. "You are the first person I have found extremely attractive, and my body reacted. I didn't know what to do. I'm sorry, I shouldn't do that. You are my rescuer; you have been wonderful and kind and—"

I pressed my finger to her lips to keep her from talking any further. I didn't want her to feel guilty. I didn't want her to tell me it was a mistake and she would never do it again. I was fucking elated that she would find me damn attractive.

There were too many times I thought of myself as less than. The wolves—they were more appealing. They looked more human. They were the right height, had the right amount of hair, they were more approachable. Me? Too tall, had tons of hair unless I kept it trimmed, my beard was too long, my face always scowled. My dick—fuck, my dick. I didn't even know where to start on that and using it with Nadia?

"Nadia, you do not need to be sorry. I find you damn attractive, too."

"You do?" Her enormous eyes locked onto mine as she pushed her glasses back up her nose.

"I don't think I would have sucked your slick off your finger otherwise." I smiled.

"Oh, my god!" She put both hands on her face to hide herself. "I thought it was a bear thing."

My mate and I were certainly different, but I had a feeling that Nadia was even more pure than I wanted to admit. She had had no sexual desires before me? Did this mean what I thought it did?

"Little bee?" I pulled her hands away. "Are you saying you have never been with anyone else? You have never been with another male or female?"

"No, I've never been with anyone. I've never even, um, have had a, uh, an orgasm before."

My heart stopped in my chest for a second time for this woman. How could she not have had a man touch her, let alone had an orgasm? My mate was stunning, the most beautiful woman I had ever laid eyes on. Men should have fallen to their feet, kissed the ground she walked on, begging her to spit on their faces.

Yet, she did not want any of them, even if they stumbled after her.

No, she didn't want them.

She wants me.

"Nadia, how old are you?"

Nadia's weight shifted in my lap, causing my cock to graze against her soft, smooth thigh. A low groan escaped my lips as I felt the delicious friction of her warm body against mine.

It felt so damn good to have an erection back, but it was torturing all the same.

"Twenty-four, if it's truly the end of January." My mate squirmed in my lap again. I groaned, holding her body still.

"What's wrong?" I gripped her tighter, and her thighs snapped together, rubbing against each other.

She blushed again, shaking her head.

Another wave of honey blossomed around us, and my body was going to explode just by the smell of her alone. It had been a good five years since I had any sort of release by my hand, but what about her? She'd never had a damn orgasm in her life, and I interrupted her in the bathroom trying to get her first one.

And I was going to give it to her. I was going to be the first to give her everything. First and last.

"Nadia," I groaned. "We need to finish what you started."

I felt her hot breath on my neck as she gasped for air in short pants. My hand traced a path across her stomach, feeling the soft fabric of her shirt under my fingertips. The heat radiating from her body made me acutely aware of the intimate moment we were sharing.

Once again, she was rendered speechless, and her hands fisted against my shirt. "Let me help you," I rasped, "it will give me great pleasure being the one to make you come first."

I laid her on the couch, hovering over her. Her eyes were wide, not in fear but in uncertainty. Her hands were on my chest, her body trembling with anticipation. "I-I don't know. I'm not sure what I was doing before, but I was close until you interrupted." She narrowed her eyes at me.

My grizzly purred, letting the vibrations of my body seep over her. She relaxed instantly, like a drug invading her system, and she calmed her body onto the couch. "Do you trust me? I won't do anything unless you want me to." My hands followed the contour of her body. She closed her eyes as I reached her bare thigh, and I pulled it over my hip.

"You don't have to think. Just enjoy what you are feeling." I kissed her neck. She whimpered, her arms wrapping around me.

"Yes, I trust you. Make it feel better."

I rolled my eyes in the back of my head, my hands sneaking underneath her shirt and squeezing her small breasts. Her breathy moans urged me on, my grizzly roaring for me to rut her on the couch. My cock strained against the curve of her ass, pressing against her. This wasn't about my pleasure; it was about hers. And I would make sure she had the best orgasm of her life without scaring her half to death.

No matter how hard it was going to be for me.

Slow. I must be slow with her. My mate had no experience, and with what I wanted to do with her, I couldn't take this so fast now.

I rose from the couch, taking off my shirt. Her eyes widened, taking in my body. I laid down on the oversized couch, enough for the both of us to lie on, and plastered her body against me. Slowly, I pulled down her shorts, and she gasped as I slung them off and closed her eyes tight.

"I-uh, no one has looked at me down there before." She swallowed and buried herself in my bare chest. Her heated cheeks warmed my chest, and my grizzly reveled in the touch of her skin on mine. This was as close as he was going to get with a naked body on him, a small piece I was willing to give him since I couldn't give him more until we were healthy enough to shift again.

"I won't look, only touch." She pulled back and studied my face, searching for a lie. Once satisfied, she nodded and rested her face back against my chest. My hand trailed up her thigh. I raised the leg closest to the couch and propped it up to give me a wide opening to her cunt.

Fuck, she felt fantastic. Her inner thigh was smooth and tender meat. I couldn't wait to sink my teeth into her skin, mark her there as well as every part of her body. Most of all, I couldn't wait to take my grizzly's tongue and lap at the honey that would spill from her.

My finger dipped into her folds. I groaned, feeling the wetness gather. She was going to soak the couch, and when she went to bed, I would find myself licking the fabric to get more of her taste.

"Good girl, spreading your legs for me. Keep them nice and wide so I can play with your pussy."

My mate whined, her chest pressing into mine. I needed more hands to play with her, but lying on my side, with her face buried in my chest because of her embarrassment, I would have to wait. The pad of my finger played with her clit. It was engorged with blood. I could feel it pulsing as I rubbed it in gentle circles.

Nadia moaned, her hot breath fanning my nipple as she panted against my skin. "So damn wet, baby, and this is all for me? You get this wet for anyone else?"

"No," her voice shook. "Only for you."

"Fuck, yes, baby, I love hearing that."

My cock rubbed against her leg as I flicked her clit with my finger. Her breath had gone heavier until she took her lips and latched onto my nipple. She was damn sucking on me, and fuck if it didn't feel damn good.

"Are you being naughty, sucking on my tit right now?" I leaned down and growled in her ear. "Keep doing it feels fucking good."

She bit down on it, and I let out a snarl, throwing my head back. Her chest pushed into me while her arousal coated my finger. I dipped into her cunt, gathering more of her arousal, and her gentle whines turned into breathy moans.

"Mmm, please. There, please, Bear."

I fucking loved it when she was begging for it. Begging for me to give her what she wanted.

Nadia let out a muffled scream, her nails grabbing my chest, leaving scratches down the skin. "Bear!" She bit down on my nipple again. I pushed my cock against her thigh, rubbing it harder against her.

"Fuck, Nadia!" I grunted. "Gods, baby, you look so damn beautiful when you come." Her body quivered. My tongue darted from my mouth, and I took my fingers and licked what arousal I could get from her pussy.

"Baby, I want another one from you." I rolled her over, caging her inside my arms. "I want more of those precious moans you just gave me."

She shook her head, panting. "I can't. I think I'll die if I do it again."

CHAPTER THIRTEEN

Nadia

It was earth-shattering. My toes curled; my body trembled. It was everything I had hoped for and more. I could see why everyone found masturbating so appealing now. It felt so good. I wanted more of it, but my body was a puddle, and if I attempted to fall into the pit of ecstasy once more, I was afraid I would never wake up.

If I did somehow wake up again, I'd wake up at heaven's gates, and who knows if they were allowed to even have sex there.

And what a shame it would be to die a virgin.

Bear hovered over me, his breath heavily labored. He was turned on as much as I was. I could feel his very hard erection on my leg. He was certainly endowed. I'd seen a dick before. I knew the average and what they looked like. I'd seen porn. I tried, I don't know how many times, to find a dick appealing, but having his right next to my leg and feeling it. God, it was arousing.

One day, I'd dare to say I would want to see his in person, but now I was insanely weak from the exertion.

Bear's brows narrowed, his lips firm. The once lustful look became scowled. I pushed back into the pillow, worried why he was giving me such a look. I thought we were on the same page, thought what we shared was amazing.

"Don't talk about dying," he grumbled. "Never say you will die, even in a joking manner."

I let out a breath, my hand reaching out and touching his sweaty chest. "I-I'm sorry?"

His forehead touched mine. "I don't like hearing about death, especially from you. You were on death's door just last week, and here you are, beneath me. I don't need the reminder of how I almost lost you."

I cocked my head to the side. Why should he care? He didn't know me last week. I'd heard them talking. It was just a favor to Delilah. I saved her, and she wanted me saved in return once she knew I was still alive.

Why would he care so much? Surely, they all weren't so saintly?

"You don't know me—not really. You wouldn't miss me that much." I let out a soft laugh, but Bear didn't; his gaze hardened further.

"All life is precious, Nadia. If I had found your heart no longer beating in your chest on that dingy cot, it would have hurt me far more than you realize."

I swallowed as I nodded, taking his words in carefully. "I'm sorry. I didn't mean to upset you." I blinked and pushed my glasses back up my nose.

He smirked and kissed my forehead, his beard tickling my face. "I know. My brothers and I are just overly sensitive with the word."

"Rogue, shifter, biker guys being sensitive? That sounds like an oxymoron."

Bear hummed, his knuckles grazing my cheek.

Bear stood up and grabbed my shorts from the floor. He tenderly placed them around my ankles and slid them up my legs without looking at my naked form, a promise he kept by not looking at my privates.

"It's time to feed you, little bee. I won't have you getting sick. Then it's off to bed with you."

At that moment, I let out a tired yawn, and he chuckled softly as he scooped me up. Damn him, he knew me better than I knew myself.

I was still a pile of goo when he sat me in the chair. My legs trembled as I sat there waiting for a steaming pile of meaty, chunky tomato sauce covering the noodles that were overdone.

We ate in silence. Luckily, I could feed myself this time. I didn't miss the glances, the twitches of his fingers that wanted to reach over and grab my fork when my hands trembled, but he let me do it on my own. I needed to do it on my own if I was ever going to get back to my old life.

Which was alone in my old apartment.

I wasn't so sure I ever wanted to be alone again, though. Two years in solitary confinement made me crave people. It made me want to be around people once I got to know them, but most of all, made me want to be around Bear.

I knew I couldn't stay around him forever, that much I knew. I could enjoy it a little while longer, though.

Once dinner was over, he cleaned up without letting me help and tended to me like a child. I tried to resist, but it was futile. Bear led me to the bathroom, showing me one side of the vanity where there was an open drawer space for tooth and hairbrushes.

My eyes were heavy as I took in the bathroom and he explained where everything was for me. Nothing was registering while I yawned, and finally, he stopped talking in his deep voice, picked up the hairbrush, and began brushing my hair. That put me into a deeper state of bliss as he brushed it, calming me further. I watched him as he concentrated in the mirror, braiding it down my back.

Bear was a serious bear, that was for certain. I'd seen how he was with his friends. He was frightening when we were around them, but with me, he was nothing but a giant teddy bear.

My lip curled into a smile as he finished, and he put toothpaste on my toothbrush and left the bathroom. When he returned, he had changed into grey sweatpants and left off his shirt. My mouth dropped as I took in his body and jerked it away before he caught me staring.

"You can stare all you want," he said cockily, coming up behind me. He wrapped his arms around my waist and kissed my neck. "But your orders are for you to get some sleep."

My orders?

I swallowed and took the shirt he held up beside me. It was one of his to wear to bed.

Bear waited outside the bathroom door, not giving me any space, and led me to the bedroom. The only bedroom in the entire cabin.

Well, isn't this a scene right out of a romance novel Mama used to read in her alone time?

The problem was I could be a blip on Bear's radar right now. Just a passing female to bide his time until his mate came along. Sure, he found me pretty, but he might just be doing me a favor because he was the only man I'd found attractive.

If I slept in that bed with him—willingly—I was gonna fall harder.

Bear rested his hand against my back urging me in.

"Come on, I don't bite... hard." He chuckled and pushed me further into the room.

Well shit.

Bear pulled back the covers and lifted me by the waist so I didn't have to crawl inside. He frowned once I rolled over, and he tucked me in. "Are you sure you don't want another meal replacement shake? I think you need to eat more."

I made a gagging noise. "No, I'm full. I'll throw up dinner if you make me drink another." Bear sighed and put another blanket on top of me. "Then I'll wake you up in the middle of the night to drink another."

Was he crazy?

"I get feral if someone wakes me during my beauty sleep," I warned and brought out my fake claws. "Rawr."

Bear grabbed my hand and looked at my nails. "Those tiny things? They will do nothing. Now these..." He took his hand and elongated his claws. They grew as long as my fingers. They were thick and black, just like a bear, and just as sharp. "These are claws."

I reached out to touch them; they were strong and sturdy and not at all weak and fake looking like I thought they would be. "Can I see more? Can I see your grizzly? Is it big?"

Bear retracted his claws, rounded the bed, and curled up beside me, making me the little spoon. I sighed happily as he curled around me, the gigantic mountain of a man engulfing me into a little ball of warmth. "I'm still healing, but soon. I think he would like to meet you."

"You speak like he is another person." I yawned.

"He is. He has his own thoughts and talks to me. It's damn annoying sometimes."

"Does he like me okay? Does he find me annoying?"

Bear's loud motor-like purring started, and my body oozed against him more.

"He isn't talking yet, but I know he likes you. How could he not?"

I smiled, closing my eyes. The warmth of his body, the noise he made with his chest was lulling me to sleep faster. I had so many more questions, and the fear of speaking was nothing but a distant memory now. I felt comfortable talking—to Bear anyway, and I was ready to continue to find out more about him.

Bear's fingers stroked my arm, his nose buried deep into my neck. Unfortunately, my plan to keep my heart away from him was failing. I was falling for the first time in my life. He had a mate out there, and the undeniable attractiveness we both had for each other was going to break me in the end.

I didn't want to give it up, not yet. Once I get stronger physically, maybe I could guard my heart better.

Fat chance.

"You think so little of me. You really thought I would never find out?" Master Cunningham taunted and circled my parents. They were tied to metal chairs, with thick ropes pressing into their tender skin. Neither one of them had their shirts on. Mama only in her bra and pin-straight skirt.

Another punch flew across Papa's face, blood spraying into Mama's eyes as she screamed at Master Shane for mercy. "Please, please, do not hurt him!"

"Then tell me," Master Cunningham asked, "who told you to work for me? Who told you to gather intel? I want the source. I want to know exactly who you report to and how you do it. I've watched you, but you both"—he wagged his finger at the both of them—"are very clever, clever indeed. I don't even know the true residence of your home, so you obviously have done this before."

This time, another masked male flipped out his knife and shoved it up Papa's ring fingernail. The silent scream was worse than hearing his throat opening up and letting out a howl. He was in so much pain, and there was nothing I could do to stop it. I was watching from the shadows, unable to watch history repeat itself over and over. It was just as bad as the first time I watched this torturous scene.

"I'm going to ask you again, who?" Master Cunningham shook with fury while unbuttoning his collar and letting the tie slide down his pristine white shirt. He wouldn't dare let the blood get on his clothes—he promised his new bride he wouldn't get his hands bloody.

"We couldn't tell you if we wanted to." Mama narrowed her eyes at him. "We were asked to check on your mansion. You were smuggling drugs and dealing with someone dangerous that could lead to trafficking humans. We were simply asked to watch, and they would contact us when the time was right."

"And you blindly followed?" Master Cunningham rolled up his sleeves with a smirk.

Papa spat out the blood out from his mouth. "Comes with the line of work."

Master Cunningham snapped his fingers and pointed to the table. Papa was untied and wrestled until he was laid faced up and tied once again. Master Cunningham shook his head and leaned over Mama's body, a cruel smile falling upon his lips.

"This is your last chance, Mrs. Kirillova. Even if you were an excellent secretary, I have my limits. You know I am not a patient man."

"Certainly not." She straightened her shoulders. "You're the worst person I have ever encountered by far, making your poor step-sister marry you. A sick and twisted pervert who only sees you as a family and not a man to warm her—"

His smack across her face echoed through the warehouse, but Mama didn't scream. I'd never seen her cry, never letting out a sound of distress. Instead, she turned her head and licked the blood from her lip. "Is that the best you can do?" She said with a heavy Russian accent. "What will your wife think of you now when she sees blood on your crisp white shirt?" My mama cackled as she saw her blood stain on his sleeve.

He cursed and strode over to the table, ordering the men to get on with the worst part of my dream. They ripped off his clothes with a knife, and I braced myself for the worst to come. Mama's chair was turned, but her head was held high. Papa looked at her and nodded—A look they both shared that I had come to understand as mutual love and respect.

They both knew they were going to die, and they both knew they loved each other without a doubt.

My eyes filled with tears, my hands holding my ears even though I knew Papa would not make a sound for at least the first few minutes. His hands gripped the table. He grunted at the surrounding men as they filleted his body and began pulling out his organs. Immediately Papa's face grew pale, and I turned away, unable to watch.

It was then Mama broke. Her screams for mercy for Papa grew louder until his screams finally faded, and the tension in my body relaxed. I leaned my head back on one of the wooden warehouse boxes, letting the splinters poke into my skin.

In these dreams, I could feel everything: my heart constricting in my chest, the tears running down my cheeks, the cries I wanted to scream. And if I did anything to try to stop the madness happening to my family, I would then be thrown into the mix. More pain and suffering for my parents as they saw me getting tortured as well.

There was no winning in these dreams.

Master Cunningham turned on his heel. No more blood was added to his shirt since he was just a spectator. He took careful steps toward Mama, the clicking of his shoes timed with the drops of blood that still dropped to the floor from Papa's lifeless body.

Mama gritted her teeth and glared up at the bastard.

"What will you do now? You've promised your wife and men you would not kill or harm a woman." Her black eyeliner ran down her cheeks, her red lips smeared from the slap on her face. Her once-perfect hair was in a tangled mess.

"Ah, but you see." He kneeled before her. *"I have a better way to get rid of my lady problems."* He took her hair and rolled it between his fingertips.

One of his men brought him his phone. It was already ringing, and an ominous voice came on the other side.

"Shane Cunningham, what a pleasant surprise." The voice was dark, evil, and I'd never forget it. *"How may I help you today?"*

"I have a problem that I can't touch, and I was wondering if you could eradicate it for me with those eloquent words of yours."

The chuckle on the other side made my skin crawl, and my eyes dart away.

"But of course, and you do have what I require?"

"I'll have it sent right away." Master Cunningham smirked. *"In fact, my assistant is the one who urged me to send it to you."* He winked at Mama.

"Perfect, I suggest you all have your headphones on, and please untie her. I'm sure you would like to see the little show she produces for you."

As always, I heard the evil smile behind the voice and wrapped my arms tighter around my body. Everyone in the room put their headphones on to block out the words that Duke Idris would say on the other line.

"Ex profundissimis animi tui somniis dimittam. terrores somniorum tuorum fruituri sunt. Praecipio tibi ut te ipsum perdas, et quia mens tua infirma et minuscula est, tenebrae te involvant et in profundum trahat te."

As he spoke, my mother fell from the chair. She fought it valiantly, trying to cover her ears. But I watched as she clawed her ears and face. Black, dark shadows pulled her down to the floor until she heard every word. The shadows released her, evaporating into the air. Her chest rose and fell until her body levitated. Everyone stopped and watched in horror, except for Master

Cunningham, who smirked as he watched.

Soon, Mama stood, her eyes red while she screamed, running around the room as if something was chasing her. Mad—she had gone mad, trying to claw at the cement walls, climbing plywood boxes and shelves. Her screams, her pleas for help were all for nothing until she found a cement wall. Her head leaned back, and she rapidly banged her head into the wall until blood fell from her face.

I put my head between my knees and waited until the thumping stopped and her body fell to the floor.

CHAPTER FOURTEEN

Bear

For the next week, my mate ate and slept well, and I had become far too accustomed to laziness. I was always with her, not giving her a second to be alone, and for the first few days, I believe it bothered her. She couldn't understand why I would not leave her, and even when she went to the bathroom, she would look suspicious when I waited outside the door.

Journey and Delilah had joked about it at dinner before, how it wasn't normal, but when our female was not by our side, that was not normal.

If I had my way, I would carry her around all day, keep her by my side, but I have found she is a very independent little human. She tried to make her own food, get her own drinks, and wanted to shower frequently. At first, I thought it was to hide her scent, that she wanted to pleasure herself, but she says she never got the chance to bathe while she was in that confinement. She still felt dirty, as she says.

It was on the tip of my tongue to ask to shower with her, maybe get in the large tub and lounge in there with her. I had yet to break through her shyness and see her completely naked. My little bee had yet to see my cock, and I was still worried about what she would think of it.

Would it be too much for her?

I could not get rid of her delicious taste from my mouth. I constantly searched for her honey scent throughout the cabin. When she slept, when she ate, I didn't know what she was doing to keep it hidden from me. Whatever she did to hide it from me, she did it well. Maybe she really was showering to keep it hidden. I wouldn't let her get away with it much longer.

I hadn't touched her pussy in a week, and it was cutting away at my restraint.

My mate had done her best to not stare at my chest or body. She only looked at my face and kept her eyes away from the low sweatpants she so loved the first day she was here. She had been distant in that regard.

I let out a low growl as I watched her sleep, curled up on the couch. Was it too much too soon? Did she not like my advances? Her cunt wept for me; her body wanted more. How could she not want more of what we did?

Too many times I had had to take my hand to my shaft and empty myself into the shower. So much seed wasted and not filled into her mouth and pussy. My cock only becomes angry, and my grizzly furious that it ran down the drain and not near my mate.

My grizzly shook himself inside me, grumbling. His fur had filled in, his muscles filling out, and his strength returning by the day. I wouldn't be surprised if by the month's end I would be able to shift into my animal form. His voice hadn't returned, but I knew what he was thinking.

He thought of me as a fool.

I hadn't told Nadia she was my mate yet, and maybe that was where I had gone wrong. She had already been through a lot in just a week, and there was never a good time to bring it up. We were enjoying each other. I was getting her healthy and concentrating on getting her well. Besides, she was sleeping and resting. That was what Bones said for her to do.

But soon I would start making my advances.

My phone buzzed in my pocket. I laid my whittling knife and block of wood on the table and reached into my pocket. I tapped the screen and sighed, seeing it was from Bones.

Bones: *How's Nadia? Have you been feeding her?*

Bear: *Same as yesterday.*

Bones: *I'm coming up for a checkup. I'm bringing a scale and vitamins. Delilah insists on coming.*

I rolled my eyes. If Delilah was coming, then Hawke would come as well. I didn't need the entire club in my den, not with my unmarked mate here. I didn't need their smells or their unwanted questions.

Bear: *You can drop off supplies. No one is coming in.*

Bones: *Pres' orders. She needs a full workup. Is she talking any?*

I sighed heavily, pinching the bridge of my nose.

Bear: *Yes.*

I snarled in frustration, the sound echoing off the walls, and slammed the phone down onto the worn leather chair with a sharp smack. The room filled with the scent of aged leather as my mate's head jerked up, her heavy eyelids fluttering open. She reached groggily for her glasses, sliding them onto her face as she released a tired yawn.

"Is it lunchtime?" she whispered.

The way she slept and ate was very similar to a bear.

I smirked and leaned on my knees with my elbows, brushing her hair away from her eyes. "Sorry I woke you. It's almost time for lunch. We have visitors coming, so it's best we feed you now."

Nadia sat up and looked to the door and back at me. Her hair was now a rich, vibrant chestnut, her cheeks flushed pink. "Who is coming?"

"Bones, Delilah, and Hawke. You remember them, right?"

She nodded and pulled the blanket around her, holding it tight. Her body immediately went into defensive mode and curled in on itself. I sat next to her and dragged her onto my lap and rested my hand on her face.

"They aren't going to hurt you. They never would. What's going on, little bee?"

"Nothing," she blurted. "I'm just not used to being around a lot of people, I guess. I'm just nervous."

I hummed in agreement. "Are you worried about talking in front of them?"

She nodded. "It's complicated." She played with the hem of my shirt. "I feel safe with you. I don't know why, and I know Delilah asked you all to help me, but with you, it's different."

I smiled, and my grizzly automatically let out that deep, rumbling purr from his chest.

"And I like that." She pointed to my chest and blushed.

"Good, my grizzly enjoys doing it for you. And don't worry, they will understand, and I will tell you more about why you feel comfortable with me later. First, let's get you fed before they get here."

"Has he treated you right? Fed you three meals a day, plus snacks? Oh, and those protein drinks?" Bones rambled while I stayed behind my mate with my arms crossed. We were all standing in the kitchen, my mate sitting at the table along with Bones. He had on his serious face with a stethoscope around his neck.

I wanted to choke him with the damn stethoscope and throw him off the cliff outside for questioning her. I had done everything to keep my mate healthy. Why would he not think so? She gained ten pounds since coming here, a fucking feat in itself for seven days.

All she'd done was sleep, eat, and watch movies. Along with sitting on the porch swing and drinking hot cocoa at sunset with me. She loved the outdoors as much as I did, and it had quickly become our favorite thing to do in the evenings after dinner.

Soon she would be healthy enough to take hikes outside, and I would be healthy enough to show her my animal and take her deeper into the woods.

My mate nodded at Bones' question. She refused to talk to anyone else but me. I took pride in that; Bones was less amused.

Bones tapped on his tablet to type in his notes. "I've brought you some vitamins. Your blood work came back, you are deficient in several areas. These are prenatal vitamins, but they have a high concentration in several vitamins you are missing, so taking these will help."

"I use those," Delilah added. "They don't upset my stomach. They're great."

Nadia looked down at Delilah's stomach. It had grown in just a week; her pregnancy would be significantly shorter than a human's, and I was sure Bones was seeing her more often than he needed to help measure for future pregnancies.

Nadia smiles at Delilah, who sits down next to her.

"How are you doing on sleep? Are you sleeping well?" Bones asks.

Nadia nodded again and looked at me like I was to answer too. "She sleeps all night and takes two naps a day. No nightmares or levitating off the table from what I can tell."

Nadia frowned at Bones. She took the paper from him he had ready for her and wrote: *I have nightmares. I've had them ever since I've been in prison. I don't know about the levitating.*

"Bee, why didn't you tell me you were having nightmares?" I picked my mate out of the chair and sat her on my lap.

She shrugged her shoulders.

Bones sighed. "You were thrashing all over the bed the night you came into the Iron Fang when you were sleeping. You even levitated off the table. It looks to be a sign of witchcraft, some sort of magic. Bear was able to restrain you, and you don't appear to have that magic control you when he is around." Bones locked eyes with me. "That hasn't happened here in the cabin, has it?"

"No," I growled. "It hasn't. I've stayed within arm's reach of her."

Nadia giggled and nodded.

"These shifters." Delilah waved her hand. "Such possessive animals, am I right?" She nudged Nadia.

"But you still have nightmares?" Bones asked. Nadia nodded solemnly. "What about?"

She took the paper again, pausing before she wrote: *Depends. Mostly watching my parent's deaths that I did not see happen in reality.*

"Fuck that's awful." Hawke rubbed Delilah's shoulders.

Delilah shifted in her seat, her hand rubbing her small protruding belly. "Nadia? Can you tell me, do you know who killed your parents?" Tears sprung in Delilah's eyes.

"Why?" Hawke snapped. "Why does that matter?"

"It just does," Delilah replied with a crack in her voice.

Nadia took the paper again. *They are in a better place now and no longer suffer. It does not matter anymore.*

Delilah broke down and sobbed, and immediately Hawke had her in his hold. "He said he wouldn't kill a woman, and he did!" Delilah held onto her mate and cried. Nadia's lip trembled, and she held onto me, not sure how to comfort Delilah.

"Was it Shane?" I asked Nadia. She nodded and pulled my face closer to her ear so she could whisper. "My mother was killed by another man. Now that I know supernaturals are real, I think he was a warlock."

I gripped her arm and squeezed for her to continue.

"His name was Duke Idris. He made her go insane."

Hawke's head snapped towards me, his eyes burning with fury. The air crackled with tension as he clutched his mate tightly. Delilah, lost in her own distress, remained oblivious to the chaos. The scent of anger hung heavy in the air, mingling with the faint aroma of deception. The revelation hit us like a punch to the gut—Duke Idris had been in cahoots with Shane Cunningham for much longer than we had ever imagined.

Hurting our mates' families we hadn't even met.

Delilah wailed again, and Nadia couldn't take her crying. She got off my lap and went closer to Delilah. She looked at Hawke warily, unsure if to approach. Hawke let go of Delilah and nudged her to look at Nadia. Nadia pulled Delilah into a hug, squeezed her, and whispered into her ear.

"Not your fault." It was barely audible for human ears, but those of us with animals heard it loud enough.

Delilah sniffed, wiping away a tear with the palm of her hand. "I think it is. Gods, I think it is, but I really didn't mean to, Nadia, I swear it."

Nadia raised an eyebrow, shaking her head.

"I knew your parents. They told me their daughter's name was Nadia. I never found out your name. If I had, I would have made you come with me no matter what." Delilah swallowed. "I heard your parents talking in Russian on the other side of Shane's office door. They were on a cellphone whispering rapidly, taking pictures when I walked in on them. I used to talk to your mother a lot. She was so nice to me. I think she understood my—issues."

"They were in Shane's office, and I asked if there was something wrong, and in that same moment, Shane walked up and asked why I was opening the door into the office, and he saw what I was looking at and found them both inside, with his desk drawers open, papers strewn everywhere."

I pulled Nadia to my side. She was stiff and unmoving as she listened.

"Shane stayed calm and had me escorted back to my room. I never saw them again after that. Nadia, I am so sorry." Delilah buried her face in her hands and began crying again.

Hawke tried to comfort her, but Nadia raced toward her and threw her arms around Delilah's waist.

"Not your fault." Nadia shook her head. "Not your fault."

Warmth filled my chest at how selfless and caring my mate was, but my anger bubbled beneath the surface that I did not do more to the asshole that was within my grasp just two weeks ago. I should have done more, made him suffer more.

Now we had to take care of Duke Idris, who was now in control of the East Coast and quite possibly working his way back to the west.

I peeled Nadia off of Delilah, brought her back to me, and inhaled her scent. "I can't have you touching other people for so long. It will wipe my scent off of you."

Nadia giggled, rubbing her face on my chest.

Hawke grumbled, his hand caressing Delilah's stomach.

"Like I said, these shifters are something, right? Just wait until you get your marking bite, and you are officially mates, then it really gets crazy?" Delilah sniffed, wiping away a tear.

I froze, the hair on my neck standing up.

Looking up at me, Nadia's eyes widened, and the lenses of her glasses reflected the bright sunlight. "What?" she mouthed.

CHAPTER FIFTEEN

Nadia

Not once, but twice, I was hit in the gut.

Delilah was not at fault for my parents' demise. Delilah was a prisoner in her own home, and she had every right to open a damn door to find out a curious noise. It was my parents' fault for not being careful enough.

Right now, I was more stunned about Bear. *He was my mate?*

All this time, I thought I was just the human he was protecting. The chemistry we both shared I thought that was all it was—chemistry. I've never felt a sexual or spiritual connection with anyone, but ever since I woke up, I've felt something towards Bear I couldn't deny.

My heart would race every time Bear was near, and a warmth would spread throughout my body whenever our eyes met. It was as if an invisible force was pulling us together, intertwining our souls I had never experienced.

The physical effects of these emotions were undeniable. Goosebumps would rise on my skin at the mere touch of his hand, sending shivers down my spine. Every time our bodies brushed against each other, a surge of electricity coursed through me, igniting a fire of uncontrollable lust.

But it wasn't just the physical sensations that left me wanting more. There was a deeper connection I felt. It was as if our souls were dancing in harmony, resonating within each other that I couldn't describe. Bear seemed to understand me in a way no one else ever had, effortlessly deciphering the unspoken desires and fears that lay within me.

As time went on, the lines between protection and desire blurred, and I couldn't help but question the nature of our relationship the past week. Was it possible that the chemistry we shared was not purely coincidental? Could it be that Bear, the one who had sworn to keep me safe, also harbored the same feelings?

Our moments together were sacred to me. With each passing day, the intensity grew, surpassing the boundaries of mere friendship. At least, to me they were.

Yet, amid this emotional whirlwind, I had my doubts. I questioned whether these feelings were one-sided, whether my perception of Bear's affection was merely a projection of my own desires. He had a mate, and he never once brought up that I was his.

The fear of rejection weighed heavily. I didn't want to bring it up, so I kept anything sexual between us off-limits.

I'd kept my distance, trying not to harbor more feelings toward the giant. I'd let him hold me, I'd sought his warmth, slept in his bed, and let him coddle me. Let's face it, I was too selfish to give it up and deny what he wanted to give.

I just saw it as he had a strong sense of looking after the weak. Protecting those who needed help. That was the Iron Fang's motto.

I admit, I let it slip getting turned on the first night and succumbed to his body and his filthy words, but I didn't know what to do. I wanted to experience my first orgasm, but after that, I knew I couldn't let that happen again. I would become too attached, and then what? His mate would come along and take him away.

Where would that leave me? With a broken heart. And I didn't want to be the *other woman.* The one that had to be talked about with his new significant other, his soulmate.

Bear stared back down at me, his eyes glowing bright yellow and his brows furrowed. His eyes snapped back up to everyone else in the room, where it had gone silent, and growled.

And for the first time since I'd let him touch me, I didn't hide the tingling between my legs. I didn't run off to the bathroom to take a shower to hide.

My fingers tightened around his shirt, and I looked at the rest of his friends. They looked absolutely petrified at what they saw.

Fabric ripped behind me, and my hands that held onto the fabric of his shirt fell away. My heart thrummed in my ears. Now I was too fearful to look at what they saw.

"We should go," Hawke finally announced, dragging Delilah behind him. "Delilah, get to the truck." Delilah nodded but was shifting in her bag and pulled out a phone, not keeping her eyes off Bear.

"Nadia, phone." Delilah slowly raised it up, showing it was just a phone, put it on the kitchen table, and slid it across. "Has my number and Journey's in it."

Whoops, I guess I haven't called her this past week.

She followed Hawke out the door, and all that was left was Bones. He continued to sit in his chair, his hands raised. I took that moment to look up at Bear. His eyes were black, the seams of his shirt ripped and hair, so much hair, had grown on his chest that he had recently shaved just for me. He was now covered in it.

And it was *hot* but also freakishly terrifying seeing him half man half animal. The longer he stood, the more animal-like he became. "Nadia,"

Bones spoke slowly. "I need you to talk to your mate. Calm him down. He sees me as a threat."

I swallowed, slightly panicking. His face was shifting the last I saw, and I didn't think I was quite ready to face it again.

What the heck do I say?

"I am unmated. Bear's grizzly is in charge and very angry. If I make the wrong move, he will rip me to shreds. Grizzlies do not take kindly to unmated males near their females."

Claws elongated from Bear's nails, and I gasped. They were thicker than the other night. Dark brown hair sprouted out of his hands, partially covering his nails.

"Oh my god," I whispered, watching Bear's hands reach out in front of me.

I was caged, and I swore his body was growing behind me.

"Nadia," Bones whispered. "Say something."

I fisted my hands together, my eyes shutting tightly, gathering the courage to see what was behind me. Would he be fully shifted now? Would he be a giant grizzly? Would he hurt me?

Questions swirled in my head, and I wasn't sure what I was getting into, but I knew I had to help Bones. Putting it all aside, I twirled around and stared up at Bear. His eyes were on Bones. Bear's shirt was gone, his pants barely hanging from his waist.

He was just a very hairy male with long claws, big, ferocious teeth, and a foot or two taller than he should be.

"Bear?" My voice shook more than I wanted.

He snapped his head down at me. Golden brown fur had sprouted around the sides of his face, and his teeth enlarged, taking up most of his face.

Under all the hair and the scary face, his dark eyes instantly softened when he saw me staring at him. I concentrated on those dark pools because the rest of his face I hardly recognized. That's when I knew my big teddy bear was inside the big grizzly. "Hi, Teddy." I wiggled my fingers in a wave, and his heavy breathing immediately stopped. I fiddled with my fingers and tried to keep eye contact, but the stare–those deep onyx eyes stared straight through me. "Can we let Bones go? I just found out you are my mate." I gave him a shy smile, and he picked me up and brought me to his chest. "Oomph!"

His nose went straight into my neck, and his body vibrated as he held me against him. The door slammed open and shut, and Bear immediately held me closer. He stomped the door, opening it and letting out a roar that resembled the animal he was named after. I pinned my head against his chest, my hand covering my other ear, and waited for whatever animal issue he had to release.

He slammed the door shut, locking the handle as well as using the other locks he equipped the cabin with. Turning on his heel, he huffed and puffed like a petulant child and went straight to the bedroom.

Oh shit, what happens now?

Is he gonna bite me?

Is he gonna claim me?

My pussy fluttered, just like it did on spaghetti night.

Bear continued stomping into the bedroom. He slammed the door shut, going from window to window in the room. These windows boasted beautiful views, but he went to each one, pulled down blackout shades, and then pulled the curtains, leaving the room in nothing but darkness. He held me close to his torso and grabbed blankets upon blankets, then finally fell on his side in the middle of the bed.

He curled around me, pulling the covers over us, his nose pinned to the top of my head. I let him do what he wanted as I didn't feel threatened or that I was in any danger. I don't think Delilah, Hawke, or Bones would have left me. Or at least, I hope they wouldn't have.

Bear had control over his grizzly with me, right?

"Bear?" I whispered into the darkness.

It was so dark I couldn't see with my hand in front of my face. It was exactly like we were in a cave.

Of course, it would be a cave. Bears liked caves. They liked the dark, like they were hibernating. This was his den where he felt safe.

The grizzly grumbled back at me, his arms scooping me closer to his body. His body radiated more heat than Bear's. He was burning up, and I didn't hate it. I was anemic, that much I knew. I was anemic before I was starving, and the heat was quite welcomed by me.

"Not Bear?" I tried to look up, to face the half grizzly human, but I was held so tightly it was hard to move.

He grunted, sighed again, and let a whoosh of heated air over my hair.

I bit my nail, trying to figure out how to talk to this thing. It was sort of funny. I was the one that couldn't talk, and now, here was the grizzly that wouldn't talk.

"Teddy? You're my Teddy bear, right?"

He didn't huff back; instead, his heart slowed, and the excitement of having others in his home was wearing off. I rubbed his chest, letting my fingers go through the thick fur. It was soft, not coarse like I thought it would be. There were patches not full, like Teddy was still recovering. Bear said his grizzly had been gone a long while, and maybe this was why.

"You are getting better, aren't you, Teddy? Are you growing this nice thick fur for me?"

Teddy half grunted, half whined, and his body had gone less tense. I felt his face come close to mine, and his rough tongue licked my cheek.

My nipples grew hard, which surprised me. It was just a lick, but it didn't stop there. He continued licking my cheek. Tasting the different areas of my skin near my face. He even nibbled on my ear, his teeth grazing on my earlobe.

I let out a moan, my hands reaching for Teddy's chest and grabbing hunks of his fur. The purring grew louder, and he went lower and down my neck. His claws had shortened and grazed my skin just at the waistband of my pants.

Teddy's sniffing came louder and more frequently. His purring turned more into grunting and whining. He was frantic, searching. His licking stopped until he sniffed between my covered breasts, then lower and lower still until he reached between my legs.

Yikes, he was smelling me. There.

He could smell me, my—

He took a deep breath, his nose pushing in deeper between my clothed thighs. He rubbed his nose, a deep vibration tickling my clit.

I let out a whimper, my legs trying to clamp shut, but he pushed them further away so he could get whatever smell he could.

"Honey," a deep, gravelly voice said. He didn't sound like Bear at all.

Teddy took long licks on the inside of my leg. "Sweet honey."

"Teddy, wait, you don't want to do that." I panicked, not really sure what Teddy's intentions were. I didn't really know the grizzly, didn't know what he could do to me.

He hummed, his big hands wrapping around my thighs. I no longer felt the thick fur on his legs or face, just the beard I knew from Bear.

"Can I talk to Bear first?" I squeaked. "I-I have questions."

Teddy hummed, his long thick tongue sneaking past my underwear and grazing part of my pussy. My eyes rolled back in my head, and I bit down on my lip to stop letting a moan escape.

Teddy crawled up toward me. I couldn't see him in the dark, and maybe

I was more okay with him touching and licking me there, but it was all so new, all so... I don't know, it was still scary to me. I wanted Bear to walk me through it.

Teddy's claw gently caressed my cheek. "Don't be frightened, little bee. We will take care of you."

I let out a long breath, and I wasn't sure if it was from relief or wanting, because I wanted both. I wanted both so very much.

Teddy's warm, heavy breath lightened. The darkness of the room settled in, and I tried to scoot away from his hold around me, but I couldn't move, and I panicked.

"I need to move," I panted. "I need to move!"

It was so dark and silent. Teddy wasn't talking, and now it just reminded me of my dreams. The warmth of someone breathing on my neck and then plunging their nails into my skin for me to feel the pain.

Had I fallen asleep again?

"Please!" I raised my voice for the first time in ages, and immediately, I was let go, but one warm hand stayed on my wrist.

"Baby, it's me. I'm right here. I'm back. I'm so sorry." Bear's baritone voice was the light I was looking for. I reached for him, found his neck, and wrapped my arms around him.

"You've got a lot of explaining to do." I chuckled anxiously.

Bear petted my hair and stood up from the bed. He immediately turned on the light on the bedside table. "I know, baby, I know I do." His expression was soft and apologetic.

CHAPTER SIXTEEN

Nadia

His face was back to normal. No fangs, no black onyx eyes staring back at me. The graveled voice that let me know that his grizzly, whom I had dubbed the name of Teddy, all had faded away, and now I wanted my answers. I felt like I had been very understanding. Partly because I was a bit put off, maybe even fearful because I wasn't sure how to act around a unique personality, but I was finally comfortable now that Bear was back.

"That was your animal. Your grizzly, right?"

Bear smiled, his fingers combing through his tousled hair. "Yes." He cupped my hip with his enormous hand. His nose was flaring, looking down my body, repeatedly squeezing my hip.

I couldn't help it. My body was reacting too. Bear was nearly naked; he might have some really stretched-out underwear down there. The light was still dim, and my eyes had not yet adjusted, and we were still beneath the blankets.

"He got angry that Delilah blurted out that you were our mate. We were waiting for the right time," Bear said, his voice filled with embarrassment. "He got so riled up. I wasn't expecting him to lash out like that, and I lost control of him. He got so strong, so fast."

"You mean Teddy," I added. "Your grizzly's name is Teddy."

Bear smirked and shook his head. "You females are all about naming our animals. The others warned me."

I frowned. "What? Warned you of what?"

"Grim and Hawke. Shifters don't name their animals, but human females do. Our second chances have all been humans, and they name them. I didn't think you would, but you named mine all on your own."

I blushed and shrugged my shoulders. "I think he named himself. He responded to it. But we are getting off subject," I scolded. "We had all week to talk. You could have even told me our first day here, and you didn't. Why?"

Bear laid on his side and pulled me on top of him. It was a position that I was used to. He was like my own personal mattress. I could hear his large heart beating in his chest, the thunderous purring, and it lulled me right to sleep in an instant.

"I thought it was too much. Too much information in one day. I didn't want to overwhelm you."

I rolled my eyes. "We really don't know each other. You shouldn't just assume. Just because my body is physically weakened doesn't mean my mind is all messed up, too."

Bear sat up and leaned his back against the large bed frame. The bed frame wasn't simple at all. He'd carved out a family of bears walking through the forest and headed to a stream with a cave on the other side in it.

"I do not think you are weak, my mate. Not in the slightest. I just thought it was a lot. You just saw Hawke shift that morning. That is a lot for a human. That is a lot for anyone who has never seen such a thing. Journey nearly passed out when she saw Grim half shifted."

I pursed my lips and crossed my arms as I sat up.

Bear laughed. "You are cute when you try to be angry." He tried to tickle my jaw with his finger.

"Am not!" I slapped his arm. "You've managed to ignite a fiery anger within me." I glared at him. "Ah, such big words for a tiny bee."

It was hard to stay angry, especially when he moved his pecks back up and down. I covered my mouth, trying to muffle the laughter, but he obviously saw right through me.

"See, you are not angry." He pulled down my arms. "I admit I should have told you sooner. It was hard to find the right time. I was barely holding on with not touching you the way it was. I wanted you so fucking bad, and then you weren't letting me touch you as much as I wanted. I thought you were pushing me away. I thought you didn't like how I pleased you. I didn't know what to do. I don't think I could take another rejection." He pushed a strand of hair behind my ear.

I frowned. "You thought I didn't like you touching me, like the first night?" The light was dim, but I could see the tint of red on his cheeks. "Bear! Did you not think I liked it?"

He shrugged his shoulders. "I didn't know."

"I liked it a lot." I cupped his face. "All those showers I took, I was trying to cool off. I didn't want to be near you so much because I was always so… hot and turned on. And I knew you had a mate, and I didn't think it was me. Now that I know, I'm more…" I paused, my cheeks darkening with embarrassment. "Receptive."

Bear sighed heavily. "Thank fuck." He crashed his lips into mine. At first it was hard, wanting, passionate. Then he backed away and pressed tender kisses on my swollen skin.

Was it so bad that I was getting my first kiss at twenty-four? I never wanted my first kiss to be some lukewarm deal with a guy or girl I wasn't attracted to. I wanted it to be with someone I had heat for. And the waiting—was well worth it.

Bear grabbed the back of my head, pulling on my hair to lean my head back. My lips parted, and he slipped his tongue into my mouth. He tasted like a mountain spring as he rubbed his tongue next to mine. My hands—I had always wondered what I would do with them, but they found their way around his neck and tugged at his tousled hair.

Bear groaned, his grip tightening on my back, his other hand sneaking its way to the front part of my body and squeezing my small breast. The darkness of the room only added to the atmosphere as he kissed me. It was dark, quiet, only our breaths intermingling with each other. The sweet kisses grew needy, and my pussy fluttered, my body becoming greedy, wanting more, and my questions falling further into the back of my mind.

I knew he was my mate now. Nothing else really mattered. I've waited for my younger years to experience my sexuality, and damnit, I really wanted it now.

My hips moved and landed on something hard, harder than I expected. Bear grunted, his hand roaming down to my ass and squeezing hard, and he rubbed me up on his length.

"Fuck, baby, are you needy right now?"

"Mmhm, please." I nipped at his lip with my teeth, causing a growl of approval.

"Good girl, how do you feel about me tasting you? Letting me lick that pretty pussy and tasting your honey?"

A shiver ran down my spine, my body both excited and terrified at the thought. It felt amazing when Teddy took one lick, but to have Bear continuously lick it? How would that feel?

I nodded, and Bear smiled in the dim light of the room. He shifted the both of us, laying me on my back while kissing me, keeping me occupied before I changed my mind.

"You got this, baby. I'm going to make you feel so good." He kissed my neck, his hands roaming up my shirt and squeezing my nipples. "Let's take this off, hmm? Let your Teddy have a look at what's his?"

He rolled me over, and I held tight to the sheets, still worried about how I looked. I didn't have large breasts; in fact they were on the small side. Bear shook his head and kissed me again. "You're my beautiful mate. As long as I have a tit to suck on, I'm one happy bear."

I giggled, covering my eyes.

Bear returned to the shirt, ripping it from top to bottom. I gasped, covering myself, and he shook his head. "Let me see what's mine, baby. I want to see all of you. Every mole, birthmark, and love bite I'll leave all over your damn body."

Shit.

Dropping my hands away, Bear growled approvingly and took his tongue and swirled around my nipple. My hands wrapped around his head as he sucked, licked, and nipped.

"Mmm, so good. I'll have to play with these more later. Right now, I'm hungry." He winked at me, let his nose trace down my body, and pulled the shorts down my legs ever so slowly.

Kill me. He was going to kill me.

With the frequent trips to the shower, I'd been able to shave, and thank god I had. It was still dark in the room. At least I didn't have a bright light staring at my now trimmed lower parts, but I still felt utterly embarrassed and wrong for someone to look at me down there.

Come on, Nadia. Be bold, be sexy.

"So fucking beautiful." Bear pushed my legs wider, and I squeaked.

He was going to have me do the damn splits.

"Look at you. You're all wet, practically soaking," he rasped. "I've waited to do this since I first smelled you."

"You-you can smell me?"

"Mhm, I smelled you in the kitchen your first night here."

Oh my god, no he didn't.

My breath hitched, and that was when I felt the first lick. He licked from bottom to top, his rough tongue grazing my clit, and I let out one long whine of a moan as I gripped the sheets.

"I told you I would make you scream, didn't I?" He smirked as he hummed into my pussy.

My body trembled as the ecstasy washed over me. My body didn't know what to do with itself and the pleasure it brought me. He sunk his tongue deep inside me. There was no way it was a normal human tongue. Surely it wasn't his bear's?

I could hear the slurps, the humming of satisfaction. His eyes were closed unless he felt my eyes on him. Bear would smirk and flick my clit with the utmost care.

I was rising, becoming so close to an orgasm, but then he would back away, and I would cry in frustration. "No! Please, I'm so close!" I cried, trying to pull away, but then grabbed his hair and pulled him closer. I didn't know what I wanted. I was so confused.

I was sensitive.

Wanting.

My body was on fire.

His hands pushed my legs further and further apart, and he stared at me with such lust. There was so much stimulation I didn't know what to feel, where to look, what to do.

"I'm in control. Let me take care of you." He laid his hand on my stomach, pinning me in place.

Bear wrapped his mouth around my clit and sucked, flicking his tongue on my clit. I silently screamed, my back rising off the bed. His claws raked the bed beside my hips while I finally let out a strangled cry.

He licked his lips, satisfied, and rose over me. "We're not done. You went days without me, and I will not let my mate go unsatisfied."

Um, okay, won't fight that.

He latched onto my nipple with his mouth and sucked, his finger wiggling its way into my pussy. I gasped at feeling so full. "Fuck, you are so tight, little bee. I'm going to have to stretch you so you can take my cock."

Bear pushed inside. His fingers were large, and I winced. "Wider, I want you spread, or I'm going to tie you up."

My eyes snapped open, and there was no lie detected anywhere on his face. I widened my legs more, and somehow I felt my arousal coat his fingers even more.

"You like the idea of me tying you up? Me having my way with you?" Bear smirked.

I swallowed and bit my lip.

Well, only Bear tying me up, no one else.

"Noted, but not for your first time."

I winced as his finger slid in and out of my body, and when he tried to add another, I let out a cry. "Baby, your hymen is still attached. I can only get one finger in." Bear growled possessively. "I'll take care of that later."

"That's only one finger?" I whined.

Snakes on a plane, I was so damn full with just one. What was I going to do with his monster dick?

Bear continued with his *one* finger, plunging it inside me over and over, curving it in my body. "I can't wait to bury myself inside you, Nadia. I'm going to mark you with my come, claim you so no one else can."

His possessive words brought more desire. I wanted to feel more of him. "Bear," I moaned, wrapping my legs around him. He bit down on my nipple, and I fell over the edge again, feeling him pound me harder.

"Fuck, Nadia, I want you," he snarled. He took his finger from my body and ripped the remaining material that covered his dick.

He still hovered over me. I couldn't see below him; the light was still too dim. He grunted while his hands stayed between his legs, and he pulled on his cock.

I wanted to see so badly, see his dick up close. For the first time in my life, I wanted to hold one, taste it, make him feel good.

Before I could ask if I could, Bear let out a roar, and his head flew back, his come landing on my stomach and my breasts. It was so much; it kept coming for the longest time. He kept pulling, tugging at his cock until he finally stopped and hovered over me with both his arms on either side of my body.

He rubbed his come between my breasts, massaging it into my skin like it was lotion.

"You're ours," the gravelly voice of Teddy said as he nipped my shoulder with his sharp teeth.

CHAPTER SEVENTEEN

Bear

As my mate lay on my lap, curled up into a tiny ball, I could hear the faint sound of her soft snoring. I relished this quiet moment with her, that she was completely and utterly mine.

Nadia was only taking one nap a day, spending most of her morning letting me take my breakfast between her legs. I still hadn't let her touch me yet, too fearful of what she would think. Even my brothers thought I was huge. What the hell would she think?

Nadia was getting tired of staying inside. She was ready to go for walks and be out in the forest. But she was still thin, and I didn't have the proper attire, so I ordered more clothing. However, after my outburst days ago, I doubted Bones would be in any hurry to come up to the cabin to bring it to me.

I stroked my mate's hair, happy that she was with me. I didn't think I had ever been so happy in all my life. I never got to meet my mate. She chose another before I even met her. She didn't even give me a chance, just decided whoever she had chosen was going to be better than who I was.

At the time I was furious that she hadn't waited to meet me. But now that I had Nadia, that faded behind me. Now I got this tiny little human to protect and keep for myself.

The front door handle rattled with keys in the lock. I snapped my head towards the noise, emitting a low growl from deep within my chest. My mate stirred beside me, seeking refuge in the warmth of my embrace. I tightened my hold on her, my lips gently brushing against her forehead. My grizzly companion, ever vigilant, employed his acute hearing, attuned to the faint footfalls outside. Finally, we caught sight of none other than Anaki. His head appeared cautiously on the other side of the windowpane.

"Bear!" his muffled voice came through the window. "You double-locked your door." He pointed to the door. "Let me in!"

I shook my head and flipped the channel on the TV, snuggling further into the couch. I would not get up. I was comfortable and had my mate in my arms. What male would give that up?

That didn't stop Anaki, however. His slender fingers fiddled with the window lock with a pick, and he pushed up the window.

I pulled the blankets over my mate's head so he couldn't see her, and he ran from the window to the front door, grabbing bags and setting them inside.

"What a wonderful host you are," he mumbled and shut the window. "You don't see your best friend for almost two weeks and don't even get up from the couch, not even for a 'hello,'" he mocked.

"Shut up, you'll wake her," I growled, shifting her in my arms.

Anaki rolled his eyes and took the bags of food into the kitchen. He knew this cabin like the back of his hand. He was the only one from the club that knew the layout. Anaki and I were closer than most of the brothers thought. He would come up here when he needed time to himself, even if I wasn't with him. Dragons didn't need a thunder, just as bears didn't need sleuth or pack. They just needed them from time to time but could be alone for longer periods. Anaki would come up here to accompany me at times, just to get away from the loud noise of the canines prowling around the bar.

Packs were just damn noisy.

It was time for him to get away. I suppose I had been selfish but fuck; I had my mate now. I needed my time, too.

"I had the kitchen prepare some casseroles and fresh food. Especially some green things. Humans need ruffage. They need fiber."

"Bones didn't say that," I muttered.

Anaki scoffed. "Of course he wouldn't. He doesn't spend enough time around humans. I serve them all day long. She needs some fiber. It's a better diet than just carbs and protein. It will help her absorb the vitamins better." He pushed the fridge shut and picked up the other bags off the floor. "I know I can't go into your bedroom. I can smell your scent from out here." He made a disgusted face. "I'll leave them by the door, but I have all the clothing you ordered."

I nodded in thanks, and he set them by the door. When he turned, he had the cheesiest fucking grin on his face, and I knew then he was going to say some dumb shit like he always did when he messed with other shifter's mates.

I still don't see how Hawke hadn't punched him in the face.

"Don't," I snarled.

Anaki just smiled and sat down in the giant La-Z-Boy rocker. He cocked his blonde hair to the side and gave a wink. "Bear, whatever do you mean?"

"Don't give me your shit."

He gasped. "I would never give you any of my shit. Now, it's my turn to hold her. Please let me. You are hogging her." Anaki held his hands out, ready to cradle her in his arms.

"She's not a fucking baby. She's my mate!"

"Funny… you hold her like a baby. Let me hold her. I'm sitting in a rocking chair. That way, you can go get some work done around the house. I am great at this domestication shit." He fluttered his lashes. "I can even burp her if you want."

"She's not a baby!" I stood up from my seat and hovered over him. My mate poked her head out through the blanket and yawned.

"OhmygoshshesocutecanIholdhernow?!" Anaki squealed and held his hands up to his face.

Nadia held her hands to her ears and winced. I glared at Anaki, and he leaned back into his seat.

"Shit, sorry." He covered his mouth.

"Her ears are still sensitive, you asshole." I sat back down on the couch and grabbed Nadia's glasses from the table, handing them to her. She put them on and blinked several times until she saw Anaki sitting on the chair. She gave a small wave. "Do you remember Anaki? He brought you a grilled cheese sandwich and—"

"Cake, I brought you that chocolate cake you didn't eat." Anaki frowned and leaned on the arm of the chair.

"She was full. She ate all that damn food, and her stomach could only take so much, don't make her feel bad," I snapped at him.

Nadia nodded frantically.

Anaki moved his eyes, assessing us both. "It isn't because you don't like chocolate, is it? Because women who dislike chocolate are dangerous. They think differently. They are a different breed of woman. They are like Scorpios or some shit like that—women I cannot handle."

My mate's eyes widened, and she shook her head again. She pulled on my shirt and whispered. "I like chocolate."

Anaki pulled out a Hershey's Kisses from the front of his club vest pocket. "Prove it." He tossed it towards her. She caught it with ease and unwrapped it.

"What the fuck are you doing? She doesn't need to—"

Nadia unwrapped the chocolate and shoved it into her mouth. She gave a pretty little moan and a thumbs up, showing Anaki how much she approved of the candy.

Oh hell. That moan.

"Okay, I believe you." Anaki sat back in his chair. "But you will eat some dessert tonight. It has chocolate, and a lot of it, just to be sure you aren't faking it. I only gave you a little."

I rubbed my hand down my face. *Why the fuck does he have to be here? He is too damn much sometimes.*

"Bear makes me hot chocolate when we sit on the porch swing in the evenings," my mate whispered. She looked at me as if wanting approval.

I grabbed her hand and placed a gentle kiss on her wrist. I'd make her all the hot chocolate she wanted.

Anaki grunted and stuck out his lip. "Bear, you never make *me* hot chocolate."

So much for the damn moment.

"You are a grown adult, Anaki. You can make your own damn hot chocolate."

"She's an adult too, not unless you guys are into age play and you treat her as a baby. No kink shaming. But I wanna play too, so I can get my hot chocolate."

I leaned my head back on the couch. "Fucking goddess above, why are you testing my patience?"

Nadia giggled until it turned into a full-blown laugh. She laid her head on my chest and patted it lightly.

"Anaki, you're hilarious. I'm guessing you are close with Bear?"

"Close? I'm his bestie!" He stuck out his chest.

I knew nothing about being his *bestie*. We were close; we shared our woes, and sure we got along. I was the grumpier one, while he was the one that did funny shit that would make me laugh… sometimes. I think most of all it was that we weren't wolves. We needed time in the forest. He had a cave around here near a lake he would often go hide in, and he would come here for dinner or watch television with me.

Anaki was a strange one, bright and happy on the outside but dark within. I knew he had his own demons he fought that no one else knew about. He was weak, just like the rest of us, and he craved a mate more than anyone at the club.

Anaki cleared his throat. "Anyway, I have some things I need to speak to the both of you about if you guys could be serious for once."

I growled, and Nadia started laughing again.

"First off, Bones is really pissed at you, Bear. He wanted me to let you know you are an asshole and that the next time you try to take his last ball off, he would put laxatives in your beer."

Nadia snorted and covered her hands with her mouth until she gasped.

"Wait… only one—"

"Yes, he only has one nut," Anaki droned. "Those communal showers you get to see everyone's scars and junk. Poor guy. That's probably why his mate rejected him. Less potency maybe? I don't know. I'm not into all that anatomy stuff."

"That's so sad. And that can't be the reason. He could still impregnate someone." Nadia's voice was so tender as she spoke of Bones with such sympathy.

It pissed me off.

I didn't want her to give anyone else any sympathy.

Especially to that one balled doctor who tries to talk to my mate alone and can't follow orders.

I'm her mate. No one else.

I counted in my head, trying to remain calm.

I shook my head. "Shifter world differs from the human one. They see it as a deformity, a weakness. I don't know if that is the reason. Our rejections are private stories. We don't share them. We just know he only has one. He jokes about it, but I wouldn't be surprised if it was part of his rejection."

My mate's demeanor turned sad, and I shifted her face to mine with my finger. "Don't worry, he will find his mate. Journey, who has a direct line to the Goddess, promised. Now that I have you, I really believe that."

Nadia smiled, and I leaned down and gave her a kiss.

"Anyway!" Anaki raised his voice. "He also said he left his bag here. It's got birth control pills in it. Wink, wink, wink."

Nadia turned her head into my chest. I could feel her heated cheeks against me.

"That's enough. Don't embarrass her," I growled.

"What sex is normal? Don't you want to do the down-and-dirty, little miss? I bet he will fill you up real good, especially with that anaconda between his legs. Let me tell you the horror stories in the communal showers with that thing—" He laughed and slapped his knee.

I placed my mate on the couch and stood up over Anaki, gripped his neck, and pulled him from the chair. I tightened my grip around him, my claws extending. My vision went red, and I could feel my grizzly in my head chanting to kill him.

"Disrespect," he snarled. *"No one disrespects our mate."*

I tried to push him back, but his strength was strong. The rush of adrenaline, feeling the fur extend down our arms, our legs, I could even feel the shirt ripping as our muscles expanded.

"Bear, please no!" Nadia's voice grew louder, her arms wrapping around the one holding Anaki by the neck.

Anaki choked, holding on to my wrists to hold himself up.

"Please, Teddy, don't hurt him. He was only joking. I like him as a friend, please don't. Let him go, please!" my mate begged.

My grizzly snapped his attention to Nadia. The pleading in her eyes, her touch, her scent caused the grip in our hands to loosen. Anaki fell to his knees. He coughed, rubbing his neck, half coughing part laughing.

"Good job, Teddy." Nadia smiled and reached up for me to pick her up. She wrapped her legs around me as I held her, and she kissed me on the cheek. "What a good big Teddy Bear you are!"

Anaki snorted. "Ha—Teddy Bear."

"Shut up, Anaki. I saved your life." Nadia wagged a finger at him.

My mate put her hand in my hair, massaging my head, and then she smiled wider. "Look at these big ears! Oh, look how cute they are!"

Nadia grabbed them with both of her hands and wiggled up my body. I cupped her ass with my hands, squeezing her cheeks. Not that she cared. She was transfixed on them, so I flicked my ears, and she cooed at them.

Fuck.

I wouldn't mind this so much if Anaki was here, but he was staring at me, his face completely red, trying to hold in his laughter. I was going to get ragged on so bad for this at the bar later, and my mate wouldn't let me beat anyone's ass.

"Little bee, I think that's enough," I begged.

"But look at them! Can you keep them out all the time? I just wanna bite them. They are so adorable! Nom, nom, nom!"

Anaki rolled onto his side, away from me, his entire body shaking.

I sighed, closed my eyes, and counted to ten.

At least she was not scared of me; she found me attractive, and she wanted me. That was all that mattered in this.

"Little bee, how about you soak in the bath, and I will prepare dinner. Then we can start our movie marathon? Would you like that?"

Please say yes to end this torture.

She slid down my chest, her breasts pinned against me. "I can help with dinner. You never let me help."

"I need to talk club business with Anaki, and I bought you some girly bath bomb shit that Journey and Delilah said you would like."

Nadia reluctantly agreed when I led her to the bathroom. I gave her one of my shirts, despite spending a fortune on new clothes for her. Once I set up the bath and gave her a towel, she tugged on my shirt before I left.

"The club business isn't to beat Anaki up, is it?" She narrowed her eyes at me.

I scoffed. "No."

She put her hands on her hips.

"Fine, I won't beat him up. This time."

CHAPTER EIGHTEEN

Bear

Anaki wasted no time badgering me before I could shut the bathroom door. His gossip about the club invaded my ears, even though it was completely unrelated to either of us. Who might be mated to who, what females had strolled into the bar lately, and whose health was waning.

No offense to any of them, but I wasn't concentrating on any of my brothers right now. I was concentrating on the female who was in the bathroom at this very moment, completely naked.

Usually, I stood outside and waited. Now that I'd seen her naked, I preferred to stand inside the bathroom, but she always made me turn around. It wasn't like I hadn't seen her nakedness in the darkness of my—our bedroom, but I don't think she had grasped that I could see in the dark.

My mate was still self-conscious about her body. She was still quite thin despite the calories I gave her. I didn't want to rush her or put any more stress on her mentally as she healed from her time in that damn prison.

I still hadn't talked about her parents. I knew that would be a difficult and potentially problematic situation to navigate. I needed to know why her parents worked at the Cunningham estate and if Nadia was working there when her parents were killed. Were they working there as a family?

Were they captured and forced to work there?

With Delilah's hold on Shane, I would think not. Delilah had rules she wouldn't budge on and to keep families and women out of harm's way. Shane would do almost anything to make Delilah happy, to make her love him.

"Are you even listening?" Anaki waved a ladle in my direction and grabbed it in front of my face. "I was telling you that Delilah just entered the equivalent of the human second trimester and has the cutest bump." He rubbed his non-existent belly and waddled his way toward the fridge. "We are all taking bets if it will be a boy or a girl. What do you think it's going to be?"

I heard the water in the tub shut off and Nadia's tiny moan as she slipped into the water. I grabbed my cock and turned away so Anaki didn't see me adjust myself. I didn't need him seeing it standing at attention and pointing in his direction.

"I hope it's a girl, too, so Hawke has to deal with the awkwardness of her liking males," I huffed and turned on the stove.

Anaki smirked and pulled a tin of food from the fridge. He lifted the foil off of it, stirred the gravy on the inside, poured it over the meatloaf, then stuck it inside the oven to warm the already-cooked loaf. "That's what I guessed. Most of the bar seems in agreement."

Anaki closed the oven and returned to the fridge, pulling out another pan. From the looks of it, he stocked the fridge with a ton of food, and I leaned over to catch sight of an overly full fridge.

Anaki was the epitome of a damn mother hen. Despite his lack of cooking skills, he had the uncanny ability to command the kitchen, ensuring food was promptly prepared and delivered to those in need. He had an impeccable talent for crafting tantalizing cocktails that delighted the taste buds. On ladies' night, he would take center stage, dancing on the bar with a finesse that mesmerized the crowd. His infectious laughter could fill the room, bringing joy to all in his presence. In times of need, Anaki would be there, offering unwavering friendship and support.

Even the times when you didn't want it but actually needed it.

Please let this pan have some potatoes in it.

There weren't any potatoes, but bright green shit was inside. I shook my head, my bear nearly gagging in disgust.

"It's kale salad. Nadia needs some greens." Anaki rolled his eyes and leaned his hip on the counter. "Don't worry, I will get your potatoes out in a minute."

Thank fuck.

Anaki's arms crossed, and he settled into a normal state of conversation. The playful banter about the club faded as his tone turned serious. Worried, I noticed the sparkle leaving his eyes and glimpsed the dull, lifeless soul inside him that he seldom revealed to anyone.

"Have you noticed that Locke hasn't been calling you?"

I nodded and mimicked his stance, my arms crossed and leaning on the opposite counter. "Yeah, I thought that was why you were up here at first. To get my ass moving and come back to the club."

Anaki placed his hand over his heart, his eyes furrowing. "You wound me, Bear. I'm here because I missed my big Teddy Bear."

I growled and rolled my eyes. "Don't. I promised my mate I wouldn't kill you while she bathes."

"I knew I liked her." He glanced at the door. "Anyway, Locke isn't doing well. In fact, he's gone downhill drastically. He's questioned Cyran's mate, frequently actually causing Cyran to nearly have an aneurysm."

I had nearly forgotten about Cyran, too wrapped up in my mate. Vampires were certainly different when finding their own mates, different species, different cultures, but I heard it can be quite drastic. I couldn't imagine what Locke had done to piss off a vampire.

"Has Cyran claimed the female?"

Anaki shook his head. "Locke forbad it. Said she could be a spy."

"What?" I said incredulously. "That's fucking insane!"

A mate has immunity. A mate can be claimed no matter what circumstance, especially if it is a second chance. That was the new law of the club to save those who were dying. The rest we would figure out later.

Anaki laughed, rubbing his chin. "Yeah it is. Grim and Journey finally stepped in and had to overthrow Locke's decision."

I ran my hand through my hair, letting out a ragged breath. Things were worse off than I thought. Grim was second in command of the club, along with Journey, since she was his mate. Technically, Grim could overpower Locke because Locke had no mate and was making the wrong decisions.

"Did Locke find anything out by the questioning? Anything that can help us with the Cunningham estate? Duke Idris?"

Again, Anaki shook his head. "Not a lot that can help us. Cyran's mate had only just arrived a week before. She doesn't have a firm grasp of the house. She was only allowed in certain rooms and was mostly a kitchen maid. What she knew was they were targeting women with no families. She grew up in foster care, like most of the women taken to work in the mansion. She heard a lot of them were going to be shipped off to auctions, put into online sex chat rooms like Journey, planned meet-ups, taking them to parties and strip clubs. The Duke is expanding, getting creative." Anaki's nostrils flared. "I wouldn't be surprised if he is reaching out to just our kind, not humans. Humans are weak. Use them, dispose of them, or keep them around until they are used up."

I gritted my teeth in anger and banged my fist on the counter. Shane wouldn't get into this sex trafficking because of Delilah. He promised her before he forcefully married her. He became friends with the duke after they had been married for a few years, so the duke could run that side so Delilah would never see.

"Do you think the duke knew Shane wasn't coming back when he ran after Delilah?"

Anaki pursed his lips. "Possibly. The duke could have talked Shane into signing his estate over to him in the event of his death. That was why the duke didn't show up to help save him. You found it odd that Shane didn't receive backup right?"

I hummed in agreement. Oddly, he was supposedly buddies with Idris, but Shane fell so easily.

Duke Idris wanted Shane out of the picture.

"Are we sure that Shane was so stupid to put Duke Idris in his will? Shane was part of the largest crime syndicate on the East Coast. He couldn't possibly be that stupid," I replied.

"How did he pay for his vampire abilities?" Anaki added. "That could have been the payment."

I pinched the bridge of my nose. "One way to find out. We can get Switch to dig up the will online and see if Delilah is on it. It should be filed by now."

Anaki pulled out his phone and started a group text with the inner group, minus Locke. An awkward churn in my gut resonated there. I didn't like leaving Locke out of group text; he is our president, but hell, if he is making poor decisions and keeping mates away from each other, it means he's going rabid far quicker than any of us thought.

"What does Journey think?" I say without bringing up Locke's name. Anytime we bring up Journey, it's automatic to think of someone going rabid or a mating chance. We once used to go to Bones for that, but Journey is a direct line to the Goddess now. She would know better than any of us.

Anaki shoved the phone into his pocket and picked up the tongs, letting out a slow breath. He stirred the salad with the tongs, adding some dressing to it. "Journey is hopeful. She says we need to be watching him but not put him out of his misery yet."

"Yet?" I whispered. "So, he may not have a mate?" No one liked that. We hadn't put anyone out of their misery since Journey came along. We have had a few pairings here and there, usually the ones that are close to losing it.

Anaki sighed. "It depends on his mate. Even his mate has a choice, Bear." Anaki took a somber breath, his nipple piercings more prominent against his dark T-shirt.

I never understood nipple piercings, but each their own I guess.

"Journey says his mate is at a crossroads. All we can do is hope."

Anaki pulled another container from the fridge and lifted the foil off. Baked potatoes sat in the tin, and my prior excitement about having them dissipated. I worried about my friend; I worried for the Iron Fang.

If Locke doesn't get his mate in time, what does that mean for the rest of my brothers?

I'd kept my mate here for so long I'd missed much and needed to get back to help the rest of my brothers. Bringing my mate back, unmarked into the club had my grizzly letting out a deep growl. He didn't want any unmated males or females near his precious gift.

Anaki turned around and stared at me, and looked over my head. "Ah, your ears are showing." He covered his mouth, laughing, turning his back to go back to the potatoes.

I covered my head, cursing to myself that I couldn't contain the damn things. I didn't look cute or adorable. I looked like a damn fool.

"Put them away," I grumbled to my grizzly.

"Our mate likes them," he huffed.

"She isn't here right now."

"You weren't paying attention. She's right behind you."

As I inhaled deeply, the sweet aroma of ripe wild blackberries and the essence of fresh honey filled the kitchen, overwhelming my senses. At that moment, my heart skipped a beat, causing me to pivot abruptly. Unfortunately, my sudden movement caused me to collide with Anaki, who was carefully holding a pan of meatloaf with his oven mitts. As the pan slipped from his grasp, the sizzling gravy splashed against my body, scorching my skin and eliciting a fierce growl of pain. Meanwhile, Anaki struggled to maintain his grip, desperately trying not to let the pan slip from his hands.

"Easy there! Back up Nadia!" Anaki stepped in front of her, his legs spread to take any spills or drops of the meat. He was able to save our dinner and leaned his head back, saying a silent prayer to the Goddess. "I saved it!" He squealed in delight, looking back at my mate. "Now you can taste my meat." He winked at her.

"Anaki!" I snarled, stepping forward.

He huffed and put the meatloaf on the counter. "Sorry, sorry." He threw the mitts at me. "No fun at all. Now, go take a quick shower while I finish the potatoes. You are all covered in gravy, not unless you want your little minx right here to give you a tongue bath."

Nadia blushed, covering her face. "Anaki, nooo."

I could see the little smile beneath her hands, but I would not embarrass her. Not now anyway. I stepped toward her and laid a kiss on her forehead. Her hair was still damp, and I petted her hair. "I'll dry your hair when I get out of the shower so you don't get chilled. Why don't you sit on the couch while Anaki finishes dinner?"

I led her to the couch and bundled her up with a blanket. She smiled up at me, her enormous eyes sparkling more each day. I couldn't wait until she didn't have to wear them anymore, and I could see straight into them without the glass. Once marked, she'd be just like me, a shifter with thicker skin. I wouldn't have to worry about her getting hurt all the time or getting sick with human illnesses.

"Be good, little bee." I playfully bit her neck where I would mark her one day. I hoped that it would be sooner rather than later.

She laughed loudly, not a care in the world that the sound she made would hurt her. I loved that she didn't have a care in the world, that she felt safe here, and that she was mine.

"I can't wait to make you mine, permanently," I whispered in her ear.

She rolled her lips into her mouth, biting them with her teeth. "How does all that happen?"

I grabbed her hair at the back of the base of her neck and leaned her to the left. With my other hand, I tickled her shoulder. "I'll bite you here, sink my teeth into you while my cock is buried deep inside you."

She panted heavily, and I could see her nipples harden under her shirt. I pulled the blanket around her and tightened it. "Stay here. Don't let Anaki see your hard nipples, or I'll have to dig his eyes out with my claws."

Her eyes widened, and I laughed, running to the bathroom to shower as quick as I could.

CHAPTER NINETEEN

Nadia

"Quick, come with me!" Anaki jumped over the couch and reached for my hand.

He didn't rip the blanket away from me, force my hand from the covers, or drag me by my feet. Anaki greeted me with a smile on his face and a sense of urgency in his voice. "Come on now, let's get you out of Bear's clothes and get you into some of yours that he ordered you. Come on, little miss!"

I tilted my head to the side, a curious expression on my face, as I slid my hand out from under the blanket and reached for his. His smile broadened like he won the lottery, pulled me to standing, and raced me across the room. Bags were dropped on the floor I hadn't seen before. He ruffled through them, humming to himself, and grabbed several articles of clothing.

"Technically, Delilah and I picked these out, but Bear is going to love it. Now, go put these on, quick, before he gets out!" Anaki shoved the clothes in my arms and pushed me into Bear's bedroom. He shut the door and slapped the wood. "You have three minutes before I come in there!"

I quickly took off Bear's shirt, slightly disappointed I was taking off his clothes. It smelled like him, the masculine, musky scent, but I was curious what I would wear that would fit my figure.

I've hidden myself in Bear's clothes. I had almost forgotten what I would look like in feminine clothes.

I pulled on the white cotton panties with a single blue bow in the front, then the pale blue shorts that were way too short. They could pass off for underwear, really. Next, the white shirt with a teddy bear on the front with a leather vest that says, "Don't mess with me."

It was cute, but not something I would wear in front of someone, anyone. This is something I would wear alone in my apartment on a rainy day with nothing to do.

This has to be a joke.

I scoffed and cracked the door, Anaki practically dancing with excitement. He grabbed my hand and the knee-high white socks that were held in my other. "Put these socks on while I do your hair," he ordered.

"I don't think this is for me." He forced me to sit down on the stool in front of the couch.

"Certainly, it is." He brushed my hair that was down my back and parted it with a comb. He twisted them into two pigtails and began spinning one side. "Bear will love it. He has been hiding your body in those big T-shirts. This is what Bear's woman should be wearing. Something innocent yet sexy. Once I heard you call him Teddy, I knew this outfit had your name written all over it."

"Oh dear." I fiddled with my fingers as Anaki finished.

He pulled me up to stand and brought me in front of a door-length mirror near the bedroom door. I didn't want to look. I haven't looked at myself in a while. I think I was too afraid to. The first time I did, I looked gaunt, still too skinny to look at, but when I looked in the mirror this time, no longer hiding under the big bulky T-shirt, I saw myself for the first time.

"Ah, see there you are." Anaki smiled. "Look how beautiful you look?"

My hair was done up in space buns, too large space buns because my hair was so long. My mother used to do it for me when I was a child. She did it for me well until middle school because she knew it made me happy.

"You think so?" I blushed, staring up at Anaki.

"Little miss, I would never lie," he said seriously. "I think you're gorgeous, and Bear will think so too. You even look like you have big teddy bear ears, just like Bear!"

I bit my lip to keep it from wobbling. I didn't know why that felt so good to hear. All I wanted to do was blend into the crowd, to be invisible. Look like everyone else and not draw that much attention. My parents said it was vital for survival, and so I lived by that.

The doorknob turned, and steam fell into the living room. Bear had one hand on his hip, holding a towel to his waist. "I forgot my damn pants," he announced. He pivoted on his foot, and when he did, his eyes fell on me.

Both of our breaths escaped our lungs, disappearing into the cool air. Water cascaded down his drenched figure, forming small puddles at his feet. The passing seconds seemed to stretch as I fixated on him, and my senses heightened. His knuckles clenched tightly around the damp towel, his lips slightly parting as our eyes locked, a silent exchange of emotions. I no longer felt Anaki beside me; it was just Bear and me in the room.

Did he like what he was seeing?

I swallowed heavily. I could hear my heartbeat thrumming in my ears.

"Mate," he breathed, his voice barely a whisper.

The word carried a weight that surpassed the significance of my actual name. It was as if a surge of electricity coursed through me, igniting every nerve ending. My body surrendered to the power he possessed, feeling irresistibly drawn towards him. His voice, like a siren's call, urged me to step closer, yet my self-consciousness held me back, my foot refusing to lift towards him.

And that was when he let go of his towel.

Immediately my eyes went straight to his dick. Because what woman *wouldn't* look?

And it was enormous, it was the biggest one I have ever seen. I wasn't completely humble, I had seen ranges of dick sizes in my life. I'd seen snippets of porn when I was trying to get my engine running, and none of them compared to this.

The thing was massive, and apparently, I had a type, and that type was girthy and the size that would move your internal organs.

"Oh dear." I licked my lips and looked back up at Bear's face, who had done nothing to hide himself from me.

His face was nearly stoic, except for his eyes darkened with lust as he stepped forward, his dick hardening by the second.

Wait it gets bigger?

His hand was on his shaft, gripping it tightly. I backed away until I hit the prickly wall of the cabin. He raised his free hand, pinning me against the wall. I had only one escape, but I wasn't going anywhere. I wasn't afraid to move; I was far too entranced where this situation was going, too far gone to see what he was going to do with me.

"Are you afraid?" His baritone voice shook me to my core.

I swallowed. My glasses were going to fog up from the heat of my body, which was certain.

"N-no." My face reddened, and I pinned my eyes on him instead of his dick, which was level with my chest.

I'm sure I could give it a handshake if I wanted.

"You don't think it's too big for you? Are you worried I might hurt you?"

My jaw went slack, my eyes darting lower down his muscular chest and getting a closer look. It was certainly larger than normal. But if I was to be his mate, some goddess said I was his, it would fit, right?

"No, I trust you," I whispered. I stood up a little straighter, holding my shoulders back.

I wasn't weak. If I was going to get impaled by something that monstrous, I was going to go out like a freaking queen. What was the saying, *go big or go home?* Besides, I trusted him with my life. He was my big Teddy.

Bear let out an enormous sigh, his hand running down the wall. He backed away, and immediately I felt the loss of his heat.

Wait a second, was that it?

Anaki sat at the kitchen table with a frown on his face. "That was the most anticlimactic scene I have ever witnessed. If I could get a hard-on, it would have deflated immediately."

Bear had already stepped into the bedroom and shut the door. When he emerged, he had grey sweatpants on and a shirt in his hand. He draped the big shirt over me, and I frowned, seeing the shirt swallow me and no longer showing off my cute clothes.

"Let's go eat, little bee." He pulled my wrist to his mouth and kissed it like he wasn't just standing there naked and led me to the table.

"What the actual fuck," I whispered, and Bear stopped and stared down at me.

"What was that?" Bear narrowed his eyes. "I don't think I've ever heard you curse like that. What is going on?"

I took my hand from his, rounded the table, and sat next to Anaki. If Bear didn't know what he did wrong, he could figure it out.

"I don't know what I did," Bear muttered to himself.

"Is he talking to himself?" I nudged Anaki.

Anaki chuckled, sliding a piece of meatloaf onto my plate. He decorated the table with potatoes, a salad, and an extra-large meatloaf, along with bread. "He's talking to his animal. His animal is trying to tell him what he did wrong. Shifters have their own form of schizophrenia, I guess you could say."

I huffed and crossed my arms. "Well, I hope his animal can talk some sense into him. Because he really left me hanging," I mumbled and took a bite of potato.

"I am also here." Anaki pointed a fork at me. "It wasn't like Bear was going to carry you off and fuck you into oblivion." Anaki perked up and looked out the window. "I take that back. He would have done that." He shook his head. "But he shouldn't have covered you with his clothes. He should have at least complimented you first."

"You are mad because I did not compliment you on your clothes?" Bear's voice was soft, his eyes pleading for me to answer him.

I lowered my shoulders and fork so I could wipe my hand down my face. Bear had no clue what he did wrong at all. Bless his big teddy bear's heart.

"It's okay, I guess. I'm more upset that you were just so intense, and then you cut it off like a light switch." I wiggled in my seat. "You had me, all hot and bothered, and then covered yourself up and then covered me up and led me to the table like nothing happened." I moved the food on my plate shyly.

Bear raised an eyebrow and looked to Anaki for help.

"You gave her blue vagina," Anaki deadpanned. "Males get blue balls, but you just gave your mate blue vagina. You got her all wound up showing off your man log that I'm guessing you haven't shown her yet, and then you did the whole booktok lean and got her panties wet. You basically asked her if she was scared to take your dick, and she said no, inviting that anaconda into the snake cavern, and you just backed away! Goddess almighty." He slapped his hand on his forehead.

My jaw dropped, and my face flushed. Bear was no better; he shoved a large piece of meatloaf into his mouth and looked everywhere but us.

I waited until he swallowed.

"I—thought you would be afraid seeing it. Most people are scared of it. I hadn't prepared myself to go further with you after you saw it for the first time. You—took me by surprise." Bear shoved another forkful of meatloaf into his mouth.

Awww, he thought I was scared of his one-eyed monster.

"Anyway, Nadia." Anaki raked the kale salad onto my plate. It was bright green with beautiful ripe red tomatoes and peppers. It was the first time I'd seen fresh food in a long time, and my mouth instantly watered. "How have your dreams been?"

I stuck my fork into the salad, my body instantly seizing at the opportunity to stuff the fresh stuff into my mouth. Growing up, my family ate a lot of cooked vegetables. It was good, but I loved a fresh salad, anything green.

"I still have them, but they aren't bad when Bear is nearby."

As I eagerly plunged the fork into the vibrant green kale, a burst of colors danced before my eyes. The crispy leaves whispered as they entered my mouth, filling the air with a satisfying crunch. The tantalizing aroma of the iron-rich kale and the tangy sweetness of the tomatoes enveloped my senses, making my mouth water with anticipation. A pleasurable moan escaped my lips as I savored the harmonious blend of flavors, urging me to take another bite without delay, my taste buds reveling in the nourishing goodness.

"Have they eased up any? Any changes in scenery to the nightmares? Are they mostly your parents?" Anaki's voice changed, obviously uncomfortable with my moaning, but I didn't care. The salad was just absolutely delicious.

"Ah, I have a new dream that has popped up this past week. Not really much of anything, though. This salad is amazing by the way." Which it was, but I was getting tired of talking about my dreams. I pointed at the large salad tin with my fork. "Are you going to eat any more of this?" Bear and Anaki both shook their heads, their eyes wide as I took the whole container and ate from it instead of pouring it on my plate.

Bear cleared his throat. "What does this new dream have, little bee. It's important for us to know. Dreams are important in the shifter world. They can show glimpses of the past, a future that may be—"

I covered my mouth, finishing the mouthful of kale. "I certainly hope not. Because the last two years have been utter hell."

I put my fork down, losing my appetite. I didn't wake up tired, feeling mangled from the scratches of some monster ripping me to pieces in my dreams when Bear was with me, but I wouldn't ever forget the memories of the last two years of my stay in that confinement.

It had been nice only seeing the nightmares, not feeling them. Bear not bringing it up was a wonderful break, but now that Anaki was here, I wondered if his friendliness was only to bring us to this moment.

Bear stood from his chair, his growl shaking the table as he rounded it and sat next to me. He pulled me into his lap, and immediately the loud motor purr took over. I leaned my cheek into his chest and felt the calming sensation that radiated from it.

Anaki frowned, tapping his finger on the table. "Nadia, I didn't mean to—"

"Bear likes me how I am. I don't want to talk about it," I whispered.

Bear rubbed the side of my face, his head resting on top of mine. "Baby girl, Anaki is trying to help. He's as worried for you as am I. I haven't brought it up, and I should have. We need to break whatever spell or curse is laying on your mind. Don't you want to get better?"

I sniffed and rubbed my nose.

It wasn't like I was planning on staying away from Bear, and the nightmares would come back at full force, but I guess we would never know. I'd rather stay awake until he came back to me now that we found each other. There was always a chance we would get separated, wouldn't there be?

I sighed and slouched in his arms.

"Most of the dreams are the same. My parents murder or me in the dark, and my parents are screaming for me to find them. This week, though, I've had a new dream."

Bear and Anaki looked at each other and waited for me to continue.

"I'm a baby." I scrunched my nose. "I'm being carried by a man, a tall man. But I can't see his face or who he is. There is a plane, and my parents are there waiting at the bottom of the stairs, waiting to climb aboard. They reach out for me, and as my mother grabs me, the monster that invades my dreams, the one that claws at me each night, covers the scene, and I don't get to finish it. I either wake up, or it goes back to my parents being murdered."

I stared up at Bear, who was looking at Anaki thoughtfully.

"This black monster, this entity, it's the curse that is laid on your mind," Anaki said. "Duke Idris put it on you before he had Shane Cunningham put you in solitary confinement, didn't he?

I nodded. "When Shane found out that I helped his wife escape, he couldn't break the promise by physically harming me, so he had his friend Duke Idris come in, and he told him to curse my mind. Everyone thought he was joking. I thought he was too. Everyone said smoke came out of his fingers. I never saw it, didn't see any of it. But I see his fingers, his claws in my dreams. I always thought it was all in my imagination, but now, knowing you all exist, that witches and warlocks exist, I guess it's true."

Bear squeezed me tight. "Deep down, I think you knew. You knew something was wrong. You took finding out that we were shifters far better than I thought."

I rolled my eyes. "Or the fact I was your mate... that might have something to do with it.”

Bear chuckled and nuzzled his nose into my neck. “Say it again.”

“Say what again?”

“That I’m your mate.”

“You’re my mate.” I grinned and wrapped my arms around his neck. Still, the tears from talking about the dreams leaked down my cheeks.

I could see Anaki shaking his floppy blond hair in my peripheral, but he said nothing as Bear and I had our moment. He just took another big bite of his meatloaf and grinned.

CHAPTER TWENTY

Bear

Carefully, I laid my mate on the soft couch and cocooned her in the warm blankets. I wrapped it around her head and body so she couldn't escape the warmth while I finished cleaning after dinner. My mate tried to wiggle free, but I gave her a stern look, and she stopped only to smile back up at me.

"I can't change the channels if I'm all wrapped up like this," she chided.

I loosened the blankets, giving her only enough room for her to use the remote to settle on a movie. She rolled her eyes and flicked through the channels while trying to shake her head.

As I entered the kitchen, I could see that Anaki had taken care of the majority of the cleaning, leaving me with the perfect opportunity to whip up some popcorn. He tossed the disposable tins into the trash, opting for a hassle-free cleanup, and gently rubbed his eyes. He was exhausted; his stamina was dwindling by the day.

"Get some rest on the recliner. I'm sorry I don't have a spare room," I grumbled as I grabbed a bag of popcorn and put it in the microwave.

Anaki waved his hand, a smile spreading across his face. "I'll go to my cave. It isn't far." Anaki leaned on the counter while we sat in silence as the popcorn made itself known. "What do you think of her dream, Bear?"

I cleared my throat and rubbed the back of my neck. Nadia didn't understand how profound dreams were in the shifter world. Many humans don't. Human dreams could mean nothing, but once you were around someone who was your soulmate, the Goddess could bless you with information you never thought possible.

My mate had been cursed with nightmares, the images vividly playing out in her mind like a horror film. She would never want them to be real or decipher them.

"I know what you're thinking." I gazed at the back of my mate's head. "But I think you are pulling at some strings here."

Anaki tilted his head, giving me a *you're such an idiot* look. "Seriously? She's handed off to her 'parents'"—he air quoted—"by another male and put on an airplane. I'm surprised that as smart as she is, she can't figure that out on her own. Nadia was obviously handed off to someone else that is not her family."

"She doesn't believe in dreams or the meanings behind them. Can you blame her?" I tried to reason. The popcorn dinged, and I removed the bag. "She's got enough going on in her life right now. Her dreams are cursed, she has fucking nightmares, she's mated to me, she's been alone for two years. She's holding on to whatever normalcy she has left. The people that raised her as far as she is concerned are her parents. They gave her love, they are her family."

I swiftly tore open the bag and poured its contents into a massive bowl. Anaki reached into the fridge, his hand brushing against the cool metal as he grabbed a beer. With a quick twist, he popped open the cap and chugged it down.

Anaki maybe a bartender but he was a lightweight, he would be out within thirty minutes over the one beer.

"I'll find out why she was in that mansion, if the people that raised her put her there or if she went in there on her own. It's all in time, Anaki. My mate is fragile and it's all I can do to hold on and claim her right now."

Anaki nodded, wiping his mouth. "I understand. I am happy for you, for the both of you." Anaki grabbed my shoulder and squeezed. "But what about that salad? She woofed it down, huh?"

I took a handful of popcorn and shoved it into my mouth. She eagerly ate that salad the same way I used to hunt deer. She was ravenous, moaning like no one's business.

Who gets that worked up over a damn salad?

"Let's go see what romance chick flick movie she's picked." Anaki patted my back, deterring my thoughts.

As we walked into the living room, my mate turned and smiled. "I've picked one. You guys ready?"

Seeing that radiant smile effortlessly lifted the heavy weight that had settled on my shoulders. The soft glow of contentment filled the room as my beloved mate found security within the confines of our home. I was determined to continue to fill her happiness, providing an unwavering sense of safety that shielded her from the haunting nightmares that plagued her each night. It amazed me how resilient she truly was, for not once had I sensed her restless movements in the darkness.

There were no timid whimpers or tearful cries when I held her close, only the soothing silence of steady strength. With unwavering courage, she confronted each dream head-on, refusing to let fear consume her. I'd remain by her side as we relieved her curse. I was hoping our bond would erase it so we wouldn't need any further magic. I feared she wouldn't want to tolerate any more magic from Tajah or Bram, but it may be unavoidable.

We were not a quarter through the movie, and my grizzly was restless.

"You should have thrown her over your shoulder and fucked her in that fake cave you've created," my grizzly huffed.

Throughout dinner, he couldn't sit still, pacing and shaking his fur incessantly. Reprimanding me for the choice I had made. Luckily, I had become strong enough to resist his forcefulness to take over our human form and take her to our makeshift cave in the bedroom.

I just hadn't thought through how to handle my mate's pussy. I didn't want to hurt her. I didn't want to scare her. She was precious, still healing from years of abuse.

When going into a rut, there were females who had rejected me because my cock was too large, and they thought I would hurt them. I'd often had to take rutting root to soothe the pain and take care of it myself. It was still painful, but the rejection and humiliation were worse.

When I dropped the towel, it was too late to go back. I needed to know if she was afraid. I'd kept it hidden from her despite the many orgasms I had given her with my tongue and fingers. She wanted to see; she wanted to touch and feel the mass behind my sweats, but I was like a damn cub, too fearful of rejection.

To my surprise, after I asked if she was afraid, she was not.

I had no plan B. I was expecting her to say she wasn't ready, or that she was frightened, and we would have worked on that, slowly, but no.

She wanted it.

And taking every bit of restraint I could, I walked away. I went against every part of my instinct to rip off the tiny bit of fabric she wore and shove my cock deep inside her. Soak her with my come, claw her backside as I pushed her into the wall.

"Should have fucked her, marked her." My grizzly growled again. I rubbed my hand down my face. Now I wished he would have stayed asleep.

He flashed pictures of my mate's glorious tits, her pussy leaking with her honey, begging for me to lick.

My cock grew hard, and I shuffled in my seat, trying to pay attention to the movie.

My animal was a fucking menace. He was an asshole to me, to other shifters. Overall, he made us look like we had the overall personality of the color brown.

Damnit, I was so damn hard.

Anaki was snoring in the oversized rocking chair, curled up into a ball like his dragon likes to sleep. A thick flannel blanket keeping him warm because the fire wasn't heating his reptilian skin well enough. For a water dragon, he must produce more heat, and I didn't think he could stay in the cave on his own anymore.

I should add that extra bedroom so I could look after him better.

Suddenly, a hand rubbed up my inner thigh, stopping at my ever-growing shaft. My breath caught in my throat when a tiny hand gripped my cock and wrapped around it. It was thick. I could feel it throbbing beneath her hand. My head leaned back and pushed my hips upward, feeling the tightness of the hold.

"Baby, what are you doing?" I rasped as I looked down at my wide-eyed female. Her cheeks were tinged with pink, her lips bruised with her teeth marks.

I lowered my forehead to hers and repeated my question. "What are you doing?"

"I'm feeling aroused again," she whispered and squeezed her thighs together.

Damn those thighs and the socks that go straight up over those knees.

I pulled her from the blankets, having her straddle me. I pressed my lips to hers and kneaded her ass with my large hands. I pulled her cunt over my cock and had her rock into my throbbing erection.

She whimpered, threading her fingers into my hair as I ravaged her mouth. I broke away from her, lifting my shirt over her head. "Do you want to know why I put my shirt over your clothes?" I breathed.

I tossed the clothing to the floor, and she responded with a headshake.

"It was to hide your body, so I didn't take you over the kitchen table and fuck you in front of Anaki." I cupped her breasts, taking my thumb and rubbing her nipple over her thin white shirt. It hardened beneath my touch.

A wistful moan left her lips, and I pushed the tight shirt over her breasts. She gasped, feeling the cool air brush over them. Her breasts were small and dainty, but I wouldn't change them for the world. I loved how small they were and how tiny she was.

I licked the other hardened tit while I pulled on the other. Her arms wrapped around my head, and her hips moved in unison on my cock as I sucked hard against her nipple.

"Fuck baby, you are going to make me come the way you rub me like that." I sucked harder, her moans coming louder.

"Shh, don't wake up Anaki," I ordered.

She quieted, tugging at my hair for me to stop.

"I-I want to taste you, like you taste me."

Fucking hell.

"Baby, you don't have to do that." I brushed a lock of hair away from her face.

She pouted. "Please, just tell me what to do."

I cupped her face, my thumb trailing around her mouth. I tickled there until I stopped right over her swollen lips. She opened them, taking my thumb into her mouth.

"Suck baby, suck my thumb," I growled.

My mate wrapped her lips around my thumb, then lowered her head. She swirled her tongue around it. I moved her hips along my shaft, feeling her hot pussy rub up against me.

"What a good girl you are." I pulled my thumb out of her mouth.

With her breasts exposed, her knees bent in those tiny damn shorts, and her sucking on my tongue, it was too hard to say no to a damn blow job. I grunted, and she smiled, wiggling her ass between my legs while I spread them and pulled down my sweats.

My dick sprung free, hitting my stomach. Fuck, it felt good to let that fucker free. My come was already soaking the front, my balls feeling damn heavy. I groaned, grabbing the base and giving it two good jerks.

My mate stared in curiosity, both her hands rubbing up and down my inner thighs. I could smell the arousal between her legs, the sweet, wild honey I hoped would soon be dripping out of her.

"Grab at the base, baby. Hold it steady."

Her tiny hands grasped it and squeezed. Her breasts heaved, and another thick, heady smell of her honey filled the air. She glanced at Anaki, who was still snoring.

I chuckled, petting her head. "He won't wake up as long as we are quiet," I whispered.

She licked her lips and immediately licked the tip of my dick. My cock jerked. Her tongue was warm and wet, and I nearly let my claws release to grip onto the couch.

"Fuck baby, gods, you feel damn good. That's it, just play with it, get used to it."

She took her hand, squeezing it, taking her tongue, and licking it from tip to base. My cock was going to explode, but I would hold it back so she felt comfortable.

"Why is it so hard? Are all of them like this?" She rubbed her hand up and down my shaft again, and I stopped her before I came all over her.

"Do you know what a baculum is, sweet girl?"

Her eyes grew wide. "Animals have those. It's a bone inside their—"

I nodded. "I've got one in mine." I smirked. "Keeps me harder, for longer, and makes sure my mate is satisfied."

Lust swirled in her eyes. I reached down and cupped her breasts, pinching her nipple. Her thighs squeezed together, and I leaned in for a kiss. "Now are you going to suck my cock, baby, or do you need further instruction?"

She whimpered, grabbing hold of my cock again.

I leaned back, watching my mate come closer to the couch. She had to grab several pillows to give her enough height, and she licked the tip once more, and I grabbed her head to lean her lower on my dick. Once her mouth engulfed the head, I was a goner.

"Fuuuuck, baby girl, that feels so damn good. Good fucking girl."

She bobbed, getting a good rhythm until I pushed her head lower. "Be a good girl and show me how much you can take. Show Teddy how much you want this."

My mate went lower, she gagged, and I nearly lifted my leg at the sweet sound. She sucked me like a damn vacuum, humming as she went. Her tongue swirled the tip of the head as she came up.

"Shit, baby, you gonna kill me," I hissed, gripping her hair. "Fuck."

Her free hands held my balls, massaging them. The tingling behind my spine slowly rising, ready to explode.

This was embarrassing, but I wasn't going to last. "I'm going to come, baby. If you don't want to swallow—"

She hummed, pressing her breasts to my thighs. My mate was so hot, so damn warm. "Fuck, baby, I'm coming, fuck, fuck, fuck!"

I let go, letting my load coat her throat. "Drink all of it. Drink every drop." My grizzly spoke and my mate gripped her nails into my thigh. Her honey scent grew, and more of my come spilled into her mouth.

My mate gagged and broke away before locking onto my cock again. Her hand continued to milk me dry as she swallowed more.

Sweat dripped down my forehead, my body shaking from the weeks of pent-up sexual tension. I'd jacked myself in the shower more times than I could count, but I was never satisfied. I always came out harder than before, wanting her.

I sat up, ready to check on her, and when I did, I found my come dripping on the side of her mouth. She took her tongue and licked it away, swallowing it before I had a chance to clean her. Her breasts had droplets on her chest, but I wouldn't fault her for that. It was a hell of a lot.

"Did I get it all?" She fluttered her lashes.

"*No, she missed some.*" My grizzly pointed out.

Asshole.

"Baby, you got enough," I panted and pulled her into my lap.

I kissed her, tasting myself on her tongue. I pressed her tits against my chest, wrapping my arm around her torso. "But I still want more."

"Yeah?" she panted. "Me too."

I cupped her pussy. She was fucking soaked.

"You're mine, Nadia," I growled.

Her arms slid up my chest, and she climbed into my lap.

I pulled her closer to me, her breasts on my bare chest, her drenched shorts on my dick. I was losing every bit of resolve that I held back for her.

I'd snapped, I'd gone off the deep end. I wanted, no needed to claim her. Especially before my grizzly took over my body and did it for me.

My cock twitched, my claws lengthened, and I dug them into her backside.

"Bear?" Her wistful breath heaved in my ear.

"I'm going to fuck you, little bee. You have no say in the matter. I'm going to take this virgin pussy. I will be the first and last cock your cunt will ever see. I'm going to claim you with my cock, my seed, and my teeth. No male will ever get the chance to know you like I will. No enemy will get the chance to touch you because I will destroy them before they even think about getting to you."

Her eyes widened, her heart thumping rapidly in her chest.

"I will not wait any longer," I snarled.

My teeth elongated while I took my claws and ripped the shirt that bunched up above her breasts. She gasped, trying to cover herself.

"You want to know why, little bee?" I stood from our seat, wrapping her legs around my waist.

"Why?" she whispered.

"Because you are fucking mine."

CHAPTER TWENTY-ONE

Nadia

Bear finally snapped. The sweet bear of mine that coddled me for so long finally lost his cool and has turned into a possessive male ready to claim me.

My body trembled. My fingers could barely hold onto his shoulders at the excitement for what was about to come. I knew he would never hurt me or put me at risk.

He kept his gaze on me as he trudged through the house to his bedroom. Using his shoulder, he swung the door open, closed it with a forceful kick of his foot, and swiftly locked it all in one motion.

Bear's hands roamed my body and kissed me while his body purred louder and louder. I couldn't decipher if it was between a growl or that motor-like purr he constantly radiated. The vibrations pushing between my legs from his wide trunk of a body rested on my pussy. I rubbed myself shamelessly on his body, ready for my fix.

"Goddess, you are so beautiful." He stroked the hair back that continued to fall away from the buns on my head.

By the time this was over, I expected my hair to be a tangled mess.

Shouldn't I be scared? Bear was much larger than me. He wasn't being gentle and treating me like glass as usual. I was being treated like a woman that was going to be claimed. I was in a possessive hold, his fingers digging into my ass that would soon hold bruises.

His beard scraped against the skin while he kissed, nipped, and bit every part of me. Goosebumps rose, my nipples hardening against his ripped body as he carried me to the bed.

His head lowered. "Mine," he whispered between my breasts.

He was treating me like I was desirable despite me being so small. I didn't have a womanly figure. I was flat in all the places a woman should have curves. For once I felt pretty, beautiful, everything I never thought I was.

Finally, I felt the fire and passion a couple who cared deeply for each other should feel. I'd desired it, wanted it for as long as I'd understood it. And now I had it. He was right here.

Damn, I was lucky. This goddess he believed in, paired me with this bear. Our souls? A perfect match? It must be true because I couldn't imagine being attracted to or more comfortable with anyone else in my life.

Thank you, thank you for this.

Bear growled, making noises far from human. My clit throbbed; I swore I felt it pulsing between my legs as his hands became rough, and he leaned over the bed and pushed me onto my back.

Bear's eyes glazed black, gazing at my naked chest and tugging on my tiny shorts. His claws elongated and ripped the shorts off my body with the swipe of his claws. Bear's knees fell to the floor, and he pushed my thigh-high socked legs apart.

He wasted no time burying his face into my pussy. I flung my head back at the immediate attention to my clit. "Fuck, this honey is going to be the death of me, baby."

The low, dim light of the room added to the atmosphere. The small lamp eluded enough light to play into his dark hair. It was enough so I could see the reflection of his dark eyes staring right at me as he meticulously licked my clit.

"Eyes on me, baby." He took a tentative lick as more of my arousal seeped from my body. I panted, gripping the sheets to keep my body pinned to the bed.

So badly I wanted to arch my back as I came to my first orgasm, but he put his enormous hand on my belly and pinned me there. "I said look at me. I want to watch you," he snarled as he wrapped his lips around my swollen bud.

I closed my eyes anyway. I couldn't help it. It was all too much.

He shook his head and lifted my hips off the bed. He kneeled on the mattress and brought my hips to his mouth. My legs lay on his shoulder, and he licked me like I was ice cream from a bowl.

Oh my god.

I didn't have time to think; instead my body shook with pleasure. My eyes may have been open, but I saw nothing as a burst of wild colors bloomed in my eyes. I couldn't see him, I couldn't see the dimly lit room, but a supernova of ecstasy washing over me.

He laid my body back on the bed, and Bear shoved his finger inside me, his tongue not letting up. "One more. I want you wet enough for my cock."

I whined, shaking my head. I was too sensitive; it was too much, but the incessant fucking of his finger that found my G-spot was enough of a difference to spark my body again. "Spread your legs wider. Come on, be a good girl."

I spread them wider, wanting to please him. Wanting to do everything he wanted. He'd brought more pleasure to my body than I ever could, more than anyone on this earth ever would. He was it for me. I wouldn't find anything more than him.

Somehow I knew that. Deep down. My soul knew it, and I think that was why I accepted this all far easier than I should have.

"That's it, baby, damn, look how wet you are. I can slide in two fingers now. Perfectly pink, all puffy and soft," he rasped, shoving his fingers deeper inside.

Bear straddled me, still finger fucking me, and I screamed as he moved his fingers just right. "Good job, pretty girl, so good," he cooed as he brought me down from my high. He pulled his fingers from my pussy and brought them between us. "Open your mouth for me."

I opened them, and he stuck them inside my mouth. "Now suck."

It didn't taste just like me; it tasted like him, too. Was his tongue that far up inside me?

"See how good you taste? That's why I'm so fucking addicted to you."

This. Bear.

Bear's hips rocked against me, his thick cock rubbing in my arousal that coated the bed. He was leaking so much precome, to a normal human, it may have looked like he came already.

"Here is what's going to happen." His voice came in raspy and strained while my arousal coated his hard, thick shaft.

He leaned his head back while putting his forearms on either side of my body. "I'm going to fuck you, and it's going to hurt. Going slow only makes it worse."

If it were ever possible, I just got wetter.

Bear's nose flared, and he smirked.

"I am going to take you over and over until I don't think you can take any more." He continued to rub his cock over my clit, and I wrapped my legs around him.

I moaned, moving my hips along with him.

"When I come for the last time, I'm going to bite your shoulder and mark you as mine," he snarled and showed me his fangs.

Instead of feeling fear, a zing of pleasure shot to my core. My body accepted it willingly, my heart taking it for what it's worth. It felt... right. Call it destiny or fate, but I knew it was supposed to be.

"Yes, please." My voice shook with excitement. "I want you to. Make me yours, please."

This was absolutely crazy, totally insane. I was doing this, completely and utterly doing this, after knowing someone for only two weeks.

As the rush of sensation coursed through me, I marveled at the unexpected surge of emotion. Instead of feeling fear, a zing of pleasure shot to my core. My body accepted Bear so willingly, my heart and soul taking it for what it's worth. All of this felt so... right. It was a moment of clarity that was supposed to be. Every doubt and apprehension I ever had about him melted away. These moments left me with an overwhelming sense of joy as if the universe itself had whispered to my soul, assuring me that this was where I belonged. It was a profound, almost mystical connection that defied explanation, and I couldn't help but smile through the tears welling in my eyes.

When your body and your heart knew—it knew.

I just pray it wasn't the magic talking, but what sort of nightmare could give you these sorts of magical feelings?

Bear groaned, slipped his dick lower, and I braced myself for the inevitable.

I screamed, wrapping my arms around his head when he thrust inside me. He stretched and prepared me well beforehand, but the painful sting was still there. Tears pricked my eyes, but I could handle this sweet torture. I wanted it. Hell I was craving it. His girth was thick, any man would be jealous of.

I held my breath while taking him, not wanting him to stop. I couldn't let him stop halfway. I wanted him fully inside me. He may see me as his honey, but I saw him as my home.

Bear groaned as he settled himself to the hilt. He breathed heavily as he hovered over my body, kissing my cheeks and my neck, nibbling my ear, whispering sweet nothings.

"The bad part's over, little bee. You did so good."

Once the tears stopped, he kissed them away and gazed into my eyes. "I'm so sorry." It was the first time in his possessive rage since coming to his room that his eyes had softened.

As much as it hurt, I was still incredibly wet. I could feel my pussy flutter around him, and his hips moving slightly was driving me mad.

"Don't lose that fire, Teddy Bear. I think you promised to claim me," I muttered.

Bear's smile widened, and he pressed a feverish kiss to my lips. He pulled out only to slam back into me again.

He was slow at first, watching my reaction, but his pace quickened when my legs wrapped around him. His torso was far too wide for me to wrap my legs around, but I did my best to dig my heels into his sides.

"Fucking hell, so damn tight, baby."

I was tight? He was so big!

I could feel the heat of his cock rubbing against my walls, every vein, every pull and push against me. My body contracted around him, my nails raked down his biceps that urged his fucking to go frantic.

The slaps of our skin echoed into the room. It grew hot. The smells of sex and our arousal infiltrated the air. My body was on fire with Bear's heat radiating around us. My body succumbed to his as I screamed his name when I came.

I didn't know if the bone inside his cock really made a difference since I didn't have anything to compare it to. I just damn knew he had stretched me to my limit, and I was going to be so incredibly sore tomorrow.

He followed just after with a roar and filled me with his come, his breath ragged as sweat dripped from his brow. He was far from finished, however, as he flipped me over on my stomach and grabbed pillows from the other side of the bed.

"I've dreamed of fucking you from behind." He slapped my ass, and I jumped with a squeal. "Bears love fucking from behind. I hope you'll like it too because I'm going to do it often."

He shoved the pillows under my hips, making it high enough so he could kneel on the bed. He traced up my inner thigh with his finger, then shoved it inside me. "As much as I enjoy watching my come leak out of your pussy, I want it to stay in your body."

I turned around and watched him palm my ass, spreading my cheeks while he bit his lip. I was so... exposed.

"Don't look at my...butt hole," I cried out.

Bear growled approvingly. "It's such a nice ass, little bee... once you are more comfortable, I'd love to put a plug in it. Fuck you with my cock in your pussy and a plug in your ass. You'd be so full."

"I'm already full now!"

Bear chuckled darkly and slowly shoved his cock inside me. I groaned, laying my head on the mattress.

No way, no way I could feel more full than this.

He slammed inside me harder this time, my body slumping forward. Bear pulled my hips back up and steadied me, his fingers digging into my hips enough to leave bruises. I loved how rough he was, how he didn't treat me fragile now. He treated me possessively, claiming me.

It felt so damn good.

His grunts and groans turned into noises that no longer sounded like him. They were deeper, more feral, more animalistic, like a bear.

He released my hips, and his chest met my back, his body so large his face met my ear. "Mine," he snapped. "Always mine. Mine to have. My mate, my soul, forever."

My pussy contracted, squeezing him like a vise. The possessive growl and the hold he had on me was unbelievable when he wrapped his arm around my torso.

"Say you are mine, and I am yours." His teeth nicked my ear while he continued to pound into me.

My pussy fluttered, my eyes closed, and I screamed out as my arousal coated his cock.

"Say it!" he roared, releasing yet another load into my womb.

"You're mine, Teddy," I panted. "And I'm yours."

Teddy rubbed his head next to mine, his purr long and loud. Spurts of him continued to spill down my leg, soaking the bed and the sheets.

"That's what I want to hear." Teddy kissed my cheek.

His hand rubbed up and down my thigh, massaging the come dripping down my leg. Teddy cupped it and shoved it back into my pussy. "Not going to waste it," he whispered huskily.

Do I dare tell him I am on birth control right now?

I continued to pant, sweat dripping down my forehead. I'd lost count of how many orgasms I'd had. I didn't know how many more times I could go, but it didn't look like we were stopping just yet.

Bear was still admiring my backside while I lay my head on the mattress. I was too tired to move or care. He was playing with my pussy with his fingers, shoving come back inside me. Some weird part of me thought it was hot; the other part just let me believe I got a little bit of a reprieve.

As I looked behind me, I saw Bear's cock looking angry. It was still thick, a big vein ran around the shaft, the head was a deep throbbing red and still leaked come like a fast dripping faucet.

"Mmm, I think my mate wants more of me." Bear took the pillows out from under me and peppered kisses down my neck and back while he gently lay me on my side. His hands massaged my breasts, his lips followed, and sucked them tenderly while I moaned into the sheets.

"You are so quiet." He bit my nipple playfully. "Or did you wear your voice out when you were screaming my name as I fucked you?"

"Ahh!" I grabbed his hair and tugged on it as he continued to play with my breasts. "You aren't getting shy now that I know most of your body, are you?"

"N-no," I whimpered.

I liked that he was in charge. He knew the right moves to make my body explode. I wish I knew how to make his body come like he can with me.

I'm sure there are some books I can find for that—

Bear hummed, letting go of my nipple, and crawled back up my body. He reached around me and held me tight before rolling on his back and had me sit up and straddle him.

One bun of my hair was gone, and the other was halfway there. I was the epitome of a hot mess.

"How's your pussy? Can you do one more?" Bear's strained voice from growling and yelling was the hottest thing I had ever heard. My legs squeezed his body. He ran his hands up my thighs and cupped my waist. If I wasn't careful, I think he would flip me over and fuck me all over again right now.

"It's sore, but a good sore," I said, covering my breasts. I felt so damn exposed above his body.

Bear lifted me up by my hips and had his dick in front of my pussy. It was still as hard as when I first gave him his blow job.

"Ride me," he ordered and petted my sock-covered calves.

Christ.

"W-what?"

Bear lifted his knees to help push my body up and over his dick. My pussy was dripping come, and my arousal, and Bear spread my labia and pushed his cock inside me. "I want you to fuck me like you mean it, baby, I'll help you."

Bear lowered me onto his cock, not giving me a chance to back out. I let out a long moan, my body feeling so damn full, I swear my insides had to move to accommodate him.

I planted my feet on the mattress, moving my body so I could move up and down to test myself.

"Good girl, look at you riding your mate's cock. You make me feel so good, baby girl." He gritted his teeth while he looked at me like he was trying not to flip me over and finish the job.

Please do, because I have no idea what I'm doing!

I moved my body faster, trying to match the pace he liked, but I was not as strong as Bear. There was no way. "Faster, help me," I begged. "More."

Bear chuckled, putting his hands on my hips. "Only if you pinch your tits at the same time."

This dirty bear.

I complied because my legs were shaking and my body was turning into goo... or come because my insides were completely coated in it.

He thrust his hips upward, roaring at the same time until he decided to flip me over instead. He pressed my left leg above his shoulder, leaving me so wide and exposed.

There was no time to feel shy. Bear, or Teddy, was salivating at watching my breasts bounce as he moved my body up and down while he pounded me relentlessly. His balls slapped my ass. As if that wasn't enough, he leaned closer, wanting to take a deep smell of my neck and let his teeth graze between my shoulder and neck.

The heat of his breath sent shivers down my spine as my pussy contracted, and I cried out his name. Bear reared his head back, roaring a deafening cry of claiming, and before I realized what he was going to do, I felt his teeth sink into my shoulder.

There was no time to scream. His sharp teeth broke into my skin. My hands immediately went to his head to pull him away, but he only pushed his fangs in deeper. Slowly, the skin numbed until I could no longer feel it, my body surging with warmth and a connection I couldn't comprehend.

My breath hitched, my hands dropped away from Bear's head, and my breathing evened out.

I gasped, feeling a heavy intensity in my heart and soul feeling so—full. Was I supposed to feel this? Is this what the mark does?

"Bear?" I whispered.

He dislodged his teeth, pulled away, and looked down at me. My blood coated his mouth and teeth. He stared at me with a look of complete and utter confusion.

"Nadia?"

CHAPTER TWENTY-TWO

Bear

She was awake.

Why was she awake? She was supposed to be sleeping. At least that was what I thought would happen.

"Mate," I panted, licking away the blood from my lips.

She cocked her head to the side, her eyebrows furrowing.

"Did you feel it too?" Her lips grew into a smile, but I couldn't concentrate on what she was saying.

My body thrummed, my heart racing, and my soul was connected to hers. I could feel it, but she shouldn't stare at me wide-eyed and awake like this.

Humans couldn't handle stress. Their bodies became weak after a bite, and the bond overtook their bodies, weakened their minds, shut down, and made them sleep.

Why was she awake?

I glanced back down at her neck. The bite I inflicted into her skin was deep; blood still seeped from her skin, but I could already tell it was healing.

I knew it was normal after Grim and Hawke explained it to the rest of us. They fell asleep, a few minutes to hours.

Maybe the bite wasn't deep enough.

"Bear?"

My mate's voice was full of doubt when I looked into her eyes, and that it should be because I stared right through her.

I brought my thumb to her face and smiled, stroking her cheek. "Yes, little bee, I feel it. It will only get stronger over the next few days."

The bond would hit her like a ton of bricks if she had passed out and woke up. Now the bond was just a dull humming between us.

"Are you not... tired?" I asked exhaustedly. "Did I not pleasure my mate enough?" I tried to joke.

My heart raced with a feeling of dread as I realized I might have done something wrong.

Unless Anaki's suspicions may be true. That her human parents weren't really her blood after all. Worse yet, she may not be completely human.

No human could stay awake after a bite. The only species that could were supernaturals.

My mate's cheeks reddened, and she shook her head. "N-no, I am worn out enough. I am tired, but that bite and then this warm feeling all over my body... it surprised me. You didn't tell me it was going to feel that way." She smiled softly, her fingers running up my chest and cupping my beard.

I kissed her wrist, nuzzling into her hand.

"I'm going to be honest, little bee, you should be sleeping. Most mates would be by now."

She blinked for several moments. "Well, I can go to sleep if you want..." she trailed off and turned her head away.

I chuckled and shook my head, kissing her uninjured neck. "No, that isn't what I meant. It's just that, the other human females, they passed out while their bodies changed, and you haven't."

I pulled my cock from my mate. She winced as I did so, but I kept my body close to hers and pulled her to my chest. "I was expecting you to be asleep. It is my job to take care of you while your body changes. Our bond will grow, your body will also change. You are to become like me. Stronger in body as well, you will no longer be human."

Her eyes widened. "I'll be a shifter too? A bear shifter?"

I nodded.

"Uh, probably should have told me that." She pressed her lips together into a pout. "You're lucky I think that's awesome."

I let out a burst of laughter and lightly stroked her back.

There was a loud knock, excessive knocking on the other side of the door. "Bear! I just got a text from Journey! Congratulations!"

I rolled my eyes and growled. It vibrated my entire body including my cock that was nestled between my mate's delicate folds. My mate arched her back, her mouth opening letting out a sweet little moan.

Her sweet sounds stirred my arousal yet again. My grizzly rubbed our shaft next to her pussy, wanting to see her come again.

"Come again, one more time," he rasped.

Her fingers dug into my forearm, and I swallowed her scream as I kept my cock vibrating and used my hand to pull her ass closer to me so her pussy could rub against me.

Fuck I love how she gets off so damn easy.

She yawned, her eyes losing focus until they eventually closed.

"Keep doing that, and I will fall asleep."

Hell, I fucking will. Maybe I will try some of that *fuck your partner while she is sleeping thing.*

I hummed, pressing kisses on her forehead. "I need you to sleep. Your body will change a lot. I'll take care of you, and I will not leave your side.

I'm hoping our bond will take care of your nightmares."

She hummed, nuzzling into my chest which had nearly grown all the hair I had shaved away the first time she had seen me.

"And little bee?"

She hummed again in response.

"If you have that dream again about the man handing you off to your parents, try and get a good look at his face. Will you do that for me?"

She opened her eyes, only to close them again, and nodded silently as she fell asleep.

With my mind reeling about her being awake after my bite, I held my mate in my arms. Her shoulder was still covered in blood, we were both covered in come and her arousal and the room reeked of sex.

My nose ran up her neck, already smelling my scent coating her body, and soon it would be embedded into her skin, and I would never have to worry about any male doubting who she belonged to. Even if her mark was covered or not.

I struggled with the idea of just laying here the rest of the night but ultimately decided to bathe my mate since she was still susceptible to germs in her weakened state. I pulled her glasses, which were clearly bent now, off her nose.

She won't be needing those anymore.

I was sure Anaki was on the other side of the door, waiting for me to emerge.

I picked up my mate, able to hold her in just one arm, and pulled a blanket from the bed. I smiled, seeing the small patch of blood on the sheets.

It wasn't much, she had been stretched enough, but fuck it felt good to see it. It was damn stupid to be proud of something so trivial. It didn't matter; I was her first, and knowing no male had touched her and no other male would...

My grizzly stood on his hind legs in my mind, his roar letting me know his approval as well. He would have killed any bastard that had touched her too.

I cracked the door, seeing the lights were out and the dim light of the TV was still flickering. Anaki was curled up on his favorite chair under the blankets. I could almost see his blue dragon's tail curled around him. I bet it was fucking adorable.

I hoped he found his mate soon, and I was sure he would. Out of all of the Iron Fang, I think he deserved it the most. Maybe I could put in a special request or some shit, but I was sure the goddess had some master plan.

As I bathed my mate, she didn't stir. This was going more to my original plan after she was bitten. I'd never been so surprised that she was awake and talking after our bonding.

It still disturbed me that she didn't go to sleep right away, and I was going to have to speak with the magic deities of the group to figure out why.

I gently bathed her in my arms, and she stayed curled up beside me, moaning softly. The mark on her shoulder had already healed quickly, and I pressed a soft kiss on her cheek as I let the warm water wash away the soap.

Once she was mostly dry, I put a towel over her body so she didn't catch a chill. I didn't need my mate getting sick because of my carelessness. I took one more sniff of her hair, already smelling our scents intermingling with one another. I smiled, excited that I finally had her. She was completely mine.

"Is she okay?" Anaki sneaked up on me as I opened the door to the bathroom.

I was still naked, but of course, my brother didn't care. "Uh, yeah." I held my mate close. I didn't think it was possible, but I'd become more territorial over her. I didn't want Anaki near her, but I also knew he was like a blood brother to me and would never do anything to hurt her.

"Sorry I bothered you." He scratched his head. "I just got excited for you. And you did it while I was here, and I was like the last to know."

I frowned. Yeah, that was pretty shitty of me.

But what was I to do? Wake him up and tell him I was going to go fuck and claim my mate?

"Yeah, sorry." I cleared my throat. "I do need to tell you something that the others don't know, though."

Anaki perked up.

"She didn't fall asleep right after the bite."

Anaki's eyes widened. "She didn't? Maybe you didn't wear her out enough."

Little fucker.

I shuffled my mate in my arms. "No. That can't be it. She's taken this, all of this." I turned to my bedroom that I treated like a cave. The way she submitted so beautifully to me, how she hardly fought the bond, she sought my touch, accepted who I was, who the Iron Fang was so easily. "I'm starting to think you are right. I don't think the parents that were killed were her birth parents. I think that maybe she might not be human after all—or at least not all human."

Anaki covered his mouth. "It's… possible. Maybe genetically altered like Shane?"

"Or maybe it's natural? Born half supernatural. I don't know. I don't know what else she could be. Only supernaturals have the ability to stay awake after bonding is completed and feel the connection formed," I countered. "When she wakes up, we need to go back to the club."

Ankai nodded frantically, then snapped his fingers. "The salad. She freaked out when she ate that salad. Like it was the best thing she ever ate."

I gazed down at my mate, gazing at her features. She looked like a human, except she was exceedingly small, but that could be the human side as well. Or she could just really love salad.

Fucking gross.

"I don't know, maybe she likes salad." I shrugged my shoulders.

"I don't know, maybe she likes salad," Anaki mocked in his girlish tone. "She wolfed that salad down, man. I think she might be a fae or a fairy."

I stood there dumbfounded. "Fairy's are small. How would that even work? It would have to be a fae."

Anaki rubbed his chin. "Fine, a fae. A fae had some relationship with a human, unbonded, and produced a half-human fae child, Nadia." He pointed to her.

"You're speculating. We don't know yet." I turned and headed to my room. The bed was filthy and unmade, and I wanted her to rest in clean, soft sheets.

Anaki came over, nearly bouncing on his toes.

"Can I hold the baby while you domesticate your cave?" He held out his arms and wiggled his fingers. "I won't drop our love child, I promise!"

I growled, causing my mate to stir, feeling my unrest.

"She is not our love child, and we are not an item. Don't test me, Anaki,"

I snapped.

Anaki pouted but continued to hold out his arms. "Understood, Teddy. I'll rock her in the chair while you clean up the mess you both made." He fluttered his lashes, and I continued to growl, ready to damn smack that smirk that was threatening to escape.

This was Anaki, however. I trusted this unmated male with my life and with my mate's life. He was the only brother of the club I would ever lean on.

I let out a breath and gently put my mate in his arms. He held her like she was the most precious thing to him. He didn't stare at her body; he cradled her head, held her tightly to his chest, and immediately took her to the rocking chair, draping a blanket over her.

My grizzly stayed hidden in the background, watching intently. "I'll be quick."

I kept the door ajar, peering through the crack to make sure my friend was still in view. He stood staring blankly ahead with an unreadable expression on his face. I knew that look all too well—it meant he was deep in thought.

Most likely thoughts of his old mate, like most of the Iron Fang. Anaki was different, though; he had a big heart, and he loved much. With such a big heart, I was sure his rejection was heavy.

I walked back into the living room to find Anaki sound asleep. My gorgeous mate lay in his arms with her hand resting on his chest. The moonlight beamed through the window like a spotlight cast on them, creating an ethereal glow around their bodies. It was as if they were both caught up in some dreamy world of their own.

I didn't have the heart to move either of them, so I lay on the couch beside them both. I grabbed her ankle and held onto her, and we all slept together in the living room until dawn.

CHAPTER TWENTY-FOUR

Nadia

"You have to take her. She isn't safe here," a male's voice said inside a large tent.

I was looking at the scene from a distance, but I could hear everything so clearly.

The snow was coming down in thick white blankets, blanketing the land in soft, fluffy pillows. The tents were scattered around, tucked into the sides of the massive trees, like little specks of color against the evergreens covered in snow. The fire was blazing in the center, providing warmth and light to the area of the thick surrounding forest.

Men and women were bundled up in furs, coats, and jackets. Their faces were nearly white with pink noses and sharp cheeks that almost sparkled green in the light. I squinted to get a closer look as they huddled next to each other. Those who didn't have a warm body nestled closer to the trees that surrounded the small clearing.

As I got closer to look at their faces, a baby's cry came from inside the largest tent. I winced at the pitch of the sound, but I wasn't deterred to stay *away. I was even more curious as to why a baby would be in such harsh, cold conditions.*

An argument broke out, and fists banged on the table when I entered.

"He is looking for her. The babe is putting all of us at risk. Do you not understand that? It's for the greater good that she is taken away." The tall male hovered over the table that held a map pinned with ornate daggers at each corner.

At a glance, it looked like a map of Russia, but none of them were speaking Russian nor had an accent like my parents had.

A woman at the back of the tent was shushing a baby; a hood covered her face, and she was whispering, cooing at the baby she was rocking. The woman was smaller compared to the others in the room, reminding me of my own height.

"Ignore, Shhkuk," a woman who sat next to the asshole said. "Listen, Nina, the baby won't be able to stand the cold out here," she soothed, "and we don't have enough magic to conceal Kraven's looks and keep you and the babe safe. Our kind is only safe in larger numbers. This is no place for a child, especially one that is more human." She stood, and the hood that concealed her face fell, showing an angelic face. She had specks of green sparkle on her high-pointed cheekbones.

The baby cooed, and my attention was brought back to the couple that were holding each other. The male, Kraven, held them both tightly. "I didn't want this. I didn't want us to be separated." He shook his head. "Are you sure there isn't anything else we can do?"

Shhkuk, who was cloaked in white that blended in with the surrounding snow, scoffed. He had a stern face, crossed arms, and his lips curled into an arrogant sneer. "Yes, you can break this pseudo bond sickness you have on this human and let her go with the monstrosity child you have created."

Kraven's jaw clenched tightly, and his eyes blazed with fury as he grabbed the man's neck. The tent erupted into chaos with voices rising in anger and fear. People shouted and scurried around looking for safety, pushing and shoving to get away from the confrontation.

The baby cried, and the mother held the baby tight against her chest. She bounced the child, singing, and tried to stay away from the chaos.

The woman who had sat gently across the table came to comfort the mother. Her hand grazed the baby's forehead. She whispered to the mother, calming her, then whispered to the baby. I moved closer, trying to listen to what she was saying.

"She has no pointed ears, no coloring in her cheeks. The babe will look just like her mother." She smiled up at Nina. "She will be safe with other humans, I promise you."

The woman waved her hand over the baby's forehead and said, "Usana cripta senna kamora tena siepta retum human lam." And a burst of light illuminated over the baby's forehead.

Kraven let go of the offending man, shoving him aside and went to stand by his partner. His hand rested on top of his baby's stomach.

A horn blew somewhere in the camp. Everyone froze as if waiting for a pin to drop. Then another blow came, and everyone gathered their supplies from the table.

"It's time." Kraven picked up the mother of his child and led them out of the tent.

I followed, watching the panic. Everyone was pulling their tents down, stomping out the fire. Within seconds, the camp was torn to the ground. Cloaks were wrapped around their bodies, the supplies were on their backs, and they were all running.

Nothing was left except footprints in the snow.

Kraven attempted to take the child from Nina, and she cried out.

"No, please, I just can't leave her." A sob broke from her.

Kraven appeared to be just as heartbroken as her. She reluctantly gave the baby to him, and she stroked the tiny child's cheek.

"We have to. We will find her again, I promise." His voice cracked. "If we keep her here with us, he will find her. There's just not enough magic, my darling. Not enough help for us."

She sniffed and placed a kiss on the baby's forehead. I still couldn't see her face. A darkness hovered over her. I wanted to rip it away; I wanted to push the shadow, the remnants of a nightmare, darkness, whatever it was away. But I was too afraid.

Who were these people? Why was I having this dream instead of a nightmare?

Panic rose in my throat.

Could this all be linked to me somehow? Bear was so adamant that dreams were so real in his world. That once we were bonded, my eyes would be opened. That I should pay attention to the dreams that I was given.

I wanted to laugh at that. Who would want a nightmare to be true? Who would want any of that to be true?

But this wasn't a nightmare or a dream. This was history.

I could feel the icy chill tingling on my bare feet, the crackling of the dying fire, and the gritty touch of ash on my face. This history wasn't mine... was it?

Just like when I was replaying my parents' death each night. I could tell it was real. I could tell when I entered a dream and tried to stop their punishments when they were fake.

I knew what was real, what was fake.

And this was real.

My hands clenched tightly, the knuckles turning white. I observed the couple, their eyes locked on the baby, their faces filled with a mix of love and sorrow. As I stood there, my breath caught in my throat. I could hear the faint sound of their whispered words of farewell.

"Be safe, my sweet Nadia," her mother said.

Oh my god.

My eyes popped open, and I blinked several times. It was the first time I didn't have a nightmare.

I guess it would depend on what degree of nightmare I just witnessed because it wasn't necessarily a pleasant dream or a dream at all. It felt utterly real, and it wasn't sunshine and roses.

A tear dripped down my cheek; I rubbed it away quickly.

My life the past two weeks was nothing but a whirlwind.

Right now, I didn't want it tainted. I found someone I truly cared about. Bear should be my focus. I shouldn't wake up crying about a past I could not control. I should be happy that I had a man that I had deep feelings for.

I rubbed my chest, feeling warmth spread through my body. It was an odd feeling. It wrapped me in a blanket, an immediate sense of comfort, of love. I'd yet to say the word, but I felt it.

I let out a breath. The panic that had risen from my past quickly dissipated. One step at a time. Bear would help me through this. I knew he would.

The dimly lit room enveloped me, casting shadows across the space. Before me, a slumbering figure emitted deep, rhythmic snores. Pressing my face against the massive, furry form, I inhaled the unmistakable scent of Bear. Familiar and comforting, it mingled with the air as I became attuned to his distinctive, motor-like breathing, a constant presence in my life.

The room didn't reek of sex anymore. In fact, it smelled quite nice. My eyes adjusted, and it wasn't completely black. The sun was streaming in through the small slats of the blinds and curtains, but even with the tiny streams of light, I could see more.

Like the grain of wood in the table, the swirls and intricate designs, almost like it was telling a story about how it grew. From plentiful watered years to years of drought and clouded skies. I shook my head, staring at it. Why would that come to my head?

I cocked my head and also wondered how I could see that so well in the dark. Then I touched my nose to scratch it, and I realized... I didn't have my glasses.

My vision had been... corrected?

I placed my hand on my chest, laying away from Bear. Not that I was trying to get away, but I had a lot of information to unload here. A lot to sort through before he woke up. How would I explain this to him?

I had parents. I grew up with them. They were not of my flesh and blood. Looking back, how could I have not seen it before? I never looked like them. I was short; they were tall. I had darker hair; theirs was lighter.

They were adamant I should always blend in, never stick out. I thought it was because of their jobs. They may have looked like your typical secretary and driver for a well-attuned family in New York, but when I got older, I knew better.

The skills they taught me when I was younger were no random hobbies or their love for James Bond movies.

I huffed and shook my head.

Damnit.

I'd been blind for so damn long it was almost sickening. They were trying to protect me. I hoped it was more than a job. I wrapped my arms around my legs.

Now, who was hunting me, and why did my birth parents have to get rid of me?

Bear rustled beside me. He stretched and groaned until he sat up and gazed around the room. "Mate?!" He turned to me, and his eyes softened. He rolled onto me, his nose going straight into the crook of my neck.

I laughed. My worries faded as soon as his body was in contact with mine.

"I felt your worry. It woke me." He nuzzled further into my hair, his entire body covering mine as he lay on top of me. "What is wrong? Are you sore? Would you like me to give you a tongue bath?"

My eyes widened, and he chuckled.

"For your pussy. My saliva has great healing properties," he added, licking his lips.

"As fun as that sounds." I smiled. "I'd like to talk to you about something."

Bear rolled us over so my body was lying on top of his. He scooted up and sat up against the headboard and had me straddle him. His dick was already hard. I nestled my pussy right against him. It took everything in me not to rub along his length.

I had a shirt on, but we were both naked from the waist down. This was straight-up torture. I took a deep breath and tried to concentrate.

"This is hard," I whispered.

"It is most of the time," Bear agreed. "Imagine trying to walk with a big bone between your legs." He rolled his eyes.

I slapped his chest playfully. "No, bad Teddy. I need to tell you my dream."

Bear's face grew serious, and he nodded. "You believe in them, little bee?"

I nodded as his finger traced where my glasses should be. "I see that toothy grin, even in the dark."

"Already?" He wrapped his arms around me, pulling me back down onto the bed. "I guess I can't stare at you in the dark anymore. It might get weird."

I explained my dream in detail. At first he was intrigued, but as I continued, his face grew more serious, his brows furrowed until he scowled like he had done at the Iron Fang the first day I woke up. Until he looked angry like he was ready to punch a hole in the wall.

"Who the hell sends a baby away?" he growled. "A shifter would never do that, never. And what about the woman that blessed you? You said she had sparkles on her cheeks. What about her ears? She mentioned that your ears weren't pointed." Bear continued to throw out questions left and right.

I shook my head. "Everyone's ears were covered with hoods or hair. I didn't see them. Are there many species with pointed ears?"

Bear grasped his beard and played with it. "If they were tall, they were fae, most likely. If they were clothed in heavy cloaks and all freezing, they weren't winter fae. Most faes are grouped into seasons, or light or dark. Light fae are extremely rare. I'm not sure if there are any left."

I tilted my head, listening intently. It was all fascinating, and I may be part of that species.

"You said the one female had green sparkles on her cheeks, right?" he asked.

I nodded.

"Then spring or summer would be my best guess. Why a clan of fae were hiding in Russia is beyond me. I know little about fae, but the extreme cold would dwindle their power and leave them extremely vulnerable. What I find interesting is that your parents have bond sickness."

"Yeah, what is bond sickness? I thought a bond was supposed to be strong. Ours will be strong; we won't get sick, right?"

Bear held me closer and grunted in agreement.

"No, our bond is secure. Bond sickness means they *need* to mate. In our world, if you are meant to be mated to someone and do not complete the bond within a certain time, the bond will force you to be closer together. If you separate, you become deathly ill. You need to be with them at all times until you complete that bond." Bear scratched his head. "But why wouldn't they complete it?"

I shuffled in his arms, trying to get more comfortable. All I could think of was that mean fae that didn't really like my father or my mother. He would rather her go off without Kraven, even called their bond fake.

"That fae didn't like them. Remember? They must have forbidden it because she is human?"

"Shit." Bear leaned his head up on the headboard. "You are absolutely right. It is just recently we have come into second chances. They are on the other side of the world."

"Couldn't they be first-chance mates?"

Bear shrugged his shoulders. "I don't know. It's possible, but I have never heard of one. Most likely, your father was rejected, and your mother saved him. It's that idiot fae leader of the clan that is just too blind to see."

In a bittersweet way, I was following in my mother's footsteps. I was the second chance for my bear.

I let out a large breath. This was a lot to take in. The people who raised me, I would always see them as parental figures. They kissed my knees when I fell. They taught me ways to survive, and they taught me to help others to save those unable to help themselves. I would never forget them. I would always love and be grateful to them. I would always see them as the parents that raised me.

I now may have a chance to see the parents who didn't want to let go of me. Find out where I came from. Find closure, find out who I really was. Let them become bonded.

"Bear?"

Bear pulled me down to his chest, cradling me. "We are going to find them."

I smiled, rubbing my face into his hairy chest. "How did you know I was going to say that?"

He chuckled. "Our bond, little bee. Soon you will feel my emotions and read my mind as I can read yours. Right now you are a ball of nerves and cannot clear your head, but it will come, and we will speak to each other as we do out loud."

I groaned and tapped my head on his chest. "This is a lot."

"It is." He sighed. "And it may be a lot more complicated now that we know you are half-fae. I don't know if you will shift into a bear or if you will become a full fae."

That's too bad because I wanted to be a bear. It sounded more badass.

Bear let out a bark of laughter and rolled to his side. He petted my hair and placed a kiss on my forehead. "It will all work out. You do not worry about anything. It is my job to take care of you. We will take all of this one step at a time."

I hummed, rubbing my face into his chest to seek his comfort. The more I felt his skin, the more at ease I felt.

"May I ask you another question, mate? If you do not feel comfortable answering, I do not mind waiting."

I huffed and sat up on his chest. Bear thought it would be too invasive to ask me a question? After eating out of my body, pushing his dick inside me? Biting me? Claiming me as his? How could he think I wouldn't answer a question and not confide in him?

"The people who took care of you—who exactly were they?"

CHAPTER TWENTY-FOUR

Bear

My mate was tired after I pleasured her again. Her body was still healing and using my tongue to lick her swollen pussy helped her relax and brought her back to sleep quickly. I wrapped her in blankets filled with my scent and placed a kiss on her forehead.

I wanted to stay with her, stay wrapped up in this cave, and not leave for the entire day, but I wanted to work on a surprise I would conduct for her.

Bear shifters had connections all over the world. Though we were mostly solitary creatures, bears came together at sleuths several times a year to trade, network, gather for potential mates, and for news in other parts of the lands on Earth. Now that we had come into technology amongst humans, it had become more useful to connect with other bear shifters around the world, such as Russia.

Before I left my sleeping mate, I wrote some emails and texts to my home sleuth to see if I could find this clan. Russia was a large place, but there were plenty of bear shifters in Russia who liked the cold winters there, and I was sure over the years they had heard of at least one traveling fae clan. If I was lucky, I could hear something within days.

What I couldn't wrap my head around was how my mate was part fae. How I couldn't smell any part of her being other than human. Was there more magic around her body than we all realized? Even with my bear nearly healed, I couldn't smell an ounce of fae on her body.

I slightly opened the door, allowing my mate's soft snores to trickle into my ears. As I glanced upwards, I caught sight of Anaki's wide grin, his fingers wrapped around a steaming cup of coffee. The aroma of rich, roasted beans filled the main part of the cabin, mingling with the metallic scent of the two thick strips of bloody steak resting on a porcelain plate.

"Sleep well, teddy bear?"

I growled, pulled out the chair to the table, and immediately started cutting into the meat. If Anaki wasn't here, I would have cut it with my claws and shoved it into my mouth.

"When do you want me to schedule a meeting with everyone?" Anaki took a sip of his black coffee. "I'm sure Locke, in his state of near demented mind, will love the idea that Nadia's adoptive parents were hired Russian spies paid to protect a half-faeling."

I let the meat slide down my throat, tasting the bloody taste of the raw meat settling in my stomach. "Did you sit at the door and listen to our entire conversation?" I raised an eyebrow.

Anaki smirked. "You know it."

I groaned. "You are a fucking bastard. We need to talk about boundaries now that I have a mate. It's damn wrong. We need privacy. I'll build you a bedroom, but you can't be spying on us."

Nadia didn't know from the dream that they were Russian spies, but she figured out they were as she grew older. She pieced the puzzle together when they taught her how to load a gun, throw knives, and sneak in and out of spaces undetected. Hell, she knew her way around a computer, some security cameras, and her favorite: how to tell if someone was lying. That was how she trusted me so much, not just the bond, but because I had also given no signs of lying to her.

Her adoptive parents, the Kirillovas, started working for the Cunninghams when they moved to New York for side money but found out incredibly early that they were running drugs and guns. Using their expertise, they launched their own investigation.

Unfortunately, they were eventually caught giving away pieces of information when Delilah discovered them. Nadia figured they must have found something extremely incriminating against Shane with the type of torturous death they were given.

After their *untimely disappearance,* my mate was given a letter telling her to flee the city and stay away from the Cunningham Estate. Of course, she did the opposite and settled with a job there to find their killer and get revenge.

I couldn't imagine my mate trying to kill someone, but if there was enough rage, I was certain anyone could do it.

Anaki snorted, the aroma of freshly brewed coffee wafting up from his cup, and took another sip. "I didn't listen to you guys doing any of your mating stuff. Just the pleasant conversation. It gets boring out here all alone."

I frowned as I stuck another large piece of juicy meat into my mouth. I couldn't fault him for that. He didn't have a mate. Hell, he'd been alone more than I had. Each shifter went through their own length of time to how fast their animal would go rabid. I wished there was a damn timer over their heads that would let me know when their time would come, but we just didn't have that.

Anaki had been a rogue longer than I had. He deserved a mate before me, and I couldn't kick him out. I couldn't be an ass to him. He helped me find the Iron Fang. Anaki found me in the woods outside my old cabin, writhing in pain. He waited until I was done wallowing in my misery until he picked me up and told me about a club that would help people like us.

Without him, I wouldn't have Nadia. I wouldn't have had the support system I had now. I owed Anaki my life.

When my sleuth found out what had happened to me, they wanted me to stay. They called my phone for days, telling me they would send food, even take turns having someone stay with me. Bears were loyal, even to the rogues, which was rare in the shifter world. Then again, earth bear shifters differed from those of the shifters from the Elysian realm, where most supernaturals came from. We were different breeds.

We have hearts.

But I didn't want to be a burden. I followed Anaki, and he has been my brother ever since. I wouldn't give up on him now, and I would take care of him until he found his mate. And give him hell when he found him or her.

"Just don't listen to us when we are mating." I stuck another large piece of meat into my mouth. "And stop feeding me like some mother hen. I can take care of my mate and myself just fine."

Ankai shook his head. "I'll do what I want, Teddy, and your ears are showing, and uh, your claws?" He gestured towards my trembling hand as a thick layer of fur slowly engulfed my arms and chest, the sensation sending a wave of heat over my body. The rapid growth of fur intensified, causing my heart to race, its beats echoing loudly in my ears.

Adrenaline surged through every fiber of my being, setting my heart racing and my breaths shallow. A wave of panic engulfed me, leaving me bewildered and unaware of its cause. My eyes darted frantically around the room, taking in the blurred images in a whirlwind. With an involuntary jolt, my body sprang up from the chair, toppling it over in the process.

Amidst the chaos, Anaki's concerned voice pierced through, but it reached my ears like a muffled echo from beneath the depths of water.

My back curled, and my bones cracked audibly as if a symphony of tension was being released. The sensation pulled at my muscles, elongating them like taffy. It was a rare occurrence, a transformation I hadn't experienced in what felt like an eternity.

At this moment, I was acutely aware of my connection to the grizzly bear within me. Its panic reverberated through every fiber of my being as my body contorted, surrendering to its primal instincts. The usual exhilaration that accompanied our change was overshadowed by an unfamiliar sense of alarm.

It was not our own bodies causing this unease but that of our mate. We could feel the distress coming from her, radiating from our core, intertwining with our own turmoil. The air crackled with tension, charged with the scent of fear and urgency. The world around us faded into insignificance as we focused solely on what our mate was feeling.

Fear.

We leaned our head back, golden brown fur unfurled around our body. Our sweats ripped, our legs lengthened, and claws scraped into the rug on the floor. Anaki took steps back until he was curled onto the floor in the kitchen, making himself as small as he could. It was all he could do. When my grizzly was in charge, everyone was at his mercy.

We landed with an enormous thump. Our fur was thick and heavy as we landed. We huffed out a breath, our ears pricked up at the scream of our mate from the crack in the door, and we turned our large, six-hundred-pound body and barreled into our cave with heavy grunts and growls.

As we entered, we saw our mate, her back to the headboard, breathing heavily, sweat dripping down her face, and eyes wide with fear.

In front of her stood a sinister black shadow, its elongated tendrils extending on either side of its body like eerie fingers. Its head loomed large, revealing a gaping maw filled with razor-sharp teeth. No eyes or nose were visible, heightening the sense of dread. The figure's slender body gave an impression of an otherworldly, demonic appearance.

The shadow-like creature never turned. Not seeing me as a threat. It kept its body in front of my mate.

I let out another thunderous roar, saliva spraying from my ferocious jaws. With a powerful leap, I soared through the air, swiftly reaching the bed. But just as I was about to sink my teeth into the shadow creature, it suddenly dissolved into a swirling void, vanishing into thin air. In a strange twist, it swiftly bolted straight into her forehead.

She blinked, slapping her forehead several times until she gazed up at me.

"Teddy?" her voice shook. "Y-your a big bear now?"

My grizzly hovered over her. I was only a bystander now. My animal had pushed me too deep into the recess of my mind. He was too far into his element to protect our mate, to destroy whatever had entered her mind.

"Mate... what was that?" he tried to link her.

I let out a breath of unease. Surely Nadia wouldn't be able to have her mind open after such a damn traumatic event—her mind was just impaled by a damn demonic creature she...

"Teddy? Did you just talk to me?" Her voice was a jumbled mess, filled with tremors and uncertainty.

I'll be damned.

Anaki's presence caught my animal's attention. He darted his head and found him knelt by the doorway, his neck bared in a submissive bow, and his eyes closed. "Nadia, are you alright? Bear sensed something was wrong, and he shifted. This is the first time I've even seen his grizzly and uh..." Anaki swallowed. Fear radiated from his body and resonated into the room.

My grizzly didn't mind him. Either he didn't find him a threat, or he knew I found him as my brother. I hoped for the latter, but we hadn't talked about it. We never really were the talking type.

Anaki stood slowly. "What happened? Did you levitate again? Do we need Journey, the witch, and the warlock?"

My grizzly snapped his head and roared at Anaki. *"We will protect her!"* he yelled inside us. He turned our massive body off the bed and toward Anaki.

"Easy there, Teddy Bear!" Our mate's gentle hands grasped our colossal head and pulled us back toward her. "Come here. Don't you want to stay with me?"

Nadia rubbed her face next to ours, and instantly, she became the song that calmed the beast. Even me with my worry about a fucking nightmare being stuck in her head, she put that worry away to ease our rage and take care of us instead.

Fucking hell, I didn't deserve her one damn bit.

We followed her as she sat down, our head laying on her lap, and she leaned against the headboard.

"That was a nightmare that haunts me. It was out of my body. It's never done that. I woke up, which normally I can't wake up from a nightmare—and it was there in front of me while I was awake." She shook her head. "It was mad at me. It scared the hell out of me. Then Teddy came in roaring, and it jumped back into my head!" She rubbed her forehead, the slight crease forming between her brows.

My animal rose from her lap, making the bed creak, and licked her forehead. She smiled and rubbed behind his ears. "Nom, nom," she chuckled.

Anaki shifted from foot to foot in the doorway. "Bear didn't stray too far. Besides, we both thought since you actually had a nice dream, your nightmare had gone."

Nadia pursed her lips together and continued to pet rub our ears. "To be honest, I thought so too."

CHAPTER TWENTY-FIVE

Nadia

The rush of panic and fear had long evaporated, leaving me in a state of calm as Teddy enveloped my body. His massive head rested gently on my lap, his velvety ears nestled between my breasts. With each breath, his chest rumbled, emitting a comforting purr that resonated between us. In this serene silence, no words were exchanged between us.

We didn't need to. There was a direct line of emotions going through each other. It was the strangest feeling that I was still getting used to. He held fear and anger, and, most of all, he felt helpless.

It made me acutely aware of the power emotions held and their ability to transcend barriers and bridge the gap between two individuals. And as I navigated this new territory of raw vulnerability, I couldn't help but wonder how our shared emotions would shape the path ahead between us.

It will either help or curse us.

There was a nightmare inside my head. A demon, maybe a phantom that cursed my dream world while I slept. It wasn't Teddy's fault it was back in there, but he thought he could capture it with his teeth, but obviously, that would not happen. Was there a chance Teddy would now see him in my dreams since we were so emotionally connected now?

Would he feel my fear while I slept? There wasn't anything he could do, no physical being he could latch on to.

Teddy snarled. I could feel his lip curl as he raised his head.

Anaki backed away from the door, reaching his hand in his pocket, and began dialing. Teddy lifted his head again, taking his massive form to go after him. I gently tugged on his ear, guiding him back towards me. "Nuh, uh, come here, big boy." He groaned and plopped back on the bed, and the bed squeaked beneath us.

I need some air, I thought.

Staying in this dark room only reminded me of the dark shadow that hovered over me when I woke up. I didn't need that reminder. I needed the sun on my face, the cold air wrapping around my body, and the leaves crunching under my feet.

Teddy snorted, his deep rumble vibrating through the room as if his body was burdened with weight. He mustered the strength to descend from the bed and tenderly cradled my hand in his massive jaws. He was delicate with me, pulling me to the closet and opening the crack in the door.

Bear's clothes lined one side, while mine lined the other.

I let out a laugh and ran a finger through the sweaters, jeans, and jackets. "Guess you are letting me outside, then?"

Teddy huffed and sat down, waiting for me to change.

It was the first time I'd been outside, I mean, really outside in years.

The air was typical of the upper Northwest, which I had learned in my early years in school. Wet, damp, and cold, but not cold enough for it to snow much. The leaves weren't crunching beneath my feet; rather they were wet, but that didn't disappoint me because I could still see the light from behind the clouds, and I could see the hints of green moss behind some of the trees.

Teddy was easily concealed in the woods. The cabin quickly hid between the trees, thanks to the year-round evergreens, pines, cedars, and spruce.

"I hope you know where we are going," I nearly whispered because of the surrounding nature. It was peaceful. I didn't want to disturb the nature around us. The birds were chirping despite the fog and the giant grizzly that walked beside me.

"Of course I know where we are going," he grumbled. *"I would not lead my mate blindly."*

Boy, he was a real winner on personality.

"I heard that."

I giggled, rubbing between his ears.

"You know what I meant. You are still angry about that nightmare?"

Teddy let out a low grumble, his fur bristling as he reared up on his hind legs. With a mighty swipe, his claws connected with the enormous tree trunk, sending a shower of rough bark flying through the air. The sound of the impact echoed through the forest, reaching the ears of nearby creatures. The scent of freshly exposed bark hit my nose, mixing with the earthy aroma of the surrounding forest. As Teddy's claws dug deep into the meat of the trunk, the force of his strike left behind sizable divots, like deep scars etched into the tree's flesh.

"Teddy!" I scolded, putting my hand on the tree as he moved away.

The sheer power from just a tiny swipe of the tree was deep, reminding me how powerful Teddy was. It still hurt to see that a tree was an innocent bystander.

Teddy turned and huffed, steam rising from his maw and nose.

I half expected to feel pain from the tree, knowing what I was, a half-fae. I mean, I was supposed to be connected with nature, right?

"It is the circle of life within nature, little bee," Teddy finally said, turning around to look at me. *"Animals use the plants in the forest to mark their territory, to eat, to make their homes. If a fae could feel the feelings of a tree or in their food, I think they would be in pain a lot."*

I laughed nervously, taking my hand away from the bark.

It was just a thought.

Teddy chuckled and waited for me to walk alongside him. *"I'm just messing with you. I know little about fae. I know they can heal trees, and I know they can feel the pain of trees that are ruined by human hands."*

I nodded and kept my hand on Teddy's back as we strolled. As we went deeper into the forest, the tension in his body released, but Teddy was ever vigilant, looking at every sound he heard. Even my ears had opened and listened to the noises, such as the cracks in the branches, the running of water in a nearby stream, and the brushing of the pines in the wind.

I didn't have to concentrate or worry someone was going to speak too loudly. A problem I didn't have to deal with while growing up but had only dealt with since coming out of solitary confinement.

Now I wondered if all my differences were somehow connected to my heritage.

"As a baby, you had grown accustomed to louder sounds," Teddy said, interrupting my thoughts. *"Your body naturally became accustomed to and adjusted. Since you were in solitary confinement, your body wasn't used to sounds anymore and magnified the smallest of noises. You will adjust. It is much better than when we first met, isn't it?"*

I nodded and huffed out a breath, watching the steam from my nose rise. "You getting in my head is kinda annoying. When can I read your thoughts?"

"One step at a time, mate. First try talking to me without moving your mouth."

I held my shoulders back and closed my eyes. *"Can you hear me now?"*

I could feel Teddy rolling his eyes at me. *"Yes, female. Now open your eyes so you don't fall."*

"You aren't as fun as Bear. You are quite grumpy. I do like your name, though. It gives the illusion you are a big teddy despite your personality." I poked at his cheek.

Teddy lifted his maw. Even though it showed off a row of teeth, it looked like a handsome smile.

"I am the logical one. I am to keep you safe. You are my everything, and I will do everything in my power to do just that. Even if that means to kill everyone in my path." Teddy stopped and turned to me.

He held no humor on his face. Teddy was an animal. He was nothing like the name he held dear that I had given him. Every word he spoke was the truth. The massive strength in his body, the sharpness of his teeth, his claws, and paws proved he was a lethal weapon. He was a damn grizzly, probably the strongest land mammal on the continent.

His piercing eyes, devoid of any mirth, bore into my soul with a chilling intensity. When Teddy spoke, his words resonated with an unwavering certainty, leaving no room for doubt or interpretation.

But it was not just his words that command attention; his physicality was a force to be reckoned with. The sheer size of his body was awe-inspiring, muscles rippling under his thick fur. His imposing stature, reminiscent of a mountain in its strength and solidity, left no doubt that he was a formidable adversary.

And then there were his teeth, sharp as knives, gleaming in the dim light. With a single snap, he could tear through flesh and bone, leaving a trail of devastation in his wake. His claws, like razor-sharp daggers, capable of slicing through anything that dared to challenge him. His paws, massive and powerful, ready to deliver a crushing blow at a moment's notice.

Teddy, the name that once evoked images of a soft and cuddly companion, was just a name for how I saw him. To others, he embodied the essence of a grizzly, the epitome of raw power and dominance, a living testament to the indomitable spirit of the wilderness.

I wasn't scared of him.

My very soul rejected the idea. From the first moment he picked me up from that cot to this single moment where he said he would protect me with every fiber of his being, I felt utterly protected by him, cherished even.

I stepped forward and wrapped my arms around his thick neck. Teddy pulled me closer, and the rumbling of his chest vibrated around me.

Witnessing death over and over again to the people I loved had hardened me to the harsh reality of the world. I didn't want it to happen to me, to Bear, Teddy, Anaki, Delilah, or anyone at the Iron Fang who had been through so much already in their lives.

If it meant Bear and Teddy had to get a little bloody to protect those he cared about, so be it.

"You don't scare me, Teddy." I pulled away and played with his ears.

"You're my big Teddy Bear, and I'll always be right here for the both of you." He huffed out a breath, his eyes searching mine until we continued our stroll through the woods.

It was a comfortable silence as we strolled until we came up on a roaring stream with fish.

I sat on a nearby rock while watching Teddy fish and pawing at the water to sling fish onto the embankment. It was strange to see that Bear was really two different beings. Like he had schizophrenia, but not. There really was an animal inside him, but he was also human.

The animal had feelings like a human, talked, and had complicated thoughts and concerns. Bear, his human side, had animalistic traits of claiming, protecting, and having a cave.

Teddy, once satisfied with his catch, came on shore and grabbed a fish. He gazed at me, offering a raw fish. I shook my head and waved my hand for him to eat. I had plenty to eat before we left, anyway.

I watched in awe how he devoured each one and let my mind wander while watching these animal qualities. How fun it would be to roam a forest, swim, play, and not have a worry in the world. A place to escape.

I smiled as he went to eat another. He wouldn't really hurt one of his own, would he? Anaki? Bear had such powerful feelings, a brother bond to Anaki. Would Teddy really hurt Anaki if he felt threatened? What about the rest of the Iron Fang?

I pursed my lips at that thought. I believed every word Teddy said. He would kill to protect me, but what if he was in a rage like he was earlier? I had to pull him back to protect the one other person I'd really made friends with here.

Teddy turned back to the stream and put his face into the water, cleaning his snout and paws from the remnants of his lunch.

I jumped down from the boulder and yawned. Teddy was right there beside me and rubbed his body up against me. *"Climb on my back, and I'll tell you a story."*

"Is it a happy story?" I joked as I climbed on.

His fur was soft and fluffy. I thought it would feel uncomfortable when I straddled him because I would feel his spine, but it was the opposite. I think I could fall asleep on the giant ball of fluff. I laid my body down and wrapped my arms around him.

"Afraid not, but you get to find out what Bear's true name is."

"You mean, it isn't really Bear?" I giggled.

Teddy let out a chortle. *"If you thought it was, then you aren't as smart as I thought you were."*

I rolled my eyes and gripped his fur tighter.

"No, Bear had to pick his name for the club. The Iron Fang all pick alternative names because they leave their old lives behind when they come into a club full of rogues. They want to forget their old lives because their families and friends want to forget about them. Bear's background is different. Bear shifters, well, Atticus' sleuth is different. They wanted to help him when he became a rogue."

I picked up my head from Teddy's back. "Why is that?"

"Bears are a different breed in this realm. They help each other. Even though bears are more of a solitary animal, they still have strong family values," Teddy explained.

"Wait, different realms?"

"Ah, right. Getting ahead of myself. There is the Earth realm, and there is the Elysian realm. Elysian holds most of the supernaturals. Supernaturals can go between the two. Humans cannot. Humans are forbidden to go there. Supernaturals must hide their true form from humans. If humans find out about supernaturals, both the supernatural and the human would be put to death."

I gasped. "That's terrible."

"It is. Which makes it all quite complicated when your second chance mate is a human. It's only just recently happened, and it is probably why your parents haven't sealed their bond in that fae clan in Russia. They are hiding because they don't know if their pairing will work. If the Royal Council in the Elysian realm found out, not only would your parents be killed but the entire clan as well. Even knowing and letting it go is an offense. Hell, I'm surprised the clan are letting the two of them be around the clan at all."

My breath hitched, and I gripped Teddy's fur tightly. *Maybe they weren't even alive anymore.*

"Grizzly!" I hear Bear come through the link. *"You are upsetting our mate. Shut the fuck up!"*

Teddy snorted and shook his head. *"Our mate needs to know these things. She is stronger than you give her credit for. You can not conceal her from pain."*

My hands loosened on Teddy's fur, and I nodded. "He's right, Bear. Or should I say, Atticus?" I smiled.

Let's change the subject.

"I let you in on this conversion because you need to hear this story as well. Don't make me change my mind," Teddy said to Bear.

Bear snarled. *"She doesn't need to call me Atticus. That's my past life, and that is where I want to leave it. Besides, I was damn there. Are you wanting more commentary?"*

I covered my mouth, trying not to snicker at their bickering.

"There is more to the story than you remember, Atticus," Teddy said softly. *"I purposefully blocked it from your memory."*

I opened my mouth in shock. Bear said nothing. He was silent for a long while as Teddy continued to walk slowly on the path back to the cabin.

"This is our story," Teddy said. *"Our real story, and how I would never*

take Anaki's life, even if I was ever in a full fit of rage."

CHAPTER TWENTY-SIX

Bear

What the actual fuck?

I wasn't the deep, thoughtful type. I wasn't the type of shifter who would ponder life and wonder why I was dealt the cards I was dealt. I was grateful I didn't have a long, drawn-out, dramatic rejection. I moved on, thanks to Anaki. He helped me pick up my sorry ass and took me to the Iron Fang.

My life was going to be shorter, but at least I was going to do some good with it before I left this earth.

I yearned for my soul to be completed before I met Nadia. Once my stubborn ass accepted that there were second chances, I took that bull by the horns. I had hope again.

But why in the hell would my fucking animal block out my memories? Why would he need to, and how the hell was that even possible?

"Grizzly," I growled.

My mate was confused, her heart palpitating in her chest as she rose into a sitting position on our back. Her thoughts tumbled through her, thinking she should jump off and let us fight on our own, but she was going to stay, not leaving our sight.

Even my animal was ready to wrestle her down and keep her with us as we fought with ourselves.

"*Stay,*" we both growled at her as she tried to dismount us.

"This is so weird. It's like having two boyfriends."

"*Mates,*" we both replied. "*We are your mates.*"

She blew out a breath.

"*I did it for your sanity, Atticus. For both of our sanities. Why do you think you did so well when I slumbered? You need me as much as I need you.*"

"*As much as you are an ass?*" I snapped. "*I did fine without you because you weren't yapping in my ear all the time.*"

My grizzly snarled back at me, and our mate pulled on our ears. We both howled in pain.

"That is enough. Oh my god, it's like a bunch of toddlers," she said exasperatedly. "Teddy was trying to help you, Bear. Just understand that. Teddy, as much as you were trying to help, it hurt Bear, okay? I'm glad you are coming clean now. Let's do that instead of fighting."

Grumbling in unison, our mate guided us with our ears towards a tranquil clearing covered in velvety moss. With a graceful movement, she swung her leg over our body and gently pressed us into the plush surface of the moss. As the sunlight pierced through the dissipating clouds, its warmth enveloped our fur. Leaning against us, she tenderly ran her fingers through our thick, golden coat.

"Are we calm now, you two?" she lightly scolded.

My grizzly let out a huff, and that led me to be the only one with a reply. "Yes, little bee, we will be good." I wanted nothing more than to nuzzle my nose into her neck. I took control of my grizzly's head and did just that.

She was kind of hot being a controlling, angry little tick mouse.

She laughed, feeling the cold nose run up against her skin, and she caressed our face. "I can't imagine how tough it is to have two people inside one body. Just try not to fight because now I have two of you inside my head."

My grizzly huffed again. "Just wait. If you gain a bear, then you will have your own bear soul latched onto you, too."

Our mate put her forehead to ours. "Oh, dear."

"Not a deer, a bear," my animal replied.

I sighed heavily. "Again, with just throwing random shit at her?"

"Our mate is strong. She can handle it."

Our mate laid back onto our body. "I'm ready for my story now." Her emotions settled, and her head nestled into our fur. She wasn't fearful, and she wasn't overly stressed like I thought she may be. *Thank the Goddess.*

She's far more accepting than she should be. A trait she must gain from her mother because a fae would never.

My grizzly gave me an "I told you so" nudge and cleared his throat.

"Atticus," my grizzly, emphasizing my old name, began, *"was splitting wood near his home. He was planning on taking a truckload of cedar to the sleuth gathering later that week. They weren't far. In fact, many were in the area already mingling to find mates."*

Our mate snuggled deeper into our fur. Our purr radiated into her body, and our mate took comfort in our touch. I didn't want to pay attention to my animal. I wanted to concentrate on our mate. She was so beautiful, so serene when she gave up all her will to us.

Our mate felt protected and cared for and never felt scared despite our size. There weren't many females that did, even during sleuth gatherings.

"I could sense our mate's arousal and a male in the area. I sensed them a mile away. Atticus, being the ever-focused one, didn't notice. He continued to chop. He was bare-chested, sweating despite it being close to winter and

the snow coming down. Bear shifters rarely hibernate, the human part of ourselves too restless to sleep. We do however, eat heavily, and Atticus had put on much weight and muscle that season."

I saw our mate smile out of the corner of our eye. Her fingers tangled into our fur. When she slept, I noticed how she would absentmindedly thread her hand through our chest hair.

Maybe I won't shave it. Show all the wolf shifters some females like a hairy one versus a shaved one.

I had always been more self-conscious about it. My brothers made fun of me often for it, but I brushed it off. If I showed I cared, it would just spur them on more. Along with the size of my body and my cock—I just had to own it. Males were not allowed to show their emotional and vulnerable sides. It was weak and unnatural.

"Atticus continued chopping while the female approached our territory. Atticus would remember nothing beyond this because this is where I have blocked his memory."

I felt Nadia's grip on our fur tighten and my throat thickening.

"After a few more chops, he perked up his head and sniffed. I stayed silent for a while, hoping he would return to finish our task, but he caught our mate's scent and her arousal. He thought it was a chase, a game. His heart quickened, and I tried to gain control of his body. It didn't feel right. It felt wrong."

"How did it feel wrong?" I asked.

My grizzly laid his head on my mate's lap. She played with his ears, keeping quiet as she listened. I couldn't imagine how she felt about all this. Listening to how I was rejected by the person I could have been originally mated to.

She took it in stride. All I felt from her was worry for me.

"I smelled another male's arousal and his scent all over her. You weren't

listening to your instincts; you were listening to your human side, remaining optimistic and not using your senses."

I scoffed. He was right. That was me, back then anyway.

"You ran toward her scent. I tried to talk sense into you, but you didn't listen. You came upon a scene I will not describe to you, and I will not break the wall I've barricaded in your head." He sighed and put the full weight of his head in our mate's lap. *"It broke you, it broke me, it broke the territory that we had claimed years ago. They did it on our land, to our face. If they meant to, we will never know, but they were officially bonded."*

My heart constricted itself in my chest, but it did not break. For our heart was whole because we had Nadia.

Had I seen them, my mate that was supposed to be my other half, however, I think I would have broken.

"That stupid bitch." Nadia sniffed. "How cruel." She leaned her head forward and kissed our head.

I chuckled. *"It doesn't matter now, baby. We have you, and you are a million times better than she ever was,"* I told her. *"I'm glad I have you. I'm glad we have each other."* And I meant that. I felt nothing for our previous mate.

Nadia's tears continued to cascade down her cheeks, moistening our fur. The sound of her gentle sobs nearly broke me. Seeking solace, she pressed herself closer, enveloping us in a warm embrace. The scent of her fragrant hair mingled with the comforting touch of her arms around our neck.

Damn, she smelled so good.

"I'm not done yet," my animal huffed. *"Once they had completed their bond, and we withered. On the ground, feeling our soul break and sever. The male wandered over and leaned over us with no compassion as we continued to feel our soul crush into thousands of pieces.*

"I could feel your emotions. You were giving up. I could feel every part of

you wanting to die right there, Atticus.

"Since you were a cub, that was all you wanted. To have a mate like your parents, and this had to happen to us. You were ready to give up because there were no second chances, but I knew it wasn't over for us. I knew we couldn't give up just yet."

I used to think my animal was an ass all this time, but now I'm realizing that my grizzly did have a heart. He was hard to get along with, more stubborn than an ox, but shit did he have a heart.

"That's when I blocked your memories when you were at your weakest. I couldn't do anything else because our body was weak. I could see that male was reaching out for us, but there wasn't anything I could do but protect you—our mind."

My grizzly's head perked up, his heart racing in his chest. *"That's when that crazy little fucker came out of nowhere."*

"Anaki!" Nadia smiled.

"Anaki." My grizzly laughed. *"The bastard jumped out like a spider monkey, took out a dagger, and plunged it into that bear's forehead. The other bear fell backwards, slit his throat, and did a lot of other crazy things to the body."*

Our mate sat up and slowly shook her head. "Innocent Anaki did that?" her voice shook.

"Anaki is a sea dragon. They may be slender, but they have a nasty bite and are fast little fuckers." I held my mate closer. *"I just didn't remember him doing any of that,"* I said softly.

"Because I blocked your memory," my grizzly reiterated. *"Afterwards, our former mate died a painful death because of her new mate's demise. I put you to sleep and explained to Anaki that I blocked your memories to keep you from going into a depression. Anaki said he will keep you safe.*

"He told me about the Iron Fang, and I told him to keep you safe and

take you there. I had a good feeling about it. Shortly after, you know what happened, I fell into my slumber. And then, when I woke, I met our sweet mate right here."

We purred loudly, and Nadia smiled despite the tears drying from her cheeks. She held sadness from our past life, but the spark of light in her chest told me she was happy that it happened and she was with me.

I was happy to have her, happy that my life turned out the way it did. I had her, Anaki, the Iron Fang. The Goddess worked in mysterious ways, I suppose.

"And I just woke up and concluded my mate was mated to someone else?" I asked.

"Basically," my grizzly replied. *"Anaki filled in the holes for you and dragged you back to your cabin. He was very efficient, not getting any blood on him. Those dragons are pretty skillful."*

"Woah, woah, woah." Nadia stood up and held up her hands. *"Why am I just now realizing Anaki is a dragon? How cool is that?"*

We both blinked several times.

"Like a real dragon? How big does he get?" She jumped up and down. *"Does he fly?"*

"He's a water dragon," I said, slightly annoyed. *"He swims. He has a flattened tail, kind of like a shark. I've never seen his dragon, just what he has told me."*

"We need him to find his mate so I can see!" Her eyes brightened.

I was worried our mate would be upset that we were talking about my past mate, but clearly, she seemed unperturbed. Now that I claimed her and could feel her emotions, that didn't seem to be the case.

She was happy that she was with me. She was happy she had Anaki as a friend, and she didn't have to worry about my animal hunting him down due to their bond.

But still, we felt—jealousy.

We growled, and my animal let me come to the forefront. I stood on all fours and came closer to my mate, who was no longer smiling and jumping for joy to see Anaki and his animal.

"Uh, oh. Are you mad?" She backed away slowly until she was propped up against a tree. "I was just excited to know there are dragons and that I know one is all."

She didn't radiate fear but excitement. I could smell her arousal pooling between her legs. I licked my maw and could remember the flashes of images of her orgasming around my cock just the night before.

Would it be too soon to take her again? Would it be too cold for her body to strip her now and fuck her against the tree?

"Mad?" I rasped. *"I'm not mad."*

I let my body begin its shift back into its human form. The bones popped and ground together as they rearranged. My mate made wincing noises until my body was back to its original form. Her eyes widened when she saw me, and her fingers gripped against the tree.

I was already hard. Hell, I was always hard around her, but this time, I was ready to fuck her and not give her a chance to run away from me.

"Y-you look like you're mad?" She looked me up and down before looking at my face and licking her lips.

"I'm not mad, little bee." I cupped her cheek. "I am feeling something, though. I want you to feel it. Concentrate."

She closed her eyes hesitantly and shuffled through our bond. Soon she could pick it out right away. Once she opened her eyes, she smiled in realization.

"Jealous? You're jealous? And Horney. Oh, Teddy Bear, why?"

I chuckled darkly. "You getting excited over any other male is going to make me jealous. And whether Anaki saved my life or not, I'll still kick his ass." I raised a brow.

"Now that isn't fair." She pouted and stuck out her lip. "How can I not make you jealous anymore?" She put her hands behind her back and swung her chest from side to side.

I pinned her against the tree with both my hands on either side of her head. "I can think of a few things."

Her hands roamed down my chest, her bravery coming in waves. I let my thoughts and desires be loud so she would know how much I wanted—needed her touch.

She took her time, kissing my chest, biting, nipping until she latched onto my nipple. I didn't know why the hell it felt good, but it did. She took it into her mouth, sucking while her hand trailed down my sides to my hips, and her hand took hold of my cock.

Her hands were warm, even with the cold air surrounding us. She wrapped her hand around it, and her lips left my chest and trailed down my body, licking all the way down.

This bravery, it was hot as hell.

"Fuck baby, you know how to touch me just right."

She cast a seductive gaze, her eyes peering through lowered lashes, now unobstructed by her glasses. As her lips drew nearer to my cock, she sensually traced the tip with her tongue before eagerly engulfing it. The rough bark of the tree pressed against my gripping claws as I moaned in pleasure, my head thrown back.

"Your mouth feels so damn good. Keep doing that."

I loosened my grip with one hand, sliding it to the back of her head. Her movements were perfectly synchronized, but the touch of my hand on her hair amplified my control. I firmly grasped her silky strands, and as she moaned against my erection, the vibrations sent shivers down my spine.

"Good girl," I moaned.

Her hands reached around and landed on my ass, her nails dug into my skin, and her mouth took more of me.

Goddess almighty.

"I need to come, and I'm doing it in your cunt, baby," I rasped.

I pulled her off my dick and pressed my lips to hers while I pulled down her pants. She smiled and laughed while I grunted, trying to pull off the bottom half of her clothes.

"Damn boots." I ripped them off, threw them to the side, and pinned her against the tree.

I took myself in hand and rubbed myself against her pussy. Fuck, she was soaked, and I hadn't even touched her yet.

"Do you like sucking on my cock? Does it get you wet?"

She nodded and whimpered. "I like it a lot."

"What else do you like?" I rubbed her clit with my thumb as I entered her.

She gasped, and I felt her tight cunt wrap around me. It was just like the first time taking her, feeling her squeeze me, holding me into her body, sucking me in. Not once had she complained I'd been too big, and I couldn't understand why. When I felt her emotions through the bond, all I could feel was her pleasure, how much she wanted it, craved it.

It made me want to fuck her more.

I pulled it all the way out to push it back in again.

"I like it when you play with my breasts." She moaned when I pushed it back inside her.

Hell, I enjoyed sucking her tits, too. I bunched her shirt over her breasts and lowered my head, and started sucking them. But soon, my cock took control, and I realized I needed to come soon.

Our skin collided with a resounding slap, intensifying the moment. The exquisite tightness of her cunt engulfed me, overpowering my senses.

As she took me in, her delicate fluttering pulled me in deep, amplifying the pleasure coursing through our bodies. Her arousal coated me, leaving an intoxicating scent in the air. Her ecstatic screams pierced through the forest, causing the birds to scatter from their perches, startled by the raw intensity of our connection.

"One more," I grunted. "Give me another. We do it together."

She wined. "I don't know if I—"

"You can. I know you can. And if you feel the urge to bite me...do it. You won't hurt me."

I thrust into her several times, hard. The bark of the tree trickled to the forest floor. Taking one last thrust, I groaned and held her close to me. Nadia cried out as she came with me and sunk her teeth into my shoulder.

As her teeth sank into the muscle, a wave of exquisite pleasure washed over me, engulfing my senses. I could hear my own gasps mingling with the rustling of leaves underfoot. The air was heavy with the scent of passion and desire, fueling the intensity of the moment. My release surged forth, a torrential outpouring from the depths of my being, filling her body to the brim. It overflowed, trickling down her leg, leaving a glistening trail amidst the foliage.

I panted, holding her there, and she dared not to let go of the bite into my skin. I was grateful, holding her head onto my shoulder, still not sure if I should release her.

I felt her tongue licking the blood. An act a human wouldn't normally do. My hand rose from her head, but she kept her teeth lodged inside me. I waited, not sure if she was waiting on her body or some higher force, such as the Goddess, to tell her to let me go.

So I held her, kissing her neck, keeping my cock lodged into her body, and whispering to her for the first time, "I love you, mate."

CHAPTER TWENTY-SEVEN

Nadia

It all felt like a dream. A wonderful dream.

From first waking in his arms, to the plane, the Iron Fang, Hawke shifting... it was all surreal. And now, as I tasted the metallic tang of blood in my mouth, my tongue instinctively explored the deep wound on Bear's body. The scent of the surrounding woods filled my nostrils as I realized we were completely alone, ravaged by passion, without a single worry in the world.

I dislodged my teeth and leaned my head back on the tree. In a sea of lust, *I just bit him.*

I bit him hard enough to make him bleed. As a human, I never thought to hurt anyone unless they hurt me or my loved ones. Only out of will to live or save someone, but Bear was bleeding, and I had caused it.

I took deep, laboring breaths, and my tongue slipped out of my mouth and lapped at the blood on my lips.

To add the cherry on my sundae, Bear admitted he loved me, all while I had bitten his shoulder. That wasn't something you should just say after someone has impaled you with their teeth.

He turned his head. He had a wide grin on his face and placed kisses up my neck. "Good job, baby. You did great."

I did great?

"I-I don't know what I did?" My fingers wrapped around his biceps and squeezed. My world was becoming dark the more I continued to breathe. I was going to pass out.

Bear wrapped his arms around me and placed his hand on the back of my head. "Breathe, baby, it's okay. You marked me, just like I did to you last night," he cooed.

Still, my heart pounded in my chest like a relentless drum, and each breath felt shallow and inadequate. I could feel the lump in my throat, like a boulder obstructing my airway, as I forced myself to swallow hard. Gripping onto Bear, I could sense the warmth of his fur against my trembling fingers, seeking solace in his presence. Being pinned against the tree was suffocating, the air heavy with an unexplainable tension that pricked my skin. I yearned for more of his touch, the reassuring weight of his body grounding me in reality, providing a much-needed anchor amidst the chaos within me.

"Close your eyes, Nadia," Bear soothed. "Close your eyes and concentrate on me. Listen to the sound of my heart, feel my emotions. What do you feel?"

I closed my eyes, not releasing my hold. Bear backed away from the tree and continued to walk through the forest, leaving my pants and boots behind.

"I feel your warmth." My body shuddered.

"Keep going," he linked.

"Your love, your concern." I dug deeper, laying my head on his shoulder, on top of the shoulder I had bitten.

I didn't care if there was blood smeared on my cheek. It had stopped bleeding, and I could feel the skin folding in on itself, leaving my scared bite marks bright and white on his skin.

"Close your eyes, my mate. It's too much for you to be looking around right now." Bear rubbed his hand up and down my back, whispering in his deep baritone voice.

I whimpered, closing my eyes again. This time, when I closed them, I felt not the skin of Bear's shoulder but the fur of Teddy. He was right there with me when I shut my eyes to the real world, and somehow, he was with me when my eyes were closed.

"I see Teddy," I told Bear. "He's right here with me."

"He and I will always be here. When you are awake and when you sleep."

"And what if that nightmare comes back?" I sniffed, holding onto him tighter.

I could hear Bear's feet step onto the wooden porch of the cabin. The creaking of the screen door opening and Anaki's sharp gasp didn't deter me from opening my eyes. I had Teddy and Bear with me at the same time.

"That's not happening again. We are leaving now. Anaki, get the vehicles ready to leave," Bear barked.

Bear strode into the bathroom again and stepped into the shower. Cold water rained down on us, causing me to jolt my body away from him.

"We are getting that thing out of you today," he growled. "I've been prideful, thinking I can do it on my own, but I can't. I'm going to be an asshole. I don't want people touching what's mine, but now that we are bonded, I'll try my best to be on good behavior."

My chest rose, and my nipples hardened at his sharp tone. Possessive Bear was certainly a turn-on.

I nodded and placed my head on his chest. "I love you too, Bear," I whispered while he set me down. He tilted my head back by pulling on the hair on my scalp and placed a chaste kiss on my lips.

But now, as the realization of the depth of my feelings crashed over me like a tidal wave, a sense of overwhelming vulnerability washed over my entire being. It was both exhilarating and terrifying.

I had accepted this life, the shifters, the Iron Fang, Bear, this unconventional love, with open arms. The acceptance came effortlessly, a testament to the undeniable bond that had formed between us. It wasn't just physical attraction or a fleeting infatuation; it was something far more profound. Our souls were intertwined, calling out to each other across the vast expanse of time and space.

I wanted to enjoy it now, and with this nightmare inside me, it wasn't going to happen.

"You are doing what you think is best." I swallowed.

Bear shook his head. "I love you with all my heart and soul, Nadia. I'm going to protect you, no matter the cost. I'm a fucking idiot. I thought I could keep you safe." The water rained down on us, washing away the dirt, blood, and the arousal between our legs. "I'm going to fix this, I swear it."

I leaned against the large shower that could easily fit three of him. I didn't cover myself. I wasn't at all shy about my body now. It was mostly because I was tired, but he knew all of it anyway by now. I grabbed the girlish loofah Anaki had brought and put on a scentless body wash.

"Thank you for calming me down," I whispered.

Bear never left my side. Some part of his body was always touching me: his hand, his leg, his foot. When he left my side to grab the shampoo, my body chilled, and panic swelled inside me.

"We will need to stay close as the bond ties us together. You will also see your bear emerging soon. Most likely in your dreams, as long as that nightmare stays away." Bear's brow furrowed. "I will stay with you while you sleep. How are you? Tired?"

I nodded. With the water streaming down my face, he couldn't see the tears threatening to fall, but that didn't stop him from rubbing his thumb under my cheeks. "Let's hurry. The quicker we get to Tajah's shop, the quicker we can get this thing out of you."

By the time we reached Tajah's shop, the sun was nearly set. It was a nice-looking town, small with coffee shops, a bookshop, grocery store, apartments. Overall, quiet.

The streets of the town were mostly deserted except for the side of town where the Iron Fang bar sat. The bar was the only area that looked animated at night, with the lights glowing around it. The door was old and wooden. It gave it a tavern look and was rather large to look like a bar. But I guess that was because there was a whole compound in the back that housed the clinic where I stayed. It was much more than just a biker bar.

Anaki helped me out of the truck, squeezing my hand as I jumped the last step out.

Motorcycles revved and parked in their designated spots a few blocks down from Tajah's shop. They lined the streets. There had to be at least thirty bikes all in a row.

I didn't have to cover my ears, but it was still loud, and I winced when someone revved an engine too loudly. Bear wrapped his arm around me and sent a loud growl down the street. Several men perked up their heads and gave a curious wave, taking a few steps closer to us for a greeting.

"Not tonight," Bear yelled down the street. "Later." His voice clipped, and he wrapped his arm around me. "Anaki, make sure no one comes in except the inner circle."

Anaki gave a mock salute, opened the door for us, and gave me one last wink.

The open sign was flipped to closed so no one else could enter. A beautiful etched glass was at the front of the store so customers could look inside that I didn't get a view of. The manikin at the front held clothing of old gypsy clothing, a round table, and a crystal ball.

"Is this her?" A woman, much younger than I expected, pushed over hanging beads that separated the back and the front of the store. "Took you long enough to bring her here, Bear," she scolded.

Bear wrapped his arm around me and stood in front of me. "I had to claim her." He gritted his teeth. "I didn't need anything happening to her."

I saw the hair rising on Bear's arm, his body heat doubling as he stood near the woman in front of us. I put my hand over it, rubbing it, trying to calm him. "It's okay." I looked up at him. "Everything is fine now."

I sure hope it was.

"Really, I am okay. When Bear is near me, I don't have any problems sleeping," I whispered to her. I felt small, utterly small around the tall woman in the room.

"Except she still has the nightmares," Bones butted in when he opened the door.

Bones, Hawke, Delilah, Grim, and Journey all came in at the same time. Anaki gave a little wave and stood inside but continued to stay at the door, watching. Who I didn't see, that surprised me, was Locke.

"I agree, this is strange," Bear linked to me. "Where is Locke?" Bear asked

everyone.

Hawke cleared his throat. "Locke is indisposed right now. Let's handle one crisis at a time, shall we?" He wrapped his arm around Delilah, who smiled and waved excitedly toward me. Oblivious to the tension in the room.

Grim grunted in agreement with Hawke and nodded for Tajah to continue.

"First, let me introduce myself to our newest member here before I get my magic on her," she smiled and wiggled her long, manicured fingers.

Bear scowled and pulled me back behind him.

"I was only teasing. You aren't any fun." Tajah put her hand on her hip, showing off the intricate detailing of a black corset that tied up the front with a lace buckling. Her knee-high boots matched the corset and the long cape she wore made her look like a complete badass for a witch.

Tajah lowered her shoulders, glanced around the room, and sighed until she leaned against the counter. "I guess it 'tis to be expected that everyone is acting like a stick is up their ass with everything going on. Anyway, Nadia. My name is Tajah. I am the resident witch and long-standing member of the Iron Fang."

Tajah didn't offer her hand to shake, and I'm guessing it was on purpose. Bear had his arm around me tightly, and he wasn't going to let me budge.

Tajah continued. "The Iron Fang and its physical properties are all protected by sanctions of protection spells to keep out spirits. They also keep us hidden by certain entities of dark magic." She clasped her hands together. "The reason I tell you this is that we thought a curse was laid upon your mind, but now that we know a spiritual being has come out of your head and reentered you, we believe we are dealing with a spirit. A spirit or demon can only enter a protected area if they are inhabiting a living body."

As Bear's hand gripped my shoulder, I could sense the waves of anger and worry emanating from him.

"Wait a minute." Hawke raised his hand. "You mean to tell me we may be in danger?"

Tajah shook her head. "I didn't say that. I still need to ask her a few questions first. I'm trying to explain to her that this is very serious."

"Duke Idris already knows where we are." Journey spoke up from the corner of the room. "Remember, there was a tracker on me?"

Hawke crossed his arms. "He would have burned us to the ground by now if he did know," Hawke said.

"He was bluffing," Grim snarled. "Or he has forgotten when he was burned to a crisp the first go around."

Bones groaned. "Did we even check Nadia for a tracker? It was a clean sweep, no alarms tripped, only a couple of guards dead, and no trail left behind when she was retrieved. It was almost too easy. I bet Idris gave her to us."

I held onto Bear's arm tighter, listening to everyone's rising voices. I wasn't scared, but Bear's rising anger was fueling mine. I wanted to snap at all of them. It was a new emotion I was experiencing, and I wasn't sure I liked it.

"Cyran's mate had a collar. Nadia would have had one too. She just has that thing in her head," Hawke argued back. "Let's calm down and have Tajah look at her and go from there."

Bones rolled his eyes. "If Bear wouldn't fight me all the time, this wouldn't be an issue." He raised his voice and came closer to the both of us. "Then I hear from Anaki that this nightmare demon came out of Nadia's body and was hovering over her. Bear, you can't handle that shit on your own. She should have been here, at the Iron Fang, getting care from people that know what they are doing!"

Bear snarled.

"Just because you have your mate doesn't mean mating and bonding her can fix her. You need to learn to trust people, trust me!" Bones shouted.

Bear's hair was turning to fur. My body reacted as well as I stood in front of him. My lip curled, my front teeth lengthened, and I felt my mouth expand until I jumped in front of Bear and right in front of Bones.

I took in a breath and let out a roar so loud the other people in the room took a step back, their eyes wide with shock. Hawke grabbed Delilah, forcing her behind him. Grim smirked, holding Journey by his side as she smiled along with him.

I continued to roar, letting out a torrent of frustration and agitation.

Bones stumbled backward, bumping into Hawke, who helped him stand back up.

Once I calmed, my face contorted back to its original form. I patted my cheeks and mouth and felt my teeth still had little points.

"Oh dear, I'm sorry," I whispered, turned around, and buried my face into Bear's chest.

It took him several moments before he wrapped his arms around me and whispered in my ear. "That... was unbelievably sexy, baby."

"Hell yeah, that was fucking awesome!" Anaki shouted from the door.

CHAPTER TWENTY-EIGHT

Bear

I didn't care if my cock was about to split my jeans open. My mate was unbelievably hot when she was angry.

My usually shy, tiny little bee took charge and snapped at a male. Some may find it emasculating, but fuck, I wanted to throw her on the damn table and rut her there.

I pulled her closer, pushing her ass into my erection. "See how you make me feel?"

Nadia groaned and shook her head. "I didn't mean to do that. It just came out."

"You shouldn't be shy about your feelings and who you are becoming," Tajah said as she put down her bag. "The bond you solidified earlier today will work quickly, especially since you already have the blood of a supernatural working through you."

I lifted my head where I was pressing soft kisses into my mate's hair. "What will become of her since she is part fae?"

This question I knew bothered my mate. What would she become?

Would she remain part of her fae heritage and not accept a bear spirit? We are entering unfamiliar territory regarding humans as mates, and now we have to worry about the genetics of halflings.

Tajah shrugged her shoulders. "Your guess is as good as mine. However"—she traced her lips with her long fingernail—"I cannot sense any fae genetics in her at all. If she hadn't had the dream of her past and her appetite for fresh greens, we would have never known. Her sensitivity to hearing, we could have written that off as psychological from being in solitary confinement."

Everyone agreed, nodding.

"With that act of aggression we just witnessed." Tajah smiled. "I would say we have a bear overpowering fae genetics."

Nadia stopped squeezing me and turned to see everyone looking at her. She blushed and touched her teeth once again, finding them dull.

If my mate continued to be fae and half-human, I would still love her. If she became a full fae, I would have never cared. I just wanted her soul. Interracial species and same-sex pairings exist now. We have that proven with Tajah and Beretta, a panther shifter.

Journey stepped forward, Grim pressed up against her backside. He never lets her go far, and I would be the same with my mate. Journey was but three feet away, and it was unsettling having anyone near my mate, but I knew Journey would have the answers we sought.

Journey was the direct line to the Moon Goddess of pairings, and I believed with all my being she would help us where we needed it most.

"Hi, we haven't officially talked yet, but I'm Journey." Journey gave a little wave, forgoing the handshake. She had learned since coming to our world that touching freshly paired mates was not wise.

Nadia waved back, their interaction almost comical. Journey had always been quiet as well, but she spoke loudly and often to put people in their place when the goddess needed her to.

"I hope to become good friends, and I know you are really nervous..." Journey paused and then chuckled. "About everything."

Nadia laughed, too, and my heart squeezed tight in my chest.

"But the Goddess wanted me to tell you, your destiny was to meet Bear, to become like him." She glanced at me and smiled. "Your parents gave birth to you the way it should have been. I can't give you the reason why that is or anything. Even the Goddess can't give me all the answers." Journey shrugged her shoulders. "I just know this was how she wanted it. What she thought would be best for you."

I wrapped my arms around her, my nose rubbing into her mark. She shivered and rubbed my arms that were tightly wrapped around her.

"And what about my parents? Are they—?"

"I'm sorry." Journey shook her head. "That's all I can give you." Her eyes softened, and she placed a hand on Nadia's arm. "Let's concentrate on getting you better first."

Nadia's shoulders deflated. "Thank you," she whispered gratefully.

The room stayed reverent as Journey backed away. Tajah flicked her fingers, illuminating the lights and turning off the electricity in the room.

"Right, Nadia," Tajah began. "Bones has given me part of your diagnoses, and Anaki has been kind enough to update us on what's been going on in the cabin. With Bear's permission, of course," she added, "I would like to ask a few more questions about this nightmare. It will give me a better understanding of what we are working with." Tajah smiled, looking at Journey. "And congratulations on your mating."

The rest of the room grinned and nodded, all except Grim. The idiot never smiled, only at his mate while he was ravaging her senseless.

"Um, thank you. And yes, we are... together," Nadia said quietly.

Her fear was building, so I automatically picked her up, began purring, and cradled her to my chest. I rubbed my face into hers. She smiled and let out a silent laugh.

"I think hell has frozen over," Bones whispered to Hawke. "He's purring, and he's being... nice, and what the hell are those?"

I ignored Bones and concentrated on my mate. Her heart slowed, and her breathing eased. "Are you better?"

"Yeah, I'm just. I'm sorry. I should be stronger than this. Its—"

I growled louder, my grizzly's noise taking the entire room. "You've been through a lot of shit, Nadia, and still have a lot more to go. You are allowed to be overwhelmed. You have someone to lean on now. Besides, you are exhausted from not sleeping. I think that gives you an excuse."

She pursed her lips and fisted my shirt.

"Hey, I'm serious." I moved her chin to look at me. "And I should have taken care of this earlier. I'm an ass and wanted you to myself. Forgive me?"

My mate rolled her eyes. "It was better you took me away. You gained my trust. I would have been kicking and screaming if anyone tried to touch me."

I sighed and pressed a kiss to her forehead.

At least she didn't think I was an ass.

My mate reached up and touched my grizzly's ears. *"And thank you for bringing out your nom nom ears,"* she linked. *"They are my favorite."*

We were interrupted by Beretta who came from the back. Her dark skin glistened in the candlelight as she carried in a portable padded table and opened it up in a cleared part of the room.

Beretta smiled at my mate. She had bright green cat-slit eyes and long claws on her fingers. "This is my mate, Beretta," Tajah said. "She's a panther shifter."

Beretta gave a slight bow and backed away to give my mate room.

"Bear, this table will not hold your weight. It's for Nadia to lay on during the spell. Nadia, do you feel comfortable sitting here while you give me a brief explanation of your nightmare?"

I swallowed and nodded. I was reluctant to let go of her, so I didn't. I kept my hand on her thigh and stood right beside her. I blocked the rest of the bodies in the room so my mate wouldn't feel overwhelmed.

They were here for support, to show that my mate wasn't alone. I appreciated their efforts but knew my mate still had trouble in sizable crowds.

"Are we still not going to talk about what's on his head?" I heard Bones whisper to Hawke again.

"Nadia calls them her nom nom ears. It's damn adorable. Don't bring it up to Bear, though. He gets kinda pissy about it," Anaki whispered.

I rolled my eyes and counted to ten, trying to ignore the idiots behind me.

"Nom, nom," Nadia linked and bit her lip.

I squeezed her leg and gave her a wink.

My anger slipped away, watching my mate put on a brave face and speak with Tajah. She explained how she could wake from the nightmare now and how she hadn't done that before. Tajah attributed it to being bonded to me, that it gave her the strength to break away from the dream.

This nightmare entity was angry that it did not have a hold on my mate like it used to. Nadia was able to wake herself as she grew stronger with her animal growing inside her. Tajah explained it manifested itself in front of her to try and scare her in her awakened state, to make her faint so she could not wait up so easily.

As my mate carried on describing the beast, my claws lengthened, and I put my hand on the nearby desk to hold me upright. My anger was growing by the minute. I had been careless when she was first brought here, too stubborn to see that I would have never been able to help her.

Tajah sighed and patted my mate's hand. "I have an idea, and it is what

Bram believes it to be as well." Tajah rounded the table and went to a large cabinet holding various elixirs and bottles. Parchments of papers were neatly stacked on one side and a tray containing several bottles, candles, and a black folded tablecloth.

Everyone was silent as we watched Tajah set the tray on the table where I had my hand. She eyed me, seeing the grooves of claw marks I accidentally pushed through the wood. "Bear, it was wise of you to have bonded with her." She took the bottles off the tray. "All in all, I believe the bonding has strengthened her body to reject this entity, and with the fae blood running through her, the Goddess was truly on her side."

Nadia's warmth of encouragement came to me in waves. She never blamed me for taking her, but I knew Bones still did.

Some doctor mentality shit.

Tajah meticulously arranged more flickering candles on the cool, polished floor, encircling the cushioned table where my mate peacefully rested. By her side, I remained, intertwining our fingers, tenderly pressing my lips against her delicate wrist. The soft glow of the candles danced in the air, casting a warm glow around the room.

I didn't know what this witch was going to do, but I prayed that it wouldn't be painful.

Tajah dusted off her hands. The candles lit in a perfect circle around my mate. "Next, I'm going to have you lie down on the table, darling. I'm going to explain everything in just a moment."

"Are we going to know what this is before you rip out whatever is in her head? Do we need to get our females out of the room?" Hawke spoke up.

Tajah scoffed. "It's perfectly safe, and I bet your *females* take offense at that. They are as strong as any of you *males*."

Nadia giggled when she saw Journey and Delilah sticking their tongues out at their mates. "Lay back, little bee." I put my hand between her chest and cradled her head until she lay down completely.

My mate trusted me completely. She succumbed to my voice, and her hand rose to hold my wrist to keep me there. I knew she was leery of Tajah and most of the people in this room through our bond, but I would trust these souls with my life.

"Duke Idris has cursed her with a sleeping demon, or a nightmare demon, if you want to call it. It's a simple name but can cause a punch to the mentality. If Nadia was fully human, she wouldn't have survived it. It can make a human go crazy in a matter of weeks, maybe months. Replaying memories or creating new ones. They are graphic and violent, you feel like you are there. You can feel emotional and physical pain, and when you wake, you can still feel the remnants of what you have just seen."

Delilah sobbed in the corner of the room.

I held my mate's hand tighter and brought it to my lips.

"Nadia, you are so strong," Tajah said. "I know you feel you are weak, but what you have been through, I can never imagine."

My mate swallowed. "I'm better now, though. If Bear is with me, I don't feel the pain. It doesn't hurt as much."

"Because of the bond." Tajah petted her hair. "And now that you are bonded, your mind is stronger. And we are going to rid that demon once and for all, alright?"

Beretta came to Tajah's side, grabbing the black tablecloth. I was instructed to release my mate's hand, and I watched as they laid the cloth over my mate's body. A pentagram lay in the middle with various symbols at each point.

Bram entered from the back of the room. His gait was slow, his hood drawn as he entered. He stood on the other side of the table, reached over my mate's chest for a blue elixir bottle from Tajah, and downed it in one go. He smacked his lips and gazed down at my mate, who looked up at him with much uncertainty.

"I'm Bram. Former high warlock of the Elysian realm. I'm here to assist with your nightmare."

Nadia's eyes moved to me, and I nodded. "He's okay, baby. Right, Bram?" I raised an eyebrow.

He knew what I was referring to. His mess up with Delilah. He proved himself useful in protecting Hawke and Deilah, sheltering them when Hawke went into his rut to keep them safe and away from Shane. But he failed to give them the proper birth control, resulting in Delilah's pregnancy. He mixed up the wrong shit.

All in all, the pregnancy was a blessing. The club was excited to see a pup running around, but now we were dealing with my mate's mind.

"Of course. I've proved myself wrestling with a damn half-rabid wolf all morning. It put some hair on my chest, that's for sure." He threw the hood off his head.

I growled lowly, my hand wrapping around my mate's leg. I wasn't in the joking mood anymore. There was too much magic, too much at stake right now. Like my damn mate laying on the fucking table.

"Bram, demon extraction, focus. Bear isn't the joking type, especially freshly mated," Tajah clipped.

I growled again, and Bram cleared his throat.

"Right then, have you explained this is a multiple-step process and not a once-cure-all?" Bram settled a candle next to my mate's ear.

I hovered over my mate, ready to pull her into my arms. "No, she didn't. What do you mean, multiple steps?"

Tajah, undeterred by my rising anger, brushed my mate's hair from her forehead, letting the hair hang down from the table. "Once a day until the demon is fully extracted. Imagine a piece of gum getting into your hair," she explained. "At first, it is somewhat easy to get the gum out. As time goes on, more and more hair gets into the gum until it's just a giant wad of hair stuck to it. Each time we do the spell, we are ripping away pieces of hair, just as we are ripping the demon away from her mind.

"This demon is embedded in her mind. It's not supposed to keep its host alive this long, so its claws are deep."

"Shit." Hawke rubbed his chin.

Nadia kept her eyes on me, and mine were on hers. She was determined to get through this.

"Each extraction will be painful, more painful than the last. The dreams are more vivid, vibrant, violent. The last dream, he will panic and try his best to stay attached to you," Tajah said.

I bring my mate's wrist up to my lips and kiss it. "I wish I could do this for you."

Nadia shook her head. "I'll be fine. It's almost over."

My brave little bee.

It still did not settle the anger rising in my gut. It came from a unique part of me, fueling my anger and throwing gas among my flames. I wanted to let loose my animal and tear everything apart for her.

"The last will be the worst," Tajah warned. "It will try to hold on to you, but it knows its end is near. It will try to take you with it, it will—"

Nadia's outward appearance was calm, but a dam broke inside her, and I was about to go with her. She pushed the cloth aside and gripped my forearm, claws sinking into my skin.

"Enough!" she snarled, her voice echoing through the room like a thunderous roar. The sheer force of her anger reverberated, causing the bottles on the shelves to quiver and collide with a resounding clash. The metallic scent of fear hung heavy in the air as everyone instinctively took a step back, creating a cautious distance between themselves and her fury. Yet, I remained steadfast by her side, unable to tear my gaze away from her, captivated by the raw intensity and overwhelming desire that emanated from her. At that moment, a sense of undeniable pride welled up within me, intertwining with the electrifying atmosphere that surrounded us.

I could feel her bear rising.

"Just get it out! Enough talk, just... do it!" she panted, pounding her other fist on the table.

Gazing around the room, I found it filled with smirks and nods of approval.

I grunted and leaned forward, and kissed my mate on the lips. "You got this baby."

Tajah didn't motion me to stand back. Instead I stayed in the circle and kept my hands clasped around my mate's that lay on her stomach. I held onto her tight, and the room grew darker as the sun set outside.

The candle's light lowered still, and Tajah and Bram placed their hands on my mate's head. They chanted, nearly silent, and my mate's eyes closed, and she fell into a deep sleep.

We all watched with bated breath. My mate's skin ran cold, and twitches and spasms in her body began. Her throat constricted, her eyes raced behind her eyelids, and I could feel a headache forming in my head.

I could feel her pain.

The chants grew louder and louder, the brightness of the room by the candles alone so bright even a lightbulb was beyond compare. As soon as they said the last incantation, my mate opened her mouth to scream, and all the lights went out with a roar of the wind, and we were left in darkness.

CHAPTER TWENTY-NINE

Nadia

It was one of the several repeated dreams I'd had in the past. This one where I was alone in the dark, hearing the parents who raised me screaming out for me. The demon's claws raked down my skin until it pulled away, howling in pain.

I woke up, my body covered in a sheen of sweat, the cool droplets trickling down my face. As I stirred, Bear's strong arms wrapped around me, instantly pulling me away from the table. The sound of his racing heartbeat reverberated against my chest as he held me close, providing a comforting embrace. I felt a sense of security, grateful for his presence. Finally, a wave of relief washed over me, and I let out a slow, calming breath, knowing that the first of many exorcisms was now over.

That's what this was, right? An exorcism?

They seemed more simple in a movie.

The rest of the people in the room sighed in relief. Delilah especially, still feeling guilty. I again reiterated she shouldn't feel guilty. I was the one that went back to the mansion. After seeing all those women wanting their escape and were fearful of asking for it, I knew I was meant to be there all along.

I made the right choice because look where it led me to.

After the first extraction, Tajah requested we come at sunset each day for the next several days until the demon was finally removed. I needed to get as much rest as possible in between, but that was proving difficult.

Did they seriously think I would want to sleep after that? At least I had Bear by my side before we started this mess, and it wasn't so painful. Unfortunately, we have angered the demon now. Who knew what the entity was going to try now that we were trying to pull him away?

As Tajah said, the nightmare was going to be frantic. Trying to hold on to what it could to keep me.

Tajah ruffled through the bag she had brought in earlier and gave Bear and me several items. She kept her voice but a whisper, but I knew most of the people in the room could hear it. The mated ones, anyway.

It was all about birth control. The human birth control pills I was taking wouldn't work anymore now that I was gaining a bear. I immediately bowed my head and looked away from Bear, but Delilah, Journey, and Anaki were laughing in the corner.

Bear continued to listen, taking whatever Tajah gave him, and listened to the explicit instructions on how I should take it. He was acting like some big hovering figure taking care of all the adult stuff, but hell, I didn't want to know what that bag full of grass he had in his hand was for.

She held out another bag that was specifically for Bear. He cleared his throat and shoved the sack into his pocket, seeming to know what it was.

"What's that?" I nudged him when Tajah turned away.

A pretty blush came to his tanned cheeks, and I pursed my lips to hide my smile.

"It's to help with my rut and with your heat. I don't want it to start before

we get this demon out of you, " he linked.

Right, shouldn't have even asked.

Bear nodded at Tajah and Bram and thanked them for their time. The rest of the room, there for moral support, was helpful but difficult to accept. These people welcomed me so easily, and they had no other ulterior motive. It was refreshing, nice, and for once, I felt accepted.

Delilah gave a thumbs-up to me as we walked out the door.

Yeah, they were all really nice. It was... wonderful.

"Damn, I'm starving," Anaki groaned. "How about we go feed little miss here and get a round of drinks? We could all use it after today, yeah?"

The men grumbled in agreement, except for Grim. He latched his hand on Journey's ass and playfully bit her on her shoulder.

Bones continued to glare at Bear, but Bear didn't seem to care one bit until he slapped Bones upside the head.

They were all one big, crazy family.

Two days later, I was sitting in the Iron Fang Gym. Bear had a thing for literal names and couldn't come up with anything creative. If we ever decided to have children, I would need to make sure I was in charge of naming the child; otherwise, it would be called cub, baby, or kid.

Was I really already thinking about having kids with Bear?

Seriously?

I snickered as I watched Bear try to fix the boxing ring that sat in the middle of the gym. It was much larger than a typical human one; this one was three times as large. The ropes, I was told, were taken down years ago.

Bones said that the Saturday and Sunday night fights needed to be suspended when everyone was getting sicker and no one could heal themselves like they used to. With everyone getting mates and their souls healing, it was time to put it back up and begin sparring once again.

In order to fight, you needed to be mated and bonded and have your animal close to being fully healed. They didn't want any accidental deaths.

"Morpheus, throw that blue rope this way." Bear motioned for Morpheus, a large dark-skinned man with a shaved head and raging muscles, to toss it his way.

Morpheus picked it up, muttering, "Back for two days and already bossing me around."

"I believe this gym is mine," Bear snapped back.

Morpheus' lip curled into a smile. "That it is, but I take care of it more than you."

Bear said Morpheus was a midnight black lion who supposedly had a thick, black mane. I had a hard time seeing it since his head was shaved, but if Morpheus said he had a mane when shifted, then he had a mane.

"I think we should wait longer. Not even a quarter of the club have mates yet." Morpheus handed Bear the next rope, who then stretched it and tightened it, checking for its stability.

Bear grunted and sat up, wiping his forehead. "We won't start fights yet. It's just for practice for those who have their mates. Don't worry, we won't start official fights until you get your female." Bear slapped Morpheus on the back. "Want to make sure my biggest rival gets a piece of this." Bear flexed his chest and arm muscles to Morpheus, who scoffed.

Bear glanced at me and had a playful look in his eye. I couldn't help but blush and pull up the hood of the hoodie I was wearing to hide my face.

The others lifting weights, always looking and watching Bear and me, took notice.

"Oh! Look at her blush!" one called out. "I hope my mate blushes when I talk about her!" The one man had tattoos running up his neck and had a leaner, athletic build. It made me wonder what animal he shifted into.

Another guy nudged him. "More than likely she's gonna have a collar around you, and you are going to be kissing her feet."

It was then his turn to blush and mumble something, slinking away to the locker room.

Bear barked out a laugh and grabbed another rope to finish the boxing ring.

"You guys don't look like you are into boxing. You look like you are just into beating each other up." I spoke up as Bear and Morpheus finished up.

Morpheus lifted his head in acknowledgment. "That's right, we aren't. We use our fists, teeth, and claws." He held up his fists and kissed them.

My face paled. "What?"

"Don't act so surprised. We are a bunch of animals, sweet thing. It's how we train. Before we lost part of our souls, our packs and prides would do it all the time. When we moved here, well, we learned quickly we couldn't do it the same way. We lift, run, use a punching bag, train with guns at the shooting range..." He frowned. "It's only natural for Grim wanting to get this ring back up. He wants to spar like old times."

They were animals. They had a lot of testosterone, animal-driven instincts to fight and defend their territory. I guess it was only natural that they wanted to fight with each other. But could they at least do it safely? With some gloves?

"Little bee, we heal fast once our souls are healed. A scratch can heal in seconds, bones minutes to hours. Our pride, well, that might take several days," Bear joked.

It was a new concept, one I was going to have to get used to. I was sure I would become better acquainted with this new culture of shifters as time went on. I knew my body was changing. The growling and my shortened temper was already tested.

Over the days sitting in the gym, I'd come to know several of the other men, from a distance anyway. No one could come within five feet of me, or Bear's claws would be out in mere seconds.

Bear was extremely territorial over me, a warning he had given me coming down the mountain from his cabin. I knew this, but it still surprised me when he gave everyone else a completely opposite personality to the one he gave me.

Kind and sweet versus grumpy and grouchy.

The brothers of the club very much looked like the typical biker gang. They all had tattoos, piercings, vests that they call cuts that had the club's logo on the back, along with their road names on the front.

A lot of the guys go shirtless in the gym where Bear and I had been the most since he owned it, and he had been toying with the idea of making a new rule to make everyone wear a shirt when I was in the building.

I talked him out of that one because it was insane to enforce a rule like that. I just needed to make sure I was always looking at their faces, but sometimes, that was hard when they had these nipple piercings staring at me when I was so short.

Despite everyone having tattoos, piercings, strange haircuts, weird colored hair, and deep scowls on their faces, they all had a story. They had their jokes and unique personalities. They were waiting for their second chances.

Some of them even smiled when they saw Bear lifting me from the padded seat he carried around and made me sit on while he worked in his gym because he wouldn't let me out of his sight. His single brothers wanted that, too.

It was both sweet and heartbreaking at the same time.

"Don't call my mate sweet thing," Bear grumbled and pushed Morpheus away. "Why don't you go flirt with that punching bag over there? Your chest and muscles need a workout."

I looked down at Morpheus' bare chest. He did *not* need to work out. He had some major man boobs going on.

He flexed one man boob, then did the other, making them jiggle.

My eyes widened, and I looked away.

"I think your mate was admiring my body. I don't think I need to work out." Morpheus ran his hand down his torso. "I take that back. Let me do some pushups right here."

What the hell was he doing?

Bear growled, the gym growing silent as Morpheus whistled as he did his workout in front of me. I kept my head away, trying not to look to avoid any confrontation, but obviously Morpheus wanted it.

"Or maybe your mate would like to see me do some sit-ups? My abs need a workout today."

Morpheus flipped over, his sweaty body leaving sweat marks on the cement floor. He rolled up his body, his abs contracting with each crunch.

"Ahh, um." I looked to Bear, to Morpheus, and the silently laughing members of the gym.

Bear's face was nearly purple, and he had a vein twitching on the side of his forehead.

Bear was not amused.

"Ah, Morpheus, he's gonna shift if you don't stop."

"That is my plan. I wanted to see how big his bear really is. I want to show him I can beat him even in my human form." He continued to do his sit-ups.

"But you can't, uh, heal very well," I added.

Morpheus shrugged his shoulders. "A little pain will feel good."

Oh dear.

Again he went to do his sit-ups. I rose from my seat, my hand reaching out to calm Bear. I had to do something. He was my responsibility right now. Teddy was coming up fast, and I wasn't going to let him rip someone to pieces.

As soon as I took my last step, a cool body ripped me away. Anaki whispered in my ear with his minty breath. "Come on, let them have a little fun," he said playfully.

"But Morpheus—"

"Is a big kitty. He can handle himself."

Morpheus shot him a look. "I resent that."

Bear let out a thunderous roar, the sound reverberating through the room as his powerful back bent and fur billowed outward, filling the air with a musky scent. The crowd erupted in cheers, their voices mingling with the sight of Bear gracefully landing on his front paws, causing the ground to tremble beneath him. As he vigorously shook his fur, a wave of excitement and awe rippled through the room.

"And that is what we needed," Anaki said proudly. "To get everyone's spirits up."

What the hell was going on?

My mouth hung open while I watched Morpheus laugh and run around the ring, jumping inside. Bear slung his head back, saw Anaki had me, and backed away. Bear nodded, crawling inside the ring and roaring again.

"Anaki! He can't do this!" I yelled over the cheers.

A group of rowdy men burst through the gym doors, their laughter echoing off the walls. They carried trays of ice-cold beers, the condensation dripping onto the floor. The air was filled with the scent of freshly popped popcorn and the faint aroma of roasted peanuts. The scene was a chaotic spectacle, resembling a circus.

"It's high time this club had some fun, and you get to witness some of it. Are you ready to see your man in action?" Anaki winked at me and pulled me to the chairs that were being lined up around the boxing ring.

Bear rebuilt the boxing ring all morning, all for someone to piss him off so he could fight in it?

"Why couldn't you just ask him to fight instead of pissing him off? That wasn't very nice," I asked.

Anaki put his arm around me and gave me a to-go box from the bar holding a large salad with a chicken breast on top. "Eat up." He jutted out his jaw. "For one, it's funnier this way, and two." He sighed. "The bar needs a distraction, and an illegal fight is the way to do it."

Journey sat on my side holding a bag of popcorn, while Delilah sat beside Anaki, handing him a bag as well. "You ready for this?" Delilah shouted over the noise. "It's my first fight. I'm super excited. My pup is all squirrelly right now, knowing his daddy is about to take a chunk of Bear's butt."

"Hawke is fighting?" My voice rose to a squeal.

"And Grim." Journey popped some popcorn in her mouth. "He's last, though, because he will probably make the biggest mess."

"Mess? What kind of mess?" I gripped the salad that I had a feeling I would not want to eat.

"Probably with pulling chunks of fur off some animals, ripping clothes off a vampire, maybe some blood? Either way, it's all in good fun. Everyone taps out when they've had enough."

I could only let out a sound that resembled a toad croaking escape my throat.

CHAPTER THIRTY

Bear

Everyone had been pushing my buttons all day. The snide remarks about how sweet my mate was. How precious and small. They all wanted her. To touch her, talk to her, to see her mark.

She was patient with them, answering their questions about how she was doing. If I was treating her right as a mate. Why the hell would they ask her such questions? Did they question my loyalty to her? Did they not think I protected her with every fiber of my being?

They all looked at her, talked sweetly, softly, like she was something precious to them.

I fucking hated it.

She was mine.

This was why I didn't want to bring her from my cave yet. I knew I wouldn't be able to control my possessiveness over her. We have just bonded. Other mated shifters had more time with their mate.

That damn demon was forcing me to stay close to Tajah. If something happened, I needed to know that the witch and warlock would be close by to take care of her.

And on top of it all, my mate and I must consume heat and rut suppressors until she healed.

Throughout the morning, I desperately attempted to maintain composure. I meticulously donned a façade, concealing my true emotions, all while suppressing the furious storm brewing within me. The anger simmered as Morpheus, with insistence, offered his assistance in assembling the boxing ring.

He was by my side, his feline scent aggravating my nose.

My mate was still trying to understand our bond. She could only feel the surface of my emotions. She could not dig deep inside me unless she concentrated, and I didn't want her to dig deep. Not now, not when she was battling the demon inside her.

We had all the time in the world to figure out our bond.

I wanted her to relax as much as possible.

But then this mother fucker had to mess with me.

Morpheus' taunting, batting his paw with my grizzly, and now I was angry. Too much pent-up frustration, anger, and worry was now ready to be unleashed.

I shifted and made sure Anaki took care of my mate as I climbed into the ring. I was ready to take on Morpheus and teach him, as well as everyone else, a lesson. I would not kill him, but I would make sure he knew not to mess with me.

Two more unmated males entered the ring. All three were unarmed, circling me, jumping at me from all sides.

Do they really think they can do anything to me? It was comical.

My animal was pissed but not worried in the slightest. My brothers were weak, and if they wanted to test me, we would teach them a lesson.

My grizzly stood tall, its brown fur bristling in anticipation. Its head raised high, ears perked, and its eyes narrowed in focus. Its claws were unsheathed, and its teeth bared. The crowd around the perimeter of the ring was loud and wild, many standing to get a better view, holding beers and popcorn. Money was being tossed around, and there was an air of excitement and tension as everyone waited for the fight to begin.

Damnit, this was all planned.

"Come down here and fight me!" Morpheus and two other males grabbed my leg. I easily shook them off, and they flew out of the ring.

Everyone laughed, and I huffed, letting out a roar.

I guess if we were going to have a fight, let's have a fight.

My mate was sitting in the middle of our friends. Anaki on one side, Journey and Delilah surrounding them. They all waved, but my mate was sitting in shock with her mouth hanging open.

"You okay, baby?" I linked.

"M-me? Are you okay?"

I snarled at the crowd hanging on the ropes. Morpheus got back in the ring, punching me in the side. I reached around, grabbed him by his arm with my teeth, barely clamped down, and slung him around a bit.

"Fine, are you okay watching me spar?"

I dragged Morpheus around the ring. He was laughing, yelling as I pierced his skin.

Crazy fucker.

"As long as you don't get hurt," she replied.

Damn, she's cute.

I threw Morpheus over the ring again. He landed in the crowd. They moved away to let him fall straight onto the floor. They all pointed and laughed at him, throwing their popcorn and peanuts on his unconscious body.

"Not possible, not with you as my prize."

I could feel my mate's blush from here, and the front door to the gym opened. The cool air washed over the heat of the room when Hawke, Grim, and several other mated brothers strode into the gym.

I stood on my hind legs, my arms up in the air as I roared. My voice echoed throughout the gym and around the ring, my eyes blazing in defiance. The crowd was alive with anticipation, their hands clapping along with my roar. They all seemed to come together as one, rising up with a loud cheer as the new opponents approached.

Hawke smiled and took off his vest. "It's been a while. I might be rusty," he said over the crowd.

The transformation was a sudden and violent flurry of motion. His bones crackled and contorted as he shifted into a sleek black wolf. His eyes blazed in the darkness, his fangs gleaming white as he snapped at the air before his teeth clamped down on the back of my neck.

I internally smirked and rolled to my back, squashing his chest. I heard the bones crack and a grunt fall from his maw. One wolf and one grizzly wouldn't work, and he knew that very well.

I rolled off Hawke, and he crawled away from me, shaking his fur. He snapped his jaws at me, wagging his tail. Grim entered the ring and shifted faster than Hawke. Now two might take me down. Grim was a fucking savage.

I rose up on my two hind legs, the crowd going wild. I fell on both my front legs again, shaking the ring. The wolves lashed at my neck at the same time, but I swung my paw at Grim first.

I looked over at Grim, who had gone limp against the ropes. A sigh of relief escaped my throat as I noticed he was still alive. I turned my attention back to Hawke, whose eyes filled with desperation and dread as I turned and snapped my jaws and seized his head with my jaws.

Hawke was now defenseless against my teeth, his skull quivering beneath my jaws.

Gently, I squeezed his head with my teeth, letting him know he couldn't escape. He whimpered the sign of submission, and I let him go, though I kept close watch on both him and Grim in case either decided to take a cheap shot.

I heard the crowd buzz with excitement as they realized that the match was about to come to an end. All eyes were fixed upon me as I looked at each opponent before snarling a warning not to come any closer or risk being attacked again.

I released Hawke, and he tucked his tail between his legs and jumped out of the ring.

Grim snarled, saliva dripping out of his maw when he rose from his corner of the ring. He looked damn rabid even though he wasn't. It wasn't a deterrent, not to me.

I was still fueled by everyone pissing me off this morning. They goaded me into fighting. I wasn't doing this for money or pride; I was doing this to show my strength and let everyone know I'd kick their asses if they touched my female.

"Look how pretty Bear's mate is!" someone shouted. "I think she might be turned on too!"

I paused, jerking my colossal head toward my mate. She was sitting between Anaki and Journey. Her eyes were wide watching me. She looked so damn small, staring up at me in the front row. Her legs were held tight together, squirming in the seat.

I took a deep breath and inhaled a mix of scents: the bitter smell of beer, the sharp aroma of alcohol, the sweet fragrance of food, but I hunted for one scent and one scent alone. The noise of the crowd faded away, and all I could focus on was her.

And there it was, her sweet honey smell of arousal.

Beneath the hoodie she wore, I could almost see her sweet nipples harden. I licked my lips, and lust clouded my mind.

She found my fighting, my strength, my stamina to fight these other animals arousing.

My grizzly puffed with pride, only to feel sharp teeth seep into my back.

A fucking panther? Beretta? Where the hell did she come from?

I reared back, head butting Grim in front of me and then shaking the feline that embedded her claws in my back as well.

The crowd released a collective "Oooh" as Grim's body connected with the padded pole. I watched as he stumbled back, obviously in pain but still struggling to keep his footing in the ring. I growled and tensed up, ready for him to make another move.

He did not disappoint. He quickly lunged forward, claws and teeth bared. I shifted my weight just enough to dodge his attack and then spun around, sinking my teeth into the scruff of his neck. He yelped in surprise and attempted to shake me off, but with a grizzly bear's strength behind me, there was no chance of that happening.

Beretta let go of my back, seeing that it was doing nothing to me, and rounded the front of my body. She growled, taking her claws and reaching toward my face.

I dropped Grim, batted them away with my claws, and pounced on her chest with the other paw. I roared into her face, my saliva dripping onto her fur. Roaring several more times before she made a whimpering noise, giving the sound of surrender.

That was when I felt Grim leap onto my back, digging at the healing wound where Beretta tried to rip open my skin.

When I took another deep breath, ready to take out Grim, my mate's scent invaded my nose.

"Once I win, I will take my prize," I linked her.

"A-and what is that?" she asked with a breathy moan.

I chuckled internally when I stood on two legs, letting Grim dangle while he continued hanging onto the scruff of my neck. The crowd gasped when I let myself fall backward.

Grim let go at the last second, but I crushed his hind legs in the process. *"You, my mate. On my desk, in my office."*

I turned around the best I could, gripped his neck with my maw, and closed around it tightly. Grim didn't whimper; he growled and shook his head, trying to pull me away.

"Grim, let it go!" Journey yelled in the ring. "You guys picked on him long enough!"

Grim growled again, snapped his jaws, and tried to wiggle free. I clamped my maw around his head tighter, but he still didn't give up.

"Grim!" Journey screamed again for him to forfeit. She wasn't scared for him; she knew I would never hurt him.

Still, he didn't give up.

I could see my mate in my peripheral, squirming in her seat. The surrounding males were staring at her intently, not even paying attention to the fight.

I know it isn't her heat, but is her arousal that strong to them?

My jaw slacked as I got a better look, and Grim wiggled free.

He put his teeth around my jugular and grabbed on tight, ripping and pulling at the muscle. My muscles and meat are thick there. It hurt, but it didn't register. I grunted, my feet dragged me across the ring, and I stared right into my mate's eyes.

Fuck, I think she's damn soaked her fucking underwear with how strong she smelled.

I can feel her want and desire through our bond.

A male stood from his chair behind her and went to touch her shoulder. I was dragging Grim, who continued to thrash around my neck, with Journey continuing to scream at Grim to let me go, but I paid no mind.

Some fucker was about to touch my female.

The crowd watched and parted as I climbed over the ring. I snarled, carrying Grim with me until the shadow of my grizzly finally reached them except for the fucker trying to touch what was mine.

I roared, and the fucker finally looked at me, pissing himself. He toppled over, trying to run away while the rest of the brothers laughed and pushed him around until he fell to the floor.

Chairs were upturned as unmated brothers scrambled away. Yet this male hadn't moved, and I was in a fucking rage. With Grim still hanging onto my neck, I took my paw and swiped at the male's chest. He screamed, his shirt ripped, and blood now stained his chest.

"Easy!" Bones came out from nowhere and pulled the unmated male away. "He's learned his lesson. Go take care of your mate!" Bones dragged the now fainted male away, and I carried Grim back to our females.

"Hi, Teddy," my mate whispered, but I heard her loud and clear.

"Grim, drop him. Er, uh, let go." Journey tried to pull Grim off, but he didn't let go. He thrashed again. "He's not gonna let go. You know how Grim is," Journey said to everyone.

Grim growled again, getting a better grip on my neck.

Nadia shifted in her seat again. "What happened? Why is Bear out of the ring now?" Nadia looked around and saw that everyone had backed away.

"Little miss, your arousal has gotten pretty strong." Anaki plugged his nose. "The unmated males have been hovering over you, and Bear was getting pissed."

Nadia's face turned bright red. "Oh dear. I—"

I snarled and started my shift. The room was rearranged again, getting ready for another fight. Grim kept hold of me until my body had shifted back to my human form. Grim stayed in his wolf body and huffed, slinking away and staying by the ring for the next fight.

I stood there, completely naked, in front of my mate.

"It's the fucking hairy anaconda!" someone yelled.

"You're naked," she whispered, pointing at my dick. "Do you want me to get you a towel?"

I shook my head, picked her up, and threw her over my shoulder. My brothers cheered, various catcalling and whoops echoed in the gym. Nadia squealed, yelling, begging for me to let her down.

The next fight had already started by the time we got into the hallway that held the offices. Once we reached mine, I slammed the door and locked it. I was ready to claim my prize now, and no one was going to disturb us.

CHAPTER THIRTY-ONE

Nadia

The thought of animals fighting in a ring, the barbaric ways of showing who was more powerful than the other should have disgusted me. At first it did, but then when Bear said I was his prize, that he was fighting for me, a switch flipped in my head.

I realized I was in fact, turned on.

Bear was large; he was a grizzly, for heaven's sake. Men, wolves, and a panther tried to take him down all at once. Their bodies were much smaller but quicker, more agile in their movements. They could jump him all at once and were faster, but Bear was so much stronger.

His massive body picked them off one at a time. His thick fur covered his muscles, but I knew what was beneath that fur.

Anaki threw popcorn in his mouth. The ladies that I had come to know the past few days were all cheering, smiling for their men. I sat speechless with a salad on my lap, unable to eat.

Greens, salad, chicken... it didn't seem as satisfying even in a state of hunger.

The large sweatshirt that covered my body was also seeped with Bear's scent. It only added to my arousal. I continued to breathe deeply, thinking how rough he was, how much I wanted him to be rough with me.

With our bonding just days ago, he had been gentle, even if he said he was rough. I know that now. The bear I saw now was a damn savage, and I really wanted him to be savage with me.

My breasts felt heavy and constricted with the bra I wore. I felt it digging into my sides, my body itching to take off my clothes as my body heated. It only got worse when Bear shifted back into his human form, standing in front of me, completely naked.

The crowd disappeared in my peripheral when he stood. His dick always looked larger each time I looked at it, and with the bright lights of the gym, I could see it in all its glory.

My pussy fluttered anytime I thought about it being inside me. Each time was better than the last. Now that he had shifted, I knew what he was going to do. He was going to claim me, and I wasn't sure if I would even protest if he took me in front of a crowd.

But as he threw me over his shoulder, the slow-motion, lust-filled gaze faded, and crowd cheers entered my head. It was loud, pounding my head, and I screamed in embarrassment. His thick, chiseled ass was all I could see, my hair covering my blazing red blush while he headed toward the hallway that held the offices of the gym.

It wasn't long before the door shut, the crowd already turning away and placing bets on the next fight.

Bear picked up the pace, running down the hallway, and my bravery rose the more I saw his stunning backside. I placed my hand on one of his ass cheeks and squeezed. He groaned in surprise, and he pushed the door open with a slam.

I peeked my head up, my vision disoriented, but he flipped me so I was straddling his waist mid-air. He slammed his lips onto mine and fisted my long hair at the back of my head.

"You're mine, Nadia. No one touches what is mine," he linked.

I'm not arguing with that.

He pushed me roughly against the wall, lifting the sweatshirt over my head. Beneath is just a crop top looking bra, and he growled approvingly, pulling it up and immediately latching his mouth to my nipple.

"Ahh!" I leaned my head back, my fingers tugging at his hair.

My toes were pointed, my body arching against his lips while his hands held me tightly against his body.

"Mine, damnit, do you hear me?" he yelled at me.

"Yes!"

He kissed up my chest and sucked on my mark, causing me to instantly orgasm. The man hadn't even touched between my legs, and I was already coming.

"Fuck yes, baby. Let's get those panties soaked."

He continued to suck on my mark, and his fingers trailed down my black leggings. I heard a rip between the apex of my thighs, and I gasped.

Bear slid my body up the wall, resting my legs on his shoulders. More ripping and tearing until his face was buried in my pussy.

The man didn't even take off my leggings, he just made a damn access point.

"You are already so damn wet. Do you get turned on watching your mate fight for you?"

I whimpered, ready for him to take it. Ready for him to just give me what I had been craving for the past half hour.

"Answer me, mate." His lips vibrated against my pussy.

"Yes, yes, it turned me on so bad!"

Bear chuckled darkly. He looked up at me with those dark lashes, and gold flashed in his eyes. "Good girl for answering your mate so sweetly."

His tongue dived in without warning, and I screamed, humping his face without any humiliation. I came instantly, my panting breaths causing me to be dizzy.

Bear didn't let up. His body is moving along with me. I needed more. I needed him inside me, and for the past few days he hasn't given it to me like I wanted it.

Too soft, too sweet.

"Because he thinks you're fragile." I heard a faint voice in the back of my mind.

I barely registered it. The pleasure too overwhelming.

"Tell him what you want," the voice cooed. *"Tell him you want his fat cock in your cunt, and you want it rough. Tell him to breed you."*

I. Could. Never.

A sensual purr came from my chest, and Bear gazed up at me, my arousal glistening from his lips. He lowered me to eye level, licking his lips.

"You want me to breed you?" He raised an eyebrow.

I shivered against his body. I could lie to myself. The thought of him filling me up, trying to get me pregnant with his child, was... arousing.

Of course, I didn't want it now, and I don't think he did either.

"I don't want one now, but—"

"You like the idea." His voice was full of hunger, want. "And you want me to be rough with you? Take this cunt like I fucking own it. Because I'll tell you something right now, I do own it. This pussy is mine." He cupped it gently, then shoved a finger inside me.

He pumped his fingers in and out, my eyes rolling into the back of my head.

"I'll treat you like my little bee, but if you want rough, I'll give it to you rough. Especially now. With all those damn shifters out there talking about how sweet you are. They need to know you're mine. I'll mark you over and over, coat you in my come, let them smell my scent all over."

This. Bear.

My body trembled. "Please."

He smiled, fangs descending from his mouth. Bear took two long strides to the desk I had just organized for him yesterday and cleared it off with one swipe of his arm.

He ripped the rest of the leggings free, his dick bobbing as he did so. I could barely control myself, my body shaking in anticipation while I watched the come drip from the angry head.

It was red, dripping, and my mouth instantly watered.

"I think you need a taste first, hmm?"

I nodded, but instead of him lowering my head and putting his cock in my mouth, he gathered the come that was now at a constant drip on two of his fingers.

He growled, letting his arousal sit between us. "Open your mouth, little bee."

My lips parted, and I sucked his fingers and felt his cock rub against my inner thigh.

"You want it rough, don't you, baby? You want to feel me when you walk out of this room?"

I hummed around his fingers, letting go with a pop. He tilted me on my side, grabbing my ass cheek and moving my leg so he had the perfect view of watching his dick disappear inside me.

"You are always ready for me, so wet."

His dirty words were like a drug. I never thought I would like dirty talk, but the way he spoke to me made me mewl for more. I pushed my chest out. He immediately latched onto my breast with his calloused hands.

"I like this position," he grunted, sheathing himself deep inside me. "I get your ass, your tits, your face, all right here," he said reverently.

My throat constricted before a voice not of my own growled, "That's nice and all, but why don't you hurry and fuck us like we really want?"

I slapped my hand over my mouth and stared at Bear in shock. His eyes widened for a moment before he smirked.

"Seems my mate has a sassy bear inside her." Bear sank his fingers deep into my skin. I groaned, feeling his possessive hold on my body. I took hold of the edge of the desk, already predicting where this was heading.

I'm going to be thoroughly fucked.

Long, deep, heavy thrusts hit my cervix. I cried out at the stretch of his cock. He must have held back before because now I felt my vagina stretching far more than it ever had before.

My back arched, and Bear's animalistic snarls and growls only made me wetter. I shattered as the thick mahogany desk moved inch by inch until it hit the wall on the other side of the room. Come was spilling out of me. He'd already come several times, and he wasn't letting up.

Not that I wanted him to.

"More!" I cried, not caring if I sounded so desperate.

Days before, I would have given up by now, but my body felt stronger with more vigor than I could ever imagine.

Bear flipped me over and gripped the side of the desk, my back arching, accepting his girth. I could feel the droplets of sweat from his brow dripping on my back, and I cried out when he slapped my backside.

"Take all of me, mate. Let me in. Let me breed you. Fill you up until you are bred."

I felt my fingers tingle, and through the haze of lust, I opened my eyes to see long claws elongate. I dug them into the wood, scraping them down the desk. Hair sprouted on the tops of my hand, and I roared out a cry when he fucked me with newfound vigor.

"Bear!" My pussy was pulsing. It was feeling raw, and my heart was pounding in my chest.

I wasn't sure how much more I could take. My body was fading from both pleasure and this fresh change in my body. I was confused, aroused, and frightened.

"Baby, one more for me." I heard Bear's gentle voice when he scooted me up on the table and climbed on top of me. His eyes met mine, and I knew he saw the mixture of emotions I had inside me.

"That's it, look at me. I'm here, right here," he whispered.

His once rough thrusts were now slow and deep. My pussy still fluttered, and his lips reached mine and kissed them softly. "Everything is alright, everything is normal."

I closed my eyes and listened to his words. One last orgasm hit me at the same time as he came in me, for I don't know how many times. My body was spent, and so was his. Our bodies were covered in sweat, sex, and god knew what else.

Bear lay on top of me, barely putting weight on my body. He took his tongue and licked up my neck. It wasn't to turn me on, for some weird reason, I knew that. Bear continued his tedious licking. It went around my neck, to my chest, to my breasts, and down my stomach.

When he got close to my thighs, I shifted my legs and groaned, grabbing his shoulder to pull him closer to me. "I'm cleaning you," he whispered. He didn't lift his head to continue.

"Please," I begged him. "Just be with me."

He gazed at me and back down between my legs. He was torn.

Did he lick me clean after every time? I'd gotten into the habit of falling asleep after our first time together.

"Bear?" He made his way back on top of me, rubbing his nose into my neck. "I'm here. I know you were scared. It's all normal, I promise."

I wrapped my arms around him and held him close.

"I had fur on my hands."

He chuckled. "And you will get more, all over. With supernatural blood in your veins, I wouldn't be surprised if you could shift by next week."

I let out a breath and held him tighter.

"Hey, it's going to be alright. I'll be here every step of the way." He brushed a hair back away from my face. "You are doing amazing with the exorcism stuff too. You're so strong, little bee. It's almost over."

I hummed to answer, yet still not quite believing him.

I'd only been through a couple, but it had been better than I expected. Maybe it was because of the strength I was gaining from the bear inside me.

"Of course it is," she said with a huff. If I didn't know any better, I'd say she was perfect to test Teddy's temper.

Bear rose from the desk. There was a mess, but he didn't seem to care. He put one arm under my legs, the other around my back, and cradled me in his arms, then took me to the private bathroom in his office. It had a shower big enough for him, but he made us fit. He washed and dried me, just like always. He frowned when he cleaned the come off my body.

I bit my lip, trying not to smile. I could feel through the bond he was trying not to put pressure on me or make me feel odd. The bear inside me was whispering to me, telling me what Bear was thinking.

This could be both good and bad.

"He wants to shove his come back inside you," she teased. *"He trying to be good."*

I blushed as Bear stepped out of the shower, getting us both towels.

"Don't worry, I'll help you along the way. Your mate will do his best, but I'm here now. The Goddess placed me with you, especially."

I didn't answer. I wasn't sure what to ask or say. She just showed up, and

I had enough on my plate.

Bear returned with a towel draped around his waist, the fabric barely clinging to his hips. His skin was glistening from the shower, and his dark hair was tousled. He wrapped me in a towel, took my hand in his, and led me to the small, worn couch in his office. It was dull and had seen its fair share of wear and tear, but it still looked inviting and comfortable enough for me to want to lay down on it.

I sighed and squeezed Bear's hand.

To my surprise, Bear threw the pillows and cushions off the couch and tugged on a bar. It was a pull-out bed.

Bear quickly but efficiently set the bed, his movements precise and meticulous. He gathered sheets, blankets, and pillows from a cabinet nearby, and within a few minutes, he created a thick padded bed with crisp white sheets, a cozy blanket, and fluffy pillows.

By this time, I was swaying on my feet from exhaustion, and Bear chuckled, pulling me to his side and laying me on the mattress. "I know you are exhausted. I'll get you to sleep, and I'll stay in this room, okay?"

I hummed, my eyes closing. I was trying to fight it as I didn't really want to sleep. I still had nightmares, but I hated facing that demon that now knew I was trying to get rid of him. Not that he could do much right now.

"Shh, I'm here, and your bear is here too. You'll have to figure out a name for her just like mine, huh?" Bear purred, and it put me at ease further.

"I've got to get to know her first." I yawned and dug deeper into the blankets. "Still getting used to the idea that I have another person in my head."

Because not only could Bear and Teddy be in there... but now I had my own animal.

CHAPTER THIRTY-TWO

Bear

With Hawke leading, I strode down the steps two at a time. The basement was dark and foreboding; the walls covered in shadows. I could make out traces of a metallic scent in the lingering smell of stale blood. I couldn't remember ever smelling it before, but maybe it had always been here.

Beneath the bar where we spent our time torturing those who had ruined the innocent lay rooms where even more secrets were hidden. I was not one who was initially invited to these areas because I was not part of the inner circle, at least in the beginning.

"It was unanimous that you be brought in, now that Locke is—compromised," Hawke said as we continued to descend the steps. "We need the manpower, and we know your loyalty is beyond compare to anyone else who has received a mate since arriving here. We know you don't need the club, yet you stay."

It was true. I could leave with Nadia. Hell, could have left a long time ago, but I felt like I belonged here more than anywhere else. I wasn't planning on leaving either. As much as I needed my space, I felt like Nadia was gaining more friendship here. She needed a family, a unit. This was where we belonged.

"I appreciate that. I'll do my best to help."

The dull, plain wall seemed to blend in with its surroundings. When Hawke stepped forward, though, it became obvious that he was pressing a specific spot on the wall. A picture slid aside to reveal a keypad, and Grim and Hawke worked together to input a code before sliding the painting back in place.

"We'll get you your own code once we get you in the system," Hawke said over the click of the door.

Grim pushed on it, and we followed him inside. Fluorescent lights lit up one by one in the hallway. Screams and howls echoed toward us. It hit me like a freight train to the face. My grizzly snarled inside me, trying to offset the sound.

"We're working on closing off his cell with a barrier. Your sleuth said they have something in the works," Hawke said as we walked.

My sleuth had been contacted numerous times by the club. They were building contractors and even helped build the Iron Fang from the bottom up. I'd never helped, never knew about it until I arrived here. I was only in charge of chopping lumber.

As we reached the end of the corridor. Sizzle and Beretta are holding AK-47s over their shoulders. Bones was leaning against the wall with his arms crossed. Their eyes were narrowed on the male in the corner. His hands were bound behind his back, he was seething, his hair and beard were unkempt, and his clothes were torn.

"I said let me the fuck out. I am your damn alpha!" He snarled and spat on the floor in front of him.

The bars were coated in silver. Normally, that wouldn't deter an alpha, but with only half a soul, it would burn him to even touch them.

I frowned, looking down at the president that I looked up to, and turned away. I barely recognized the male. I knew that things were bad, but I didn't realize things had gotten this terrible.

"What the hell happened?" I asked.

"He attacked a prospect without cause," Grim grumbled. "Said the male looked at him funny. Then Locke started foaming at the mouth and beat the poor bastard."

Shit.

Locke was rabid or damn near close.

If Locke was put down, the whole club could cease to exist. Locke was one of the strongest alphas of his time. May have been a damn prince or a king somewhere. That was how strong he was.

He put this entire club together with the help of Grim to give everyone hope, a reason to live. He was one crazy fucker. He wasn't right in the head and was borderline psychotic from his past, but he had a good heart.

If Locke was gone, who would be in charge? Who would everyone look up to?

This place would dissolve. Souls would lose hope if their leader was no longer here.

I rubbed the back of my neck. We couldn't just put him out of his misery. We couldn't kill an alpha, especially not Locke. Not like the rest.

"Bear, get me out," Locke growled. "Tell them to get me out of here. *Right. Now.*"

Locke heaved in a breath, more foam forming around his mouth. He was half-shifting, hair growing around his body. Soon he would shift and never return to his human form.

I shook my head, pulling at my scalp.

"We need your help to hold him down," Hawke said reverently. "Grim's going to hold him and give him something to calm him down."

I shook my head and gritted my teeth.

Above the bar, my mate was sitting with my brother's women. They were eating, laughing. The rest of the club did not know what was going on below them. Their president was dying.

"You aren't killing him, are you?" I asked.

Bones let out a breath. "No, not yet. We are... experimenting. It's just that we need more hands to hold him down."

Sizzle came to stand beside me. "We are just going to tell people, for as long as we can, that he's sick. That he isn't taking any visitors," Sizzle said, gripping his rifle. "It's the best we can do."

"If he shifts, he could break out of here," Beretta added. "We are trying our best. Come on, let's get in there and give him that thing." Beretta nodded to Grim, pulling out a massive syringe.

I scoffed and paced up and down the hallway. This could not be happening. Locke couldn't be going rabid. Not yet.

This was worse than I could ever have imagined. I thought he was just fucked up in the head, a few misguided steps, but maybe I really was lost in my world with Nadia right now.

I stepped closer to the cell. The silver bars did nothing to my skin when I grazed against them. Locke growled, saliva sliding down his cheek.

It was absolutely heart-wrenching to witness his current state. His wrists, raw and bruised from the tight chains, were a painful sight. His body bears deep cuts, with sores and infections festering on his vulnerable skin. With a mix of determination and desperation, I firmly gripped his trembling arms, engaging in a fierce struggle, and brought him forcefully down to the unforgiving ground.

Locke struggled, and he was strong. Hell, he was as strong as a bonded alpha, and it took me time to get him situated with his face on the ground and my knee on his back. I nodded for the others to come in. Hawke pulled down the right side of his pants to expose his ass cheek. Bones gave orders on where to place the needle, and Grim slid it into his skin.

Locke howled. The needle went in deep, and we all winced at the pain he suffered.

Once it was in, everyone backed away, and I let go. He stayed on the floor. I didn't leave the cell like everyone wanted me to. I knelt beside him, my hand on his back until his heart rate slowed and Locke's eyes opened again.

"Shit." he breathed out a sigh of relief.

The tension left the hallway where everyone stood behind the bars, and I helped my alpha up and got him sitting on a comfortable couch that someone had brought in. I wanted to uncuff him. I rattled the cuffs, but Locke shook his head.

Locke shifted his body away from me. "Best keep them on. Who knows how long the shit is gonna last this time."

This time?

"Bram doubled the dosage. We are hoping for a couple days," Bones said. "We don't really know. We can take them off for now, put them back on tomorrow, give you a break with them."

Bones handed me the keys. My hands shook as I fiddled with the locks. It felt damn wrong putting my president, the alpha of the club, in and out of cuffs like this.

Locke put his hand on my shoulder. "It's for the best. Wolf's gone ape shit. Anyone got my cigs?"

Grim pulled a pack out of his cut and tossed them through the bars. Locke reached into his pocket, took out a lighter, and lit one immediately, taking in a deep breath.

"Thank fuck, that feels better." He blew out a breath. "Now, just so we are clear. Grim is taking over after I'm gone. Hawke is second in command after. Bear is now a part of the inner circle, has he agreed?" Locke raised a brow.

I rubbed my hand down my face and nodded.

"Good, now, what about Idris? Have you updated Bear on that shit with the mansion?"

Sizzle cleared his throat and tossed his gun over his shoulder. "Switch checked all the cameras again, making sure we didn't miss anything. The duke wasn't in the mansion at the time you took Nadia. However, he came back and was pretty pissed that she was taken."

"How do you know that?" I clenched my fist, remembering how my mate was on death's door that night.

"Because he killed half the house that night in charge of protecting the mansion. The other half are being experimented on. The duke brought in his own men. Witches, shifters, fae, all of his followers that work for him." Sizzle leaned up against the wall and traced one of his tattoos on his forearm.

"The humans working in the house, the females anyway, are left un-harmed so far. Who knows what's going to happen to them? We can't get any more audio."

"We need to get back out there," I growled. "We need to rescue the rest." It was part of our code. We rescued the weak and the fallen who were weaker than ourselves.

"And how do we exactly do that?" Locke scoffed as he leaned forward with his forearms on his knees. "A worthless leader who's dying, a broken pack that can't link. We are too weak as a whole to travel, to fight against an enemy across the country, Bear." He threw his cigarette on the ground and stepped on it. "I know your mate wants to help. I wanted to ask her more questions before I went downhill. I wanted to get my ducks in a damn fucking row." Locke's voice rose as he stepped closer to me.

"But our time's up," he sneered. "We aren't strong enough to save any of those women in there. The Goddess failed us once again. Surprise, surprise!" He threw his lighter to the far end of his cell. "Way to go, oh your supremeness!" He slung his head back. "Get our hopes up and then rip us apart when we believe in some shit. Can't save others if we can't even save ourselves."

Locke ran to the bars and placed his hands on the silver. Black smoke rose from Locke's hands as he grabbed the silver bars, his expression a mix of pain and rage. His eyes were wide with despair as I rushed to pull him away.

"Don't you see? It doesn't damn matter! Might as well kill me off now. Grim and Hawke will do a better job, anyway. My mind is nothing but Swiss cheese, can't come up with a plan, can't control my wolf..."

Bones rolled his eyes, grabbed a bag from his feet, and entered the cell. He was already pulling gauze and cream from his bag, and I forced Locke to sit down.

"You're a damn idiot for an alpha," I told him.

Locke glared at me and huffed.

Bones grabbed Locke's wrists. "I know you got a kink for pain, but scaring up your hands is kinda fucked up. What's your mate gonna think?" For the first time, I saw Bone's eyes soften as he gently took care of Locke's wounds.

"She ain't coming. Why do you think I'm in this cell?" Locke whispered.

The room went quiet. No one seemed to know what to say to Locke. Pretty sure they all thought the same. Why wouldn't his mate be here by now?

These experimental shots could only go so far. Where was Journey through all this? Could she give us any help, any glimpse into the future?

I stood back and let Bones wrap Locke's hands, and I wiped my forehead. I may not be able to help Locke, but we could get some help with the women at the mansion. That would put Locke at ease with something.

"Listen... I know I've been out of it, taking care of my mate, but I've been in contact with my sleuth, and they found the fae clan that Nadia's parents are from."

Everyone in the room stared at me.

"Maybe they can help us with the women at the mansion."

Hawke slapped his hand on his thigh. "And now you bring that shit up? You didn't even tell us you were looking for them!"

"I've been concentrating on taking care of my mate's demonic entity in her head. Sorry if it slipped my mind." I pulled out my phone to pull up the messages. "I haven't even told Nadia. I didn't want to get her hopes up. I didn't even know if they would be alive." I chuckled. "But they are. Most of the clan is."

Grim and Hawke came into the cell, Locke pushed Bones away, and they all gathered around my phone to see the messages.

The clan wasn't in Russia anymore. They had moved themselves to Canada, staying mostly north and far away from civilizations. I hadn't talked to them much directly; they kept their communication to a minimum.

"How many are there?" Beretta asked.

I shrugged my shoulders. "I don't know, but they are coming. All of them."

"All of them?" Sizzle growled. "How the hell are we going to keep our operations down to a minimum if we have an ass load of fae coming into town? Are their ears going to be showing? Are they going to be wearing some weird ass shit?" Sizzle's eyes narrowed, flames dancing in his eyes.

"Calm down," Locke snapped at Sizzle. "We may need this." He pointed his finger at me. "You should have told us this sooner, Bear, but this might help those people at the mansion."

Hawke held up his hands. "Now hold on there, Locke. These fae have been hiding for years. They aren't just going to jump into some rescue mission. I'm surprised they are even coming here. What did you tell them to get them here?"

"Told them I knew of a way to get rid of bonding sickness and heard that there was a couple there that had it. A human and a fae pairing. That got their attention. I then explained I knew of a child and I knew their child's whereabouts. The entire clan is coming because there are more pairings within the clan."

Beretta smiled. "Well, I be damned. Looks like we have more members joining the club then. When is their ETA?"

I let out a choked laugh, rubbing my neck. "A few days or so. Guess we better get some apartments ready."

CHAPTER THIRTY-THREE

Nadia

"Here, have another lemon drop." Delilah scooted another pretty drink in front of me.

It was in a martini glass, with sugar on the rim and a pretty little red flower on the side.

"It's the ladies' night favorite," Anaki added, leaning on the bar. "That's why they are half-price."

I took a sip of the drink and smiled, enjoying the sweet and sour taste. I was still not used to it, but these ladies loved it.

"I think you've created a fan club here." I laughed, looking around at all the women gathered around the bar. They all chatted and giggled with each other while sipping their drinks.

The atmosphere in the bar was different than usual, more inviting some-how. The bikers took their turn to be servers on the second Tuesday of the month. They were the eye candy for the unknowing human ladies of the town. It was another secret way for the guys to get closer to the women of the town and get to know them. They were sniffing them out, seeing if they were potential mates or not since their noses couldn't smell as far as they used to.

"Scary bikers being turned into normal citizens of the town. It's genius," I said, impressed by how different this place had become since my first visit there just a few weeks ago.

It was a good tactic and was quite funny seeing them lean over, trying to sniff all the women's hair without them noticing.

Anaki smiled knowingly and nodded his head in agreement before taking another order from one of the ladies at the bar. I glanced around at all these human women enjoying themselves and felt suddenly at ease, finally feeling like I belonged somewhere for once in my life.

I sipped my drink, letting the warmth slide down my throat. It didn't taste like it would get me drunk; it tasted just like candy.

"Nadia, what did you do before you started working in the mansion? Did you go to school?" Journey asked as she took a sip.

Delilah and Journey sat close to me, and Anaki was never far from our group. He was in charge while our mates were downstairs checking on Locke. He wasn't doing well, and Bear was going to find out just how bad off he was.

"I was actually finishing up my last year of training to be a midwife," I said bashfully. "I always wanted a younger sister, and my mother never gave me one, so I played with baby dolls a lot. I guess I never got over it."

And now I really knew why. It wasn't safe. Their decision to not have children was because of me.

Delilah's eyes widened, and she grasped my forearm. "Do you think you can deliver my baby?"

I leaned backward from her abruptness, and Journey burst out laughing.

"Easy, Dede, you are going to give Nadia a heart attack! Give her some space."

"But it would make Hawke so much happier having Nadia do it. Can you imagine Bones looking at my hooha? Hawke won't let him near me!" she squealed. "And Hawke won't know what he is doing! Knowing him, his animal would take over and gnaw off the umbilical cord with his teeth." Delilah showed off her fangs.

Journey and I made a collective gagging noise and threw back the rest of our drinks.

"I didn't finish my training, though. I didn't have all the hours—"

"I'm sure you got the gist of it." Delilah waved dismissively. "I mean, you saw a few all the way through, right?"

"Well, yes…" my voice trailed.

"Then it's settled. You get to deliver the baby."

My face paled. It wasn't just a baby I was delivering, but a shifter baby. I knew nothing about those types of pregnancies.

I cleared my throat. "Have you had any checkups or prenatal care?"

"Nope." Delilah sipped her coke through her straw. "The pup kicks, though. Nice and strong." She patted her tummy.

My mouth dropped.

"How far along are you?" I raised my eyebrow.

"Almost two months. So halfway."

My eyes bugged out of my head. "Halfway, you just started your pregnancy!" I shouted as soon as the music stopped. Everyone at the bar turned to stare, and I placed my head on the table, closing my eyes, hoping I would disappear.

The music played again, and Delilah rubbed my back. "Oh, sweetie, don't worry. I felt the same way when I found out. Hawke said shifter pregnancies are pretty short. Four, maybe five months." Delilah looked for confirmation from Journey, who nodded.

"Yeah, and there isn't much prenatal care, either. I feel you stressing."

Journey helped me bring my head from the table. "We get it. It's a lot. We are still getting used to it ourselves. Just think of us as animals now. Our bodies are stronger. We don't have to be looked after as much because of the animals inside us." Journey petted my hair. "We will help you every step of the way. You just need to catch the pup so Bones doesn't get his eyes ripped out by Hawke."

I took a heavy swallow. "Is it going to be a pup or a baby when it comes out?" My voice shook.

Both women looked at me and shrugged their shoulders.

Oh dear.

Anaki let out a bark of laughter and let go of the tap he was pulling to fill up a glass full of beer. "No, you will not give birth to an animal, gods." He wiped the invisible sweat off his brow. "You will give birth to a human child. Your children will not gain their animals until puberty."

Delilah rolled her eyes. "Great, so we get to deal with them going through puberty and getting an animal. That sounds so much fun."

Anaki grinned and knocked his knuckle on the table. "Hey, little miss, you doing okay?" he asked me with a voice filled with concern.

As much fun as I was having, I knew my eyes held dark circles and bags under there. Bear was equally concerned but tried not to bring it up. With the bond we shared, it was hard not to feel what he was feeling. I didn't want the extra attention or the pity, either.

In all honesty, despite the sleeping troubles, I haven't had this much fun in a long while.

The drinks had been fun. Getting to know the girls, the bar. The whole place was lively and made me forget my problems. Not having Bear here was a little unsettling, but having Anaki and the girls here was comforting enough.

But I was tired. So utterly tired. I didn't want to sleep. I didn't want to rest because the dreams were getting harder to deal with. I could wake myself up as long as Bear was around. He was always there, so I never wanted to know what it would be like when he wasn't.

"I'm fine." I gave him a small smile and twirled the martini glass with my fingers.

Anaki tilted his head down, giving me a stink eye. He wasn't buying it.

He leaned over the counter, getting closer to me. He curled his finger for me to come closer and whispered, "How did the last exorcism go?"

The same group came every day at sunset to watch Tajah and Bram cast the same spell over my head. It had been four days, and I appreciated everyone staying with me to show their support.

Each spell went on for longer and was stronger. The fire burned brighter on the candles, and my screams echoed even outside the building. They all looked horrified when I finally woke up. Bear was consumed with guilt that he couldn't do anything for me, and for at least an hour afterward, he wouldn't let me out of his arms.

And the pain I felt in my head was excruciating.

I said nothing about it. They were helping me just by being there, and that was all I could ask for.

"Hopefully, it's not too much longer. At least that is what Tajah said." I perked up.

Anaki pursed his lips and nodded. "It's okay to ask for help." He put his hand over mine. "We're here for you."

I pressed my lips together and let out a troubled sigh. Both Journey and Delilah had been through a lot. You could see it on their faces. They had a lot of physical scars, a lot of my troubles were internal, and not to say that I was hurting less than them, but I didn't want to bring down their smiles either.

The Iron Fang, these friends, had done a lot for me. I was grateful, and

I wanted to give back to them and help out in the future.

"I'm really alright. If we can get more of those women out from the mansion, soon I think that will lift my spirits."

"Can't do that yet." Anaki shook his head. "Have to get you better. The club needs an alpha if we are gonna travel. Locke's in no shape for that yet, unfortunately."

My heart sank a little. Before I could say a counterargument, the guitar from the band squealed, and everyone covered their ears. We all jerked our heads to the stage and saw one singer push over the mike and jump into the crowd.

"That's Cyran," Anaki said, annoyed.

The woman running away, I remembered briefly from the plane when I was rescued, was skirting through the crowd, trying to get away. She had midnight black hair, dark eyeliner, and bright red lips. She was stunning as she dashed toward the door, trying to escape.

The men were laughing, and the women swooned at Cyran as he grabbed the woman.

"Let me go!" she screamed, and he pinned her to the door and put her wrists over her head. He tugged her hips close to his and slammed a heated kiss to her lips.

Holy. Heck.

"And that's Winter. She's got a heart of ice. Cyran's having fun with it, though," Anaki said. "Vamps enjoy a chase. They are perfect for each other. More lemon drops?"

Journey giggled and shook her head. "Nope, I'm done. I'd like to be awake when Grim puts me to bed tonight." She winked.

Delilah didn't turn to me. She was still watching the show that Cyran and Winter were putting on. "So uh, Nadia. What's up with Bear's ears? They were damn adorable. Do you tug on them when you guys are doing the nasty? Do they pop out on command, or do they come out on their own?"

Journey leaned over, her long chestnut hair swinging in the breeze made by the people walking by. "Oh yes, I want to know this. Do you think our mate's tails can pop out like that? I think it would be hilarious if their tails could pop out and start wagging, don't you, Dede?"

Delilah threw her head back and laughed. "Oh, that would be fun! Imagine seeing them wag when we tell them what good boys they are? *Come here, boy! Come here! That's it. What a good boy you are!*" She made whistling noises. Several wolves' heads perk up and look at Delilah. They tilted their head in confusion.

I spat out my drink, laughing, watching the wolf shifters tilting their heads back and forth.

Journey slapped Delilah and pointed to the back of the bar. "Hey here comes Hawke and Grim. Let's do it to them."

The crowd was mingling while the music played, and the group came up from the basement. They locked the door and looked around the bar until our men set their eyes on us.

"You aren't seriously going to do it, are you?" I half joked.

Nope, they really were going to do it. They got off the stools and waved, whistling. Delilah wasn't even drinking and was acting crazy.

"Come here!" Delilah whistled and clapped her hands. "Who is my good boy!?"

Hawke's head jerked back in surprise and pointed to himself.

"That's right, you are my good boy! Do you want a treat? I'll give you a treat!" Delilah said sweetly.

That was all it took for Hawke to push people out of the way and beelined for Delilah.

"I've got some treats too! Because you are my extra special fluffy good boy!" Journey cooed to Grim. The crowd parted for Grim. No one touched him, and both of the guys picked up their ladies and planted big kisses on them.

Both of my friends turned them around and patted their butts. "No tails." Delilah pouted. Journey shook her head. "Can't you push out your tails or something? You know, like Bear puts out his ears for Nadia?"

"The fuck? No, we can't put our tails out. I'd break my tail trying to push it through my jeans. Can't you be happy with my tight ass?" Hawke smirked and rubbed Delilah's stomach.

Grim leaned into Journey, whispering in her ear. "Is there not really a treat?"

I snorted, trying not to laugh when I felt the large body of my mate behind me.

"What is this all about?" he gruffed and placed a kiss on my cheek.

"They are jealous I get your nom nom ears." I reached up, trying to grab the top of his head but obviously failing.

"Little bee, don't call them that in public. It's embarrassing."

Bear groaned and set me on his lap, taking my seat at the bar. "Besides, too many humans. I'm not taking them out right now. I'll bring them out in private when you're riding my cock," he whispered in my ear before taking my mouth with his. "How are you feeling?" He wiped his thumb over my cheek.

Everyone continued to ask me how I felt, and I gave them the same answer. They knew I lied, and they let me do it. With Bear, he wouldn't let me get away with it. I just gazed up at him and fought back the tears.

Tired. Exhausted.

He nodded and pulled me closer.

"Tomorrow. Tomorrow is the last session. Tajah and Bram are sure of it."

I buried my head in his chest and took in his woodsy scent.

"After tomorrow, things are going to look up, I'm sure of it," he said and rubbed his hand up and down my arm.

CHAPTER THIRTY-FOUR

Nadia

"There she is. Get her out from under there."

I tried to push away, but it was futile. They were going to pull me out and torture me like my parents.

My mother was tied to the chair, my father to the table. They were about to rip out his insides, and instead of watching from afar. I was going to be dragged into the middle of it.

This terrifying nightmare felt incredibly lifelike. The nightmare demon's presence was palpable as I sensed his hot breath on my neck, his razor-sharp teeth lingering just above my shoulder. I could even hear him sniffing me, his repugnant breath invading my nostrils, making me instinctively hold my breath, desperately hoping to avoid retching in disgust.

I wrestled with the two guards that held me. They were bringing me to the table where my father lay strapped down. He eyed me with concern. I could see the deep, creased wrinkles around his eyes, his mouth set into a firm line. He nodded at me, a signal he had given to my mother tied to the chair many times before.

She screamed from across the room, begging for them to stop the madness.

It's not real, it's not real.

"I guess you know this girl. This is the most emotion I've seen from you." Master Shane cackled and pulled a knife from his pocket. He rounded the table where my father lay and let the knife dip into the skin of my father's forearm.

My father winced, but he didn't cry out. He always had a high threshold for pain. Even as a child, I knew this. Once he slammed a hammer on his thumb and didn't even flinch.

I closed my eyes not to watch, but one guard grabbed my jaw while the other pulled my eyelids open. I cried out, trying to shake my head, but again, it was all worthless because they opened, and I found them gutting my father like a fish.

His insides spilled onto the table. I tried to wake myself up, searching within myself for the light that I could hold onto when I found myself in these situations since being mated to Bear. I could wake up, I could, I knew it.

"Where are you?" I whispered.

Where were Tajah and Bram?

They were supposed to end this, make it go away before it got this bad. This was worse, far worse than the times before.

Now, my parents were screaming, and my ears couldn't handle the high pitches of noise. A roar left my lips, trying to counter the pain in my ears. I slumped when my father's heart no longer beat in his chest.

"See, that wasn't so bad." I raised my gaze to Shane. His eyes weren't the same. They were pitch black, his teeth long, sharp black points.

The nightmare demon.

I let out a breath and hung my head. This was worse, so much worse than I expected.

I was dragged to my mother. My knees took every brunt of the cement on the floor. On top of all this, I didn't know if I was even wearing any clothes. One rarely paid attention to that in a dream, but I felt so utterly naked.

Or was it my vulnerability?

My mother sneered and spat at Shane. He backhanded her, and blood dribbled from her lip. She wasn't as feisty or talking back to him like the other dreams I'd had of her.

This was wrong. It was different. The nightmare had taken control of this dream completely.

With the wave of his hand, the demon replaced my mother with me. I was tied to the chair, and I wiggled against the restraints binding me.

"Where is she?" I nearly sobbed.

I knew exactly where she was. She was dead. She was no longer with the living, but I couldn't help myself but ask where she was. In this dream, my parents looked more real to me now since the last time I saw them.

"Gone now," Shane said with a tilt of his head.

His deep voice echoed in the room, filling me with fear and dread. I looked around, desperately trying to find a way out, but the room was dark, and the only light came from a few flickering candles that now surrounded us in a circle. I could feel the sweat on my forehead and my heart pounding in my chest as I tried to calm myself down.

Shane walks slowly towards me, his eyes never leaving mine. I can see the darkness in them, the hunger and the thirst for power. The power over my mind, to kill me.

Shane chuckled a low and menacing sound that sent shivers down my spine. He leaned in closer, his breath hot against my ear.

"I'm not going to let you go," he rasped. "Your mind is mine, and I will fulfill my purpose."

I jerked away. His cackle echoed in the darkness of the room.

"You haven't killed me yet. You've just tormented me for years, but you

don't have the power to kill me," I yelled.

The nightmare turned around, and the body he inhabited melted. Skin, muscle, bone—it all dripped to the floor. I screamed, watching it drip, and tried to push my chair away.

The nightmare floated toward me. The dark silhouette the same as it was when he hovered over me. I could wake myself in Bear's bed. The nightmare demon's dark fangs hovered dangerously close to me. "It may have taken me time." He tilted his head quickly like a buzzard finding the perfect spot to sink his beak into dead flesh. "But in this final dream I will make sure not to let you go. I will take you with me."

"T-take me where?"

"To the depths of hell, of course." He smiled manically. "Where I will continue to torture you and the rest of the souls I have acquired for all of eternity."

A bright light shone above us. My body sank in relief, feeling its warmth. Tajah and Bram were here, just like the times before.

The nightmare cried out, shielding himself from the brightness of the light. I moved my body, wishing for the ropes to fall and immediately they did so.

"No, they won't, not this time!" The nightmare demon grabbed hold of my arm, its claws sinking deep into the flesh.

"I'm done, I'm done, I'm done!" I chanted to escape the dream, to wake up from this awful nightmare.

The demon hissed until the light was so bright that its shadow faded into darkness, but his hand still remained.

I screamed, shaking and pulling at his hand until I felt it let go. I squeezed my eyes shut tightly and opened them, ready to see Bear and my friends on the other side. Instead, darkness was still surrounding me when I opened my eyes.

I grunted, trying to move because my arms were bound and my head locked by an immovable force.

"It's me, baby, it's me!" Bear let go and cupped my face. Bear pulled back and stared down at me. "You were screaming, crying. Fuck, I couldn't take it. I had to hold you."

Bear was sitting on the table. It was bowed, getting ready to fall in on itself, but he was sitting on it, anyway. Tajah and Bram were wrestling on the floor, holding onto a black jar, and they both screamed orders at each other.

"You do the locking spell!" Tajah snapped at Bram.

"No, you, you are stronger than I am!" he replied.

A deep purple light surrounded the bottle, casting an eerie, magical glow in the room that illuminated Tajah and Bram as they continued to roll on the floor.

The purple light pulsated in the darkness like a living thing. It seemed to swirl around the bottle, enveloping it in an ethereal glow. The light illuminated Tajah and Bram as they struggled to control it, casting an eerie shadow across the room.

The bottle was small, encased in the purple light that glowed around it. It hummed and vibrated as Tajah slammed her hand over it, the light fading away afterwards.

"There it's done," Tajah said breathlessly.

I panted. "What's done?"

Bear pressed a tender kiss to my sweaty forehead. "All of it's done. The demon is out, baby, no more nightmares."

I closed my eyes and pressed my forehead to his chest. He chuckled and held me close to his body.

The rest of the room hugged each other except for Anaki, who came in and gave both Bear and me a hug.

"This is amazing. I knew you could do it, little miss. Now you get your surprise!"

"Anaki," Bear growled. "Let her recover first."

"Surprise? What surprise?"

If that surprise was a shower, I think I would be perfectly happy with that.

Bear, understanding what I was thinking, shook his head. "No, better than that. Only if you feel up to it, little bee. We can do it tomorrow. In fact, I think we should hold off until tomorrow." He glared at Anaki.

"No!" Anaki snapped. "You can't do that. She has to come see now. Come on, Nadia. You have to see."

Exhaustion hung over me, but with Anaki's excitement and smile, who could tell that man no? And who could say no to a big surprise, anyway?

Bear took extra care of me, wiping the sweat and the tears away from my face before we left Tajah's shop. Everyone was going to the bar, and it was hard to keep my eyes open.

I wanted to sleep, but Anaki said this surprise would be better than any bed or sleep that I would have in the next few days. If it was that important, then I suppose I could stay up a little longer.

Bear cradled me in his arms. He was light on his feet as our friends went into the bar ahead of us. The bar was closed to outsiders tonight, no humans in sight, with a sign outside that claimed a club meeting.

Bear set me down on my feet while everyone went inside, took out a blindfold, and put it around my eyes.

I giggled. "What are you up to, you big bad bear?"

My own bear shook her fur, and I could see the amusement on her face as she was also blinded by the light.

"I've been working on this. I didn't think your surprise would arrive so quickly. The timing is almost too perfect for this since you're free of that nightmare, but I think the Goddess had a hand in it."

I put my hands over the blindfold to set it more evenly.

"What did you do?"

I felt Bear reverently brush my cheeks with his thumbs.

I tried to read inside his mind. My bear was trying to do it too, but even she couldn't break through whatever barrier Bear had put up. She growled and let the claws lengthen.

"Little bee, I'm going to lead you inside. Trust me, okay? Let it be a surprise. If at any time you want to leave or feel overwhelmed, tell me, and we will go."

My heart skipped a beat.

What was coming?

I wrapped my hand around Bear's arm. The door creaked open, and whispers filled the room, instructing everyone to be quiet. I couldn't hear the clinking of glasses or the shuffling of feet. It was eerily quiet.

"It's her. I know it is." I heard one woman say. It was faint, but I heard it loud and clear, and it sounded so familiar.

"Bear?" I grabbed his arm tightly, and he pressed a kiss to my head.

"It will all be okay," he whispered. "I'll be with you the whole time." Bear patted my hand gently and removed the blindfold.

As I slowly opened my eyes, the dimly lit room came into focus. The air was heavy with the scent of stale beer and cigarette smoke, mingling with the faint aroma of leather from the bar stools. I could see my friends and fellow members of the Iron Fang gathered around, their eyes fixed on me with a mix of caution and concern.

The figures were tall, slender, and dressed in long white cloaks with white fur around their heads. Their faces were pale with glittery specks of sparkles scattered across their cheeks, and their ears were pointed and delicate. Their eyes were large and bright, with a hint of mystery in their gaze.

Some sat at tables, while others stood around the bar, mingling with the brotherhood, but two of these souls stood out from the rest.

The first one I recognized immediately. His hood fell back, showing off his pointed ears and his long blond hair with deep green highlights underneath it. His face was filled with awe as he stared at me.

It was Kraven—my biological father.

Beside him was the shorter woman, my height. Her hair was brown, just like mine, and she held almost the exact same features as me, completely human. She looked older than Kraven, with wrinkles and bags around her eyes. But she still looked beautiful to me—my birth mother.

I gasped, leaning into Bear. "Do they know me?" I felt the tears pooling in my eyes.

Kraven stepped forward, his hand outreached toward me while the other pulled my mother with him. "Of course we would know our daughter. We could spot you out of a crowd of a thousand souls."

CHAPTER THIRTY-FIVE

Nadia

My breath hitched, and I squeezed Bear's arm.

They were here? How?

Bear pulled his arm away from me and laid his hand on my lower back. "I put out a call with some other shifters," he whispered. "They found them, and we asked for them to come here."

I let out a shaky breath and stepped forward. My parents, my biological parents, were here in the flesh. My father was a fae. He had pointed ears and a flawless face. He smiled, and small fangs glinted in the overhead lights of the bar.

"We are so sorry." He kneeled in front of me. "So sorry we had to send you away."

My mother held her cloak close to her body. She could barely look at me. Did she not want to be here?

"There were complications with your birth. You caused quite a stir. A powerful being found out about your existence and, well, threatened our clan. Unfortunately, we couldn't come with you because fae are stronger in numbers, and I needed to stay hidden," my father said.

I nodded, already understanding this. "Your mother took it the hardest." He pulled my mother by the hand to stand closer to me. She had grey hairs mixing with her dark brown tresses.

"We never gave up hope. We wanted to come find you, but our kind is rare in this realm, and to be found out would be certain death. We all have had to remain a secret, and I am sorry we failed you."

I shook my head, sniffing.

"You have your mother's eyes. Nina, please come look."

My mother lifted her gaze with tears streaming down her face. "You're all grown up." She sighed. "My little baby doesn't really need me anymore, does she?"

I stepped forward and pulled her into a hug. She gasped when I took her in my arms and wouldn't wrap her arms around me. "I still need you," I sobbed. "I'll always need you." Finally, she pulled me closer to her and buried her face in my shoulder.

A thinner man with glasses and a messy T-shirt, who I had come to know as Switch, stumbled out of a security room. He was panting and cursing until everyone was staring at him with concern. "We have a problem, a big one. Everyone needs to get into—"

The shot pierced through the bar windows with a loud cracking sound. Shards of glass scattered in all directions, cascading down onto the floor like crystalized rain. Everyone around me was ducking and running for cover, yet I remained frozen in place, my eyes wide in shock and fear.

"Get down, Nadia!" Bear leaped forward and tackled me to the floor, along with my parents.

I heard more gunshots piercing through the air like a swarm of bees. They created a flurry of sparks on the floor and walls as they ricocheted off. The screams and shouts of people in panic followed as they scrambled to take cover. Amid the chaos, Hawke and Grim shouted out orders for their men to arm themselves.

The smell of gunpowder hung heavy in the air, accompanied by the metallic scent of fear and adrenaline. An underlying scent of fresh blood filled the room, mixed with the sweat and fear for those who remained.

Suddenly, I felt warm, sticky liquid on my hand. I pulled it up to my face and saw that it was blood.

Whose blood?

"Stay down!" Bear ordered me. He crawled several feet away. The blood that had trickled over to me was Switch's.

Bear flipped over his body, swore, and put his forehead on Switch's. He took his fingers and closed Switch's eyes.

Oh my god!

The lights went out, and my parents grabbed my hand. My father pulled us to the other side of the room. My mother sobbed, but not for reasons that it should be. This was supposed to be a happy moment.

"Who did you say was after me?" I yelled over the thunderous footsteps, the guns clicking, and magazines being shoved into weapons.

My mother pulled me closer, covering me with her body. "Duke Idris, he was a fae, a powerful one. He messed with dark magic and wanted to use your body like a blueprint to fuse our genetics with humans."

What?

Bear roared, his massive body taking up more than half the bar. Other mated, bonded shifters were shifting too and their clothes dropping to the floor. Hawke had a gun on him, the only one that hadn't shifted. Delilah was behind the bar, and Journey was in the process of shifting as well.

All went silent as we watched the door. The fae and the innocent by-standers had all crawled under tables and chairs. "We're surrounded. How did we not see this coming?" Hawke yelled, running through the crowd toward the door. "Everyone have a weapon that needs one?"

Tajah and Bram stepped from behind the bar. Tajah has a swirling orb of fire, while Bram had a blue ball of electricity. A black panther stood beside Tajah; I assumed it was Beretta.

"Magic, dark magic. Much stronger than Bram and I alone," Tajah said ominously. "I think we both know who that is."

"So the bastard found us. How?" Hawke barked into the crowd. "Was it you fucking fae? Did you rat us out? After all the shit we're going to do to help you?"

Hawke grabbed my father by the collar, pulling him up. Bear roared in front of Hawke, seeing my distress.

"I didn't say a word! I told you what I knew. I knew the duke wanted our daughter. I didn't know how they got here!"

The door slammed open with such force that the walls shook. A dark figure stood in the doorway. The only light in the room from an exit light reflected off their black pinstriped, three-piece suit. They were tall and broad-chested with a narrow waist, a large hooded cloak obscuring their face and casting an ominous shadow over the room. A longsword hangs by their side, its hilt ornamented with strange symbols.

"Fire!" Hawke yelled.

The figure raised his hand, and all bullets ceased in mid-air, dropping to the ground. The male slowly walked in, clicking his shoes against the worn wood of the bar. Beretta slunk around the corner of the bar and got behind him. She was so stealthy I barely saw her among the shadows of the bar. She lunged forward to get him in the back of the neck, but the man turned at the last moment, gripping Beretta around her neck.

Tajah screamed, holding her neck. The fire orb in her hand dropped to the floor and faded away. Beretta struggled against the hold until a resounding crack resonated into the room.

I screamed a blood-curdling *no!* My hands slapping the floor.

I darted my head to Tajah to see her reaction, but there was none. Because she had fallen to her knees and now lay on the floor as well.

What happened?

"You can't live without the other half of your soul," Teddy said through our mind link. *"You stay away from the fighting. Do you understand me?"*

I whimpered, squeezing my eyes tight. This couldn't be happening. No, everything was supposed to get better.

"Bravo, bravo. I have to say that one almost got me." The male wagged his finger. "But a cat? Really? I thought I would have been at least taken by a wolf." His smooth voice was chillingly calm after killing a panther with just one hand. His long, black fingernails added to his menace as he stared down at the massive creature's lifeless body.

"Who the fuck are you?" Hawke cocked his gun. "Or should we just go ahead and kill a mother fucker before you get a word in?"

The male chuckled until full-blown laughter echoed into the bar. Everyone was silent, waiting for the man to calm himself before we did anything.

"Why don't you come pull off my mask and find out, Hawke? Or should it be Grim? He's supposed to be second in command? Why do you let Hawke do all the talking anyway?" he hummed.

Grim snarled, his large wolf's body full of muscles. He leaped forward only to be stopped mid-air by a flick of a wrist, then slung to the back of the bar area. Shards of glass from the liquor fell on his fur. Grim huffed and jumped onto the bar, growling.

"Tut, tut." He wagged his finger. "Haven't started the killing... yet."

Hawke raised his gun and pointed it at the intruder. "Duke Idris, the mask is getting a little old."

"Right, right, it is, isn't it? Still took you long enough." Idris took off the cloak. It slid to the floor in a glorious manner. He took a bow and raised his head. Dark eyes shone back at us. I could find no soul in the fae's eyes, and I knew we were all in trouble.

"If you aren't all ready to die, I'm just here to collect one person. One person and the rest of you will be spared, for now, anyway." Duke Idris chuckled and clasped his hands together. "Now, do we have a deal?"

My heart sank. He was after me. This fae has been chasing me my whole life. The fae clan had to be dispersed into the cold. My friends were dying left and right because of me.

I let go of my mother's and father's hands. Their hushed whispers begged me to come back down into hiding. I couldn't do that, however. Too many people were at risk. After all, it was better for me to give myself up than let everyone die because of me.

Once I stood from under the table. Bear snarled and got in Duke Idris' line of sight.

"Get your ass back under that table," Teddy ordered. *"Or I will spank that ass later."*

"I can't let everyone die because of me. I'm not worth it."

"You are worth it to me!" Bear boomed and stood on his animal's hind legs.

Idris didn't move, watching my bear hover over him.

"We don't give up our own. It's all or nothing." Locke opened the door from the basement. His clothes were in tatters, his hair a mess. "Fucking attack him and the fuckers outside."

More of the enemy ran into the bar, jumping through windows and coming in behind Idris.

Gunshots rang through the air again. I was pulled to the floor with a jerk of my arm. People were running everywhere, screaming and shouting, trying to find cover. The smell of gunpowder hit me like a wave, making my eyes water and my nose sting. My father's grip on my arm was tight, but

I barely noticed it amidst the chaos.

I looked up at my father. His face was stone cold, his eyes scanning the room for any sign of danger coming near. I could tell he was scared, but he was doing his best to hide it from me. It was clear that he was trying to protect me from whatever was happening in the bar.

I couldn't very well sit here. I had to help. I couldn't let the innocent die.

"Let me go!" I struggled against my father. He shook his head and pulled me to his lap. My mother held onto my feet just for something to hold on to.

Bodies were lying on the floor, blood pooling around them. I turned my head away, unable to look at the gruesome scene.

"Get up," I told myself.

"*Yes, get up!*" the bear inside me screamed. "*Let's get out there. We shift and help!*"

My lip curled into a snarl, and I snapped at my father. He let go of my waist in surprise, and I sprung to my feet and straight to the war that was now traveling outside of the bar.

The street was being painted in blood, the bullets no longer flying but zaps of electricity, fire, and golden parchments of paper zooming through the air. Journey and Grim were circling Idris, but he gathered his fist and punched it to the ground. A shockwave beamed around him, going outwards, and everyone in its radius was shocked and had fallen to the ground.

Are they dead?

I shook my head and ran straight toward Hawke. He had a knife in his hand, going for Idris until a dark black smoke wrapped around his neck, and Idris choked him. He was being hung up in the air, far above the ground.

"Stop!" I screamed, watching him gasp for breath. "Put him down!

Please!"

Idris took his time looking at me, letting Hawke dangle above the ground. Fighting continued around us. Blood spilling, spells casting, my body trembled as I felt the bear inside me stir to life.

I felt my shoulder snap, and when I looked over it I saw bone piercing through the skin.

"*We are going to shift,*" my bear snarled. "*We are going to take him down, get rid of him once and for all.*"

I groaned, falling to the ground. My knees hit the scattered gravel and my hands scraped against the cement.

"*Nadia!*" Teddy and Bear roared in my head at the same time.

Too many sounds, too much light, darkness.

Hawke was tossed like a rag doll and skirted along the pavement. Delilah was there in an instant to check on him, cradling her stomach with her hand to protect her baby.

I lifted my head, and Bear's golden fur shook as he ran toward me. Idris snarled, his long black fingernails pointing at Bear. "Take a load off." An electrical black charge of purple and blue lightning hit Bear. He froze, groaning until he toppled over.

"No!" I choked, feeling another bone break and fur sprouting over my arms.

Idris made his way toward me. The steps were slow and calculated, and his vision set on me when I lay my cheek on the cement.

This was it. He could take me. Get away from the people I loved, and no one would get hurt.

"*Don't you give up on me,*" Bear and Teddy spoke at the same time. "*You finish the shift, and you get up. Don't let him take you!*"

"*I can't let him hurt anyone else!*" I sobbed. "*What if—*"

Locke came from out of the shadows. He was bare-chested, with two daggers in either hand. The glint of the moonlight reflected against the blades. "Stay behind me, Nadia, or I swear to the Goddess, Bear is going to teach you a lesson."

"Locke, no, you can't! Let me go to him. Let this madness stop!"

Locke chuckled as he stood in front of me. My mouth elongated, rows of teeth sprouted, and I lost my ability to talk. I huffed like an animal in distress.

"Here's the thing, sweetheart. The madness won't stop." Locke didn't look behind to check on me.

Locke coughed, dropping one of his knives. He brought his hand to his mouth, and when he pulled it away, I saw blood staining his hands. He fell to his knees, his back breaking and fur sprouting over his body.

"Nadia, look what you have done. You have let another friend die," Idris said, unamused. "And I didn't even have to do anything to that one." He walked past Locke, not even taking the time to look at him, and came toward me.

I gripped the cement with my clawed paws and let out a painful grunt of a roar.

Bear and Teddy roared relentlessly within me, their cries reverberating like thunder in a pitch-black abyss. The agony was tangible as if their struggle against the bindings of dark magic sent electric jolts through my soul.

"Nadia!" he screamed to me, trying to dislodge himself again.

It felt like time had stopped. I couldn't tell if it was Duke Idris's magical powers or if I had somehow slowed down the world around me. Just when I thought life would be looking up, I was so terribly wrong. Everything was coming to an end.

"Nadia, it isn't over," I heard the strain in Bear's voice.

"We are going to be fine, I swear it," Teddy soothed.

Idris curled two fingers to someone behind me. "Oh, it is most certainly over."

I let out a whine, my body exhausted. My clothes were torn, and my body was covered in fur. I was a bear now, but I couldn't take any time to see who I had become. The voice inside me had become silent as well. Wasn't she supposed to walk me through this?

I groaned, trying to gain my footing on all fours, but it was far more difficult to manage.

A howl came from behind me. A wolf so feral, with red eyes and patches of fur missing from its body, ran into the battle on the street and beelined straight into the woods.

Locke... was gone.

Our president, our alpha and leader, just ran off!

"Now that you have shifted into your animal, you have become useless to me. I was hoping to arrive before that had happened." He tsked, and guards dressed in all black came forward. Their faces were covered with the same cloak that Idris had held earlier, and with them were my biological parents.

I let out a groan, steam rising from my maw into the cold night air.

"Your half-human and fae genetics were the missing link I needed, but now that is wasted since your bear decided to shift. Congratulations, you get to watch your parents, as well as everyone else you hold dear, die instead."

My father's face was stoic and determined, his body straining to shield my mother. His eyes searched mine, speaking silently of a love that could outlast even death. Tears slipped from my eyes as the guards pulled their daggers, the glinting metal reflecting in his eyes. He smiled at me one last time before the blades slid into his throat. My mother screamed, still holding onto his hand until they ripped her away, taking her life as well.

My roar echoed through the air as I watched their bodies slump to the ground. Idris turned and looked at Bear and gave me an evil smirk. "Hmm, how slow do I want to kill the Teddy Bear? That way, you both can feel each other's pain?" Idris grins wickedly.

CHAPTER THIRTY-SIX

Bear

"Something is wrong!" I growled and placed both my hands on the table.

Tajah and Bram placed their hands on my mate's forehead. Where her skin used to be, now black and brown fur was sprouting. Her nails had become claws, and her bones were breaking and reforming, shifting underneath her fur.

"What the fuck is wrong!" I pulled on the hair at my scalp, turning to find my friends behind me in as much shock as me.

This session was taking far longer than any of the others. My mate was usually out for fifteen, twenty minutes at the most, and we had been going on for more than thirty minutes. On top of it all, my mate had been crying, twitching, shaking her head and calling my name in her sleep despite me holding on to her the entire time.

My touch was doing nothing to ease her pain, and even I could feel the heaviness of her soul weighing me down.

My ears pricked, and I noticed her clothing ripping and a bone breaking through the skin. Tajah and Bram had tears of blood streaming down their faces, but they pushed forward in their chants, determined not to give up on my mate or me. They knew how important it was for us to keep this transformation from happening too quickly or too painfully for my mate's sake. Finally, after what felt like an eternity, the change was nearly complete, and what remained standing before us was no longer human but half a bear.

"She's fucking shifting, and I can't do a damn thing! What is the demon doing?" I roared.

Tajah and Bram could not break concentration. They were chanting like they always did. It became louder and louder, the brightness of the candles becoming brighter and brighter. This time, the candles did not give way, and neither did they while I continued to throw out curses.

My friends stood in the corner, unsure of what to do. Hell, even I didn't know what to do. She was force shifting under duress. My mate was due to shift soon, luckily due to her genetics, but I had hoped I had more time after this demon was permanently out of her system.

It was a damn dream. How could she shift because of a dream!

"Fuck, fuck! What is going on?"

My mate let out a scream, her body shaking as it completes the shift.

"Shit, she forced a shift." Bones ran up to the circle, jumping over the candles that violently waved at the wind he created. He grabbed my hand and forced me to touch her with both of my hands. "Keep your hand on her. I'm going to get some water; she's burning up, and she's barely breathing." Bones leaped out of the circle, being careful not to touch Tajah and Bram.

Panic welled inside me. My body, my heart, and soul were crushing with every second that passed. My life was on this table, my damn world. My mate had taken these exorcisms so well, and fuck, she came out smiling every time.

They were worse than what she was telling me. Was I so blind to, or did I not want to know what she was suffering? I was a fool, yet again.

"*You are not a fool. She was—is too damn strong. She wanted us happy too,*" my grizzly tried to calm me. His anger rose. "*I will always be in her mind after this; she will never have any privacy,*" he growled. "*Now stop being a prick and beating yourself up. This is harder than all the others. This demon has saved all its power until the very end. It damn well knew what it was doing.*"

I snarled, my body shaking with anger.

I closed my eyes and let my fingers sink into her soft fur. It wasn't supposed to be like this. She was supposed to be awake, to enjoy her body changing into her animal. I had plans, wanted to talk her through this, to let her become one with her bear.

Damnit!

My eyes darted toward Bones as he burst into the room, clutching the bucket of water. My chest tightened with a sudden sense of urgency, and I knew that I had to act fast.

"What are you waiting for?" I snapped at Bones. "Pour it over her! Do it now!"

Without a second thought, Bones dumped the bucket of water over her limp body. I watched with bated breath as the water cascaded over her, her fur now matted against her skin. But nothing happened.

I couldn't believe it. Was it possible that this demon had finally succeeded in taking her life?

"Come on, little bee," I whispered, my voice choked with emotion. "Don't give up on me now."

And then, just as I was about to lose all hope, I saw the slightest movement from her chest. A gasp of air.

"She took a breath!" I shouted, my heart swelling with relief.

Bones grabbed a stethoscope and put it over my mate's small body. "Her heart is still slowing." Bones shook his head.

The chanting continued, and Tajah looked up at me with hopelessness in her eyes. They were giving up.

"No, the fuck you are not," I whispered. "You keep doing your voodoo shit!" I yelled.

I turned to Journey, who was coming toward me already. The Goddess had to do something. This wasn't the end. I couldn't have my mate give up. I would not give up, not when I just found her.

"Please, Journey." I kneeled before her. "Please don't let this thing take my mate away. I just got her. I'm not ready to give her up. She doesn't deserve it. Nadia deserves to live more than me. What can I do? I'll pray more. I'll do damn anything."

I pulled on Journey's arms, hearing a growl from Grim, but he did nothing when I tugged on Journey's arms more. I would never do such groveling to anyone, but I couldn't let my mate be taken. Surely Grim had to understand that.

Journey got on the floor with me, her lip shaking along with mine. Nadia had become a friend to Journey as well. Surely she could see that.

"Nadia thinks it's real. She thinks the dream is real. You have to make her see that it's fake, that it's a dream," she said.

Nadia had told me countless times before she could tell when it was fake. Why did she feel that it was real, and how could I stop it?

"What do I do?" I begged again. "What will the Goddess have me do? Tell me, and I will listen!" I pleaded with Journey, but she shook her head.

"Even she can't give all the answers." Journey squeezed my hand. "She's the goddess of pairing; she-she can't do everything."

I balled my hands into fists and beat them onto the floor. "You can't--give me the answers or won't?" I yelled.

Grim grabbed his mate and pulled her back. "That's enough," he growled. "My mate and the Goddess can't help you."

"Easy for you to say! You have your mate. She is living, breathing!" I threw my hands back at them. "Put yourself in my position! My mate is dying on that table; what would you do!?"

Bones hunched over Nadia's body, gently pouring water over her again. The dark fur on Nadia's back was matted and clumpy, and the soft brown fur on her chest was still dry despite the water. Her chest rose and fell softly with each breath, and I could see my fingers trailing lightly over her fur.

My mate was running out of time. Going through a dream she thought was real, and I couldn't help her. But if there was a way I could get inside, I could just tell her it was fake, that none of it was real, if only I could get in her dream.

I raised my head and darted to Journey. Grim was holding her tightly against his chest. The rest of the room was solemn, not sure what to make of the situation. But now I had a spark of hope. Maybe I could get to her, tell her it was a dream.

"Can I enter her dream?" I said out loud to no one in particular. "Can I get in her head, just like a mind-link, while she's sleeping?"

The room was still quiet besides the chanting, the candles that surrounded the table where I stayed with my mate all but nearly burned out or put out by the water that continued to spill over the table from Bones trying to keep my mate's body temperature lowered.

"It's possible," Bones muttered as he spilled the last bit of water on her body. "I've read about it in the other realm."

Grim held onto Journey, her eyes glazed over with an opaque film over them. The last time I saw them like this was when she was speaking with the Goddess.

"You need to be connected to her physically to do this." Journey spoke, and her eyes cleared.

Anaki cleared his throat. "Should we leave the room, then? Give them privacy?"

My friends glanced at each other and shook their heads. "We aren't leaving," Hawke spoke up. "We will turn our heads, but we won't leave when our brother needs us. I don't fucking care if it's awkward."

I blew out a breath and shook my head. "Idiots. No, a bite. A bite is stronger. The mating mark is stronger. That is the connection we need."

Journey nodded, and everyone in the rooms backed away. I took off my clothes, watching my mate twitch on the table. She'd grown worse in the few minutes I had been talking, trying to figure out what to do.

I was so fucking messed up. I could feel my soul withering away while trying to figure out what to do, to save her, to save us.

Part of me wanted to shake Journey, to tell her to give me the answers, but the other part knew I had to figure it out for myself. In the end, I needed to know I could protect my mate on my own, that I had the power to do this myself, not rely on others. I was strong enough for both of us.

I stood naked in front of my mate, the candle light flickering on my body. I shifted, letting my body take over. My grizzly, now large enough to straddle the table and not move my mate while I hovered over her. She was still so damn small, a sun bear and a grizzly together. It was perfect for her small form.

I nuzzled into her neck, the side where I had graced her with my mark just nearly a week ago, and opened my maw. The chants were loud as they continued to hold her forehead. They gave me enough room as I took my teeth and quickly sunk them into my mate's shoulder.

My mate winced, feeling my teeth sink into the muscle and straight into the bone. The mark pulsed between us, energy flowing through both of us, binding us together. As the energy intensified, a warmth spread throughout my body, and I saw flashes of light before everything went black.

I felt the jolt of pain she felt inside her dream. I was transported into the dream itself, and it was a war zone I could have never imagined.

It was a bloodbath, and it was real, so very real that I thought I was standing just outside the Iron Fang. My friends were lying on the cement in their own blood. I didn't take the time to look at the bodies of my friends. I knew I had little time.

I ran through the bodies and right up to the scene I could hardly stomach. My mate, in her bear form, lying on the ground, crying, whimpering as she saw my grizzly sprawled on the ground with blood surrounding its neck. We were bleeding out, and she was trying to crawl to my lifeless body.

It all looked so damn real it could have fooled me.

That was when I saw Duke Idris laughing, gloating that her life was over. I took a step back, seeing the bastard. He looked exactly how I saw him months ago when we helped rescue Journey. This time I got a better look at him, and he was as terrifying to me in the dream as he was in real life.

I balled up my fists, feeling the heat of the fire on my face from the Iron Fang burning beside us.

There was no way my mate could do this on her own. This demon was powerful, wearing my mate down for years for this moment to finally take her life and soul away. Even with the bond, I could see that the demon was waiting for a moment like this. She had nothing to lose before. He was waiting until she had everything: a life, a home, a family, a love, so it would be easier to pull her into the depths of hell.

Not today. The demon wouldn't win.

The demon must not have realized I had entered the dream because he paid no attention to me.

Watching my mate's animal crying in despair at my lifeless body, I sprung into action and roared a battle cry far larger than I could have ever done while I was awake.

My mate jerked her head to the noise, and I let her watch me as my human form took shape, then I sunk my claws into the chest of Duke Idris and pulled out his black, beating heart. The demon who took on his form melted the skin and muscle and turned into the smoke and shadows of what I saw hovering over her bed a week ago and screamed out a pitiful cry.

My mate's animal cried out, whining, huffing, and crawling to me as I stomped on the heart with my bare feet.

"Baby, it's all a dream." I ran to her, scooped up her tiny bear form, and cradled her to my chest. "It's all a dream, baby girl, it's all a dream. Believe me. He's wanted you to give up. Please believe me." I rocked her back and forth, trying to keep the emotions from welling in my throat.

My mate had to believe me. She needed to know this was all fake.

"This isn't real?" she linked me.

"No, none of it." I breathed into her fur. "It feels like it, but it's not, I swear it. All your friends are alive. No one is dead. This is a dream." I wrapped my hand around her neck and scratched the fur there. "I came from the real world. I bit into your fur so I could be here with you in your dream to save you, little bee. Please believe me. I'm here to save you, okay?"

A bright light came from overhead, and I looked up, hearing the screams of the demon being ripped apart.

"Do you hear me? Do you believe me?"

"A-are they alive? Our friends?"

"Yes! Yes they are, believe me! I'm here, that isn't me. That isn't Teddy. I'm right here holding you!"

She sobbed like a tiny cub, and I knelt to the ground. The screams of the demon were so loud it nearly pierced my eardrums. I didn't know how my mate could withstand the screams, let alone the pain of these dreams, but I was angry she had to endure this alone.

Why hadn't she confided in me? Why had I never entered her dreams before?

The light shone brighter and brighter until the sun could not even compare. My mate screamed along with the demon until the light was so bright it blinded the both of us. When the light finally faded we were brought back into the dim lit room of shop.

CHAPTER THIRTY-SEVEN

Bear

My eyes popped open. The table now collapsed on the floor, the pieces of wood lying haphazardly around us. I was on top of my mate's body, which was now in the shape of a small bear. Her fur was soft and dark, her snout pushed against the floor, and her breathing steady. I felt my skin, noting that it was no longer covered in fur but smooth skin. Relief washed over me as I wiped away beads of sweat from my forehead.

My mate was still in her animal form. Her body breathing steadily, her heart pounding rhythmically in her chest.

"Is she alright?" Tajah asked from above.

Tajah and Bram had dark circles under their eyes, with drops of blood seeping from their tear ducts. Their bodies were slumped with exhaustion, and their faces etched with worry. They moved slowly as if they had no energy left. Both of them placed their hands over my mate's body gently and with care. They stayed in the same position for a few moments, calmly and quietly.

"Is it gone? Is it out of her?" I rasped, placing my hand over the brown patch on my mate's chest.

My mate had a beautiful shade of black and brown on her chest and maw. The perfect coloring for a sun bear. They were extremely rare, small, and, of course my mate would be one, just like I suspected. She was damn special.

"Yes, it's out. I don't detect any evil presence in her." Tajah pressed her hand to her forehead again. "Do you Bram?"

Bram, being the more experienced with magic, pried one of her eyes open with his thumb and put his eye next to hers. He stared deep inside and shook his head. "There is nothing. She's safe."

"And where is the demon? It's not roaming around the room, is it?" I pulled my mate into my arms, cradling her to my chest. She weighed just about a hundred pounds, almost as much as her human form.

"It's in hell." Bram broke the silence. "You can't contain a nightmare demon on the living plane unless it has a host. If the Duke was here, I'd cast it in him."

Tajah rolled her eyes. "You don't have the strength to do that."

"If I did..." Bram smirked. "I'd do a lot more than give him a nightmare demon."

"That's enough." Hawke stepped from the shadows. "Bear, Bones, what can we do to help Nadia? What can we do to make her comfortable?"

I didn't pay attention to any of them. I let my bond take over and seep into her. I didn't care if I was naked, didn't care if I was cradling my mate, letting my purr resonate throughout the room.

Keeping her in my arms, petting her, holding her as best as I could fucking do. "I've got you," I whispered. "I failed you, but I got you." I pressed kisses next to her ear, and she let out a purr that matched my own.

"Magic aside, she's in the clear," Bram said.

Bones leaned up against the counter and let out a sigh. "She's going to be exhausted. She has had no sleep. We all know this." I nodded, squeezing my eyes shut. "And who knows what kind of emotional distress she is going to have after this?"

"What do you mean?" I held her tighter.

"Think about it. She will not know what is real or what's fake? Is she dreaming or not?" He shrugged his shoulders. "I don't know what you saw in there—"

"It was so fucking real." I pinched the bridge of my nose. "Duke Idris was there, the bar was on fire, you guys, me were all dead, and I swore I saw her fucking parents were there. That demon took everything from her in that dream and made it so real."

Delilah and Journey silently cried in the corner, my brothers shaking their heads.

"It's going to take her time, Bear. I'm here. Her family is here. Nadia is battling something mental and emotional, not physical, not what we are used to. That doesn't make her any less strong," Bones said.

I never thought she was weaker than me. Never, not the first moment I met her. But she hid things, thinking she could do this shit on her own. I was her mate now. I wanted to be there for her. I should have pushed. I should have talked to her about these dreams, asked her what they were about.

"You shouldn't blame yourself." Hawke knelt beside me. "Nadia's quiet. The girls have noticed that too. She doesn't want to be trouble."

"She's my mate," I growled. "I should've known. I should have known everything she needs."

Delilah scoffed. "Yeah, tell that to Mr. Bossy. He thinks he knows every-thing, but women are different. We carry a lot more emotions than you men. We think about anything and everything twice as much. You men just don't understand."

Hawke turned and glared at Delilah. "You keep shit from me?"

Delilah paled. "Just stuff you don't need to worry about."

"Like what?" he grabbed her by the waist and pulled her to him.

"Um, just stuff. Like thoughts of I might not be a good mom," she whispered.

Hawke growled, and they had their own silent conversation.

My mate stirred in my arms, her nose burying itself into my neck.

"Nadia's smart," Journey added. "The people who raised her taught her to be secretive. We just need to show her she doesn't have to do things on her own anymore."

My mate should have known all along that she wasn't alone. I just needed to be more persuasive.

I had been a foolish male.

"Don't beat yourself up." An exhausted voice filtered inside my mind.

I perked up my ears and nuzzled closer to my mate's soft, damp fur.

"She knows how to hide pain. She hid it from me, too, and I'm supposed to help her. I'm her animal, her protector, and I couldn't speak, couldn't move... I feel like I have failed her." A purr resonated from her body, and I felt my eyes well with tears.

Fucking hell.

"Does she feel like we all have failed her?" I asked.

Through the bond I felt her animal shake her head. *"No, she feels this is her own doing, her own fault she isn't strong enough. Nadia feels she has brought this upon herself. She hasn't. She was in the wrong place at the wrong time."*

"To the wrong damn innocent people," I snarled.

People moved about the room as I talked to my mate's bear. Someone put a blanket around me and my mate, but I was so consumed by keeping my mate safe that I didn't notice who. I just knew that the souls around me were safe. My brothers and sisters that were here would keep us safe for the time being.

To think my mate witnessed their deaths and mine, I couldn't imagine what sort of heartbreak she endured. If I saw her die in a dream, I'd feel like dying too.

Tajah knelt beside me, her robe drenched in sweat and blood still dripping from her eyes, nose, and mouth. Fuck, my worries for my mate were all-consuming. I barely thought to thank her.

"Thank—"

Tajah held up her hand and shook her head. "For my brother, no thanks is necessary."

Tajah raised her other hand, and in her palm was a necklace. The pedant on the chain appeared to be half of a small dream catcher, minus the feathers that usually dangled beneath. It was a circle with webbing on the inside of it, made of a precious metal I was unfamiliar with. It was dark, and with each twist of the metal to form the circle, slits of green and blue showed through.

I thumbed it when Tajah placed it into my palm. It was small in my hand, but on my mate, it would sit on her chest and would be very noticeable.

"Bram brought it from Elysian, from the Caves of the Divine." Tajah paused, waiting for some sort of effect of gasp from the room, but none came. We all stood waiting for her to explain.

"They wouldn't know." Bram spoke up from the corner. "It's for high-ranking witches and warlocks, but in those caves, the metals are powerful. They can hold spells, specifically protection spells, and ward off evil. They are expensive, but I could secure some before I left the realm. With Tajah's help, we were able to create this for Nadia this past week. It isn't much, but it will put her at ease."

"At ease?"

Bram hummed in agreement. "The spell is for those who have been cursed with a demon before. This pendant, as long as she wears it, will ensure she will never be possessed by any demon ever again."

I urged my mate's animal to shift her body into human form. Luckily, her animal was compliant and not leery of me. My grizzly was purring against me constantly, speaking to this sun bear, calming her because she needed it after witnessing such a dream. Now, if only I could talk to my mate's human side, that would make me feel more at ease.

Anaki helped us get home that evening and stayed in his cave not too far from the cabin. I told him he was welcome to stay inside, but he was determined to stay away to give us space.

He knew I needed it, but knowing what he had done for me in the past, I owed him everything. He still went on his way, and I watched his back disappear into the night out the back door while I held onto my mate's still naked body, wrapped in a series of blankets.

She still had not awakened, and I wasn't about to let her go.

Her body was damp from both sweat, and the water Bones had thrown on her to get her body temperature down. Now she was physically healthy, but emotionally, I didn't know what I was going to do when she finally woke up.

Time, she was going to need time.

I headed to our single bathroom and started the water in the massive tub inside, adjusting the temperature. The water rose, and steam filled the room as I undid the blankets and adjusted her in my arms.

She moaned, her eyes fluttering open, and stared up at me. I braced myself for her to flail her arms about, ready for her to yell and scream. I was ready for the emotional turmoil to rise to the surface. I was prepared for all of it, but all she did was stare at me blankly.

"Nadia?" I whispered and continued to cradle her.

She said nothing, and I think I preferred for her to yell and cry. At least I would have some reaction.

"Goddess, say something to me," I pleaded with her.

She blinked several more times, and her hand reached out and cupped my face. "You saved me."

I let out a breath and pressed a firm kiss to her forehead, then lowered us into the steaming hot bath. She sighed and pressed her face against my chest while I took the cloth and stroked her back with it.

"How did you do it? How did you get in there?" she whispered.

"I bit you, used our bond. You were giving up, and I wasn't about to lose you, baby."

She balled up her hands on my chest. "It was just... so real. I could handle it before, but that—"

I growled and pulled her up by her shoulders. "No, I don't care if you could have handled it, Nadia." Her eyes grew wide. "I should have made you tell me from the beginning. I should have asked what every dream was like. There were a lot of things I should have done and didn't. No more."

Nadia narrowed her eyes at me. A fang peeked through her lip. "It was my dream. I had to deal with it."

I snarled at her. "No, that is not how this works. You are my mate. We work together. You don't hide shit from me. I take care of you. You got me?"

Her bear flickered behind her eyes. Her bear held anger in her personality. Most bears do. Now that she was one with her bear, it filtered through my mate's being. I liked the feistiness but not when it came to her safety.

"You. Could. Have. Died. You tell me when you are in pain, when you are sad, when you are scared or lonely. When you fucking stub your toe. That is what I am here for." I softened my words when her body no longer tensed. "You aren't alone and will never be alone anymore."

My mate looked away. "I'm not used to showing and telling my emotion. I'm not supposed to stand out. I'm supposed to hide it."

"Oh, baby, you stand out more than you realize." I cupped her face and kissed her. "You consume me. I've stayed out of your head, forced my grizzly to stay out of your head to give you time to adjust, but no more. I'm making sure your emotions are met, making sure you are better taken care of."

"And getting fucked more often," my grizzly grumbled.

My mate let out a bark of laughter, but it soon turned into a cry. It was then a dam broke inside her, and I pulled her to my body to seek contact with mine.

It was the emotion that I expected to see when she first woke up, and now that the dam had broken, I was happy to see she was finally letting me have the side of her no one else had ever seen.

"You died. You died in front of me," she wailed. "Everyone did, and I was so sad, so lost. I wanted to give up when I didn't have you."

I rocked her, gripping her tightly. "I know, baby, that was scary. But that will never happen, do you hear me? That will never happen. The duke can't get here. He doesn't know where we are."

"He burned down the bar. He killed my real parents. He hurt everyone

I ever cared about." Her claws lengthened, and I felt them puncture my skin. I held her closer, not caring about the pain.

"Let it out, baby." I kissed the top of her forehead. "Let it all out. Just know it was a dream, and it will never, ever happen. I'll always be here to protect you, always."

CHAPTER THIRTY-EIGHT

Nadia

I cried myself to sleep.

Or I passed out from crying.

It's the same thing, right?

I wouldn't have purposefully fallen asleep. I knew that. I never wanted to sleep again, yet here I was, laying on Bear's chest while he flipped through the channels on the TV. He was bare-chested like he always was. I could hear the thumping of his heart; it was a smooth rhythm that kept me asleep, along with the TV being muted.

"I know you are awake, little bee." His hand tickled my back, and it gave me the shivers. "You've slept nearly twenty-four hours. You needed it."

My mouth gaped open, and I lifted my head. I was draped in a large T-shirt that hung off my still too small frame, and my underwear peeked out from underneath. On top of both of us was a thick, worn blanket that smelled of nothing but him.

"I have?"

Bear hummed, seeming pleased with himself. "Out like a light, and no bad dreams to speak of that I could tell. I'll make sure you don't have any more of those. I'll be sure to chase them away."

I wanted to question what he meant by that, but as I rose from his chest, he winced, and I looked down to see a necklace hanging from my neck. It appeared that the chain had pulled hair from his chest.

"What's this?" I held the pendant in my hand. It was circular, with thin webs wrapped around it. I'd say it looked like an incomplete dream catcher.

"It's from Bram and Tajah. It's a protection necklace. No demon will ever be able to get into your body again as long as you wear it. It is also shaped like that to capture any bad dreams. At least, that is what they told me." Bear fiddled with it and pulled his chest hair from it. "Maybe I should trim my hair a bit if you are going to be sleeping on top of me because that shit hurt."

"You aren't being a little pussy, are you?" I tried not to smile.

"Excuse me?" He raised his infamous arched eyebrow. "I'm an alpha male. I just didn't want you pulling my hair. If you think I'm being a pussy, I won't shave it."

I snorted and shook my head with a smile.

"That's what I like to see," he said, rolling over the overly large couch and landing on top of me. "My mate smiling after a good rest. Please tell me, do you feel more rested? And don't think about lying to me either. I'll know."

I nodded and ran my fingers through his beard. "I do feel more rested, better even." I licked my lips. "I still feel... raw?" It was the only word I could find that described how I felt, but it was true.

The proverbial wounds were still incredibly open, and the slightest breeze, bump, or nudge would bring them bleeding again. Even thinking about that damn nightmare could set me off, and I wasn't about to cry again. I wouldn't. *I won't.*

"What can I do to help you feel better, then?" Bear said seriously. "Besides feeding you because you are obviously going to need to be fed."

He rose from the couch and led me into the kitchen. I padded along with him, and he pulled out a chair, which I sat in obediently. Even if it had been a day since I had last cried, I felt like it was just minutes ago.

My throat was raw, and my eyes still felt swollen. I thought I had my emotions under control, but obviously I didn't. I was meant to deal with this, do things on my own, but I wasn't prepared for this sort of... magic and demonic presence in my life.

"The club got carried away." Bear cleared his throat. "They brought a lot of red meat, which is good for your bear, salad, which strangely sounds okay to eat..." His voice trailed, and he pulled out a container full of greens. He took out a leaf and stuffed it in his mouth. "Hmm, not bad. Must be the dressing or something. Bear set it on the table and pulled out more food."

What just happened?

He continued to pick out salad from the bowl until the plate he filled with a large amount of food was heated, then he set it in front of himself. He crooked his finger once he sat down and had me sit on his lap, and began cutting and placing food in my mouth.

"I can feed myself," I said with a full mouth.

"And each time you tell me that, I say I'll feed you." He placed another generous portion of steak into my mouth. Lunch, dinner, breakfast, whatever meal this was, he fed me like this until we both had our fill. It was the most I had ever eaten in one sitting, and I ate until I was completely stuffed.

Once Bear was satisfied, he turned my body to straddle him and rubbed his gigantic hands up and down my thighs. "Now, what do you need? I know, but I want you to say it. We are working on communicating verbally." He lifted that infamous eyebrow, and I tried to close my legs shut.

He chuckled darkly. "You like it when I get serious, don't you? Don't you lie to me or omit any information, you understand?"

I pursed my lips together, nodding.

Serious Bear was sexy.

"What do you need besides your physical needs, little bee? Your body obviously can't hide anything."

This. Bear.

"Um, I know they are alive. But for my sound mind… can I see them?"

Please don't make me say all their names. There were so many I remember lying lifeless in cold blood on the ground. It was a dream. I knew they were alive, but I just needed to see them.

Bear rubbed his warm hand up and down my body and pressed a kiss to my temple. "Course, which one first?" He lifted his phone off the table and unlocked the screen.

Locke came to mind, and Bear's fingers paused when I said his name. "I'm going to be honest with you about Locke, Nadia. Locke isn't doing very well. He's changing, going rabid like I told you about. His animal is taking over, and soon, there won't be much human left in him."

"Just like in my dream," I muttered. "He turned into a wolf and ran off into the woods and left us all." I lowered my head, but Bear grunted and lifted my chin. "That won't happen. Bram and Tajah are working on some experiments that are helping. I just want you to know that he isn't the same Locke you first met. He's giving up, baby."

I nodded, and he made the call. It rang several times until it finally picked up. When Locke answered, it wasn't the same man. Locke was… unhinged when I first met him. There was an air of crazy to him, but this was different.

He was unkempt, with a hint of animal residing under the surface. Locke's eyes were dark, and his fangs hung over his lips. Luckily he was still there, though, still human. "Nadia." He gave a crooked smile. "Glad to see you are alright. Knew you'd make it." He chuckled and blew out a ring of smoke.

"You shouldn't smoke," I blurted. I covered my mouth, wanting to smack myself for saying such a thing, but Locke flung his head back and laughed.

"I know I shouldn't, sweetheart, but where's the fun? Anyway, glad you're back. Bear needs someone to hold his balls and keep him in line. You promise me you will do that, right?"

I nodded, but Bear said nothing, hardly looking at the screen.

"I gotta go now. Gotta take a piss, but you take care." The phone was cut off before I could say goodbye, and that call disturbed me more than it comforted me.

"He's not well. We are hoping his mate comes soon." Bear squeezed my thigh.

"And how will he find a mate when it looks like he is locked in a cell?" In the background, there was a stark contrast of dull, grey cement walls and a prison-like atmosphere. The cot had seen better days—its blankets tattered and torn, and the couch in the corner was worn and frayed. The room had an eerie stillness to it as if the air itself carried with it a sense of dread.

Bear just shook his head. "I don't know, baby."

We spent the rest of the day video-calling. I said we should just drive down the mountain and visit everyone at the bar that night, but Bear was adamant we stayed at the cabin making awkward video calls so I could make sure they were really alive.

"Hey, honey, oh yes, Tajah is fine," Beretta purred over the phone. It was dark in their bedroom, but she turned the phone light on to show Tajah's sleeping form. "I could wake her up, but she might light the bed on fire. She's done that several times. I must keep a fire extinguisher by the bed."

I gasped and giggled at the same time as Beretta stepped out of the bedroom. "But hey, to save you time, let me get Bram." Beretta flipped the camera so it was pointing away from her and opened a door.

Steam billowed out from the bathroom, thickening the air. Bear suppressed his laughter as Beretta pulled open the curtain in one swift motion. Bram stood there in the center of the room, his naked body illuminated by the light. He screamed as sparks of electricity flickered around his fingertips, and Beretta cackled in delight. Bram frantically waved his hands and reached for the curtain, pulling it shut so he could conceal himself.

"Feline, what the hell are you doing! I am naked. You do not need to see this!" He yelled.

"Trust me, I don't. Dicks don't do it for me," she deadpanned.

"Obviously not!" He glared at her. "Good gods, are you recording me? If you are making an Only Fans page, I want the cuts. You can't be giving this stuff away for free." He waved his hand lower. "Hey, wait, I used my magic; you can't give any of this away!" He wrapped the shower curtain around his waist, pulled it off the rod, and stepped out of the shower to chase her.

My sides hurt from laughing by the end of the call, and by nightfall, I was feeling better knowing I had seen most of the Iron Fang. However, there were thoughts that lingered in the back of my mind that this all could still be a dream. I tried to push them away.

It's like I'm waiting for Duke Idris to walk through the door of our cabin or for the demon to appear and tell me this was all false hope.

Bear set the phone down and nibbled on my shoulder. "Do I need to bite your shoulder and let you know this is real?" He playfully nipped me.

I bit my lip and shook my head. "I keep trying to tell myself this is real. Over and over, I keep saying it in my head."

"I know, it's annoying!" my bear said, and that got us both to chuckle.

"I think it's just going to be a process. I need lots of reminders."

Bear played with my necklace. "And I'll give them to you. My grizzly and I will do that plenty. And once you are feeling better, I'll be sure to give your ass what it's owed." He kissed my shoulder again like what he said didn't mean anything.

"I'm sorry, what?"

"You heard me," he muttered on my shoulder. "Your ass is toast. I'm spanking it for not listening to me. I've warned you before, now I'm following through. Once I feel you are up to it, I'm taking this ass." He gripped my tiny butt with his hand. "And I'm gonna slap it until it's nice and pink."

Oh dear.

CHAPTER THIRTY-NINE

Nadia

"Nadia! Where are you?"

I could hear the loud slam of the cabin door as Bear stormed out onto the porch, his bare feet thudding against the wooden planks. With curious hands, he picked up the clothes I had just stripped off, bringing them close to his face and inhaling deeply, trying to catch a whiff of my scent.

"Female, you better have not gone far!" He yelled into the forest.

I snickered, continuing along a path well taken. I never go far from the cabin. I was still too afraid to be away from Bear for long. Teddy and Bear were my anchor that kept my mind wandering too far, wondering if this world was real or not.

As soon as I had doubts, Bear would either bite into my mark for an instant orgasm, or he would shower me with affection to let me know he'd beat a demon's ass once, and he'd do it again.

My nightmares were gone. I'd never felt more peaceful, even before I was given the nightmare demon. It could be attributed to our physical activities before bed, but I also give credit to Tajah and Bram.

The necklace was a constant reminder of what I had been through. I never took it off. It shifted with me when I did. The chain was magical to that effect, and it was amazing that it didn't break and mold with me. Then again, I wasn't a large grizzly with a thick neck and muscles like Bear. I was still rather small for a bear shifter.

I am pretty sure I weighed the same in my human form too.

"Nadia!" Bear's voice howled as I heard him shift into his animal. It came out with a low, growly roar, and I could hear his pounding claws hit the soft dirt.

My bear, who Bear and I decided together to name Nikita, snickered while I fumbled with my claws to climb the nearest tree. *"He's going to get you,"* she sang. *"You still haven't figured out how to climb a tree properly, by the way."*

I huffed, trying to dig my claws deeper into the bark. *"As I recall, you are supposed to be helping me with this. Why don't you take over?"*

The bark trickled down the tree and landed on the ground. I continued to skirt up the trunk and into the highest branches, knowing good and well that Teddy wouldn't be able to climb that high.

Nikita hummed. *"No, this is more fun. Besides, as much as Teddy has been working with you the past two weeks, I'm surprised you aren't better."*

I rolled my eyes and continued to climb until I reached a branch that I knew would hold my weight.

"And besides, I don't want that spanking to hurt more than it should. You should just take it like a good girl."

I gripped the limb and wrapped my body around it. I hadn't been able to get over the heights yet, but I was bound and determined not to get this spanking that was owed.

Bear mentioned in passing this morning that I was due. So as soon as breakfast was over, I darted out the door before we got ready for our morning walk.

I would not have a sore butt the rest of the day.

"Nadia!" He yelled through the mind link.

"You going to answer him?" Nikita asked.

I shook my head and held onto the limb tighter.

Crap, we were high.

At that moment, a slender vine from a neighboring tree delicately unraveled itself, gracefully slithering around my branch. Captivated, I remained utterly motionless, observing with bated breath as it steadily approached, inch by inch. Finally, a small bud unfurled, unveiling a breathtaking white flower of unparalleled beauty. Its fragrance wafted through the air, a sweet and intoxicating aroma that enveloped my senses. I couldn't help but continue to inhale deeply, savoring every delightful scent that emanated from the flower.

"Am I dreaming?" I blinked several times, and my tongue jutted out to want to lick at the petals of the flower.

Nikita sniffed as well and licked its center. *"Honeysuckle."* She moaned. More and more, the vines came closer. I backed away, putting my butt against the trunk of the tree, and more and more flowers came blooming.

Winter was fading, the air more tolerable, and spring was around the corner, but these flowers shouldn't be here. Not for another couple of months.

"We aren't dreaming," Nikita said, licking a petal. I hummed when I felt the taste of honey and decided to eat the flower whole.

"There you are!" I heard the twigs snap at the base of the tree, and a furious-looking grizzly was staring up at me.

Nikita chuckled. *"He's mad, but let's eat this real quick before he gets up here."*

I snorted and licked the inside of the flowers, keeping my arms wrapped around the branch.

"What the hell are you eating?" He stood on his hind legs and sniffed up the tree. *"Get your ass down here, or it's toast."*

"It's already toast. Does it matter at this point?" I continued to lick the petals, my tastebuds dancing in appreciation. *"And since when do honeysuckles bloom so early?"*

Bear huffed, steam rising from his nose, looking thoughtful. He glanced around us for a moment before sitting back on his hind legs. *"Fine, finish up, and then I'm coming after you."* Teddy growled.

I raised my head and looked inwardly at Nikita. Bear knows something I don't know if he is letting me eat these.

"Is this a dream?" I stepped back, my heart racing, as the vibrant flowers overwhelmed my senses once more. The air was thick with their sweet fragrance, and the colors blurred together, creating a kaleidoscope of beauty. Yet the panic set in, tightening my chest. This could be magic inside a dream—luring me into somewhere dark.

My Bear wouldn't just let me eat anything. He'd demand I come to him.

I felt Bear's panic rise and his claws raking up the tree. *"Little Bee, you stay there, don't panic!"*

"Why are there honeysuckles up here!? That doesn't make sense. Why wasn't I questioning it!?" My breath came in deep, quickened pants, and my arm slipped off the branch.

I let out a roar of fright, but Bear was with me before I even slipped and fell. His maw went around the scruff on the back of my neck and grabbed me.

"I've got you," he linked. *"Just hold still."*

I curled up into a ball while he kept the back of my neck in his maw, and by the time he set me down, I felt like a small cub beside him. Even as a bear, I was exceedingly small. It just wasn't fair.

Bear looked over me. Even in his animal form, I could see that damn eyebrow raise.

"And what do you think you were doing running out of the cabin without me, climbing a tree, and eating honeysuckles, hmm?"

I licked my snout. *"It wasn't to get out of a spanking, nope."* I shook my head. *"Just needed to go for a frolic is all. Then the flowers, they came out of nowhere!"*

Bear shook his fur. He had been cranky today, not toward me in particular, but his movements were strained as if holding back. Not to mention he was wearing jeans instead of his typical sweatpants the past two days, which I found odd. He hated jeans because his dick couldn't find a good way to settle in his pants.

Nikita hummed thoughtfully inside me. I could almost see a claw tapping in her head. *"Do you think he's taken his rutting medicine?"*

I cocked my head and stared at my mate. I wasn't sure if he was taking rutting medicine or if I was. Bear was the one who handled everything. He literally did everything for both of us, which was downright overbearing and weird.

But I liked it.

Bear grunted and picked me up by the back of my neck again.

"Hey! What are you doing?" I let out a groan in my animal form, swatting my claws to hit him. Bear huffed and continued his pace, heading straight back to the cabin.

"Giving you what you are due and then some."

"This sounds promising," Nikita says. *"You should ask him about his rut. See if he's close."*

"You can't just ask someone if they are going to rut," I hissed at her. *"That's private."*

"Well, just so you know, I'm getting ready to release your heat. I think it would be perfect timing," she cajoled.

"Heat? Like what cats do? When they get all horny and stuff? That's for animals and stuff. We don't do that, do we?" My voice trailed when Nikita started to laugh.

"We are animals, and they have fed us these herbs for so long, and I guess Bear hasn't fed them to you to keep your heat away. He's kept one away, so that's good. No cubs yet. We still need to get some more fat on us."

Bear trudged up the porch and pushed the door open with his snout. He placed me on the plush carpet and stared down at me.

"How will I know I'm in heat?" I asked Nikita, and I felt a fire between my legs. It came on so fast and then buried up through my inner thighs and up to my stomach.

It was nearly painful, and my body leaned back onto the carpet as I moaned.

Like a cat in heat.

"I bet you want those spankings now," she damn purred.

"You are so going to get it after this." I cried out a long, breathy moan.

Bear's angry glare softened, then heated in a matter of seconds. His nose flared, and saliva dripped from his maw.

"Mate," he muttered. *"Mmm, you are going into heat."*

Pretty sure I was already there. Now I felt bad for the stray cats that used to walk in the streets of New York. Always yowling, crying out. Did all female animals go through this?

Bear shifted, possibly the fastest I've ever seen. His claws being the last to seep into his body, and he kneeled before me, his cock jutting heavily between his legs.

"Shift," he growled. "Shift so I can take you to our den. I'll make the pain go away."

I didn't even tell my body to shift. Nikita did it for me, and when I found my human voice, I moaned, and my hands went straight between my legs, rubbing my clit to get any friction I could.

"Why is it like this?" I cried out and pushed two fingers deep inside me.

Bear snarled and hovered over me. "It's your heat. It's part of the cycle of reproduction. You won't get pregnant now, but when it's time to have cubs, this would be the most opportune time."

Bear's cock brushed over my backside, leaving a trail of his come on my skin. I moaned again, feeling the heat against my ass. I wanted his dick. I wanted it in my mouth, in my channel. I wanted to squeeze it with my body in any of my holes.

"I've slowly weaned us off the rutting and heat suppressors, it's not good to take them for long. I didn't know your pussy would be so ready for me after all you have been through. My gods, look how wet you are. You are soaking the rug."

The call-out should have been humiliating, but it wasn't. I was absolutely soaked, ready to take him inside me without any prepping.

"Please," I begged. "Please let me have it."

Bear lined up his cock. My body was still in the fetal position, but that didn't stop him from thrusting inside me. He took me on my side. It was tight when I arched my back, and Bear wasn't gentle.

"Fuck, I've been trying to be patient, holding my rut back on my own. Thank gods you started. Perfect damn timing, baby. You are just made for me, aren't you? This pussy, this body, your mind. It's all fucking mine, isn't it?"

I cried out his name and moved my leg over so my legs could wrap around him. He pulled me up and pushed me up and down his thick shaft. He stretched me, but he stretched me every single time he took me.

"You are always damn tight. Are you okay?" He gritted his teeth and didn't stop his strong arms from lifting me up and down his cock.

My words were nothing but mumbled jargon. Nikita must have answered because the next thing I know, Bear laid me back down, threw my hands above my head, and thrust into me.

"I'm going to fill you up," he grunted. "Fill you with my seed. Put a cub in you."

I arched my back as I came, more of my arousal coating him.

"Fuck yes, baby, come all over me. Let me feel that slick."

The pain quickly subsided, but there was still a warmth between my legs. I knew it would flame to life if he didn't continue to use his body.

"Baby, you feel so good." He lowered his lips to mine and tweaked my nipple with his fingers. I cried into his lips, and he kissed lower to my neck and down my breasts.

"As long as I keep my cock in your pussy, give you all my seed, you are going to do just fine." His finger trailed down to my clit and flicked it, slowly pumping into me again.

He continued his ministrations, praising me, telling me what a good girl I was. I melted, utterly melted, with each touch, each orgasm until we had completely ruined the carpet below us.

"Can you stand for me, baby?" he rasped.

Was he serious?

I groaned and shook my head. My legs were jelly, and I lost count of the orgasms I'd had. I just knew that I was feeling a little better, and maybe this heat was about over.

Nikita giggled. *"Fat chance."*

Bear's sweaty body glistened in the low light displayed across the cabin. He picked me up, and instead of gently laying me on the couch, he put me belly-side down over the large arm and palmed my ass.

Wait. A. Second.

My body tensed as much as it could have. I was a ragdoll now, so there wasn't that much strength to move.

Bear panted, raising his hand and cupping my cheek. His cock grazed my thigh, and my body instantly shuddered. Out of the corner of my eye, I could see it was still hard, dripping with more come.

He probably needs to hydrate.

"Do you know why I'm spanking the hell out of you right now?" Bear rubbed my ass, kneading it before he slapped the hell out of it.

I gripped the pillows in front of me, feeling the come drip down my leg. "I uh…" My throat was hoarse. "Need to express my needs to my mate."

Bear breathed heavily, parting my ass and kneeling before it. He took his finger and lifted the come that dripped down my leg and pushed it inside my pussy. My back arched, my claws digging into the pillows.

"That's right, and I will do the same. Open communication, got me, baby?"

I moaned as he pumped three fingers in and out of my well-stretched pussy. Before I reached another orgasm, he pulled out.

"Nooo," I whined and lowered my head to the couch.

"It's a punishment, not a reward. However, since we are in a heat and rut, I'll fuck you after. How does that sound?

I raised my hand to give a thumbs up, and he grabbed my wrist and pulled it behind me, placing it on my lower back. He did the same to the other. I was completely at his mercy, and I loved it.

Because I knew he would take care of me… always.

"Good girl, you submit so beautifully. I'm just going to do it fifteen times."

"What?" I yelped. "That's a lot!"

And yet, my body was still turned on by it.

"Yes, fifteen, unless you say red because it becomes too intense. It shouldn't come to that. I know how to read your emotions, but you say it if you need to. Do you understand?"

I nodded, and he swatted my ass.

"Owie!"

"Words, I want communication, little bee," he ordered, with a massage on the offended cheek.

"Yes, sir, I understand!"

Bear groaned again, rubbing his cock on my thigh. "I like the sir talk. Maybe you should say that more in bed."

My lip curled into a smile until another hand landed on my backside. I squealed, my legs tightening together. My pussy pulsed with excitement.

I liked that way more than I thought.

"Spread your legs!" he barked. "I don't want you rubbing your pussy while I give you your punishment."

This. Bear.

The slaps rained down hard, but they weren't painful like I had expected. They were arousing, and my clit was pulsing with more desire by the minute. It could very well be because of my heat, but I wanted more.

I wanted to explore this kinky side that Bear was showing me. What other things could he show me?

I let out a moan, and the last spank was harder than the rest. The burn on my skin hurt, but the sting combined with Bear forcing his cock inside me was another level of pleasure.

My breasts heaved over the side of the couch, rubbing the material. With the constant sensations of my body moving along the couch with Bear's grinding and thrusting, I was coming harder than ever before.

Bear wrapped his body around me, leaning over the couch. His teeth grazed my shoulder while his hips continued to pump into me. "Mine," he growled before we both were overcome by our body's releases and slumped onto the couch.

CHAPTER FORTY

Bear

My hips bucked, feeling soft lips around my cock. A tongue licked up its underside and pushed into the head. I groaned, my hips involuntarily thrusting forward. A gagging noise followed along with the sweet scent of honey invading my nose.

Fuck, this has been the best week ever.

My hand entangled in my mate's thick, dark hair that radiated a brownish-red hue in the morning light. I gripped her head gently as she continued her work, and her scent of sweet honey carried around the room.

"Fuck, baby, what a way to wake up," I rasped.

She hummed, and the vibration went straight to my aching balls. I came, but not enough to give her a mouthful. She'd drained me dry, and I'd not hydrated enough, too worried about keeping her healthy and satisfied.

She crawled up my body, laying her head on my chest. I groaned and rolled her over to kiss her softly. "You should be sleeping," I told her and gazed at the corner of the window.

The sunlight was a warm, golden hue that streamed through gaps in the thick blackout curtains. It was mid-morning, and the air was filled with a cozy warmth, like a blanket of heat that encased us in our private cocoon.

We'd been undisturbed, consumed in our own world of passion, food, and rest. The light was a reminder that a new day was here and that I had a promise to fulfill.

Hell, it had been the most satisfying rut I'd ever been through. Even my mate had become more curious about her body, trying positions and even becoming a demanding little thing in bed.

When I continued to look at the sliver of light coming in the window, I could see the honeysuckles that had taken over the cabin. The vines had crept in and covered most of the perimeter of the house. It was far too soon for them to be blooming in weather like this, let alone take over the cabin.

Her parents were becoming impatient.

Nadia's parents arrived the day after Nadia's exorcism and with her fragile state, I wasn't about to have her meet them. She may become angry with me later for making them wait to see her, but her mental health was far more important.

My mate was broken, raw, as she said, seeing all of her friends die. It was only a few days later she told me how shocked she was that her biological parents were also in the dream. It made the dream that much harder. She had literally lost everything like the demon had wanted her to.

After messaging the inner circle, we made the decision to keep her parents, as well as the fae clan, away from my mate so she could heal. We provided apartments for the clan, but they declined. They were used to living in the outdoors, creating their own tents and cabins. Their magic had grown from so many years ago despite their hiding in colder temperatures.

Now they were in a slightly warmer climate. They said they would take to the forest that we had purchased and create their own areas to live and thrive with the rest of us.

Soon enough, Locke and Grim were going to have to purchase more land.

While I tended to my mate, Journey had spoken with the clan and the several couples who had bonding sickness. Three mixed-raced couples lived within the clan and had now been given the go-ahead by Journey and shown that they would not die, and that it was not an abomination to mix species.

The leader of the clan, known as Shhkuk, was reluctant, fearful that the fae species would shrivel and die, but Journey, somehow with her eloquent words, smoothed it over just enough to allow it. Explaining how she was once a human herself and was now a full-blooded wolf. Once Shhkuk gave his approval, all the bond sickness couples took off to the nearest wood and consummated their pairings and haven't been seen since.

Except for Nadia's parents.

They waited patiently until Hawke and Grim asked their interrogation questions to make sure the Iron Fang was safe, and Nadia was safe to meet them. Of course they passed after Switch did thorough background checks, finding nearly nothing on them in the dark web or in Duke Idris' systems.

They had lived utterly off-grid, which they planned to do now in our forest.

And come to find out, they were hiding Nadia from Duke Idris all this time. The fae that gave her the blessing was Rosalina. She was powerful and pushed Nadia's heritage so deep no one would be able to find it.

Duke Idris' list of wrongdoings was growing by the minute. Capturing him would be sweet revenge.

I twirled my mate's hair with my finger. Her purr resonated against my skin. She'd grown so much in the weeks I'd made her stay up here in the cabin. Now it was time to get back to reality, let her meet her parents, and pray that her mental wounds had healed enough that she trusted me, my grizzly, and her bear to be there to catch her if she had difficulty believing her parents were standing in front of her today.

I pushed the heavy curtain out the way of the window, seeing the vines of honeysuckle. "Why don't we go on our walk before lunch since our bears have calmed down?"

My mate purred against me and wrapped her arm around my waist. "Shower real quick?" She bit her lip and rose from my chest. Her breasts were covered in my marks, beautiful red, purple, and pink from my teeth and lips. Her whole body was marred with scratches and bruises around her hips, and her mark damn near glowed. Yet her bear didn't heal them.

"She loves it." My grizzly puffed out his chest. *"She likes being marked by our body. I bet she wouldn't mind having a tattoo across her chest that held my face."*

I internally rolled my eyes so Nadia didn't get the inclination to see inside my head. She hadn't mastered searching deep within my mind as of yet, but she was close. She had concentrated more on her emotional healing, shifting, and, most of all, communicating.

I didn't want to sit in her head at all hours of the day wondering if she was still hurting, and luckily, she had gotten far better.

"Shower then," I said, and she rose her naked, glorious body from the bed. Even her backside was covered with my handprints.

I didn't know she would like having her perky, now fully plump ass spanked so much. Her perky ass that has filled in nicely. Not that I was complaining. All the extra food she has been eating, her hips have widden that she will bear my cubs quite easily.

I slapped her ass before she got out of reach. She squealed and held her left cheek, sticking out her tongue.

Behave, I told myself. She's supposed to meet her parents in just an hour.

Then she sashayed her hips, and I saw my come running down her leg.

To hell with it.

I snarled and bolted from the bed, running after her before I made her scream in the shower once more.

Nadia

Bear's large, warm hands encircled mine, locking us together as we stepped onto the porch. His grip was firm but gentle, and I could feel the strength in his fingers while the light caress of his thumb brought a feeling of comfort and stability. His gaze was penetrating and protective, watching me for any signs of fear or anxiety, ready to take action should I need it.

The forest was now carpeted with green grass, with flecks of purple, blue and yellow wildflowers scattered throughout. The tree trunks were no longer dull and bare, but bursting with fresh, bright leaves that swayed in the gentle breeze. The sun shone through the branches, sending beams of warm light and shadows across the forest floor. The air was humid and invigorating, with a sweet scent of wildflowers mixed with the freshness of the morning dew.

It was a beautiful spring day, dare I say almost summer? I squeezed Bear's hand again, making sure he was still real. I felt his lips touch my shoulder, and I blinked once more, taking in the world around me.

Honeysuckles climbed up tree trunks and bushes, their white and red petals intertwined and winding their way up to the sun. Thousands of them filled the forest, an explosion of color and life that seemed too over-whelming to be real. The petals caught the light of the sun, creating a magical effect that made it feel like anything was possible.

I thought back to nearly a week ago when I saw those honeysuckles in the tree. How the vines uncurled, and Nikita and I lapped at the sweet honey.

Had they grown that much in just a week?

Bear tugged me along into the grass that now grew off the front porch. It covered the stepping stones that led to the cabin porch, and the vines even took over Bear's truck.

"What, what is this?" I breathed. "This... is this a dream? Is it real or—"

Bear cleared his throat and pulled my other hand to his, squeezing it tightly. "This is magic, Nadia. Please do not be afraid of it. It's not a dream."

I felt the honesty in his words. I felt it through the bond. Still, I walked with trepidation down the steps and into the soft grasses that I knew shouldn't have grown around the cabin. It was usually filled with moss, dirt, and mud.

He continued to lead me through our normal walking path. It was worn from our bare feet and claws. The scent of the honeysuckle drove me mad, wanting to taste a bit of its honey, but Bear continued to have us walk down the soft path.

"A lot has happened since I've kept you in the cabin, having you heal and teaching you about your bear," he said, keeping his hand on my lower back.

That was an understatement. My first shift was done in a dream. It wasn't a pleasant shift and filled with both emotional and physical pain. Over the weeks, Bear taught me how to shift to make it less painful, how to embrace my animal, and teaching the basics, even how to walk.

I'd come to love her and build a new connection with a new part of myself.

"Hawke and Journey have worked with a special group of souls that have come under our protection, and there are two very special people who want to meet you. They've been searching for you for a long time."

My stomach leaped.

Did he? Did he find my parents?

I halted in my steps and stared up at my mate, who continued to surprise me. After all he had done, he still continued to amaze me. He gave me more than I could ever give.

Immediately, my eyes welled up with tears.

"Woah, woah, you can't do that." He panicked, taking his thumbs and wiping away the tears. "I can't do tears, baby, not when I have no idea what's going on."

I let out a giggle and wrapped my arms around him. "They are happy tears. Women can do that."

Bear lowered his shoulders and let out a breath. "Goddess, you females are something. Now that you know you can cry in front of me, you are going to do it all the time, aren't you?"

I nodded and rubbed my face into his shirt.

"Don't cry now, because I think your parents will get pissed at me. I don't need a summer fae wrapping his vines around my throat."

I stared up at him, blinking. He smirked and nodded his head for me to look behind me.

My father stood tall, his deep green linen pants and white tunic standing out against the colorful backdrop of nature. The sun rays that shone through the trees glinted off of his long, blond hair, the dark green highlights underneath it curling around his neck. The blooms around him seemed to expand and grow brighter, and he emanated a comforting honey-like aroma.

He looked better than in the nightmare. He looked fresh, clean, so healthy. He wasn't weak or lost in despair; he was regal, and I questioned if he could possibly be a prince or a king. My thoughts of my father soon drifted away when I saw my mother. Her skin was smooth and unblemished, her dark brown hair cascading down her back in waves of golden highlights. She wore a tan dress with green embellishments swirled on the cuffs of her sleeves, her arm firmly looped around my father's. When she turned to gaze lovingly at him, two distinctively pointed ears were revealed that gave away what she was now.

A fae.

My mouth dropped, but I squeezed Bear's hand for reassurance. My mother and father, and they were bonded—together.

Don't let this be a dream.

Were we still having our rut and heat. I was passed out on his body, savoring the warmth, and I was having a fifteen-minute power nap before we did it again.

That was the only logical explanation for all of this.

"This isn't real." I placed my hand over my mouth. "This, none of this." I backed away, but Bear's giant hand stopped me.

"Baby, it's real. I promise." He kissed my mark, and the tears flowed.

They both stepped forward, arm in arm. They weren't surprised to see me at all when they walked toward me, and my mother threw her arms around me. I let her, despite the shock, and hugged her back. This hug felt warm, so much more passion than in the dream.

"It's real, all of it's real," Bear continued to remind me. I still held onto his hand while they both held me.

"We are so sorry," my mother sobbed. "We didn't want to send you away. We really didn't." Her lips grazed my cheek and kissed the stream of tears. "I wanted, we wanted, to go with you. We just couldn't."

I shook my head, peeking out from my mother's shoulder to see my father's face. He was filled with sadness at seeing my mother cry, but I gripped his hand to pull him closer to us. "You did what you had to do. I was a risk, wasn't I? To you both, to all those other faes?"

My father's voice cracked. "Yes, darling, we didn't know. We had not been enlightened about the Goddess' new gift, and our leader was fearful of what it might bring. Death? More attention to the clan? Then your mother fell pregnant." My father rubbed her belly lovingly. "It was the best and scariest day of our lives. I didn't know I could get her pregnant without completing a bond. And when you were born." He sighed. "I knew you were meant to be here."

His face turned to anger. "But then someone in our clan betrayed us."

"Betrayed?" I sniffed, pulling away.

"There was an autumn fae that begged to travel with us to Earth. We sought peace from the Elysian realm many years ago. Political reasons." My father cleared his throat. "Anyway, Aedar traveled with us. He was quiet, dutiful, always did what he was asked. He always had his nose buried in a book, and when we went to towns for supplies, he found computers fascinating. We thought it was just pure interest in human technology, but we believe it was far worse."

"He showed extreme interest in our pairing and even asked us questions about the pregnancy," Mother said. "He was kind, brought me pillows, even brought a gallon of milk... my favorite thing to drink when I was pregnant with you."

I smiled.

Kraven's voice grew cold. "Yes, but then once you were born, and you survived, that was the last we saw of him."

"You will be happy to know that he's dead," Bear interrupted. "He was one of the fae exploiting humans, exploiting Journey, our priestess now. Grim ripped him apart, piece by piece." Bear growled.

My father nodded. "Good, it was well deserved."

"That poor woman. She's come so far." My mother gripped me closer. "You didn't... have anything like that happen to you, did you? What happened?"

I gave her a crooked smile. "Doesn't matter now. I'm here, alive, happy. But no, I wasn't touched. I was just locked in a cell."

And had my mind played with for a few years, but I didn't think I'd dare tell her that. Not now, not ever.

My father's fists tightened, and he snarled and continued his story. "There were whispers among the faes; we had limited communication since there are so few of us but we heard that Duke Idris was alive through other passing supernaturals. It was almost unbelievable to hear, but we felt the truth of their words in our bones. And he was collecting."

I tilted my head in confusion.

Bear placed a hand on my shoulder. "Duke Idris was forming an army many years ago when his power was still weak. Collecting fae and witches, promising them more power but draining them of theirs. He doesn't do that anymore, but it's what he did."

What a horrible person.

"He's become powerful, but he wants to strengthen the army he has. He wants them mindless, listening to his every word, and to do that, having them be part human accomplishes that. Strong bodies but weak minds. He wanted to experiment on you. Learn your genetics, learn how to alter them for future experiments. You were one of the first halflings born. Fae genetics are hard to work with, especially when you are dealing with multiple species of fae."

"Are there others? Like what I was? Half fae?"

My father pressed his lips into a thin line.

"Yes," my mother said. "There were. They had to be sent away as well. There aren't many, and we hope they can remain undetected. Your powers were buried deep inside you, Nadia. You were given a blessing to do so. The only way a halfling powers can be revived is by a witch that knows there are powers there."

My mother's hair brushed over her face. I could see sparkles of gold strands in her hair. I wrapped my finger around to play with the long tresses.

"Are you disappointed I'm a bear and not a fae?"

They both looked at each other, smiling, shaking their heads. "Why would we be upset? You have a mate, and you are positively glowing!" My mother gleamed. "Isn't she glowing, Kraven?" My mother continued to touch my face, my shoulders, my hands.

"Absolutely." He nodded. "Surprising, since she was kept in a cabin for a week, not sleeping." He eyed Bear, and a blush spread across my cheeks.

Bear stuck out his chest. "We are mates." He pointed out. "I will protect her with my life, but she isn't fragile."

I snuck a smile at Bear and wrapped my pinky finger around his. "He's a good bear. He's saved me several times."

"But she saved me first." Bear wrapped his arms around my neck and placed a kiss on my head.

My father studied him and nodded. "Yes, as did my mate." He winked at my mother, who blushed as hard as I did.

After our grand meeting, Bear led us back to the house. There was a skip in my step. I was ready to learn all about my parents, about their lives, how they met. I wanted to know it all.

But today, we wouldn't talk about Idris, not anymore. Because he took enough years away from me and my family. Today, we would get reacquainted with each other until we had to talk about the inevitable.

CHAPTER FORTY-ONE

Bear

My mate, with her dark hair, rosy cheeks, and curves that made me drool, reached over the bar for more wine. The crop top she wore, baring her skin, made me eye her hungrily across the room, wishing I could touch her, here and now.

The others in the room—her mother, the mated women, even Anaki—seemed to sense my gaze, and all eyes turned towards me before they started giggling. Anaki, ever the wild spirit, had been teaching the women how to make fae wine, and it seemed they were all having fun.

I could see Anaki's wall of mates growing above the mantel on the bar. My mate and I were the last picture hung, hanging proudly with the most obnoxious flowered frame picked out by Anaki. There was favoritism there, I was sure. My mate and I were nestled under a honeysuckle flower arch created by her parents.

I shook my head, taking another sip of my beer.

My mate caught my eye, her gaze flickering with a heat that made me feel like I was going to combust. I smiled, taking a sip of my beer. I wanted to take her in my arms, to feel her heart racing against mine. But I knew this was not the right time. I would take her home soon, I promised myself.

But for now, I just had to sit back and watch her, my beauty, who I loved more than anything in this world.

I took another sip, the haze of smoke drifting over the pool tables. The bar was lively tonight, especially for a Saturday. Brothers were laughing, throwing each other around. We'd only had to escort three unruly shifters to their rooms and lock them up for getting out of hand.

Hawke nudged me, his phone in hand, looking at his messages. "Locke's going to come up and make an appearance. Think we can do a meeting at the church?"

The women all squealed when Anaki set a drink aflame. He downed the drink in one go, and our mates all laughed.

"Yeah." I pushed away from the wall and downed the rest of my beer. "Am I the muscle tonight?"

Locke wasn't right. He only came out of his cell every couple of days, right after the high dose of whatever shit Tajah and Bram gave him. It was not working as well, but he hadn't shifted into his animal, thankfully.

He kept up appearances for the sake of the club to give everyone hope. But when his eyes went wild, we knew he was on the brink of a breakdown, of shifting. Then it was right back into his cell.

Only the inner circle knew, and it would remain that way until we could find his mate.

I strode over to the basement doors. I could hear Locke coming up the stairs. When he arrived, he was clean-shaven with cuts on his body. He had sunglasses on to hide the dark circles under his eyes and a cigarette stuck in his mouth.

"Hey, hey, it's a party." He nodded to me, and Sizzle came up behind him.

I linked my mate that we had a meeting, and I'd meet with her later. Before I was able to take two steps, she was already bounding toward me and giving me a kiss.

"Don't take too long." She smiled wide. "You said you'd dance with me tonight."

Locke gazed down at my tiny mate, no smile or acknowledgment. He kept his face stoic and continued his walk.

I pressed a kiss to her forehead, reassuring her I would be back in time. I made a gesture for Anaki to cut out the alcohol for her, but he waved me off. Bastard better not get her sick.

Once we got to the office of the church, I stood behind Locke and crossed my arms. There was an extra seat for me, but with my president's twitchy movements, I felt this would be a short meeting. So I decided to stand behind him, crossing my arms and watching over.

I could smell Locke. I could smell his animal, an alpha wolf, and it was damn strong. I'd never been around royalty, but I'd bet my life on it he had it in him.

Hawke, Grim, Sizzle, Beretta, and Bones sat at the table, and a newcomer we'd added who had not been considered part of our inner circle but was now an ally and new friend.

"Shhkuk, glad you came." Locke nodded his head to him. "Are you and your clan feeling welcome?"

Shhkuk had an olive complexion with high cheekbones and a strong jawline. His dark eyes scanned the room, giving nothing away, and his expression was stern. There was a hint of gratitude in his gaze in spite of his firm composure. He spoke in a deep, clear voice and carried himself with confidence. "My people are grateful for your hospitality and your information regarding bonding sickness. We are truly in your debt."

Hawke and Grim nodded as they were the ones who had taken care of the fae in my absence since calling them here.

"Isn't a problem. It seems we have similar causes. Getting out of the Elysian realm, from its brutality, barbaric ways of rejecting bonds." Locke leaned back in his chair and interlaced his fingers together over his stomach. "And I hate to be an ass and request payment so soon after your arrival, but we do need your help."

Shhkuk scoffed and let down the magical glamor that hid his true form. His ears lengthened, and his slender fingers tapped the table. "Your reputation proceeds you. You don't give a shit."

"Oh, a fae that curses. What do I owe the pleasure?" Locke gave a wolfish grin.

Grim shifted in his seat. "Locke."

"I know, I know." He leaned over the table, closer to the fae. "Truth is, your clan is stronger than ever being in our climate over the weeks. They have been primed for the cold, and now with these much easier temperatures, their power grows."

Shhkuk raised his jaw. "For what. Your bidding? Ride bikes, throw beer bottles around. We are above that."

Locke didn't smile. He tapped his knuckles on the table. "Do you know what we stand for? This little cover I've created?" Everyone stayed silent, the tension palatable.

"We arranged ourselves as a club, an MC to help each other when times were dark. To live amongst humans to survive." Locke pressed his finger into the wood. "Riding bikes," he spat, "lets us feel the wind in our hair when we can't feel the wind in our fur. It's a perk." He lifted his shoulders. "But don't you throw off on the people that have come from nothing, been rejected by the same realm that you ran from."

You could hear a pin drop in the room.

Locke's forehead beaded with sweat, and he reached into his cut for a cigarette and said, "The work we have done here has brought us the redemption we sought. A second chance, second chance mates. We were granted it by the Moon Goddess. You've seen it, witnessed it. We have our own priestess. She's far more powerful than any priestess in Elysian, and you know it."

Locke's hand shook, trying to light the cigarette. Grim gripped Locke's wrist to steady him. Locke took a long puff and nodded to Grim. "The work we do here is to rescue the lesser of us. Usually humans, but we have rescued our kind a time or two. There is a mansion where Nadia was held, and it holds women, men, hope to the Goddess no children, but Duke Idris... he's in control of it. Ready to ship them off in containers for sex trafficking."

Shhkuk's face paled. "What, why? Why would he do that?"

Hawke growled. "Sex, drugs, money, that makes the world go around here. He's planning to rule it all. At least that is our guess. We just know we need to stop him."

"He's creating a new world. One where he will rule. He promises the supernaturals that join him will get a piece of the pie. How he is able to continue walking around without a mate, it's wrong," Sizzle said, shaking his head.

"Look, we don't have all the answers," Locke interrupted. "We just know we need to get those women out. Delilah used to live in that house. She knows the layout. We don't leave souls behind."

Shhkuk leaned back in his chair, his expression unreadable. "I see." He paused, rubbing his chin. "What do you need from us?"

Locke took a final drag from his cigarette and stubbed it out in the ashtray. "We need your help in retrieving his prisoners. Your people have unique abilities that can aid us in infiltration and sabotage. We need to disrupt his operation and take him out before he can hurt anyone else."

Shhkuk considered this for a moment before nodding. "We owe you a debt. Consider it repaid. We will assist you in any way we can."

"Good," Locke said, sitting up straighter. "We'll need to plan this carefully."

As the meeting came to a close, I could see the slight relief on Locke's face. He'd been carrying the weight of this operation on his shoulders, and it was clear that he needed all the help he could get. I glanced at Shhkuk, still trying to read his expression. He was a mystery to me, and I couldn't help but wonder what his true motives were.

As everyone filed out of the room, I caught up to Locke. "You okay, Pres?" I asked, placing a hand on his shoulder.

He gave me a tired smile. "Yeah, just a lot on my mind. This is a big operation, and we can't afford any mistakes."

I nodded in understanding. "We'll get it done, Locke. We always do."

Locke nodded and started to make his way out of the room. "I'm gonna go check on Delilah. Make sure she's ready for this." He let out a shaky breath.

"I'll do that." Grim slapped Locke on the back. "Our females will be informed. Let's get you a drink?"

Locke didn't say anything as I followed them back to the bar. His steps were slow, calculated as we stepped inside. Hawke nodded me off while he and Grim stepped side by side with Locke.

My eyes trailed behind the bar, looking for my mate. She wasn't where I had left her, and a slight panic rose in my throat.

"*Whipped,*" my grizzly gruffed. "*She's on the dance floor.*"

I huffed and jerked my head to the music. The Moonlight Outcasts were nowhere to be seen, just the old, worn-out DJ stand where one of the brothers could pull from a long list of songs on a computer.

My mate was swaying with Journey and Delilah, who was now heavily pregnant. My mate outshined them all, waving her hands in the air. Her movements weren't at all with the beat. They waved violently across the dancefloor as she hysterically laughed and twirled.

I shook my head and weaved my way through the tables and chairs. The brothers all watched the females that were all way too drunk, but they knew damn well never to touch a mated one.

I trailed my hands around Nadia's waist, grinding my growing erection into her backside. She stilled, rubbing her hand over mine.

"You came back!" She lifted her head, her pretty bright eyes gazing up at me.

"Said I would," I grumbled and calmed her movements, grinding myself into her.

She purred and pushed herself more into me.

Grim and Hawke soon join their mates. Their female's eyes flickered with amusement, hunger, and arousal.

The dance floor became a maelstrom of color and motion. The single brothers sported their usual vests. The human women twirled and swayed around them, their bright eyes searching the crowd for a partner. The music, loud and infectious, filled the air with thudding bass lines and soaring melodies. Even the fae, under their glamors, joined in the revelry, dancing with their mates or blending in with the humans.

The thudding of the bass, the movement of my mate's body against my cock, my hunger continuing to grow until my hands wandered from her waist to her now delicious, thick thighs.

Her breath hitched, and her hands lay on top of mine.

"Bear." Her voice was barely a whisper, but I heard her loud and clear.

Her arousal seeped into my nose, my grizzly begging me to take her here on the dance floor. My brothers wouldn't bat an eye, but the fae, I was sure would snub their noses at it.

My grizzly forced my hand lower, and I let him, unable to resist the temptation. Her honey scent entranced me as I wiggled my fingers through the top of her leggings. My fingers were instantly coated with her slick, and I growled, lowering my mouth to her ear.

"Are you wet for me, even around all these people?"

She whimpered, her hand wrapping around the back of my neck. "I'm always wet and ready for you."

I bit her ear in approval, shoving two of my digits into her cunt. Her knees buckled against me, and I used my fingers and my arm to hold her steady against me.

"You enjoy having an audience, don't you?" I whispered.

She panted, her nipples showing through the tight, hot pink Iron Fang ladies' tee Delilah made for the mated couples.

My nose ran across her mated mark over the shirt. I bit down on the mark. My mate's head was thrown back. "Coat my fingers, baby. Then I'm going to have you suck me off."

I withdrew my fingers, gently massaging her moist, delicate clit in rhythmic circles. As she gazed up at me, her eyes partially veiled, the room seemed to fade away, leaving only the intense connection between us.

Everyone was moving in a jumbled, frenzied pattern, the music blaring and making the walls vibrate. Bodies pressed against each other, hands in the air, while some couples were engulfed in their own world. The base was so loud it was almost muffled, seemingly almost part of the atmosphere. In the middle of this chaos, we remained still as I pushed my fingers into my mate's body, making her quiver with pleasure.

"Bear," she whispered until she fell apart around me. Her pussy fluttered, trying to pull me deeper inside her.

I groaned, pulling my fingers away and sinking them into my mouth. "You always taste so damn good. Your honey drives me wild." I pulled her away from the crowd, no longer wanting her to suck me off but to bury myself deep inside her.

I took her into the hallway, leaving the crowd still bumping and grinding to the music. She was panting, still getting over her prior orgasm, but she was already pawing at me, pulling at my belt buckle.

"Aren't you eager?" I chuckled, pulling her hair back and making her kiss me.

It was deep, hard, and I fucking devoured her lips while I ripped the seams of her leggings between her legs. If someone did come back in this hallway, they won't know I was fucking her.

Maybe.

"You like knowing someone could come out in this hallway and find us?" I asked. She looked to her right into the crowd. The lights had gone lower, hands and bodies rubbing against each other.

"Maybe," she rasped and tugged on my cock.

Fuck, what a good little mate she was.

I could see her eyes darken with pleasure, and her body shudder as I slid inside her. Her head tilted back against the wall, and her lips parted as she moaned. Her legs were wrapped tight around me, pulling me closer, and her hands gripped my shoulders. I felt a warmth radiating from her core, drawing me further into her depths.

But I was in charge. She didn't command how fast or hard I'd go.

"Bear, please," she begged, bucking her pussy along my shaft.

I panted, pulling on her bottom lip with my fangs, and her breasts pushed against me.

"Fuck, your pussy is gonna suck me dry."

She whined, her claws ripping my shirt. I bucked my hips, and she smiled in gratitude.

"More! I want more of you."

What my mate wanted was what she got.

I kept my movements slow but deep and hard. My penis rubbed her clit as I did, and her growls echoed in my ear. "More!"

Nadia's nails dug into my back as her moans built to a snarl. Her eyes were locked onto mine, pupils dilated, and cheeks flushed. I thrust into her, pushing her further into the wall and sending vibrations through the hallway. Despite the change in music, our rhythm stayed constant as I kept pounding into her.

My teeth elongated, and I pulled her shirt to the side. I grazed her skin with my fangs and bit down until I broke the surface.

"Bear!" she cried. Her pussy fluttered and clamped onto my dick. I could barely pull in and out of her body it was so tight, making me let out a groan.

We both panted, and her claws still dug into my skin.

Yeah, I could definitely get used to this.

Her body slumped, and I reluctantly pulled from her body. Come dripped out of her immediately, and she gasped at how much I'd spilt.

"I don't think I'll ever get used to that," she said, leaning up against the wall.

I wrapped my arm around her waist. "I can help you get used to it. We can do it on the bar next."

My mate wrinkled her nose. "Ew, that isn't sanitary."

I shrugged my shoulders. "Delilah and Hawke did it."

Her eyes widened. "That... doesn't surprise me."

I threw my head back and laughed before placing a kiss on her forehead. "Come, let's go home so I can finish having my way with you."

My mate hummed, but pulled away and put her hand on the bathroom door.

"What are you doing?" I raised my eyebrow.

My mate looked between me and the door. "To clean up, so I don't have stuff, you know…" Her voice trailed, and a blush danced across her cheeks.

I pulled her to me and purred. "No need. I want everyone to know what we just did."

"But my parents are out there!" she argued.

Suddenly, the door to the male's bathroom opened. Her mother and father walked out, both of their hair disheveled, and her mother giggling until she saw her daughter standing before her.

"Nadia!" She placed a dainty hand over her mouth.

"Ha! Fucking in the bathroom. Who knew that the stuck-up faes would do such a thing?" Teddy snorted with laughter.

Kraven straightened his tunic and pulled Nadia's mother closer. "Sorry, we were, uh, making sure the toilets were working."

Nina elbowed him. "They knew what we were doing. Just like we know what they were doing." She jutted her chin toward us.

Kraven's face paled, and he covered his eyes. "Sweet Goddess, I saw nothing, neither did you. We do not repeat this night!" He grabbed his mate's hand and tugged her along to leave the hallway and into the dancing crowd.

"That was kinda gross." Nadia wiggled her nose. "My parents did it in the bathroom."

"We did in the hallway," Teddy linked all of us. *"Because our mate gets excited about getting caught."*

Our mate blushed. "As long as we don't get caught," she added. "I might die if that ever happened."

We heard the sound of a toilet flush, and Anaki strode out of the bathroom. "You won't believe what I had to endure." He raked a hand down his face. "Two fae going at it, and I'm pretty sure it was your parents."

Nadia laughed and nodded.

Anaki shook his head. "I need to get laid. Everyone does stuff around me, and I can't join in. It's getting depressing." He said in a light tone, but I very well knew he meant it.

He looked over his shoulder and winked. "Just like the time when Nadia sucked off Bear in the living room, and I had to pretend I was asleep."

Nadia's face paled.

I snorted and pushed his shoulder. "Asshole."

Anaki walked away with a light step, whistling a tune as I took Nadia's hand in mine. Sizzle, Tajah, and others waved goodbye to us as we got closer to the door. When it opened, we could feel the sweet spring breeze that signaled away the cold winter air. Grass and trees were all in bloom, and colors of life were brought back to the village.

Mostly, thanks to the faes of course. I was sure the area surrounding the town would be nothing but a warm spot from now on.

"Ready for a ride?" I handed her the helmet on the back of my bike, and she grabbed it eagerly.

I double-checked the straps of her helmet before she climbed on with me. I could still smell her honey scent, and now with the slit in her leggings, it would coat the seat of my bike.

"I can hear your thoughts loud and clear," she said over the roar of the engine.

I smirked and grabbed her arm to wrap around me. "Good, you were supposed to."

I revved the engine several times before we took off into the night to head home. To our home. I took a deep breath, thankful that the many obstacles that brought us here were over.

I knew that we had many more to come, including dealing with Duke Idris and Locke and his future. But we were here now, we lived for tonight.

Nadia nuzzled into my back, her arms wrapped around my waist. "Let's go, Teddy, time's a wasting."

And with that, we left the Iron Fang for the night, to live in our little cabin on the mountain.

CHAPTER FORTY-TWO

Nadia

I studied nonstop during the final weeks of Delilah's pregnancy. Well, as much as Bear had allowed me to. He was still very protective of me, and I didn't see that going away anytime soon.

He hovered, which I really didn't mind. I didn't want to be alone, especially when I slept. I hardly dreamed anymore, and I think it was because of the necklace I wore. It didn't ward off just demons, but I guess it warded off any dreams period.

Which I was happy with.

I slept in a dreamless sleep unless Nikita came to talk to me or if Bear wanted to see what I was seeing. It was strange he could enter my mind by just sinking his teeth into my shoulder. My mark, that is.

He was always checking, though, which I was grateful for.

Bones gave me free rein of his clinic. He didn't use it very often, only for the occasional stitch or two for the unmated. A lot of his supplies were carried in his bag that he carried around with him, wanting to be helpful wherever he went.

And he was.

Bones and I had an odd relationship now. The men of the Iron Fang only wanted the females to see me. Unfortunately, I could only do so much with them because I was only trained in midwifery, but Bones suggested that I start taking classes to improve my skills.

We didn't need a doctor, not really. The more serious trauma Bones could do, especially in a do-or-die situation. Bones saw it differently, however, and he wanted to take me under his wing and taught me what I needed to know because he said there may be a day he couldn't help anymore.

I didn't want to think of that. He would find his mate. I was sure of it.

For the time being, I stuck with my review on birthing babies and not knowing if it would help at all with Delilah. She had grown large in just a few weeks, and she was more and more uncomfortable by the day.

I measured her uterus today, and she was measuring large, forty-three weeks, and we did not know the exact time of conception.

"Give me the diagnosis, doc. When am I going into labor?" Hawke helped Delilah sit up on the table and wiped her forehead. She was sweating, panting, and definitely having trouble breathing because of the weight of the baby.

"I wish we had an ultrasound so I could at least have an idea how large the baby is going to be, but I'm just going to go with outside measurements. This being a wolf-shifter, I don't know if I am helping much at all." I pulled off the glove where I had just checked her cervix.

Hawke rubbed her belly and nuzzled into Delilah's neck. "Well, from a human standpoint, how is she?"

"Baby is healthy, strong heartbeat, but I worry how large you are right now. At some point, the placenta won't work properly, and we don't want that."

Hawke pressed his lips together. "What do you suggest?"

"Strip her membranes," I said matter-of-factly. "She is two centimeters dilated. It will be easy to do. My mother also has some primrose tea she could drink as well to soften up her cervix. I think we will see a baby very soon after that." I smiled, patting Delilah's knee.

"Good, because this kid is killing my ribs." A powerful kick could be seen from her stomach. I winced.

Yeah, that would not happen in a human pregnancy.

"Then let's do this. I'll have you lay back, and you are going to feel me prodding at your cervix again. It will be slightly uncomfortable."

I took my gloves off again and left the room for Hawke to help Delilah get dressed. I knew that within twenty-four hours she would go into labor. How long of a labor was the question.

"There you are. You were taking forever." Bear rounded the corner and picked me up. "You smell like Delilah and Hawke." He wrinkled his nose.

"Yeah, I've been in her vagina. What do you expect?"

Bear made a face and led me down the stairs. Grim had four square tables put together with a large map of the town, the bar, and the forest behind it. Grim was outlining areas with a highlighter and putting red dots in various places.

"What's going on?" I asked as we approached.

"We needed more land," Grim grunted. "I'm sketching out the new boundaries."

The original boundaries showed a wide extension of forest, but now it was tripled.

The fae clan, my clan I guess I should say, had not necessarily taken over the forest, but have helped the trees grow just by their presence. Fae hold more power as a group than we had all realized, and winter melted in an instant in town and in the forest.

The flowers bloomed, and the sun seemed brighter over the temperate climate. It was going to draw attention, especially how the fae were now practicing powers they had not used in many years in preparation to storm the mansion across the country.

Tajah created a glamour over the territory to keep any human wandering eyes away. Now they saw nothing but an empty forest, but it was a glamour that wouldn't last forever. Tajah created weekly castings, and with just her alone, it could take a toll on the body.

Tajah hoped that when Bram found a mate, restoring his power, he could create our territory with an unbreakable barrier so no human eyes would ever be able to find it. That was all with high hopes he found a mate soon as well.

"H-how can the Iron Fang afford all that land?" I asked.

Bear put his hand on my shoulder and pressed a kiss to my head.

Journey pulled out a chair for me to sit on. "All the businesses that Locke and Grim started and gave to members," Journey added. "Plus, Locke has a fair amount put away for a rainy day."

I twisted my mouth trying to put it together. There was a cleaning business, apartments, the gym, the bar, the magic, and mechanic shop. Even with all those businesses running, surely they couldn't afford that.

"That's a story Locke should tell," Hawke answered the rising questions in my mind.

Delilah wobbled beside him until he pulled out a chair for her to sit.

Bear rubbed my arms up and down. "Locke is a good wolf, if a bit eccentric. He protects his own even when he doesn't have the strength to. We owe him everything."

We all went silent. Locke was no longer coming up to the bar to make appearances. He hadn't shifted, but his wolf's personality had surfaced. His wolf was mean and cold. The women weren't allowed to go down to the basement anymore, and the men had a hard time holding him down to give him his shots.

Even if his mate came along to save him, they weren't sure if she would stick around for his body to heal and listen to the trash he spat.

I couldn't help but feel the deep sadness of Locke's situation. He had done so much for the club. I didn't know him very well, but he was obviously very loved and cared for around here.

I felt equally as bad for Journey. She was lucky to have Grim as her mate. Everyone looked to her for answers, but she didn't have them. She was just a priestess for the Moon Goddess and even she couldn't solve everything for us.

No one dared ask Journey at that moment if Locke's mate was coming. I believe the inner circle knew that Locke's time was limited.

But for now, I had to focus on Delilah and her upcoming labor. I needed to make sure everything was prepared for her and the baby.

As the day went on, I made a list of supplies we needed and sent Bones out to gather them. I also texted Delilah regularly, monitoring her progress and making sure she was comfortable.

The fae may have made the surrounding area beautiful and green, but it did not stop a large storm from brewing and coming into the area like a thief in the night. Lightning clawed through the sky as the wind and rain pounded against the bar.

I laid on Bear's chest as we rested in his old room, where he spent most of his time alone before me. We weren't about to stay at the cabin and risk getting stuck if Delilah went into labor.

"Do you think the reason why I didn't have a sex drive before I met you was because I was destined to be with you?" I tickled his bare chest with my finger and let out a big sigh.

"I read that the fae don't have sexual urges until a bond is locked into place, so I very much believe that."

"You read that? Since when do you read?" I cocked my head to the side.

Bear growled and flipped me over, pinning me to the mattress. "I read when you are off doing your exams on the other females."

I let out a giggle and poked his nose. "Aw, you are so sweet learning about my heritage."

I had been far too busy to even pick up a book about the spring fae, not that it really mattered. I was a bear and had spent my time prepping for Delilah's impending birth. I forgot all about my heritage. I was lucky to spend time with my parents. They were just as busy as I was. They had homes to build, training to complete.

My father was put into second in command by Shhkuk and was in charge of all the fae that were yet to find their second chances. Which were few, but my father took great pride in that.

My mother didn't even care about talking about the fae; she wanted to know how my life was growing up. I wasn't overly exciting, except for the knife throwing and ability to look at someone and find key features to see if they were lying, except in a dream they were useless.

I hadn't and would never talk to her about my time in solitary confinement. It was still too fresh on my mind, and I never wanted her to feel guilty for any of that.

"I was curious." Bear scratched his beard. "And I guess my new love of vegetables is thanks to you." Bear rolled his eyes. "Extending my pallet was a bonus. The kitchen won't run out of meat now."

Bear leaned in to kiss me, but a frantic knock rapping at our door interrupted us.

"There's water everywhere!" Hawke screamed. "Water came out of her. She said it broke. I don't know what the fuck that means!"

I snorted and pushed my mate off me, and got dressed quickly. "Playtime later. You ready to see the first baby of the Iron Fang?"

"That's it, Delilah, big breath in," I urged.

Hawke was a mess. He was supposed to count the contractions nice and slow, but he would count too fast. He wanted his mate to be out of pain, but counting faster would not have this baby come any quicker.

Hawke pulled at his mohawk, rubbing Delilah's back. "Don't touch me!" Delilah hissed. "No one touch me!"

Hawke growled, his heavy footsteps echoing through the room. Frustration hung in the air as he grunted and let out a string of curses. I could see his agitation in the way he paced back and forth, his brows furrowed. Meanwhile, I focused on my task, the sound of his discontent serving as a backdrop to my counting.

"And rest." I patted Delilah's knee. "You are doing great. How is the birthing bar? Is that better to use?"

Delilah was hanging on to it for dear life. We were using gravity to get this baby out, and it was proving effective.

I nodded at Hawke to approach. His eyes softened. I could feel how he wanted to comfort his mate, but Delilah was in an enormous amount of pain. "I need Hawke to cool your face, okay? Try to push with your body, not your face. You don't want your pretty eyes bloodshot, do you?"

Delilah hung her head, body panting.

Hawke took the washcloth and patted her face. "I'm sorry, Hawke," she cried. "It hurts!"

Hawke kissed her forehead, his purr resonating throughout the room.

I continued to watch the clock, counting the seconds until she had to push again.

Bear was at the doorway, the door cracked, his arms crossed, looking in to check on me. Not that he had anything to worry about, but as I had read about wolf births, they could be, well... territorial once their pups were born.

I needed to help Delilah birth the baby, cut the umbilical cord, and, if there was no hostility in the room, deliver the placenta. That was hopeful thinking. By that point, Hawke's wolf might be in control by then, and I might sustain a nasty bite since his wolf would see me as a threat to the baby.

It was a vulnerable situation for everyone. I trained Hawke's human side to be prepared to deliver the placenta on his own if I needed to make a getaway.

I swallowed and placed my hand on Delilah's stomach. "Ready, and push again, Delilah. This is it."

Again she pushed, and she cried out in pain. Hawke's heart broke at seeing his mate. I could feel it myself. Hawke let out a howl, and the lights in the clinic flickered in the room. Another howl echoed through the halls. It was overpowering Hawke's, and he was just right beside me.

I ignored it, concentrating.

"Deep breath and one more push!" The howls continued until I could see the blonde tuft of hair coming through.

"I see it! Your baby is coming. Keep going!"

Delilah cried out again, and with the help of gravity, I cradled the baby into my arms. Hawke grabbed an exhausted Delilah and leaned her against the pillows. I quickly got to work and wiped the baby's face, clearing out their airways.

I didn't even have time to look at the gender before I heard growling from the head of the bed. I glanced up to see Hawke, his eyes wild and fur sprouting down his neck.

"Time to go," Nikita urged.

The cord was still attached to Delilah, and I couldn't have Hawke rip the baby from my arms. I watched Hawke and spoke softly to him. "It's alright, I'm here to help. I'm going to give you your pup."

His wolf growled, and Nikita was doing her best to stay silent, but I felt the fur on my neck rising.

Bear was deadly silent on the other side of the door.

"Easy," I continued to soothe Hawke and clamped the cord. "Do you want to cut the cord?"

"Goddess, just cut the cord, damnit!" I heard Teddy roar in my head.

Bear growled from the other side of the door in warning, which Hawke didn't take kindly to.

I was still between Delilah's legs, and I leaned forward and rested the baby on her bare chest. The baby nestled into her, and I put a blanket over both of them to at least keep the baby warm. I kept my eye on Hawke as he watched me, his claws growing.

"Easy," I soothed.

Delilah let out a sob. "Hawke, look, it's a girl!" Hawke shook his head, looking at me and Delilah. I took the time to grab my scissors and lift the blanket to quickly cut the cord.

Hawke growled again when I made a fast movement, and I held up my hands in surrender. "Easy, I'm leaving. Take all the time you need." I continued to back away, not taking my eyes off him. Once I left the room, I shut the door and made sure the warning sign was up so no one could enter.

"Shit, that was exhausting," Nikita thumped our head on the wall, and I nodded.

"Let's hope there aren't any other pregnant shifters," I said.

As I stood up, I noticed Bear was nowhere to be found, and neither was Bones, who said they would be nearby.

My stomach churned. Why wouldn't Bear be here? He was supposed to stay until everything was alright. *"He knows your strong,"* Nikita said. *"Maybe he was excited to tell the others?"*

I shook my head in disbelief and made my way down the dimly lit hallway that led to the bar. As I reached the end, I leaned against the railing and let my gaze wander over the chaotic scene below. Instead of the bustling bar filled with eager members, I saw them frantically cleaning up what appeared to be a disarrayed mess. The sight of broken glass and scattered debris filled the air with a musty scent, while the sound of shuffling footsteps and hushed whispers echoed through the once lively space.

My mouth opened at seeing tables knocked over, the door off its hinges, and the large glass window destroyed.

Anaki was sweeping up glass by the bar, and my parents eyed me and gave me a solemn smile. They continued to help Anaki behind the bar.

What the hell happened?

Lightning flashed in the distance. The storm was now passing, but I feared something terrible was left in its wake.

When I came down the spiral stairs, I found Switch staring out with his black hoodie, his hands balled into fists. "What happened?" I asked.

He took off his glasses and rubbed his eyes. "It was Alpha Locke."

My heart stopped beating in my chest. The rest of the bar stopped their cleaning and gazed over at us.

"He's gone rogue," Switch all but muttered.

The glass tinkled across the floor as someone continued to sweep, and Bear stormed over. "No, he didn't go rogue," he announced to the crowd. "He didn't. He will come back."

"Well then, where did he go?" A fae asked behind him. "He was a wolf, the biggest one I've ever seen. And his eyes they—"

Bear held up his hand to silence them and clenched his jaw. I stepped toward him and grabbed his hand, squeezing it tightly. "He's gone hunting. For his mate. That is all you need to know. He will return."

EPILOGUE

Bear

Spring was warmer this year inside the forest, thanks to the fae. Luckily, with Tajah's glamor, it was hidden from the humans of the nearby town.

Cabins continued to be built by my sleuth, and they were more than excited to see my mate, Nadia. They even wished for us to return to be closer to my old cabin, but of course, we refused. That was my past and the Iron Fang was our future.

The cabins continued to be made with sturdy yet delicate wood, built with curved limbs and branches that fit the flow of the land. The Fae buildings were whimsical and mysterious by fae hands, made of an unknown shimmering material that glinted whenever the sun shone in its direction. The forest, which had once been barren and cold, was blooming with new life; wildflowers painted the ground in vibrant colors, birds sang in the trees, and the light making its way through the canopy created a peaceful atmosphere. Everything seemed to get better as the sun warmed the land, growing ever closer to resembling Elysian, or so I was told.

Darkness still beheld the territory in its shadows, and it was because of our former alpha that was still hiding within them.

Locke, or his wolf, was lost within its depths. Locke was rabid, and those who held a mate and an animal were now required to scout the territory in search of him. A rabid animal was a danger to not just supernaturals but humans as well. If Locke ventured into human territory, he could very well kill them with just a bite with his venom.

No one was to venture into the forest alone at night, and they were to remain in their homes in the confines of the bar apartments until further notice. The fae refused to leave the forest and stayed in the little town they had created. They had their own wards to keep themselves protected from wild animals.

"Look, I caught another!" Nadia linked as she pawed another trout from the stream. We were working on fishing today, then we would bring them back to the cabin for an MC fish fry.

"I think three more should do it," I replied and swatted another large trout onto the shore.

Nadia had embraced her bear, Nikita. Nadia now also confided in me when she felt incompetent or afraid. She had expressed her wish to study with Bones and train under him in his clinic while I continued to work in the inner circle.

Whatever my mate wished, I could not deny. However, if Bones touched her, I would break his fingers.

"Got them!" She swatted her paw and threw the last two onto the pile.

I puffed out my chest in pride, happy that I could teach my mate the ways of her bear. The one thing I had left to train her on was how to defend herself. In that, I did not know if I had the heart to do so.

She wished it, though, and I would not let her feel defenseless. Not when that was her greatest fear since her dream.

In the late afternoon, as the sun dipped lower in the sky, a lively gathering took place at our cabin. The Iron Fang, clad in their rugged attire, arrived one by one, their laughter mingling with the gentle rustling of leaves. The air was filled with the fresh aroma of sizzling fish as the pot luck fish fry began. Amidst the joyful chatter, the fae gracefully joined the festivities, the sparkles in their cheeks reflecting the golden hues of the setting sun. With them, they brought an exquisite array of fresh vegetables, fruits, and flowers, their vibrant colors adding a touch of natural beauty to the scene. The sight of this bountiful feast filled the air with a sense of abundance of smiles as everyone eagerly indulged in the delectable treats.

Delilah hummed, dipping hers into a large batch of tartar sauce and taking a big bite.

"I've never been a big fan of fish, but this is super good!" She licked away a stray piece of sauce from the side of her mouth.

Hawke bounced their baby in his arms and watched her hungrily. "Yeah, it's delicious."

Nadia snickered, stuffing her own portion into her mouth.

The cabin was bustling with activity. I don't think I'd ever had so many people in the cabin at once. Nadia's parents, the inner circle, Switch, the magical beings, they were all either inside or on the porch talking, trying to forget.

The bar was undergoing renovations. It had been closed for two and a half weeks, and just being around the bar was hard enough. It brought up terrible memories of Locke running out in his wolf form, eyes blazing red, and patches of hair missing from his body.

It was all a terrible reminder that we were alone without an alpha.

Grim grunted, holding Journey in his lap. "Thanks for hosting this." Grim wiped a napkin down his beard. "It's a great reminder that we are all still a family. That we are going to get through this."

I nodded and put my plate down on the kitchen counter. "Locke wouldn't want us to mope around. He would want us to continue what we started. We have to continue training, continue moving forward with the raid on the mansion…" Nadia grabbed my hand and rubbed her thumb over mine.

"I agree," Grim interrupted. "Locke wanted to rescue those at the mansion, and we will. As soon as the fae say they are prepared. Switch has a close eye on the mansion. No one is being abused. They are currently just locked up, and the duke isn't even there. Switch is working on tracking any correspondences coming out of the house. We should know something in a few days."

I grunted and pulled my mate closer.

Nadia growled. "I'm coming too." Her claws elongated and scratched the kitchen table.

My grizzly snarled, snapping at Nikita, but she growled back.

"We can talk about that later," I grunted at her.

"It's happening," Nadia argued back. "Delilah can't go, not with Hannah just being born. We all know Delilah and Hawke can't travel."

The baby cooed from Hawke's arms and slapped him across the face.

His eyes widened, and stared at her in shock. "Well then," Hawke snorted. "You are just like your mother."

We all laughed around the table and held our mates a little closer.

Journey raised her glass to our small circle. "To Locke. May he find his mate quickly."

We all stared at each other in question for a few moments. Could it be possible she knew more?

"Of course she does," my mate soothed me through the bond. *"You can't possibly think that this is the end of Locke, do you? Not after he has done all this?"*

I held onto Nadia's gaze as we looked out over our home, our den. As much as we meant for this to be a merry time, to help forget the renovations of the bar, losing our alpha, or president, there was a solemn tone to the party. The brothers still talked, still mingled together, but no matter what, I think Locke would always be at the forefront of our minds.

Journey looked behind her, her glass still raised. Grim rubbed his hand down her back and cleared his throat to get everyone's attention in our home.

With Grim's demanding presence, the room stilled. Even the people who gathered outside looked in the windows. "My mate wants to raise a toast," he growled.

Silence came over the cabin, and they all stared into the kitchen. Journey scooted closer to Grim. "You didn't need to do that," she whispered.

"This is a toast for everyone," he murmured into her ear.

Journey sighed and pulled back her shoulders. "To Locke," she announced loudly. "May he find his mate quickly."

Everyone in the room looked as shocked as we were until Grim gave a glare that promised death if they said or questioned his mate. They all raised their glasses.

"*Oh dear,*" my mate squeezed my hand.

"To Locke," we all said in unison and downed whatever bit of alcohol we had been drinking.

As I lay beside my partner, embraced in slumber's grasp, a profound sense of gratitude washed over me. I was fortunate to have her by my side, to call her mine. With gentle caresses, my fingertips traced the curves of her hips, gliding down the length of her legs. The softness of her skin met my touch, igniting a tantalizing sensation. In the darkness, our bodies aligned, and the subtle pressure of her backside against my own stirred a primal desire.

My mate made me forget, made me forget the troubles of the world that would plague us until Duke Idris was long gone and hoping our president would return.

He would return.

I slid my hand up her torso and cupped her breast, my fingers pinching her hardened nipples. She sighed and turned her body toward me. Her body was lush, her hips full and damn, her ass had filled out nicely.

"Why, Teddy, your ears are showing." She raised her arms and tugged on my ears, pulling them down, not to meet me in a kiss but lower, and had my lips graze her nipples. I latched onto them and sucked harshly, sucking them with undivided attention while she wrapped her hand around my cock.

My shaft dripped, coating her hand, and I groaned against her supple skin.

"Baby, you know how to get me worked up." I rasped.

"It isn't that difficult when your dick is literally hard all the time." She rolled her eyes.

I chuckled and let my precome coat the inside of her thighs. I could smell her honey already dripping from her pussy. I groaned, pushing the tip inside her. I swallowed her gasps with my kiss and thrust inside her. I took my time with her, letting my cock feel every part of her, feeling her flutter around me, sucking me in.

I was a lucky bastard. There were so many other shifters more deserving than I was. Somehow I was blessed, and I would step up while Locke was gone. I'd do my best to do what I had to do to make this club run, help Grim and Hawke the best way I could.

But I'd spoil my mate along the way. Because I was a selfish bear, I was an asshole, and I would not put her in any danger, just like any other shifter would with their own mate.

We both came with roars that shook our den. I continued to pump my seed inside her and felt her belly as I let my seed fill her womb. It swelled, and I snarled, feeling the pride that one day, hopefully soon when the danger passed, I would fill her with a cub of our own.

My mate and I were blessed, and soon, hopefully damn soon, Locke would be too.

MORE BOOK BY VERA

Iron Fang MC Series

Grim

Hawke

Bear

More to Come

Under the Moon Series

Under the Moon

Clara and Kane's Story

The Alpha's Kitten

Charlotte and Wesley's Story

Finding Love with the Fae King

Osirus and Melina's Story

The Exiled Dragon

Creed and Odessa's Story

Under the Moon: The Dark War
Clara, Kane, Jasper and Taliyah's story

His True Beloved: A Vampire's Second Chance
Sebastian and Christine's Story

Alpha of her Dreams
Evelyn and Kit's Story

The Broken Alpha's Princess
Melody and Marcus' Story

Twinning and Sinning From Mutts to Mates
Dax, Dimitri, and Seraphina's Story

More Books To Come

<u>Under the Moon: God Series</u>

Seeking Hades' Ember
Hades and Ember's Story

Lucifer's Redemption
Lucifer and Uriel's Story

Poseidon's Island Flower

Poseidon and Lani's Story

Thanatos' Craving

Thanatos and Juniper's Story

Coming soon!

More to Come

<u>Under the Moon: The Promised Mates of Monktona Wood Orcs</u>

Thorn

Thorn and Ellie's Story

Valpar

Coming Soon

Sugha

Coming Soon

Visit authorverafoxx.com for updates and future books!

Vera Foxx | Facebook